OF SECRETS AND BEGINNINGS

BEGINNINGS AND ENDINGS SERIES
BOOK ONE

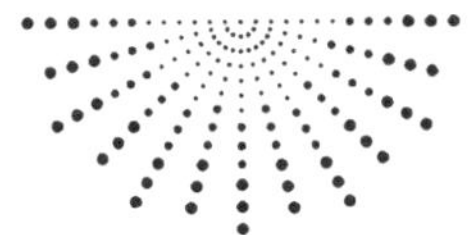

ASHLYN B. RUDD

COPYRIGHT

Of Secrets and Beginnings
By Ashlyn B. Rudd
Copyright ©2023
All rights reserved, including the right to reproduce, distribute, or transmit in any form or by any means.
This is a work of fiction. Names, characters, place settings, etc are the product of the author's imagination, and are used fictitiously. Any resemblances to real life are purely coincidentally.

Of Secrets and Beginnings is a work of fiction, however, it does deal in topics including, but not limited to: outcasting, rejection, mentions of bullying, mentions of rape, torture, kidnapping, death of a young child, assisted suicide/mercy killing, loss of a partner/significant other, and dismemberment.

This is not a comprehensive list as triggers/triggering events are specific to every person. If anything in this work puts your mental health at risk, please do not risk your safety. I appreciate your support, but you and your health are more important. Stay safe lovelies.

DEDICATION

To my friends and family, who supported and believed in me
even when I didn't believe in myself.
And to my mom and dad who gave me every opportunity on this
Earth,
so that I could reach for the stars.
I love you all.

Irropia
Cliffs of Barae
Way
Crian Mountains
Eskira
Straight of Laos
Elona
Lasaego
The Divinian Sea
Atalia's Village
The Outskirts
Basige
Cothir Forest
Western Reaches
Feardin Forest
Southern Hills
N
RHA

oors
Ophineas
Pyre Forest
Serpent's Bay
LASEA
Eastern Vale
issere
Gravelands
Malise
The Sea Smoke
The Eye Stones
Vallenia
Island of Corosa
Kingswood
Saitian
Sallin Marshes

PROLOGUE

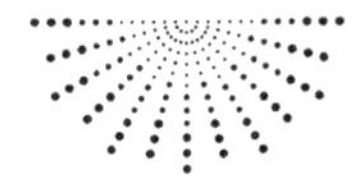

Volume one
Untitled work, Unknown author

*I*n the beginning when there were no gods or goddesses, no world-ending magics, no galaxies or planets, there was only the Cosmos and the Void. Two incomprehensible beings alone in the universe.

The Void was everything dark and empty. Calm and cold. She was the blank canvas of what would become a great vastness of creation.

The Cosmos was what all natural energy channeled through. He was the beginning, middle, and end of everything. The great painter of worlds yet to come, of creatures roaming across realms, and of beings, pillars, who were barely a spark in their creator's mind.

In an act of fate, Cosmos and Void came together, and a universe filled with planets and stars became reality. Cosmos's energy spread out across Void's emptiness, coating the darkness in color and creation. Natural energies and magics formed wherever these two beings touched.

In the very center of the universe stood the Nexus, worlds that were the very first creations, the center of everything; made with energy and magic so thick that the very atmospheres were rich with it. Cosmic energy connected them together as one, yet separated them for the benefit of the universe.

Millenia passed by in seconds. Eons flowed like river sand, unstoppable and ever moving. Eventually, the Cosmos grew weary—tired. Thousands of different worlds. Millions of wonderfully unique beings. With such a worldly fatigue, always watching and yet unable to truly join in, the Cosmos inexplicably changed the course of the universe.

He separated all the energies that he held within himself and spread them across the Nexus to hold the universe at the center of the Void.

Some energies, varying in duty and power, turned into sentient creatures or beings; others became objects to be protected and guarded by the people of the world. All were meant to hold an integral part of the power that kept the universe and everything in it safe.

Stripping himself of the last of his natural power, the Cosmos fell away into the Endless Sleep, finally getting the rest he needed and leaving the protection of all that he had built in the hands of the Nexus.

One world in particular had magic running through it like lifeblood. It flowed through the sky in every color imaginable, the very air rich with aether and energy. Creatures who had been there since the beginning of the worlds walked across grass fields shining in the light of the magics that one could feel brushing across every sense.

And on one ordinary day, nothing amiss—not a single blade of grass out of place—on the beautiful planet, Death took his first form in the skies above. With a thunderous boom, the world went dark for an entire cycle. No light shined through from the sun, no magic frolicked in the air except for the power of pure darkness. Swaths of inky blackness covered the skies, with no end in sight for the blinding power.

On the second day, Death took a physical form. The swirling mass coalescing together into a beastly embodiment of death. In this shape, Death became sentient, learning his role in this new world as well as what it was like to be someone and not just an aspect of the universe. Here he ran through the wild grasses with the predators and climbed the trees with the prey. He flew through the air on his dark wings with the birds, and fell in love with the flora and fauna. With the magical creatures he felt at peace, the way their energies sparked with life from the inside.

The animals worshiped him and his prowess, recognizing him for what he was. Predators had always tried to resist the claws of death, and in turn, brought it down upon others in order to survive. Prey ran from it, determined to see the next day. No creature could stop him; too ferocious was he in this form, not that any would have tried. Eventually everything passed through Death's gates, and so both sides bowed down to his almighty strength.

He may have been Death, an entity of unforeseen power, but through his compassion, he became the King of Animals.

It took time, no one really knows how much, for Death to take his final form. One birthed from his mind, an itch he couldn't get rid of; and so he became a man. One that could speak and think and feel, yet still riddled and run by instinct.

Even in this shape, he was still otherworldly, stronger and faster than anything that could cross the land, seas, or sky. Able to wield his power with a precision and deadliness of skill that frightened even the most greedy of souls.

He was admired and loved. Feared and respected. The sentient beings bowed to him and to no one else. And so he became known as Death: The God of Endings. Ruler of the world that hummed with magic deep in its bones.

Even with all of the wonders of the universe, Death began to suffer from the same weariness as his creator. For sentience isn't always the greatest of gifts. Knowledge of one's self, awareness of the world around you, brings with it mundane, mortal feelings. Feelings of which a being of such power maybe should not hold, and yet it is the sacrifice of such awareness—to be so awake is to be forced to witness.

To feel.

Love, anger, joy, sadness.

Loneliness.

For as much as he enjoyed the wildness of his planet, there was no one to walk along the riverbank with. No one with whom to contemplate life, and what adventures they might get up too. At least not as equals. Death was ferocious in all his glory, but underneath it all, he was just a man who wished to have someone by his side.

As if fate had been listening, a second being of cosmic energy appeared. Chaos. It did not take long for the two to become inseparable, as close as the two beings could be. Death ruled as king and god with the help of his new brother, and together they were unstoppable.

Everything was idyllic and perfect in every way.

Until it wasn't.

The unraveling crept in like a disease, an illness that could destroy the mind; Death began to lose control of himself. He began killing everything within reach, his mind clouded by an insidious madness. Even during the small moments he surfaced from the dark insanity, he was unable to rein in his fatal power. And so, Death lost himself from within.

Blood ran freely through the world, drenching the grasslands and waters; the air smelled of iron and a red mist hazed the sky. His most loyal companions, the wild beasts of the planet, withered away in his very presence. The destruction of his beautiful, magical world was almost inevitable. Entrenched in grief, Death called out, pleading, begging in a roar of pain that echoed across galaxies for the help to stop his killing.

It was at this moment that the Cosmos's most grievous error became realized. For when he had cleaved Death from himself, he had also cleaved Death away from another, interrupting a delicate balance, as there was one entity to which Death, unknowingly, had a greater bond. The two of them bound in a way not even the creator of the universe should have thought to separate.

This being had been more comfortable watching over her planet from afar, but at the call of her mate, her pair, she was unable to allow his suffering to continue.

For what was Death without Life?

What was an Ending without its Beginning?

CHAPTER ONE

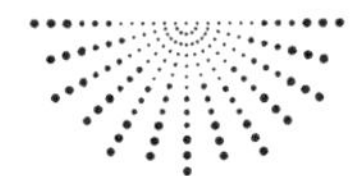

*L*ife's a bitch; a cruel mistress in a world full of cruel people. Sometimes she rolled the dice and decided whose day would be fucked. Unfortunately, she landed on me today. A cruel mistress indeed, considering she'd been shitting on my life for as long as I could remember. It's a good thing I learned how to roll with the punches—and how to punch back.

I mean, could a girl not go through town, minding her own business, without being harassed? That's all I wished for. To go about my errands without wondering whose job it was to make my life a living hell.

In my world, being the social pariah means outright rejection and alienation. Someone to be feared and avoided at all costs except when the lovely, lovely people of this deadbeat village decided to remind me that I would never be welcome among them. That I would be stared at and hated; an abnormality they couldn't wait to see destroyed.

Miserable and outcasted, that's how they liked me.

The side eyes and sneers thrown my way only served my

point. They couldn't have me getting too comfortable in my position of least wanted person ever.

I'd been out since dawn collecting the herbs that Maris needed from the east side of the forest, and now the sun had already started its downward descent for the day and the moons had begun their rise.

I could have taken the long way around and avoided the center of the village entirely, but I was exhausted and had hoped to get away with it. Blessed Divine, how dare I even consider the possibility? Of course, the minute I was spotted walking down the street, the stares and whispers started. Mothers hid their children and old grannies tsked as I passed.

I could feel their accusing eyes boring into the side of my head as I continued on. As if every move I made was just one step closer to them finally acting on their hatred and crafting some horrible accident in which I perished in the aftermath.

A very depressing thought, but one that crossed my mind all too often; yet I couldn't seem to help pulling on the short leash they liked to keep me on. Or that they thought they kept me on.

A very thin leash, given I couldn't care less what they thought of me. As if the, frankly uninteresting, insults their tiny minds came up with could ever truly hurt me. I had learned long ago that they weren't worth my time, let alone my tears. If it weren't for how they treated Maris and Geoff whenever I acted up too much for their liking, I would have told the lot of them to go fuck themselves with the sticks they had shoved so far up their asses they tended to walk crooked.

Those moments never seemed to go over well, however, so I did my best to keep quiet and go about my own business, unlike the rest of them. It was a feat of strength that tested me every day; the soreness in my jaw from where I ground my teeth together was testament to that.

They feared me. They had ever since I first came to this town, barely two years of age. It didn't matter, though; I could feel their nerves in the air. After seeing the predator inside, the one lurking behind the gaze of a toddler, they could hardly stand my presence, let alone my eyes upon them. So as I grew, they poked and prodded to make certain I knew they held some power over me, but never enough to get the beast to snap back.

Cowards.

This was why I told Maris she should be doing the harvesting. I drew too much attention, whether I liked it or not. Sometimes I thought it would be nice to blend into the background with everyone else, to get some peace and quiet while I went about my day.

Of course, Lady Life, The Divine Goddess of Beginnings that she was—my eyes were at risk of getting permanently stuck in the back of my head—thought that was asking too much.

It would be damn near impossible to fade into the everyday hustle and bustle of the village with my reputation, let alone my annoyingly obvious differences.

With hair shinier than the gold coins carried by the wealthy merchants from the capital, Vallenia, I caught people's eye even in the pitch black of night. In full sun like today, I was downright blinding, and stood no chance of going unnoticed.

No block dye could dull the gilded color, and cutting it had absolutely no effect. It grew right back within a day, falling mockingly in gleaming curls down to my waist. The unnatural coloring I possessed, especially now, painted a huge target on my back. Had I lived two thousand years ago, people probably wouldn't have looked twice, but now I stood out like a sore thumb, and hiding it was nearly impossible.

I would think, even as magic continued to leave our world at an alarming rate and two thousand years after The Divine and their Descendents had disappeared, the small remnants of power would have desensitized people to the strange and the weird. But no, it just made them that much more greedy and angry than they probably were when they realized they held no inkling of that power.

Irropia's old stories told of a world so full of magic that the sky was streaked with colors such that a human's mind could not always comprehend them. Where huge creatures roamed the plains and the trees were alive with magic.

Now barely a few wisps graced the sky on a good day, magical beasts or beings were brought to Vallenia for *safekeeping*, and only the trees in the Blackwood showed any signs of having ever been alive—not that most people went far enough in to see it.

Magic was a dying entity in our world, withering away with gasping breaths instead of a bang. It was a sad sight, even for someone who didn't know any different. I could tell though, something intrinsically connected to Irropia was disappearing —more and more each year—and it showed in the most inconspicuous of ways. It was like some dormant disease, sitting and waiting and building its strength so that it could kill the planet at its leisure.

It didn't help that every year King Starga decided to round up all magical relics, creatures, and people from the cities and towns in the realm. Babes were wrenched from their mothers' arms and hundred-year-old family heirlooms were ripped from mantles if they showed even the slightest sign of power.

Protection, the king called it. *Stealing*, the people silently screamed back, too afraid of the king's guards to publicly demand what little magic they had left be given back to them. The villagers called it the Tearing.

Looking like magic in a backwards town full of people that were jealous they no longer had any, who were enraged at having what little they did stolen by a greedy king, was a cruel twist of fate in the weaving of my life.

If they didn't hate Starga more than they did me, I had no doubt that they would have turned me over long ago to the royal guards as they made their pass each year through the outer villages with their caravan of magics where relics pulsed with power in the backs of wagons, and children no older than eight peered out of windows in the carriages. I could still see their breath fogging up the glass as tears silently fell down their cheeks. Magical creatures were more rare, but the ones pulled along were the makings of legends.

It was the one time of the year when the village had my back, when not a single soul spoke of me, and those that did were quickly silenced. I spent the entire day deep in the Blackwood, farther than anyone else would go for fear of disappearing within its depths. By the time I got back, the guards would be long gone, and the villagers would once again take their hatred out on me.

I had many societal flaws in their minds; their utter dislike of me was not just because of the power that may or may not have run through my veins, or because of my sparkling personality.

I think it was the knives that really got their blood running. Proper women didn't carry blades.

At least that's what I had been told by several men who thought it was their business to teach me what a woman's proper place should be. On her back, apparently. I decided to teach them a much more important lesson instead.

Don't corner the psychotic bitch with the daggers. It won't end well.

"Whore," a pockmarked woman hissed at me as we passed by one another, venom all but shooting from her cracked lips.

Life in the village tended to take the young's beauty far quicker than anyone ever wanted it to, whether from hard work in the fields or in the shops.

Where magic was used to help in the simplest of tasks, now most men and women had calluses covering their hands and scars dotting their faces from the sweat and blood they had put into their work, like a rite of passage they all went through.

I wasn't blind to my own looks. In a village filled with dull, work-scarred people, a woman who gleamed gold, brighter than any statue in the capital, was bound to catch hate for it. It wasn't for the lack of trying or work, but save for the few calluses on my palms from sparring, I couldn't scar to save my life.

After the first hurled insults were shouted at my back, following me as I went through town, years of blocking them out had kicked in instinctively. Except for when the woman's friend said, "Someone should teach her a lesson like they do with those wantons in Vallenia." The woman sneered as she looked over her shoulder at me, her mouth twisted in disgust.

I stopped in my tracks, barely keeping my rage in check as a gentle hum built in my veins and rang in my ears—that was never a good sign. For them anyway.

I struggled to keep my feet planted, as every part of me strained to reach across the short distance and wipe that smile from her face, but I knew if I showed any kind of reaction they would only use it to continue tormenting me.

They laughed together at the grotesque and horrifying joke. As if the idea of keeping women imprisoned in their own city was funny. If the rumors were true, those poor girls could barely get five feet out of the city gates before they were hauled back in and punished for it. Sex work was lucrative in Vallenia, but it came with a price.

Even with the reminder of what some of those women in the capital go through, I still wasn't insulted by being called a whore. The brothel workers in our own village put up with enough shit for me to always show them the respect they deserved. The things the women and men who go into the field had to do to survive—the verbal and physical abuse they endured—were brutal.

I forced myself to take a deep breath before continuing on my way, even as the feral thing inside of me stretched its muscles. What would happen if the predator in their midst got off her leash and decided to flash her iron claws?

Whoops. I didn't mean to bash their heads together; truly it was an accident. No, no, don't mind the blood.

I smiled at the thought. Wouldn't that be fun? Maybe I would try it one day just to see their reactions.

But no, I couldn't give them more ammunition to use against me. Against Maris and Geoff.

Even still, I felt the deep pit where I kept all of the dangers start to come alive inside me. I looked around, catching the gazes of others, and watched with a demented sort of satisfaction as they winced away from my heavy stare. Some turned tail and walked the other direction all together. Others instinctively moved away in fear. They knew in their very souls that the entity in their midst was not in the mood to be poked today.

With a cruel grin, I made my way out of town. They may have hated me, but they still stepped out of my path as I walked. No one wanted my attention falling upon them.

I couldn't make them like me, and I refused to change who I was to appease unworthy, unpleasant people. At least when they feared me they left me the hell alone, for the most part.

I walked across the well-worn stone of the road as the smells from the market stalls swirled all around me. The village, compared to some of the ones I had visited, was stunningly small. So small that it didn't even appear on most maps, yet alone have a name. It had been grouped together with the other two villages around these parts, and simply named the Outskirts.

All the houses and shops sat around the main area in a circular pattern, creating an outside rotunda that, during the day, turned into a thriving marketplace.

The wealth of the homes slowly changed the farther out you went from the market, the poorest living on the edges, closest to the Blackwood. The rings turned from homes with detailing and actual roofs to ramshackle sheds that looked as if they could be knocked over by a good gust of wind.

The roads between shot out like a spider's web, ending well before the last house on the row. All roads led back to the center with the only traversable way out of the village being one dilapidated path that led straight out toward the other Outskirt villages, before eventually reaching the first major city, Nastare.

We weren't a place of extreme wealth by any means. This far away from Vallenia and most main avenues of travel, no village was, but what little wealth we did have belonged to a select few who lorded it over the others with their egocentric houses and gaudy clothes. You could tell the few apart from the many quickly.

A normal day in the market center saw vendors and traveling merchants selling their wares. Workmen went about their day. Servants and maids completed errands for the few who had enough to employ them, like the prissy ladies in atrociously corseted dresses, pretending to be highborn as they went for their daily promenade—or whatever the hell they called it.

This was normal by all standards to anyone not born here, except for the lack of magical artifacts being secretly peddled here and there by the merchants like you would see in cities closer to the capital. Merchants had no chance of getting an artifact's worth so far away from the majority of the wealth on the continent.

Any remnants of the old world were completely gone from the outer villages, having been taken to the capital years ago. No new relics had popped up in at least a decade, and no one in this horrid place had been blessed with magic since I was a little girl. Now people traveled miles upon miles to the capital just to see a glimpse of magic—of true power.

Everyone wished to hold even the smallest bit of that power, to remember a time where the world was filled with it. Everyone but this village, it seemed. They sent wary glances and snide looks at the golden-haired anomaly, the weird woman who was hated by most, and feared by all. In reality, I had done nothing to deserve their spite; they just hated anything different from them. Anything that had something they did not.

They loathed me for the simple reason that I'd have fit in with the magically gifted rather than them. With my old world appearance and unhinged ability to scare the shit out of them with the lift of an eyebrow, there really wasn't ever a question as to why they disliked me so much. It still hadn't stopped it from hurting as a child.

Yes, the blatant disregard for the mundane was my fault, but in my defense, normal was often scarier than crazy. Normal meant living your life exactly as someone else has planned it, and that just didn't work for me.

I shook off the depressing thoughts that would do me no good and closed my eyes. Breathing in the warm spring air, the soft breeze blowing gently across my cheeks, the first real smile I've had all day appeared on my face. I let the toxic anger from the marketplace fade into oblivion. They tried to take every-thing from me, did what they could to chip away at me little by little, but they'd never be able to take this away: my home, and the people inside who loved me.

The little cottage sat tucked away, nestled just on the edge of the Blackwood, with its beautiful stone walls—thriving ivy vines growing up on the shaded side in mockery of Geoff's attempts to cull it back—and its warm stone and thatched roof that sometimes leaked in the rainy season.

Rays from the falling sun cast a warm glow upon the house, a halo of radiant, dream-like light. The large, ornate herb garden out front, that Maris gently tended to day and night, was soaking up the last of the warmth.

I could remember a time when Maris and I would be barefoot in the garden listing off all of the names of the plants and herbs we grew. Lavender and dandelion, milk thistle and black cohosh—although you'd never put those together—and so many more. I could still feel the dirt between my toes as I recited the long list as I walked up and down the rows.

A loud bray broke through the tranquil quiet of the cottage yard. The noise was somewhere between a horse's whinny and a goose's honk. Birds in the trees above balked in outrage at the crude sound, the bugle straining with voice cracks that made me wince in pain.

The adorable creator of the sound, a fluffy brown brat of epic proportions, leaned as far out as he could without breaking the fence that blocked him.

I laughed with a unique genuineness only this place could bring out of me. "Gideon, did you think I forgot about you?"

Another goose-whinny was let loose, his mouth open in a demanding cry.

I chuckled before walking over and hopping up onto the first slat of wood, reaching over the top of the boards to pat his head. If it weren't for his big ears that were longer than my forearm, the donkey could have been easily mistaken for a horse. Gideon stood out amongst his pasture mates within the first glance. And if you didn't notice him, he sure as hell would make it known that he was around. He was the biggest pain in the ass and thrived off drama, even more so than the townspeople. As smart as he was, catching him and the rest of the animals had become an almost daily chore after he figured out how to open the gate to let everyone out, of course.

Geoff would have gotten rid of him years ago if he wasn't so damn strong, pulling more weight than any draft or ox could. That, though the man would never say anything, and he secretly loved the big jackass as much as Maris and I did.

Rubbing the inside of his ears just the way he liked, I swatted at him as he used the distraction to nip at my basket. He rifled around inside, looking for the treat he knew I always carried for him, whimpering impatiently.

"Hold on, you big baby," I said, shoving him away, rummaging through it for the single green apple, his favorite. I couldn't help but let out another laugh as he tossed his head around and flapped his lips impatiently.

Holding my hand out, I balanced the small green apple on it, shaking my head and rolling my eyes as he took one big chomp and nearly swallowed it whole.

"You should really chew your food, you know," I recommended to him.

He looked up at me and burped his reply before sucking on his tongue, quite proud of himself. His big brown eyes clearly told me that he couldn't care less.

"Charming," I replied. With one last thump against his thick neck and a shake of my head, I headed back toward the cottage.

Striding across the vibrant wild grasses, the stalks brushing against my leather-clad legs, I walked through the cottage's well-worn door. Entering, I passed by the stairs to the second floor and the hallway that led to the workroom on my left.

The short hallway came to an end in the main room, where the purposefully mismatched furniture and colorful chaos gave the whole space an air of warmth and comfort. I breathed out another sigh of relief, finally hidden from the poison of the village.

Just as I was about to head into the kitchen to find Maris, something softly shuffled behind me. Jerking my head up, my senses sparked as the hair on the back of my neck prickled warily. The energy in my chest immediately pushed against my skin, humming restlessly, ready and alert. Gently setting the basket down on the table in front of me, I reached my hand down for my blade.

Only, it was too late. I had let my guard down and forgotten

Geoff's first rule: always check your surroundings. I was about to pay for that mistake as a large, shadowy figure appeared at the edge of my vision.

CHAPTER TWO

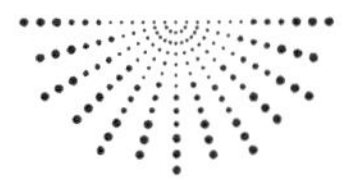

I moved to strike, but my attacker was well prepared. Reaching around with a heavily muscled arm, he pressed it into my neck, cutting off my air. Without a split second's thought, I thrust my elbow back into his stomach.

A rush of air knocked out of him, and the arm across my throat loosened enough for me to slip out of reach. I coughed, air flowing back into my lungs. Turning around, I got into a defensive stance, my body moving as instinctually as breathing.

Standing at six feet, nearly broader than the doorway he blocked, Geoff gave me a teeth-baring grin. With his suntanned skin, long brown hair—which unsurprisingly looked unbrushed—and bright blue eyes that put the sky to shame, he was without a doubt a handsome man. His broad, masculine face made you think of wild men and chopping wood; but to me, he just looked like the man who had raised me.

I shouldn't have been surprised to find him waiting for me. He liked to call it teaching me life lessons; I think the old guy was just bored as shit sometimes. Also, Geoff could never resist a good fight. His love for it was evident in the nicks and scars that criss-crossed his roguish face.

He used to be a guard at some highborn's estate in Vallenia, or at least that's what he always told me. He never gave me more than that, and I never asked, knowing I would get nowhere on the subject. Anytime the topic came up, I could almost see the shutters slamming close behind his eyes.

To anyone watching, it would have seemed an unfair fight, what with little ol' me versus a gigantic bear of a man. But I had been trained by both Geoff and Maris since I was old enough to hold myself up straight. I now fell into a good fight with the ease of a pub brawler.

I grinned back with just as much teeth-baring challenge. "Bring it, old man."

With a chuff that scared birds from their perches, my adoptive father charged. He was intent on pummeling his lessons into me, even if he had to do so literally.

Waiting until the last possible second, I tucked into a somersault, rolling across the floor before popping up behind him. I planted my fist in his kidney, the force pushing him straight into the table holding my basket.

As the table went crashing to the floor, the medicinal herbs scattering across the hardwood, he caught himself on the back of the couch. Using the distraction to get close, I struck out with my leg and hit the weak spot on the outside of his knee. I felt the muscle and tendon give out, bringing him down to the ground.

Looking over his shoulder, he held up one finger with a proud smile, acknowledging that he'd allowed me to get him into a position where I could have killed him. Returning the smile, I backed off and let him up, not wanting the fight to end so soon. Relaxing into the swell of confidence I got when fighting, I kept my defensive position up and my eyes on him. I couldn't get cocky, or he would be kicking my ass until next week for allowing myself to think I had outsmarted my opponent.

I settled into the intoxicating feeling that always filled my veins when the adrenaline hit. The same burn that preceded the rise of ... *something* in that deep pit inside, drowning me underneath its crushing weight. I normally tried to hold it back, but now I let it rise higher until I heard the humming in my ears once again. A satisfying fire lit behind my eyes as I let it rise a bit more.

We started trading blows. My fist glanced off his chin, followed by a straight jab that whipped his head back. He came back with two punches to my stomach that had me doubled over. The relentless thrumming in my ears started to pound away.

The pit flared hotter, rose further. Refusing to take but a second, I stood back up, ready to land another hit. I was so filled with adrenaline, it didn't register that I had left myself open. Without hesitating—Geoff was always about tough love—he landed a well-aimed kick to my side that knocked me off my feet and tossed me through the air.

I hit the ground with a brutal force that knocked the wind clean out of me. Going with the fall like I was taught, I tumbled back onto my hands and knees. The almost deafening drumming in my ears beat away and the edges of my vision started to blur with golden light—a telltale sign that I'd let the power grow too bright, too hot.

I took a second, my head hanging, and let the oxygen replenish my lungs as I tried to calm the raging storm brewing in my chest.

Letting the energy build during a fight kept me on my toes. It helped sharpen my reflexes and quicken my step, but I never let it out fully, too afraid of what might happen. There was always a risk when I let myself get too far into it, and now I was paying the price as the bright light passing over my gaze finally won, pulling me under the insurmountable tide.

The battlefield was brutal, the endless sea of bodies was only broken up by the dead that dotted the ground. Screams of the wounded and dying came from both sides, while swords continued to clash. The clang of metal on metal was an orchestra to which the fighting played out as anguish, hate, and desperation permeated the metallic-scented air.

Bright energy whipped through the air, crashing into lines of soldiers and creatures alike, turning what was supposed to be a horribly tragic scene into a beautiful, macabre painting of blood and color. The sky was a twisted amalgamation of magic, even as the dark funnel clouds above threatened their wrath.

A slight change in the wind behind me had me whipping my head around as a blurred figure charged me. Without thought, I sliced through him with my dagger, the dark blade longer than my forearm and sharp enough to cut the enemy in half without any resistance. He fell to the ground in two without me even catching sight of his face.

As I took in the misery and hopelessness around me, all of the death and suffering, the once green field a sea of blood and carnage, my sorrow turned to anger. Charging into the fray, my scream of rage at the endless slaughter rang across the battlefield as I sliced and stabbed away at the enemy, several at a time. Cutting off heads and ripping limbs apart with my bare hands, I fought like a demon possessed. Kicks from my legs crushed organs and shattered bones.

Where is he? I searched through the throng of people for that coward—

My sight cleared, and the worn, scuffed floor of the cottage stared back at me. The electrified sensation boiled under my skin, stretching and shifting inside me like never before. Rage that was not my own coursed through every fiber of my body.

The golden sheen spread completely over my eyes and I was helpless against my own mind, unable to control my body. The pressure only grew until I felt like my head would explode and I was being swallowed whole, drowning in a gilded sea. I reached for the surface, hand outstretched for something unknown, trying to hold on to my body as one last wave pushed me back under—and I was no more.

Snapping my head up, I stared into cerulean eyes that were wide with shock.

With a snarl fit for an animal, I lunged at the man who was soon to be dead for his audacity. Faster than the eye could see, I punched out with a fist that could rival lightning on a stormy night. I felt the man's jaw crunch under the force of the blow as he went crashing back into the wall behind him with a loud crack.

Jumping on his prone form, I pulled a knife from its sheath on my thigh and thrust it against his throat. "Who the hell are you?"

When he didn't answer, staring at me with a mixture of surprise and fear in his sky-blue eyes, I bared my teeth in a grin of fury, ready to slice his throat and be done with it. I had more important things that I needed to take care of. The white blade wouldn't kill him, unfortunately, even if I cut all the way through; but it would keep him down long enough for me to make it a permanent situation.

"Atallia!" a voice screamed out, making me whip around and meet the eyes of a woman I knew very well.

"Maris?" I asked in confusion. What the hell was she doing here?

Seeing Maris's green eyes alight with desperation, I looked back down at my attacker, whose eyes were shining with love and something else entirely.

I snapped back into my body, taking a gasping breath like I'd been underwater too long. The power rush died out quickly, fading away into nothing, like it was never there in the first place. The gilded sheen over my eyes fizzled out and I was left staring at the havoc I had caused.

What happened?

With wide eyes, I looked down in a daze, finding my iron blade pressed against Geoff's throat, a bead of blood trickling down his neck.

"Gods!" I yelled as I tossed away the dagger and launched

myself away from him. Slamming myself back against the opposite wall, I slid down and pulled my knees up to my chest. Maybe if I kept a barrier between us, I could stop myself from hurting them.

My episodes had been getting worse for months. They were mostly controllable, and I had stopped trying to remember what happened during them; but now I'd almost killed my Geoff with the same dagger he had given me.

We had sparred with real weapons before, and we may have had a cut or two that were accidental, but we always pulled our strikes, preferring to use the flat of our blades to mark a hit.

My hands were shaking as I thrust them through my hair, gripping the strands tight at the root. What the hell was happening to me? What had I just done?

Geoff, picking himself off the floor, stepped closer to me. "What happened, cub? We were having a good fight and then I lost you." His soft voice was as comforting as any childhood blanket.

"I don't know." My voice wobbled as I struggled to keep tears at bay. "It was like when I wake up from my nightmares, except different. At least then I have some awareness, but this—this time I don't remember anything at all," I say, shaking my head. "It felt like I was drowning, being pulled underneath a swell, and then nothing."

"You don't remember anything at all?" Maris asked with concern as she crouched down beside me, reaching out to gently pry my hands loose. She held them in her own, the tips of her fingers stained with the juices of herbs and berries.

I leaned my head back against the wall of the hallway. "Maybe a flash, a glimpse of a battlefield." I groaned, running my hands down my face. "I don't know, mostly just feelings. Rage. Sadness." A tight burning, unlike before, warned of my doomed fight to keep the tears back. "And then nothing, like I blacked out. Then I came to and I was holding a knife to your throat," I said brokenly, staring at the cracked wall where I must have thrown him.

Maris and Geoff looked at each other, something silent passing between them before they turned back to me with wan smiles.

"Chin up, cub. It could be worse," Geoff said in his booming voice, coming to crouch down on my other side.

I turned toward him slowly, mouth agape. He was crazy; there was no other explanation. How much worse could it get than trying to kill someone and not even remembering that I'd done it in the first place? With his hair even more mussed than usual, and the dried blood around the cut on his ne—

Geoff's huge hand came down to rest on my shoulder, shaking me from my thoughts. I met his eyes, and for the first time in my life, I found myself unable to hold someone's gaze, turning away first.

"It could be worse … Geoff, I near—" My voice wobbled slightly. "I nearly killed you. I don't remember anything, but I know what I felt and I would have done it." I could barely get the whisper past my lips. My heart clenched in pain at the thought.

He scoffed, waving his hand as if wiping away the entire incident. "Cub, the only reason I didn't fight back was because it was you." Moving his hand to my cheek, he turned my head toward him. "I was more worried about you than I was about me. All the years we've trained, I know how easily you fall into a fight. How easy it is for you to let everything go, but I've never lost you like that. And that scared me more than anything. I laid there and did nothing because the idea of hurting you hurts me a thousand times more."

The tears I tried hard to keep back fell silently as the strong arms that had held me since I was young wrapped around me.

His warm pine and rain scent was as familiar to me as the lullaby he had sung to me to keep the monsters away.

"I love you. Both of you," I said when I let go, looking over at Maris, who was still crouched by my side, tears of her own dripping down her face.

"And we love you. More than you could ever know," she replied. Geoff nodded in agreement.

I gave them a watery smile as I tried to keep the sobs in my throat from escaping.

I liked to pretend it didn't, but deep down, the slumbering entity has always terrified me. I never knew what would happen if I let it out, if I let it take me under like it did today. How was I supposed to control something I couldn't even remember doing?

What if I hurt someone? What if something like today happened again and someone wasn't there to stop me? I refused to be anything other than who I was, but what if who I was was dangerous to those I loved?

We had speculated that I was a distant relative of a Descendent. It made the most sense, but even that we couldn't confirm without an actual Descendent's help, and nowadays they were more myth than reality. My blood must have carried some spark of magic, something that made me this way, but I had no idea what it might be.

Not knowing where or who you came from could really be a pain in the ass sometimes.

Sniffing, I used my hands to wipe away the tears dripping down my face with a huffing laugh. "Well, this was not exactly what I had in mind for today."

With a chuckle of her own, Maris stood, reaching her hand down to help me up. "Why don't you pick up those plants and the table, and come help me with the tinctures while I tell you about our new patient."

"Patient?" I questioned, the healer in me perking up as I

crouched down to pick up my basket. "Another one so soon? What happened?"

"Yep, they found him this morning, and brought him in soon after you left. It looks like the same thing got him as the last one."

"Why didn't you come get me? I could have helped set him up," I said, following her and Geoff down the side hall into the workroom. The addition was added years ago to the small cottage for Maris to do her work.

She may have trained me to fight right alongside Geoff, having been the one to teach me the versatility and danger of a woman with a dagger, but her true passion was in the medicinal arts, not the deadly ones. She was a dirty fighter, a mean one if she had to be, but unlike Geoff, she fought so she could defend herself and her patients from any harm.

Along with my combat training, she taught me the practices of healers. When I wasn't in the small arena out back, I was in here, first under Maris's feet and then put to use as her assistant. Now, I was improving upon some of her oldest techniques, making them more efficient and versatile.

I loved the work as surely as I loved the feel of a dagger in my hand. The ability to both take life and give it had always felt balanced in some way.

While some of the women in town knew basic remedies for common colds and headaches, Maris and I were the only true healers in the village. Even then, most of our work was spent selling salves and elixirs to the villagers. We only ever got a true patient, one who needed real treatment, every couple of months. The last one had only been a little over a week ago.

"When they brought him in he already looked dead," she said, moving over to her workbench, which was stained with so many colors it hardly looked like wood anymore. "I honestly thought he was for a second, but then he opened his eyes. I didn't think he'd survive the hour, so I saw no reason to have you come back."

"Are the bite marks the same too?" I set my basket down on the stained butcher block in the middle of the room. Herbs and flowery branches hung from the rafters in various stages of freshness and dehydration. A collection of shelves lined the back wall, filled with little glass jars and ceramic pots holding miscellaneous barks, dried berries, fungi, and powders. Functionally organized stores of ready-made salves sat stacked on the lowest shelf ready to be picked up.

A set of windows on the left brought in the natural light Maris preferred to work with. They also allowed her to look out to the front as people walked down the lane to stop at our door, filling up on this or that for the minor aches and pains they received from their jobs—chapped hands, sore back, sunburn.

A fireplace in between the two windows helped keep the space warm when needed, and the backdoor allowed her to walk directly to the small etched-out sandlot that we used to spar, as well as the hutch where we kept any sick patients. The Blackwood was a mere thirty yards away, bordering our little cottage, but none of us had ever cared about the rumors, enjoying the peace that the woods brought.

The scent of willow tickled my nose. The smell changed in here daily with whatever was being made, but the underlying scent of spice and warmth always put me at ease. After today, I could use some easing.

"Yes, same marks. Scratches, too. I would like to think that whatever animal gave them to him is the reason he's nearly dead, but something else is wrong with him. He's just as gaunt as the last one, all skin and bones," Maris said, shaking her head in confusion as she roughly stripped the willow bark in her hand. Angry at herself, as usual, when she couldn't find the solution to a problem. She always took it hard when it was one of her patients.

"But if what the people who found him say is true, he hasn't been gone for more than a day or two. That's not nearly enough time to have starved his body to this extent."

"How close is he?" I ask, reaching over the bench to grab the bark from her before she rendered it useless.

"Very," she said with a heavy sigh. "Almost worse than the last one. I've done all I can, treated his wounds and took away his pain, but I doubt he'll survive the night."

Nodding, I stripped the bark into uniform pieces. It was the same as the last man who came in. We treated him for two days after he was brought to us from the neighboring town. Anything we tried to stop whatever was eating away at him failed uselessly. He passed away unsurprisingly the next morning.

"Is it anyone we know?"

She shook her head. "No, his name is Brendon, not that he's been able to confirm that. He was brought in by some of the traveling merchants who just happened to know him from their last stop. They'd just left his town—the same one from where the last man came from—a few days ago, and said he looked as healthy as could be. Halfway between there and here they found him in a ditch by the woods, half out of his mind and barely coherent."

My brows creased in confusion, worry starting to replace my curiosity. "Do you think it's going to come here, whatever it is?"

"Blessed Divine, I hope not, at least not until I can figure out a way to cure it." She used the old prayer, hoping to ward off the evil with her words. "Don't worry about it too much. We'll be just fine." Her warm smile gave me some comfort that we would figure it all out in the end.

"Yeah, cub, I'm sure you'll scare whatever it is away with those eyes of yours," Geoff says teasingly, coming in with some logs to start the fire for whatever tonic Maris was making. He always found it amusing the amount of times I'd made grown men piss themselves from staring at me for too long.

I scoffed in feigned outrage, shaking my head and trying to keep in my laughter. I mean, he wasn't wrong; knowing my luck, the disease would evade the town just to stay away from me.

"Oh, leave her alone." Maris chuckled, tossing a piece of bark at his head. He ducked before it could hit him, laughing as he reached into the fire pit. He shot her a warm smile over his shoulder, one she returned shyly before reaching toward the piles of herbs I had been about to twine together. "Here, why don't you let me do that and you go check on Brendon. I want your opinion on his state."

"Okay." I nodded, wiping my palms on the bench rag. "Is he spewing the same religious nonsense as the other one, too?"

"It's not nonsense, the God and Goddess created us and sustain all that is around us. They are what balance our existence." Maris looked at me in exasperation, having tried to teach me all this for years.

"So I'll take that as a yes," I said, giving her my own annoyed look back. If the God and Goddess were so important, then why had they disappeared with their Descendents and whatever magic had made Irropia so unique, leaving the rest of us peons to suffer the loss of what our world used to be?

They had left almost no trace of their existence except by written word and legend. A few old texts and relics were all anyone had left of a time when magic prospered and everyone in the kingdom bowed to the power of The Divine, and most of them were now being kept *safe* in the capital or under lock and key in some old temple.

This was a topic Maris and I had disputed for a long time. She tried to assure me that there was a reason for their leaving, but was never able to tell me what that reason was.

She sighed heavily. "Yes, he's talking like the last one."

I gave a groan of annoyance. The madness-driven rambling always creeped me out. The last man had a tendency to get loud and upset when I walked in the room. His incoherent words grew frantic, a panicked edge to them, as he stared into my eyes without flinching. Creepy.

"Great," I mumbled as I shut the back door behind me.

CHAPTER THREE

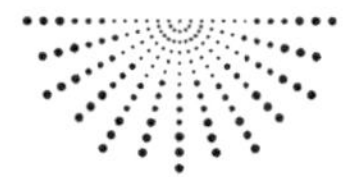

I crossed the few yards between the house and the shed where we had people stay who were in critical condition. Geoff had never liked the idea of having a stranger in the house, so he built the small building along with the cottage when they had first moved here.

Toeing the weather-worn door closed behind me as I stepped into the room, I took care to be as quiet as possible. It was bare of anything except a twin bed and the desk that Maris kept for when she needed to work near her patients. The window above lit the room surprisingly well and the white walls helped keep the typically dreary atmosphere from invading the room. A small, iron oven stood in the corner, which we used to keep the space warm during the colder winter months.

Summer had already begun to encroach on spring, so even the mornings were warm enough that a fire was usually unnecessary. As the days went on, it was a relief when the cold stone of the cottage kept the house cool.

I stepped farther into the room, trying not to disturb the fragile man lying in the bed. Hopefully, he'd stay asleep and I could get away with taking a peek at his wounds before the manic ramblings of gods and monsters began.

A creak sounded from the floorboard underfoot, and without warning, the man's head snapped up, looking over toward me at a speed that should have been impossible in his withered state.

Jumping in shock, I could almost hear the cracking and grinding of his bones as he moved. I silently cursed Maris for making me do this. The soulless eyes of the skeletal man tracked my every move as I walked to the middle of the room. His seemingly calm demeanor was scarier than if he had been shouting.

Walking up next to the bed, I saw the clean sheets had been pulled down to the man's hips, allowing me to look at the state of his emaciation.

I could see almost every bone in his body. Ribs protruded out in a sickly, stomach-turning way. His thin, almost translucent skin was stretched so tightly over them I was surprised it hadn't ripped yet, as if every breath could have the bones tear right through the wafer-thin membrane.

His arms, which lay lamely at his sides, were nothing more than spindles of decaying muscle and bone, barely wider than my own wrist. Any bit of fat the man may have had was all but gone. His face resembled a skull more than a person. The gauntness brought his cheekbones to a razor's edge, and his eye sockets had sunk in past what even the most gruesome of starvation could have caused. The last few wisps of patchy red hair lay flat and dull against the pillow. The skin of his scalp was pulled so tightly, I could almost see the sutures of the bones beneath.

The most disturbing thing, however, were the claw marks that crossed directly from his left shoulder to his right hip. Even with a poultice covering most of it, I could still see the putrid green and black ooze that was seeping from the wounds. The vile substance had made my iron-stomach turn when I first saw it. The noxious slime crawled beneath Brendon's skin, veins of it snaking out around the wound: toxic vines sucking the very life from him, every ounce of his soul slowly leeching away.

The bites covering the rest of his body wept the same tar-like liquid. The poisonous web carved its way across his entire chest, some even beginning to creep up his neck as I watched. They were growing fast, like some invasive plant that stole all the nutrients from the soil and killed everything else around it.

The poultice that Maris had made looked to have only slowed the infection rate based on the lines she had made with ink on the man's chest, marking its progress. Each line representing an hour passed. The ones closest to the wound on his chest were only separated by a few inches, but as they slowly reached the man's neck, they began to grow farther apart as the disease spread faster.

Maris was right, he didn't have a lot of time left. It was slowly covering his entire body, and soon he'd have more of the noxious black liquid beneath his skin than his own blood. It was eating him from the inside out, turning every part of him into decayed tissue.

I went over to the desk, and the man's dull eyes followed as I moved around the room. His wheezing breaths rattled inside his chest painfully, splitting through the silence in reminder of his fast-approaching death. As if we needed reminding.

His gaze, while lifeless, seemed to spark quickly for a single moment, almost pleading in its intensity. Pleading for help—or death. I didn't know which would be more merciful; even on the slim chance his body survived, would his mind ever return to what it once was? Or had it already receded beyond the barrier to the afterlife, leaving his rotting body an empty husk?

I turned back to the papers scattered about on the desk, completely covering the worktop. Some were random thoughts jotted down with distracted quickness. Others were time stamped and depicted infection patterns from both our previous patient and Brendon.

While it didn't appear to be contagious yet, thank The Divine, the fact was it came from an animal. It may not be spreading among humans, but it could carry across to other creatures, making it almost impossible to find and kill off the original carrier of the disease.

And then there was the looming dread that it would mutate into something different—something far deadlier—and then we would all be shit out of luck. There was a clock ticking somewhere, counting down the time left for us to figure out how to stop it, and I wasn't liking our odds.

Maris's notes spoke of other remedies that she wanted to try, and the infection's effects on certain organs. I knew what she was doing just from peering at the pages. Watching how it spread, keeping track of timing and placement of the wounds in relation to vital organs. Maris didn't believe one bit that she could save this patient; it was the next one she was hoping to save from the same fate. Or the one after that. She was preparing for a plague. A widespread breakout.

Riffling through the papers, so many that I had no idea how she knew where to find anything, I found pieces of bluish-gray parchment hidden under the chaos. I picked them up, growing more and more confused by their contents as I read. Mentions of energy sparks and the disease's effects on them were hastily written in bleeding ink.

Whatever a "spark" was, it looked like the infection was slowly eating away at it, leaving little behind for her to encourage a complete cure of the body with. It was dying out, although her shock at that was evident, the note underlined so many times the paper had nearly ripped. None of these had been here last week.

A map of the continent was splayed out across the desk, underneath the mess of parchment. Everything north of the

Blackwood was empty, covered in fog and the unseen curiosity of the cartographers. None had ever made it past the dark forest to see what laid on the other side. None that ever came out, that was. No ship or crew dared sail around for fear of losing their lives to the Sea Smoke or the dangerous waters that separated the continent.

Drops of ink dotted its pristine, detailed face like beauty marks on an ivory doll. They were spotted about the page in an irregular pattern, starting in clumps near Vallenia and the surrounding towns and cities on the eastern border of Irropia, before spreading out across the land in ones or twos. The more I looked, however, the more unnerving the sight became, because of the unorganized yet consistent pattern of dots jumping around the map, heading closer and closer to the cities and villages in the west. Toward us.

Tucked underneath the map were even more papers, containing detailed descriptions of the sickness from other healers across the kingdom, dated weeks ago, stating that they had all seen it spreading in random patterns through their area. It killed one, maybe two people in a few days. Other times, it took out whole families before moving on without a trace.

When had she done all of this, collected all this information? We had only seen the sickness for the first time a week ago. At least, I thought we had. Confusion and even some betrayal warred inside me; I couldn't understand why she would keep this all from me.

She lied to my face and told me not to worry about it. That we'd be fine. By all accounts, we were not going to be fine. If her map marked where all the cases had been accounted for, then our village would be hit soon.

Had Maris known about this for over a month? Looking back down at the map, the countless marks mocked me, staring up at me like beacons of evil. Maris wasn't worried about a plague forming. One had already started.

What the hell was going on?

"I give warning to the light! Hear me! They come for you!"

I jolted at the mumbled words, knocking into the desk with my hip, and dropping the papers as I twisted around. Brendon, at some point, had sat straight up, with what muscles I had no idea. The rigid posture must have been nearly snapping his spine in half with his body so weak. Given his state, he shouldn't have been able to sit up without help, let alone hold himself like that.

Staring with wide eyes at the man, I leaned back slightly as his gaze met mine. I wasn't even looking at a person anymore, nothing but dying embers. No consciousness. No soul. They were blown so wide in a panic, yet no true fear seemed to actually remain. He began to shake, shivering in terror, but his facial expression didn't change. His body was going through the motions of terror, and yet feeling none of it.

Louder than before, he yelled, "I give warning to the light! Hear me! They come for you!"

The cautionary flicker started within me again. Before, when I was fighting, I burned with rage, but now a pleasant—soothing —feeling filled me. Like a warm bath after a cold, freezing day in the snow. Shelter during a tumultuous storm.

Brendon's eyes grew even wider, and I worried they would pop from his head as they stared straight through me at some invisible monster. He shouted, nearly screaming, "I give warning to the light! HEAR ME! They come for you!"

The well of energy stirred inside me and flared in response to the man's yelling, protecting me from who knows what. The gold sheen came over my eyes once again, drowning my view in a gilded river. The chills of wariness that came with the shouted words fell away. The sweet, peaceful hum in my veins filled me from head to toe. Last time I drowned under the weight of the power, blacking out. This time, I fell into it willingly, seamlessly melding into the endless well. Without thinking, I stepped up to the poor soul who was barely hanging on by a thread, so tattered and broken.

Opening its mouth, his body bellowed, "I GIVE WARNIN—"

Reaching out with my hands, I cupped the sunken cheeks of the empty husk, its words cutting off abruptly.

Turning the poor man's head toward me, I looked into its gaze and for the first time, I felt as if I saw a person in there. A person begging for death, so tired and destroyed. A certain desperation, an almost pleading look for mercy. With sorrow and a soft feeling I couldn't describe, I rubbed my thumbs gently across his cheeks, careful not to tear his fragile skin.

As the warmth in my chest pulsed softly with heat, like a low-burning fire, it moved up through my arms. I flowed with it, letting it do what it may. The arcing power ran its course beneath my skin, spreading through my fingers before slipping into Brendon's body.

I watched as he relaxed almost instantly as the energy encompassed his being, protecting him from the infection waiting in the wings like some dark force, eating away at him little by little. For a brief moment, a flash of awareness flicked across his gaze, a look of pure relief spreading over him.

Closing his eyes, leaning his head against my hand, a single tear fell. As it flowed down over my hand, he took his last breath. The smallest of sighs, a curl of his lips in the briefest of smiles, and he was gone.

The gold sheen still hovered over my view, giving everything a sparkling glow, a soft radiance of peace and dreams that fit the circumstances. With a heavy heart and wet eyes, I gently lowered him back down onto the bed, pulling the sheets up to cover his skeletal body, tucking in the edges like one would with a child.

I floated along the endless burning sea as I sat with him for what felt like hours, holding his thin, skeletal hand in mine. I stayed contently submerged within my well, silent tears leaking from my golden eyes.

When I finally got up to leave, the sun having descended and the night sky out in full, I leaned over him. Pushing back the last remains of what was probably once a head of luscious auburn hair, I pressed a kiss to his forehead.

A slight tingling sensation came to my lips as I whispered, "May you come back in the next life to a more forgiving world." His soul deserved another chance at the life that was stolen from him.

Before I could even question it, the power ebbed away, leaving me exhausted and emotionally raw. Reaching up with a shaky hand, I wiped away the wetness on my face. Looking down, I saw the shimmering liquid lightly covering my hand, glinting like flakes of gold in water. I wiped my hand on my pants, removing the trace of my shining tears.

Walking to the door, I turned and took one last look at the lost one. His face now set in a peaceful expression, as if he had simply passed in his sleep and not in suffering—his soul finally at rest.

I crossed the short distance once again in the dark, Maris needed to know about Brendon, and I needed to get some answers as to why the hell she was keeping stuff from me. I walked through the workroom, brushing my hand gently over the hanging bundles of herbs as I walked down the hall.

I went to call out for them, however, the sounds of a heated conversation coming from the main room stopped me in my tracks. Pressing my back to the wall, I listened in, knowing Maris may catch and berate me for eavesdropping, but after finding the papers and notes—she had some questions of her own to answer for.

"We can't keep lying to her, Maris. We don't have any time left. Her episodes are getting worse, and her birthday is tomorrow." Geoff's voice was strained with exhaustion, as if an invisible weight was sitting on his shoulders, dragging him down.

"I know, but where do we even start? We waited too long. If we tell her now we might just send her spiraling."

"We waited too long because you were always against it," Geoff scoffed, anger clear in his voice. "And besides, when have you ever seen that girl fail to take on anything?"

"Don't go blaming this all on me; you know exactly why *we* didn't tell her." Her voice was stiff, clearly uncomfortable. "And that may be, but we can't do it now. We wasted so many chances to talk to her about this. We run the risk of her not believing us, or worse, refusing help because she's too stubborn. She might not even remember anything."

I had never truly known whether a heart could break, but if it couldn't, what was I feeling then? Because each one of their words, their admissions, was a dagger to mine. Some part of me had hoped that everything would be a big misunderstanding. That Maris had just been too busy and had forgotten, but I knew that was just the naive little girl that still wanted to hide under her covers until her parents checked under the bed. Now I didn't know what to think.

Maris let out a weary sigh. "I know we weren't sure about it when she was younger, but now ... we can't go against him, Geoff. He told us to protect her, no matter the cost. We don't even know what will happen. If we can't keep her safe for as long as possible, he will kill us. I don't think he would even hesitate if we failed him. And if she spirals, refuses help, and gets herself hurt—or worse, gets others killed—then that's exactly what we've done."

My hands squeezed into fists as my anger rose, the two of them having seemingly conspired to lie to me, keep secrets about *me*, for eighteen years. And worse, at the command of someone else. What was so important they wouldn't tell me? Who was so important they would rather keep me in the dark rather than go against whoever *he* was?

We had never kept secrets from each other, not in any way that mattered. At least that was what I thought, until those notes and the map and now this … now I don't think I had ever been told the truth by my adoptive parents. Had it always been lies that were used as the foundation of this family, used to keep me naive and complacent? We always knew I was different; it's not like it was hard to connect the weird dots together, but we had always dealt with it together. Or I thought we did.

Magic may have all but disappeared, but not completely. I was something, whatever that may be, and they seemed to know more about it than they were letting on.

Neither had ever really talked to me about their past, preferring to live in the present. It always led me to believe that they came from a bad situation. That they had moved to start over, but I never got an actual answer.

Most of what I knew about their past consisted of vague stories. They had moved to the village a few years before they found me at the edge of the woods, abandoned and alone. No one in the village would confirm that, but until very recently, I hadn't seen the point in digging into it. I'd always taken their word on everything, never questioning anything.

"We don't have any more time to protect her. We'll barely have enough time to get her home tomorrow. You saw her this morning. That was not normal. She knows she's not normal—you need to give her more credit. She's not stupid, and she'll figure it all out anyway. You're only delaying the inevitable because you're afraid of what will happen when she does know about everything," Geoff all but shouted, his frustration clear.

Well, at least someone was on my side. Although he was just as guilty, having had my entire life to tell me what they had been hiding.

"The bullshit we've been feeding her for years isn't going to work anymore, Maris. These past few months have proven that. Her night terrors are getting worse, and I keep finding her farther and farther out into the woods. She's already trying to get there. If we don't tell her, we are dooming her. And most likely everyone else along with her."

Having heard enough, my anger barely contained to the humming that started sometime during the conversation, I backtracked to the workroom door, shutting it loudly. Their mumbling voices cut off abruptly. Apparently, they didn't want me hearing what they were talking about. How shocking.

My heart clenched in both anger and sadness, knowing that I couldn't trust them. Not until I figured out what was going on. I shoved the emotions aside, unable to dwell on what this all meant—that my faith in them was shattering like glass in my hands.

Reining it all in, I tried to keep my face neutral as I called out, "Maris?"

"In here, honey." Her voice only wavered slightly.

I walked back through the hall and into the main room. Both Geoff and Maris were standing in the middle, trying their best to look innocent. Immediately I wanted to call them out on their bullshit, but from what I had gathered, lying had been a thing in this house for far longer than I could have imagined. I doubted they would even tell me the truth if I asked them directly. They were so practiced in their subterfuge, it must have been second nature now.

"What were you guys talking about?" I asked with a placid smile that matched their own. Knowing myself, it probably came out more brittle and bared than I would have liked, but it couldn't hurt to try. A tiny part of me was waiting for them to tell me, to break down and just explain everything to me, but as I watched them both zip everything back inside, I knew it was a hopeless wish.

I looked at Geoff, begging in my head for him to stand up for me like he always had, like he seemed to want to. I swore an apology flashed through his eyes, all but pleading with me to understand why he couldn't. Pressing his lips together in a forced smile, he let loose a pretty lie, "Nothing important, cub, we were just waiting on you to get done with Brendon. How is he?"

So I guess a heart could break; I felt my own split right down the middle. It seemed after living so long with no one in your corner that when you lost the person who stood by you no matter what, that it cracked under the weight of such loneliness. The last of my trust shriveled up into a ball, a whimpering, pitiful creature hidden deep within my chest.

Maris had always treated me with love, like I was her daughter, but I had always felt as if she held me to a higher standard than everyone else. As if I needed to act a certain way in order to fulfill an idea of me in her head. But Geoff … he was the man who wrapped his arms around me when I was at my lowest. When I woke up screaming from my nightmares, he was the one to hold me until I could fall asleep again.

I held his gaze for a split second longer, his face looking more guilty by the minute. He broke eye contact with me, turning to look at Maris, and my heart wrenched in pain. Shoving all of those feelings back into their box, I shifted my focus to her as well. Her green eyes hid secrets within lies. Secrets about me, that caused everything inside my being to rage at not knowing.

With curly black hair framing the light brown skin of her face and the slight stature of a delicate bird, strangers would consider her as beautiful and as fragile as one. But despite her petite nose and full, warm face, in reality, a wolf sat behind those eyes. It was something I had always respected about her, but now I could see how that cunning had at some point been turned on me, to hide whatever was worth breaking my trust.

"He passed away," I said, my voice flat and giving away

nothing as I stared into the eyes of the woman who had raised me since I was two. A tempest of conflict battled inside me over what I had thought I knew and what I now understood to be empty truths.

"What!" Maris's brows furrowed, eyes wide in disbelief. "I for sure thought he had until tonight. Did something happen? We heard some noise, but figured he had started speaking again."

"He was fine when I first went in, silent and calm, but after a few minutes he started shouting. Then he closed his eyes and passed away, like nothing had happened," I said convincingly, shrugging my shoulders in faux confusion as I conveniently left out the part where I was involved.

Geoff gave me a look, and I winced internally. If anyone was going to call me on my tells, it was going to be him.

"What did he say before he died?"

He had been the one to tell me that a great lie was made mostly of truths, placed in there to distract someone from what they were truly hiding. I guess he should know—they'd both been doing the same to me for years. My bitterness was apparent, but I couldn't find it within myself to care at the moment.

"Just the same cryptic words as the last guy, nothing much to make sense of. I went over to try to calm him and he just sort of …" I shrugged my shoulders again. "He just stopped."

I felt a little bad for Maris, who was clearly in shock, worried by how quickly Brendon had died. In my heart I knew I had helped him pass away somehow. That I saved him from the long hours of pain it would have taken him to do so on his own.

But I also couldn't help but feel that if she had just talked to me, included me in her research—not kept things from me—then I might have been able to help her save him, or at the very least, have come up with a better way to slow the spreading.

"Geoff, would you put together a pyre for Brendon? I know it's late, but I don't want to risk whatever this illness is seeping into the ground or air by leaving him any longer than necessary. I'll bring a message to the post to let his village know of his passing."

Geoff glanced once more at me, with his rugged face drawn in displeasure, before he lumbered outside to do as she asked. Maris looked at me, and my gaze settled on her. I don't know what she saw in my eyes, but the smallest of flinches pinched at her features, creasing the corners of her eyes.

People had flinched or winced away from my gaze for as long as I could remember; seeing something inside me that scared them to their soul. Maris and Geoff seemed to have built up an immunity to it—they eventually looked away, but never had they flinched. I knew it wasn't that.

No, this was the reaction of a woman who knew she'd betrayed someone who trusted her. A part of her, no matter how tiny, knew that keeping things from me would only drive me away—make me resent them.

With a shaky voice, Maris took a step toward me. "Talli, why don't you go get cleaned up? We don't want you carrying anything that could have gotten on you around the house. It may not be contagious to us, but let's not be too daring with it."

Staring at her, disappointment and anger mixing into an ugly concoction, I considered confronting her on her deceit, letting it all out, rather than keeping the toxic emotions inside. However, I was unwilling to be lied to again, to be placated. So, turning, I followed the stairs at my back up to the floor above that held the two bedrooms in the house.

I'd barely gotten halfway up when I heard the sound of relief come from the main room. I couldn't stop the tears of anger that welled up in my eyes.

CHAPTER FOUR

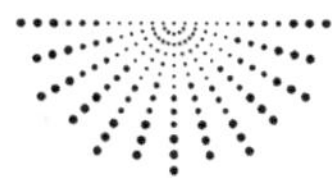

he bed was plush, a mound of pillows in every shape and color was piled on top. A soft, decorative carpet covered most of the floor, yet the cold from the stone beneath still found a way to seep through. Pretty tapestries and artwork hung from the walls. It would have been a beautiful room, had it not been a prison cell.

The bars at the front were made of a white, glass-like crystal, burning so brightly it was throwing a glow through the entire space. Veins of energy struck the crystalline bars, moving through them like a river. The currents branched off like suspended lightning. The closer I got to the bars, the more tired I felt, wading through my power as if rocks had been tied to my ankles, dragging me down into the depths. I felt it tighten up inside, nestling into a ball in the middle of my chest.

A door somewhere off to the side let out a high-pitched creak, the light from the bars obscured almost everything outside them with their intensity, keeping me from peering too hard into the darkness. The footsteps slapped resoundingly against the stone as a group approached my cell. Standing, I moved closer to the bars, despite the draining effect it seemed to have on my energy. My bare feet curled into the rug as a chill swept through the corridor.

A man stepped into view, followed by two guards, both dressed in silver armor with their faces completely covered by helmets. Their chest plates gleamed, the fronts taken up by some kind of emblem that I couldn't make out. The man's slick brown hair framed a pretty face. Striking—chilling—green eyes that held an eerie rot pierced through me.

Chiseled cheekbones and a sharp nose gave him the appearance of some bird of prey. His lean frame was draped in black trousers and a silver tunic embroidered with twisted images of skeletal creatures. The bodies were misshapen, faces crying out in silent pain. I could almost picture the dying, wounded sounds they would make.

Despite all that, he was handsome in a way that could disarm you if you let him. Most venomous creatures were pretty like that. They got you to drop your guard, so you never expected the bite. His camouflage was nearly perfect, but the sick, demented look in his eyes would turn any sane person away.

We held each other's gaze, both taking measure of the other. Just the sight of him made my blood boil, my energy fought against the glowing bars, nothing able to truly keep it down as my rage stirred it higher. I flicked my eyes around my surroundings despite the light, looking for any possible escape or weakness once the bars could no longer hold me. He was on the clock, and we both knew it.

The traitorous snake lifted his chin up in superiority, very pleased with himself at the situation before him. Me in a cage, him lording over me. His eyes filled with lust and arrogance. "Comfortable?"

I gave him a saccharine smile, honey nearly dripped from my lips. "Quite."

He sniffed his nose in annoyance, a small crack in his mask.

"You know you can't win this, right? He will come for me." I shook my head mockingly. "This will not end well for you."

He hummed in thought. "What will we do about him?" he asked sardonically, a cruel twist to his mouth. "I have a feeling he'll walk right into that cell next to you as quiet as a lamb if I ask him to." The insanity he tried so hard to keep from public view crept into his gaze.

"And explain to me the part where you expect him to go along complacently? We are talking about the same man, yes?"

"For all of his strengths, he does have one weakness." He looked at me, tilting his head to the side, anger flashing through his eyes. A sick smile appeared on his face as he held up a curved black dagger. The sickle-shaped blade was made of a similar glass material as the bars, except the blade's black depths seemed to suck the light in. "I may not be able to kill you both, at least not until all my plans line up, but something tells me the mere mention of any pain befalling you will make him do whatever I want. That should greatly expedite both of your deaths."

"I can't believe you mined the glass, you traitorous bastard." My rage built, making my power stir more. Even within the confines of the cell, it came to me, making me glow brighter than the bars.

Taking a step back, a split second of wariness crossed his face, eyes flicking between me and the only thing that kept me from ripping his heart apart, shredding it from his body. He knew there was only a limited amount of time before the crystal would drain completely from the effort of trying to restrain me.

I laughed mockingly at him, watching his face twist in rage at my dismissal of him. "You don't know how long these bars will hold, do you? It could be days, weeks before they fail, or it could be hours." I stepped as close as possible, pressing myself up against the bars. They hummed and buzzed in agitation, the light growing as it fought against my rising power. Gritting my teeth as my energy faltered slightly, I used my anger to withstand the restraining waves of energy.

"But know this." My voice promised him violence and death. "They will fail, and when they do, I will rain a hell upon you that will make you wish I had left you to him. You think he's your nightmare? You're wrong." I pressed even further into the glass, my own light battling for supremacy against the prison. My entire body stood encased in the warring colors. My skin cracked apart in areas, my spark shining through.

I laughed at his ignorance and gave him my most vicious smile, baring my teeth like the predator inside of me wanted to, whispering huskily, "I am."

His eyes widened in terror and I had the satisfaction of watching him panic over whether the bars would break this very minute. If they could hold me. Unfortunately, for now they would, but if I had it my way, they wouldn't stay up for long.

Stepping back, bored with him and ready to get out of here, I let my power drop. There was no use in wasting the energy just to continue to prove a point.

His face quickly smoothed over, and he cleared his throat as he tugged his tunic down, readjusting his unbothered appearance. A distraction. One he kept up to fool anyone who didn't know that underneath all that finery was a decaying creature of a foul and chaotic nature.

Obviously going for a different approach, he gave me a placating smile and stepped closer to the bars, almost touching them. "Must we fight, my love? I had hoped to have a pleasant conversation."

I narrowed my eyes, mouth twisting in disgust at the use of the pet name. "I'm not yours. You don't have the right to that name."

His nostrils flared, and he lunged at the bars with shocking quickness, his hands wrapping around them. Banging and raging against the crystal glass, he shook with fury, uncaring that they drained him as well. He screamed at me through them, spittle flying in all directions. "I DO HAVE A RIGHT!" His eyes burned bright, gaze wild, as his depraved, wicked insanity cracked through his finely crafted mask. "I DO HAVE A RIGHT! I DO! YOU WERE SUPPOSED TO BE MINE! YOU! ARE! MINE!"

I stood unflinching in the face of his explosion, giving him a small, secretive smile as I leaned in toward him. "Careful," I whispered, so only we heard, "Your crazy is showing."

With a furious look on his face and a delicate sniff he stepped back, and readjusted his clothes once more. "Apologies, where are my manners? Here, let me show you what I've been working on." He motioned to one of the guards forward.

The armored man stepped closer, lifting his helmet without a single word. The horrendous sight before me sent shivers down my spine. The man's lower jaw was missing chunks of skin, his mandible jutting out and open to the air. Jagged wounds sliced down his jaw as green pus oozed its way down his neck, black veins crawling under his skin and across his face.

His eyes, sunken into their sockets, held no soul within their gaze. The whites had been taken over by empty blackness. He was no longer alive, I could tell, but neither was he dead. A wraith, stuck forever in the middle of existence.

"Isn't he marvelous?" the man said, like a proud father would of his son. "They're quite easily controlled unless they become starved, and then they are as unpredictable as they are ugly." He laughed like someone told him a hysterical joke. "They'll ensure my victory." He gazed at his creation in a crazed sort of joy. As if he hadn't stolen this man's life and turned him into an abomination.

I looked at him in shock, disturbed on a soul deep level at the atrocity before me, by his actions, having distorted the circle of existence. "You're deranged. Do you know what you've done?" I whispered at him as I simultaneously recoiled from his monster and also struggled not to reach out and put the poor thing out of its misery.

He glowered at me, obviously wanting a different reaction. "You see, they tend to start falling apart unless they eat regularly. It truly is an amazing transformation; just think if they could access their other forms or magic like this."

Just as he went to continue, a piece of skin sloughed off from the cheek of the guard, falling to the floor with a wet splat; slime and other unknown substances covered the inside of the flesh. Black rotting muscle was left behind, goo dripping down its neck.

The man sighed, put out from the interruption of his tirade. "Well, I guess you'll just have to see what I mean." He turned away from the prison cell, walking back the way he came in from, he called over his shoulder to the rotting corpse. "Feed."

My brow furrowed in confusion, but in the same moment the

wraith, who had been standing complacent and docile, suddenly lunged at me with a snarl, his mouth open wide to show me a mouth of sharp, serrated teeth.

My eyes snapped open as I gasped for air, kicking at the bed sheets as I thrashed around, stuck in a state of fear as screams of agony rang in my ears. Breathing heavily, I shot upright, looking around as terror assaulted my senses. I never remembered much from my nightmares, cursed to wake in a panic night after night and not know the cause, but this one …

Flashes of a stone cell and a decaying monster ran through my head. Of a chilling green gaze, the man's face blurring in my mind until I couldn't even remember if he'd been there at all.

Looking around, I had to check that the same walls of my bedroom surrounded me as they had when I fell asleep. The light from the four moons spilled in through the uncovered window, allowing me to see through the pitch darkness.

Something was wrong. The air felt too quiet, even for such a late hour. No crickets chirped outside the window. No dogs barked down the street. No creaks came from the house, or snores from Geoff across the hall.

The pit of energy that sat in my chest fanned the flames higher as I silently tiptoed out of bed. Quickly shucking my nightshirt, I donned my leathers from yesterday. Grabbing my daggers, I moved quietly to the door.

Pressing my ear to it, I listened carefully for any sounds of life from within the house. It was completely silent, no noises reached me through the thick wood.

Moving to turn the knob, I faltered, gasping as energy pulsed outward, electricity burning through my veins. I doubled over in pain as the heat reached every deep corner within me, pushing against my skin. It simmered underneath like a river of lava, cauterizing my nerves until there was nothing but cords of energy. I fought for air, barely able to move, until it finally relented.

My breath came out in harsh relief, air filling my lungs once more, as the storm quickly disappeared. A slight hum and a pounding in my ears remained. A loud thump, coming from the back of the house, drew my attention away. Slowly opening the door, I crept out into the hallway, daggers at the ready.

Across the hall, Geoff and Maris's door stood open. Slowly peering in, I noticed the rumpled, slept-in bed. The blankets were thrown back and their clothes tossed haphazardly on the floor. Even if it weren't for the weird time of night, the whole situation would be unusual; Maris had an obsessive need to have everything in its place. Geoff's broadsword, which was nearly taller than me and usually rested on the wall next to his side of the bed, was gone.

Another thump, followed by silence pulled me away from the room and down the stairs. Keeping my back to the wall, I edged around the corner into the main room. Nothing but shadows greeted me, seeming to pull away from the wall toward me in a protective embrace.

Whipping my head toward the workroom, I moved into the darkness of the hallway, as low snarls met my ears.

Viscous growls and awful ripping sounds grew louder as I stepped into the room. Overturned jars and bottles covered the work bench, their contents scattered all about the room. Shattered glass was flung across the floor, glistening like teardrops in the colored moonlight. The back door hung from its hinges, the window in shards from being bashed in.

I passed the mess and went out into the backyard, moving toward the only sounds I could hear in the sinister silence. Following it to the side of the house, nearest to the pasture, I gripped my daggers tight, turning the corner.

The creature was at least the size of a small horse, and would have resembled a bear had its body not been malformed in so many ways. It had a patchwork quilt of shaggy, mottled brown fur, and gray skin. Pieces of bone jutted out at weird angles all along its body. It looked as if it had taken its own claws to its skin, with bleeding cuts and wounds oozing a black pus that reminded me of the infection that had spread through Brendon's body.

The beast's mangy fur was covered in the tar-like substance. Pieces of its skin hung detached, connected only by thin strings of muscle and sinew. Spinal protrusions broke through the creature's back, the white bone open to the air, looking like spikes just waiting to impale something. Or someone.

I jumped back behind the corner of the house, my heart racing, thoughts going through every scenario in which I got out of this alive. This must have been the creature that had attacked Brendon and the others.

Peeking back around the corner, my knuckles white with the grip I had on the daggers and forcing my eyes away from the beast, I looked around the ground. Blood splattered across the grass like paint on a canvas. Red blood. And laying amidst the massacre was a broadsword, the perfectly sharpened blade catching the moonlight, refracting the colors all around, even as it was mostly covered in black-green blood. Waiting for its warrior to come and pick it up once more.

Yet with no sign of either Geoff or Maris, I wondered if that day would ever come again. Heart dropping at the implication, I leaned back against the house, squeezing my eyes shut.

Don't think about it, Talli, don't think about it. Shove it down, put it back in its box.

A loud pound drew my attention back to the demonic creature, and I watched as it shoved something up against the fence post. Taking a small step closer to peer around its wide berth, I found that it was not just one creature, but two.

Well ... had been two, I think in disgust, as the bear ripped into an even less identifiable creature. More bone than actual animal, the beast must have been the one to be cut down by the broadsword, its black blood pooling everywhere as the bigger one feasted on whatever was left of its insides.

Indecision warred within me, my rage and pain making the hum in my veins louder, demanding I seek revenge for Maris and Geoff. To destroy this plague upon the world. Equally as strong was my training, my instincts, and my self-preservation. I knew nothing about this creature, that very well could have taken out both of my adoptive parents. I didn't know its strengths and weaknesses. I would be going into this fight blind, alone, and wholly unprepared.

My choice, however, was stolen as my legs gave out and I fell to my knees. Knives dropped from my hands as pain hammered at me from all sides. The burn from before was barely a flame compared to the raging wildfire determined to leave me a pile of ash. I could feel it trying to change me, morph me into some-thing … someone else.

Whoever that may have been, I was terrified to know. My blood all but dripped out my pores as the pressure pushed against my skin. My face pinched in barely contained agony, my teeth gritting against the scream trying to push its way past. Hopeless to do anything against the onslaught.

Just as I thought it would never end, the pain was whisked away once again, leaving me in a whimpering pile. Sweat dripped down my temple as I tried to pick myself up off the ground. I couldn't help but cry out as I pushed off the cool grass, my muscles feeling as if they had been trampled by a stampede of horses. On my knees, I breathed hard, chest aching as the cool air rushed in.

My thoughts had barely returned, when a low growl turned my attention back to the real threat.

"Fuck," I breathed out quietly.

The hell beast's dark soulless eyes stared into me, chills racing down my back at the emptiness within them. They held no spark of life, nothing to distinguish that the creature had been alive at one point.

Its head was round like a bear's, but it was completely devoid of any fur. Its skull pushed against the thin, sickly gray skin, the black orbs of its eyes were sunken into the sockets. Ribs popped out from all sides. The jaw hung open as black saliva dripped out between the four-inch fangs.

The beast looked half insane. Its gaze was void of anything but madness. Blank. Nothing. A shell.

A *wraith.*

A more apt name could not have been given to a walking carcass—living but not. The ravenous gleam in its eyes told me that it had one thought and one thought only.

It took a step forward, opening its giant mouth to release a roar that shook the ground beneath. Spittle flew in every direction, flecking the ground around its gnarled claws.

Pushing past the pain in my muscles, electricity racing through my veins, the hum in my ears louder than ever, I grasped my daggers and stood.

Click. Clack. Click. Clack.

The wraith's bones hit against each other, creating a rattling sound that would soon join my other nightmares. The harsh noise was a blood-curdling reminder of what I would be fighting. Not that I needed one.

Backing up as it stalked me across the field, I looked around quickly, scanning my surroundings for anything that could help. I usually preferred open ground when fighting, but the first lesson Geoff ever taught me was to assess your battlefield, and if it wasn't advantageous to you, then know when to retreat so that you could fight another day.

Out in the open like this I had nothing that could protect me. Those claws could cut me in half with a single swipe. With no real idea as to what I faced, I was at an extreme disadvantage.

I knew how to fight, and fight well, but this was definitely not the time to test it. Not if I didn't have to.

A slight shifting of the ground beneath let me know I'd backed up all the way to the sparring circle in the middle of the yard. I didn't look down, keeping my eyes on the hungry beast, trusting years of practice to keep me balanced on the sand, making the slight adjustments to my stance without much thought.

I stopped in the middle of the ovular ring, the wraith circling around me, its head hanging low. I spun with it, never taking my eyes away as I assessed every possible weak point. The gaping holes in its mottled gray hide would have been my first attack to its major organs, had there been any. I winced in a mix of pity and disgust as a dark sludge sloshed around inside, slowly leaking out of the gaps in its skin.

Whether this had once been an animal or not, nothing deserved to live this pathetic existence—cursed to fall apart and in a constant state of insanity, of hunger. The monstrous ... person, creature, from my nightmare jumped to mind, the image blurred and unclear.

Feral snarls ripped out of its throat, the sound causing skin to slide off and hang down its neck in one big piece, revealing putrid green muscle, something in the stages of rot.

I tried not to gag as I pushed aside any thoughts or feelings; this was about survival. It or me. Crouched at the ready, I held one knife in a basic grip and the other in reverse, blade pointed toward me, its double edge ready to slice across a neck if need be. I could hear Geoff's voice fly through my head, causing my heart to clench and my hands to steady.

"Sometimes it's kill or be killed, cub. One day it might come down to you living or dying, and let me tell you something; if it ever, ever comes down to it—you kill, Talli. You kill, you live, you get back up, and you keep going. But sometimes you don't have that choice, so you do whatever the hell you have to in order to survive. You get me, cub?"

Determination steadied me, bolstered by the power continuing to rage inside me. Narrowing my eyes, I quickly formulated a plan, slowly stuffing my knives back into the pockets of my trousers, sheaths forgotten in my rush.

The beast stopped circling, it's back to the woods, turning inwards—toward me. Time froze, the air standing still, not a peep from the forest or its inhabitants. The woodland creatures were too afraid to draw the abomination's attention.

Kill or be killed. Survive or die.

Coming to the same conclusion, the beast lunged at a speed that shouldn't have been possible. Thankfully, I was quicker and more adept on this ground. Kicking up sand into the beast's eyes as it came upon me, I dove to the right and out of its path at the last second.

Curling up as my hands hit the ground, I rolled into a somersault. Pushing up to my feet without a thought, I made for the forest.

The rage-filled roars of the wraith boomed through the night air. The pounding steps and snarls told me my distraction hadn't lasted long. Pushing past any weakness, the vibrations in the ground from the large bear were the only motivation I needed. Not looking back, I darted into the Blackwood.

CHAPTER FIVE

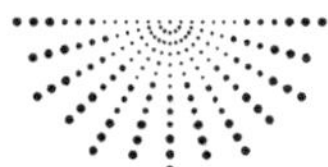

I tore through the trees, shadows coating everything in an inky blackness. I had always found a great peace within the forest's depths; the darkness and quiet had always appealed to me. However, even the lack of light was hindering me this time, my knowledge of the woods was the only thing keeping me on my feet. The canopies far above only allowed slivers of light from the four moons to peek through. Moon rays hit the branches, cutting across the darkness in colorful defiance.

Fear and adrenaline pushed me forward, and I didn't care as the branches whipped against my skin, cutting across my body. They accompanied the shooting pain searing through my very cells.

The sound of trampled leaves and branches wasn't far behind me, the ground vibrating as those hellish paws smashed against it, following me away from the cottage. I couldn't leave an entire village to the same fate as Brendon. They wouldn't stand a chance against this creature, and no one deserved what would become of them if it decided to stray into the town square—not even them.

This monstrosity may tear me to pieces, but I was going to get as far away as I possibly could before that happened, hopefully giving them a chance. And maybe, if blessed by The Divine, I could survive it myself. The horrible, retching snarls that followed my every step seemed to contradict that hopeful wish. As if even the gods were terrified of what beast had crawled its way from the depths of hell.

Turning my head back, I glimpsed the carcass only a hundred feet back. Its eyes flared in enraged hunger, its maw opening to let loose a terrible, broken roar. Whipping my head back around, I pushed my tired and strained muscles harder, running so fast the black-barked trees were nothing but a blur in my peripheral.

I don't know how long I ran for, but somehow I had kept ahead of the beast, driving myself deeper into the darkness until no light was able to penetrate the black depths of the forest. The pit of energy deep inside my core had broken out into a full blaze, its heat so mighty I could have been a drop of fire from the sun or mistaken for the stars themselves had I not been human.

But as it continued to rip everything inside of me apart, I was starting to find it hard to believe that.

The power filled every crevice and divot there was, leaving nothing of me behind. I wanted to curl up on the forest floor and let it consume me whole, but fear and survival were wonderful motivators in the best of situations. Downright inhuman in the worst of them.

The trees around me started to grow larger, and the first hints of light appeared. Their trunks were wider than several grown men, and they had a tendency to glow in the dark. The roots were streaked with luminescent maroon, like they had been painted with shining blood. The tangled limbs were thicker than my entire body was wide, and stuck up out of the ground, making them look like walking giants. The spaces underneath them varied in width and depth, some were the size of full houses and others just small holes for the forest animals to burrow under. This was the true Blackwood. The trees that lined the forest's edge were scrawny saplings in comparison to the towering sentries around me.

What most people had yet to find out was that there still was some magic in the world, you just had to know where to look for it.

The magic of the Blackwood became present the farther in you went, but given the number of people who had disappeared within its dark depths trying to see what was on the other side, there was rarely anyone brave enough to traverse the trails.

The trees seemingly came alive around you, the creaking branches and rustling leaves, the slight groans from their trunks as they held steady against the harsh winds of winter. Truth be told, the trees of the Blackwood hadn't been alive for centuries, having been one of the first things to disappear soon after The Divine had.

But sometimes I swore I could hear them whispering to me. Secrets of the forest, of the things they had seen in their long time on this world, and of the realm they were told to hold within their depths. They were Irropia's first storytellers, and I often found myself desperate to hear those tales. The glow given off by the trees' roots was very dim and almost imperceptible, and I tried not to dwell on the fact that it got duller each year.

It was some of the last magic left behind by the God and Goddess. While the trees no longer moved or spoke, they still held a magic that refused to leave even as the rest of the world surrendered to the inevitable.

Flashes of light flickered in and out of the thick brush, little bursts of radiance which I could never catch when I was little. The orbs darted in and out of the branches; the blues and greens and purples gave the forest a sense of the sentience it once held.

The bright spheres started dancing around, rushing forward toward something.

I ducked underneath the closest set of roots, turning to follow the only source of light, the opening too small for the wraith to follow. The orbs dove and flew through the gaps of the forest; following behind, I darted to the next root-laced burrow. Weaving in and out of the complex systems, I ignored the rough bark scraping against my unprotected arms as I rushed between them.

Roars of frustration followed behind me as the wraith became stuck between the tangled trees, but I continued to pick up my speed even more. The colorful spheres seemed to glow brighter in happiness before they dissipated into the forest, leaving me to find my own path.

My nerves were on fire, whether from the pit of rising power in my stomach or from the excruciating pace I was keeping, but as I ran, unable to stop, I slowly put distance between myself and the creature. Its guttural screams of rage eventually falling away.

I kept moving, weaving underneath the trees, completely lost to the adrenaline and fear pumping through me. The need to survive kept me going even as every inch of my body screamed for me to stop. Every part of my soul shouted in agony from the pain running its course through me—changing me.

I saw a glaring light up ahead, blinding me after mostly darkness for who knew how long. Running towards it, I burst straight into a small clearing as my legs gave out from underneath me, finally refusing to move anymore. The moons shone bright overhead, lighting up the grass clearing in a blaze of hues. A scream edged out of my gritted teeth and tears fell from my eyes as I crawled forward, barely inching my way to the center. Unable to move anymore, my body completely spent, I fell flat to the ground.

My breaths were ragged, lungs burning sharply in my chest, grasping for whatever air they could. I buried my head in the dirt, squeezing my stinging eyes shut. A strangled whimper of pain tore from my throat, the stabbing torture all over my body. I no longer knew where it came from at this point.

I heard Geoff's voice echoing in my head once again, telling me not to stay out in the open for long—to find cover. I wished I could listen to that voice, but I couldn't get my body to move; shockwaves of flame rippled underneath my skin, the very marrow in my bones turning to boiling river inside me. I was being skinned alive, and I had nothing to show for it, what a damn shame.

Gritting my teeth against the pain, I rolled onto my back, my throat unable to hold back the torturous scream. Through stinging breaths I looked up at the star-filled sky, a beautiful painting above me. The four moons were beacons of light, calling to all of night's creatures. This wasn't the worst view to die to, I think. I could have done much worse.

Death and me, we had a … complicated relationship. I'd never been scared of the darkness it would bring, never been scared to pass through his gate. Maris once told me that I was fearless, that I took any obstacle as a challenge and, no matter what, I would find a way to overcome it. If that meant I needed to bash my head against a stone wall, then so be it. While that may have been true, I had never been fearless. Not even a little bit.

Many things had scared me in my life, this night included, but I had accepted Death was just as much a part of life as Life was to death a long time ago. All things had a beginning and an ending, that's what Maris always taught me; despite my reluctance to believe based on sheer faith, what The Divine represented had always resonated with me.

The flow of existence was endless, like a circle, and everyone was bound to it. Who knew if the God and Goddess truly presided over that flow, but it was easy enough to grasp that everyone would pass through those phases whether they liked it or not.

So why should I fear something that I couldn't help? The best I could do was avoid the God of Endings's grip for as long as possible, and make the best of it for however long I was in this world.

My face pinched as I kept my eyes locked on the stars, the twinkling lights the only distraction from my aching body. Head-splitting pains shot behind my eyes like needles, a whimper escaping me. I knew I should be picking myself up, trying to find some place to wait this all out, but the clenching from continuous spasms that rocked through me made it impossible to think past the pain. The incinerating energy within my body was destroying and remaking everything in its path.

A branch cracked with a resounding snap, and my blood turned to ice. Multiple rumbles and snarls came from all around. My nightmare was about to become so much worse.

I closed my eyes again with a resigned sigh, dread pooling in my stomach. "Fuck."

I rolled over onto my hands and knees, my teeth nearly cracking from holding my jaw clenched against the onslaught that beat against my nerves. Pushing up off the ground, I wobbled on my feet like a newborn fawn.

Four more demonic wraiths appeared from between the trees, slinking beneath and over the entangled roots. At different levels of decay, they truly were nightmarish. Black blood dripped from the open wounds along their hides, noxious, green drool hung from their mouths. The dark thick liquid covered what little fur they had, slicked back like an oily blanket.

One of them, resembling something that could have been a mountain lion, would have nearly looked normal if not for the patches of tawny fur falling to the forest floor as it walked toward me. Black and vibrant green spittle dripped down its chin. The eyes were so dilated I could barely tell their color, and the whites had turned black.

The others resembled wolves or foxes. The worst one had barely any skin covering its frame. White ribs, bared and bright under the full light of four moons, jutted out of its body. Many had organs, shockingly, still encased inside their bodies while black fluid dragged behind them like leaky spigots. Some had flayed, decaying muscles, others showing parts of their skulls.

The original wraith stood at the front of the pack, leading the others to their next meal. The low growls and high-pitched snarls, odd retching noises that they were, bounced all around the clearing, disturbing the eerie quiet of the forest.

I pulled my knives, fingers scarcely making it around the handle, my body barely able to get in position.

Without warning, the skeletal wraiths rushed me all at once. The first one reached me within seconds, bounding across the clearing in a few leaping steps. Jumping out of the way, I turned back around, straight into the jaws of a fox. Stabbing out reflexively, both knives drove straight into its throat. Black viscous blood poured out onto my hands, splashing me across the face, and completely covered the ground beneath us in a thick, dark puddle.

Kicking out with my foot, I connected with the jaw of another animal, my leg screaming at the rebounding force. Pulling my blades free, I turned to face my next opponent, but I didn't get a chance as my feet left the ground. The wraith I had just stabbed through, who by all means should be dead, had barreled into me.

I landed hard on my side, the wind knocked right out of me. I coughed as I tried to breathe air back into my lungs, pain radiating from my ribs—probably bruised or broken.

I twisted onto my back just in time to see one of the hell

beasts lunge at me. Slashing with a blade, I dragged the edge across its throat, flinching as I was drenched in the sticky blood. With a whimper, the creature flew over me, only to be replaced by a wolf missing half of its face. The gray skull flashing before my eyes.

Gasping in fear, I threw up my arm to protect my face, screaming as it bit down, crushing my wrist between its massive jaws. The sound of my bone snapping rang in my ear. The echoing cracks of it grinding beneath the unrelenting pressure were even more horrifying.

I punched my fist into the wolf's jaw, my red blood mixing with the black, before thrusting my last blade through the side of the mouth, uncaring as I felt the tip slice into my skin. The beast, however, seemed to barely feel it as it shook and yanked my arm in its grasp like a dog with a bone.

The edges of my vision started to blur, and just when I thought I might pass out, another creature grabbed at my ankle. Pulling back, dragging me closer across the ground, it tore at the tendon and muscle until I could no longer feel it at all. Soon teeth pierced my shoulder, fangs ripping into the skin with ease.

The wraith's face was so close that rotten, green-flecked spit sprayed onto my face. Its rancid breath was toxic, the hot, harsh breaths burning my nostrils as my tortured shouts and screams of agony rippled across the woods. My voice cracked and fell silent as the beasts tore into me like a four course meal. Ruby-red blood poured out onto the ground below, so much of it that I could smell the copper tang in the air.

My leg was dropped as claws dug into my side like they were trying to reach deep inside and tear my soul straight from my body. One of them might have let go and started in on my abdomen, trying to reach my soft organs, but I didn't know, unable to feel anything but pain and the fuzzy, endless haze that was sweeping over me.

The darkness faded in and out, slowly dragging me under, and just as I was about to succumb, the fire in my stomach came alive with a fury rivaling anything I had ever experienced. Incinerating me from the inside out, the power shot through my veins. The sounds cut out all around me—the growls and snarls disappearing into nothing until all I could hear was the roaring fury of the universe in my ears. My mind broke, shattering under all the torment, unable to handle the pain coming from every direction.

I went limp and my head flopped to the side, watching through blurry vision as my arm was torn apart by one of the beasts. Small strings of muscle and skin were the only things keeping it attached, but where it was supposed to be connected, a searing golden light remained. The edges were hazy, nearly formed but not. The very little unmarred skin I could see was cracking apart like a desert floor, veins of liquid gold criss-crossing all over, revealing the glowing core underneath burning away unhindered.

A golden hue crossed over my gaze. I burned and burned until I was barely hanging on to life, until my mind was gone completely; finally, when I couldn't hold on any longer, the last bit of who I was yanked free from its confines. With a scream that pierced through the nothingness, the energy I held inside exploded out of me, destroying what was left of my ravaged body.

Encased in gold light, my form unleashed the burden it carried. My eyes gleamed as brilliant light flooded out of me from every direction. Colors of all kinds whipped past, melding with the golden force, turning it into a beautiful weapon.

I couldn't feel any pain. No crushed bones, no broken body. It was the apparent lack of sound—of sight and smell and time—that pulled my attention, as if I had turned off the very universe for only a second. The whooshing beat of the unstoppable force crashed against my skin, or what I thought was my skin. I watched as the monsters' faces screeched in horror as they burned to ash before my eyes, skin and muscle flaking off as gold hot fire ate away at its edges, and I felt nothing for them.

All I could feel was the calm. The peace. As my mind floated on a sea of world-ending energy. I watched, uncaring, as the power that erupted destroyed everything it touched.

The wraiths were gone in a flash, nothing left but dust and even that seemed to be vanishing from existence. The ones that had tried to run were caught swiftly by the chasing tide of magic tearing away at them from the inside out. Their eyes glowed as the power imploded, pushing out from between their skeletal frames, unable to be contained by such poor vessels.

Thousand-year-old trees burned away in an unseen wind of destruction and power, no remnant left of what once stood long before I was born. The ground became charred dirt and ash, eroding away in some spots to the rock below.

The bright energy whipped around me in a funnel of power. Building and building, up and up it gathered. Coming together into a pillar of light that poured across the sky, reaching well beyond the clouds, before it ripped back into me. I arched as it filled my cells, burrowing deep into my soul, warming me gently from the inside.

Slamming back to the ground, I was numb, my head laying against the ring of flowers and clover that had sprung up around me as the cool wind dried the sweat from my face; a small oasis amidst the ruins and remains of the clearing.

My head lolled to the side, my splayed arm in view, the edges of my vision going dark. The skin was pure, unmarred ivory. Not a scratch in sight. I couldn't bring myself to concentrate though, exhaustion weighing me down into a dreamless darkness.

CHAPTER SIX

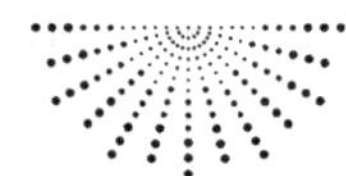

The funny thing about living in a small wooden house, surrounded by animals and forest life, was that there was always noise. A creak of the floorboards, the snores of my parents in the room next door, Gideon's goose-whinny being let loose at the ass crack of dawn demanding we feed him his breakfast. It was never silent in my home. Never.

It was the lack of noise that finally roused me, dragging me from my sleepy abyss. If I were in my bed, I would have heard Geoff cutting wood in the back, or Maris cursing in the kitchen about this herb or that. Instead, it was complete silence that greeted me, my blurry gaze taking in the indistinctive ceiling above.

I was ripped apart, had exploded into a funnel of power, and now I was laying in a strange place with no clue where I was. I felt like I had been beaten with a wooden club and then trampled by a herd of horses. My muscles still remembered the vicious spasms and overwhelming pain, but I could also feel the strength coursing through me to my very bones. As if I had been imbued down to the last cell with vitality.

The burning pit of energy that had always been contained in

my chest had spread throughout my body, leaving my veins buzzing. I felt how it had worked its way through every living part of me. Every cell vibrated with unrestrained energy; every piece having been reshaped, down to my very marrow. Even my damn fingernails felt stronger, more hearty and less likely to break.

Magic may have all but left the world, but I was proof that it still existed. I should have been dead. Down at least one arm, I thought, recalling the hanging piece of butchered meat that it had been. My wounds had been too extensive for even the best of healers to fix, but here I was feeling like I could run through a wall without a scratch.

Tossing aside the heavy fur blanket that covered me, I swung my legs out to take stock of the room. I had always been a practical person, and, as crazy as it sounded, that meant figuring out where the fuck I was first. The mental freakout about all of this could come later.

A wooden side table held an oil lamp, a glowing yellow flame throwing light throughout the room. Sitting next to it, pristine and out of place, was a white flower. The beautiful drooping petals were glistening, like they had been encrusted with diamonds or made from starlight, the golden stamen dropping shining dust onto the dark wood. Picking it up delicately, careful not to cut myself on the wickedly gilded thorns, I held it up to my nose. The breeze during a starry night, wildflowers blooming, a trace of an iron in the air hit my senses, transporting me to a different place. It smelled of new life and potential. Something warm and intangible built in my chest as a smile touched my lips.

Setting it back down gently, I couldn't help but wonder who had left it. Shoving aside the unimportant thought, I looked around the rest of the room.

It was tiny, big enough for only the bed, side table, and a small workbench, similar to the one Maris had back home.

A sharp tug pulled on my heart at the thought of Maris and Geoff. I had no idea if they were alright. They could be anywhere, injured and alone. Dead.

I pushed away those thoughts, knowing they would have hit me over the head for getting distracted in a situation that could possibly be dangerous. I had no idea where I was, or who brought me here. Were they a friend or a foe? A helpful stranger that came to investigate the disturbance in the woods—doubtful —or dangerous enemy who kidnapped a vulnerable woman? It was probably best if I figured that out when I was in a better position to defend myself. Finding a weapon was top of my list, my blades nowhere to be seen.

The only opening was a closed door next to the desk, light shining out from underneath the crack. My only option was through that door, and I was in no way prepared for what could be on the other side.

At some point someone must have changed my clothes. Instead of my hastily thrown on, bloody leathers, I was in warm gray socks and a long white nightdress that fell down past my knees. It was definitely not the most practical of outfits, but at least I could move in it if I needed to.

I couldn't do much about it right now as no other clothes had been left for me. Whoever they were, they also had the fore-thought to braid my hair back—the curls must have been down-right hellish after my stroll through the woods. The long gilded tail fell over my shoulder, brushing the top of my thigh.

Nothing of mine was left except my old boots, which had been laid out beside the bed. Jumping at the shred of normalcy, the last slice of my old life, I tugged them on over the socks. Now at the very least I could run away without worrying about shredding my feet.

Striding over to the workbench, I found nothing but a few bottles and a mortar and pestle laid out on the table. Picking up the mortar, I took a sniff. The heavy smell of valerian root hit my nose. Grabbing the small bottles, I looked at the brown paper labels: lavender, valerian root, and chamomile. All common herbs that were used to promote and aid restful sleep. The last bottle had no label, though, and had a glowing purple liquid swirling around inside. It shimmered in the dim light, streaked with color and unquestionably beautiful. Wishing I had more time to examine it, I set them all down reluctantly before moving over to the door.

Pressing my ear up against it, I was hit by a wave of déjà vu, having just been in this exact position before my life went to hell. I had a vague sense that my world was about to get flipped upside down once again. Maybe this time I wouldn't get eaten— a girl could dream. Hearing no sounds beyond the room, I cracked the door open and peeked out.

Empty.

Narrowing my eyes, I stuck my head out further. Still nothing, and a small sigh of relief fell out of my mouth. I wasn't one to complain—an impromptu meeting would probably go badly at this moment—but the seeming lack of … anyone was weird, especially if they had taken the precautions to keep me asleep.

Something told me they didn't want me awake, and I had no intention of being here to find out why. A small hallway lined up directly in front of me, a few doors on both the left and right sides, light filling in from a much larger space at the end.

Peering over my shoulder at the dazzling flower, I weighed my choices. Sit here and wait for my supposed rescuer and possibly be in the hands of an enemy, or take my chances and apologize later.

"Fuck it," I whispered out loud as I pulled the door open and quietly stepped out into the hallway. I had never been very good with patience, and as much as I hated to leave it, sitting around twiddling with a flower wasn't going to get me anywhere.

Easing the door shut behind me, I stalked down the long row, passing by other doors and assuming they were probably all like mine. After seeing the table I had an idea of where I was being held, and as I reached the large area at the end of the hallway, I confirmed my suspicions. An infirmary, and a large one at that.

Beds were lined up in rows along the walls. White curtains hung from wooden poles between them, offering some modicum of privacy for patients. Large windows across the top of the walls swathed the entire room in light. It was early morning, midday at most.

A few work benches, bottles and instruments tossed carelessly on the tables, were spread sporadically throughout the room. Cabinets with large shelves leaned against the walls closest to me, filled with glass jars and ceramics, boxes that held herbs and medicinal materials.

I moved quickly over to one of the tall shelves, peering over my shoulder every few seconds, searching through the instruments left out in the open. Probes, clamps, and more mortars took up most of the bench. Scattered herbs and crushed up powders forgotten in their jars reminded me of our workshop back home.

Other tools that I had never seen before lined some of the lower shelves. Ignoring my instinct to inspect the pristine metal tools, I reached down, pulling open drawers and digging around until I found my prize.

A thin bone-handled blade sat inside the drawer surrounded by envelopes and bluish-gray parchment. A letter opener was no dagger, but it was better than nothing. With enough force aimed at the right spot I could cause some serious damage if I needed to. Maybe to the eye or throat. If you poked enough holes eventually all the blood ran out.

Except for the occasional patient, who each seemed to be unconscious or asleep, I was completely alone, letter opener in hand like some mighty warrior. I snuffed out a derisive snort that wanted to escape. Still, I found it odd that there wouldn't be at least one healer running about checking on the ill.

The magic in my veins sparked at my unease building up inside me, pleasantly this time, as if readying to protect me. It was comforting in a way I had never experienced, too cautious about what it could do before.

Forging on, two large doors at the far end of the hall were my only visible escape. Taking one last peek to ensure the patients I could see were asleep, I darted through the main area, crouching and staying quiet as I passed the beds.

I ducked behind the work benches down the center aisle whenever I could, and the occasional snore from those lying in the beds was the only sound breaking the harsh silence. Taking my chance, I sprinted down the rest of the floor. Reaching the dark wooden doors, I gathered myself before pulling it open, opener at the ready.

Empty.

My brow creased in confusion. Surely there would have been someone wandering about. A loved one of the patients, a healer coming back from delivering news. Nothing. I was not one to take blessings for granted, however, so with a shake of my head I stepped out, closing the door softly behind me.

The long rug that spilled in either direction was weirdly split down the middle, green to the left and blue to the right. I wasn't even going to try to understand, going with my instinct and turning to the right. I moved down the hall with determination, ready to be out of this place. Reaching a turn, I peered around the corner before continuing.

A wide corridor greeted me, great big windows all along the left side brought in the light from outside. Heavy, white velvet curtains hung on either side along the cream walls. Mahogany benches sat underneath, draped with plush pillows. Tapestries lined the opposite wall, broken up by doorways. The blue and gold carpet continued, extending down the entire length of the gallery, a fresh shine to the dark wood floors underneath.

Even from here I could pick up the sounds of muffled voices, my hearing even more acute than I was accustomed to. My body warmed with the power flowing through it.

I am too gods damned nosey for my own good, I thought as I darted down the center aisle quickly, mimicking a scurrying mouse far more than I would have liked. The passageway only allowed for me to turn left, so following the wall, I prepared to shove my ass into one of the many rooms behind me. The voices got louder as I approached the turn.

Slowing to a crawl, crouching down at the corner, I peeked around. A man and woman stood talking in the middle of the hall, their hushed tones just barely reaching my ears. An apron covered the front of the woman's navy dress, an insignia I couldn't make out marked her breast pocket. The colorful stains around her fingers and the instruments lining her pockets marked her as a healer. Her black hair was adorned with a crown of flowers circling the back of her head, the long flowing locks framing the features of a classically beautiful face.

The man stood at least a head above her and held an air of wisdom to him. He was dressed in much grander clothes than she, wearing an embroidered tunic of navy blue edged in gold, dark trousers, and gleaming black boots.

His clothes were as striking as his features. His closely cropped black hair and dark skin made the colors even more vibrant. Stark blue eyes, the same pale shade as an icy storm, were piercing in their awareness. His chiseled face and wide brow gave him the appearance of someone young, but the way he carried himself said otherwise.

"Have you had any success in keeping her asleep?" the man asked, his voice carrying a soft rhythmic accent.

"Barely. Every time I put her back under she comes out of it quicker than the last," the healer explained, clearly frustrated.

"The only reason I can keep her down at all is because of how weak she is after her Awakening."

"How long do we have?"

"Honestly, she could be awake at any moment. Her energy is adaptive and is refusing to cooperate with me. Every time I try it lashes out at me, she's already blinded me once, and that felt like a warning. I recovered, but something tells me next time it won't be so forgiving. Her magic is protecting her, and I don't think it will tolerate any more intrusions than those it already has."

The man let out a weary sigh, running a large hand down his face, "Okay, just give us as long as you can, but don't endanger yourself or anyone else. The Council will just have to get over themselves and agree on what to do with her."

So definitely not as friendly as I would have hoped if they were purposefully keeping me under. Whoever the hell these people were, they wanted something from me. But why?

And then there was this *Awakening* that everyone kept mentioning, Maris and Geoff having spoken about it during their argument. If they knew anything about what was going on, where my parents were, then I needed to find out.

I looked down. With the white nightdress swishing gently around my knees, dainty letter opener in hand, I wasn't really the image of intimidation. Figuring everything out was going to have to wait until I was better prepared, and preferably more clothed.

Peeking back around the corner, I saw the healer walking in the opposite direction from the man, who was headed straight toward me. Because of course he was.

Sucking in my breath, I turned, running as quietly as possible across the floor—thankful for the long runner that softened my steps—and ducked into the closest doorway.

The room was poorly lit, but from what I could see it was an office of some sort. A great wooden desk stood directly in the middle, books covering the walls from floor to ceiling, somehow making the room seem both bigger and smaller at the same time. The dark wood flooring was overlaid with an extravagant blue and gold carpet with a similar pattern to the crest that hung on the far wall. An intricate symbol of a white bird bursting from a golden tree and shooting into the navy blue background took up the majority of the tapestry it had been stitched into.

Dammit, I thought, letting out a sigh. *Please, Cosmos, please tell me this is not what I think it is.*

Hearing footsteps just outside, I pressed my back up to the wall behind the door. Holding my knife to my chest in a loose and practiced grip, I steadied myself, breathing deeply before blowing it out, preparing to defend myself if needed.

My breath came in and out in whispered silence as I stood there praying that this wasn't the man's office. I wanted answers, and I wanted out, but I was in no way prepared for either of those things right now with my thin nightdress that could barely withstand the wind, and my tiny blade that looked pathetically small compared to the forearm-length daggers I usually carried.

Either way, there was nowhere to hide in the sparse room, and there was no escape or exit except the one that led me straight to the man who'd admitted to knocking me out. The best I had was hope, and I was not much of an optimist, so…

The steps got louder, the sound pounding through my adrenaline-fueled body. A soft whistle followed along, the man singing a sweet tune.

Don't be this room. Don't be this room, I chanted in my head as the steps slowed until they stopped. The doorknob turned suddenly without hesitation.

Godsdamn it.

I nearly growled in frustration at my piss poor luck as the door swung inward, momentarily blocking me from sight. The man barely got a foot in the door before I slipped behind him and held my tiny opener to his throat.

He froze, going as still as a spooked deer in the woods.

I pressed a little harder. One good jerk of my hand and his blood would run, making quite a mess of the beautiful carpet below. I slowly closed the door behind us with my foot, the soft click shattering through the room.

Forcing as much sternness as I could into my voice, I asked, "Where the hell am I?"

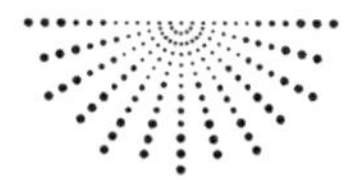

CHAPTER SEVEN

"Well, hello there! You must be Atallia," the man greeted me as if I was his friend, and not someone who was holding a knife to his throat.

"How do you know my name?" I demanded, pressing the blade to his skin a little harder.

"We've been doing a little digging while you've been asleep."

"You mean, while you've been drugging me," I added sardonically.

"Ah, well … yes, there is that bit of unpleasantness," he said, surprise in his voice. "You know, eavesdropping is quite rude."

I scoff in righteous exasperation. "Do you really believe you should be throwing stones in regards to politeness?"

"My apologies, you're right; where are my manners? You must be quite confused. My name is Cashim," he said, unfazed by how his throat pressed deeper into the edge of the blade as he talked. I thought the frozen way he held himself was because of fear, but now I wasn't quite sure. I gripped the handle a little bit tighter.

"I don't really care what your name is. Where am I and how the hell did I get here?" I was not at ease in this situation, and he clearly was, which only made me more worried. I knew nothing about this man, who he was, or what he could do. I quickly peered over my shoulder at the door, I needed to escape and quickly.

"Well, you were unconscious when we found you. We thought it best to bring you back instead of leaving you in the clearing … or what was left of the clearing," he mused almost as an afterthought.

"When you found me?" I asked, ignoring the rest and the implications of what it meant.

"Yes, your Awakening was seen all the way from the border. Nearly sent everyone into a panic over it." Cashim laughed casually.

Just as I was about to ask what he was talking about, the door behind me opened. Whipping us around, I yanked Cashim closer to me.

The healer from before rushed in, panic written all over her face. "Sir, Atallia is go—" Her words cut off as she saw me, standing there, knife in hand. Now she froze, this time in actual fear, anxiety written in her gaze.

"Atallia, why don't you drop the blade and we can all talk amicably, hm? I'll explain everything, but I'm not sure we can have this conversation comfortably while at knifepoint."

There wasn't any way that I would be cornered in a room with the only exit blocked by people who had been drugging me. Making my decision quickly, I pushed Cashim forward. "In the hallway. We'll talk in the hallway."

The healer's eyes darted to Cashim's and with the barest hint of a nod, she backed out of the doorway. Following slowly, my eyes took in the hallway once more, searching for any sign of guards or other people. No man as well dressed as him, in a place like this, wouldn't have guards.

"I sent people looking when I couldn't find you. It's just us, I promise," the healer reassured me.

I didn't have any choice but to believe her. It was that or they were waiting in the wings to rush me, and if that was the case, I needed my hands free. I shoved my captive toward her and backed away, keeping my guard up as I turned my back to one of the walls. I eyed them warily, half my attention on the two hallways on either side.

Cashim rubbed his neck, and yet where at least a small cut should be—for how hard he pushed into the blade—there was no evidence of a cut, not even a small rivulet of blood. My threshold for weird shit had been hit and passed several times over.

"Talk," I said harshly, my frustration finally bubbling over.

"Two days ago, you became a full Descendent, going through your Awakening at the age of twenty-one like we all have," he said speaking calmly.

"Descendents?" I asked them, my disbelief clear. "They haven't been seen in Irropia for centuries, let alone in the middle of the nowhere village I grew up in."

"We are not sure why you were on the other side of the border, and actually Descendents have lived in Northern Irropia for nearly fifteen thousand years; we've just been out of the public eye, so to speak, more recently," he said in his old tone, waving his hand about dismissively.

"Northern Irropia?" I paused, trying to come to terms with what that could possibly mean. "Are you telling me we're north of the Blackwood?" My shock was clear, but I couldn't help but feel the spark of curiosity flickering away in my chest.

"Yes." He nodded, looking out the window to my left. I didn't dare look with him for fear of taking my eyes away from a possible threat. "The Blackwood separates our land from the mortals, or at least it has for the past two thousand years."

"So you're telling me," I spoke slowly, still trying to wrap my head around it, "that the Descendents are still around and have been for forever, you yourself are one of them, and, oh, by the way, so am I?"

He nodded thoughtfully, my sarcasm going ignored. "Yes, that's about it."

I blew out a breath, wondering when I would exit this dream and enter reality once again. "Excellent," I said pitifully, shaking my head as a million things ran through my head. "Where am I, then?"

His eyebrows lowered, a slight frown taking up residence on his handsome face. "You're taking this quite well. I had figured you didn't know what you were, considering you lived in Rhaelyth," Cashim said, looking me up and down in concern.

I snorted in derision. "My foster parents may or may not be dead, and regardless, I have no idea where they are. Hell beasts attacked and ripped me apart limb from limb, and I spontaneously combusted, killing them all in a fiery explosion of death," I said flatly, completely fed up, the stress of the past few days bubbling past the point of reason. "There's very little that has happened to me in the past few days that I can bury my head in the sand about. To be honest, this conversation has probably been the most normal thing in my life recently."

He looked at me with tightly pressed lips and eyes filled with sympathy. "Ah ... very true, my dear, very true," he said quietly, somehow sounding older than he looked.

I blinked back the burning behind my eyes, refusing to let strangers see me vulnerable. I still had no idea what the hell was going on and whether anyone could be trusted. All I knew was that these people had been hiding for two thousand years, I didn't have much hope that they would leave their safe haven to help me find Maris and Geoff. "So? Where am I?" I raised my eyebrows in question.

"You had just crossed into our side of the Blackwood before you had your Awakening," a lilting voice said. The healer, who had been so quiet I had almost forgotten her, moved away from her spot on the opposite wall. "Soldiers were sent to investigate as nothing like what you had released had ever happened inside or outside of our realm, and all they found was ash and charred dirt for miles around. In the center of the destruction, they found you covered in flowers and vines, completely unharmed. They brought you back here to us so that we could ensure that you were healthy. Awakenings are exhausting at the least and can completely wreck a person's body at the worst."

No wonder I felt like I had been hit repeatedly by a plank of wood. "And where is *here*, exactly?" I asked, still working through all they had said.

"Allasea," Cashim said proudly, stepping in for the healer. "You're in the realm of Allasea, gift from The Divine and home of the Descendents."

Walking through the building, finally having changed out of the nightdress, I should have been questioning everything and everyone, but I was keeping it all to myself. At this point, I was more concerned about what these people planned to do with me and what happened to Maris and Geoff. If these people truly were Descendents, they might be the best option to figuring out what the hell has been happening in Rhaelyth. Those wraiths were infecting humans with something, killing them, and now my parents had vanished. Something very wrong was going on, and I didn't want to see what would happen if no one was able to stop it.

I followed Cashim back down the hallway, the healer having left to go back to her duties, turning around the corner to where I had first seen them. I took the time to appreciate the beautiful building—the vaulted ceilings and detailed metal work of herbal plants, the sconces on the walls that looked like crawling vines growing up to the ceiling.

There was a great wooden staircase, so finely carved I could see individual flower petals on the railing growing in clusters all the way up to the landing. Arched double doors of a rich mahogany stood surrounded by a sculpted marble entryway. Sunbursts and forestland decorated its beautiful grain.

Three tapestries with detailed crests hung from the ceiling in the grand foyer. The one on the right was the same one that had been in Cashim's office, the white bird stark against the navy fabric. The tapestry on the left was made of a vibrant forest green, the blooming, golden lotus shimmering in the sun's flaring white light. The last crest, larger and more prominent, hung in the middle of the room. The white fabric was edged in gold, and gilded glimmering threads shot out in every direction, a glorious starburst spreading across the material.

He led us out into the warm air, the bright burning light from the white sun forced me to close my eyes, bright spots dotting behind my eyelids. Blinking until my eyes adjusted, I looked around, getting my first glimpse of the new land outside. My jaw dropped in awe.

Even though we had walked straight out into the middle of a busy city, my attention couldn't help but be snagged by the view above us. Magic of all different colors and hues flowed through the air like a river. I was mesmerized by all the shades dancing through the sky. All my childhood stories were coming true, no one having seen anything like this in centuries. The few wisps I had glimpsed only a few times a year paled in comparison to the loom of color weaving its way alongside the clouds.

Sunlight shot through the different threads, beams of color hitting the ground around us. It reminded me of the glass sculpture Geoff had hung from my window that, when hit by light, caused a cascade of color to flitter throughout my room. The energy twirled around like leaves on a breeze, carrying with it the shimmering aura of magic.

Looking over to my right, my disbelief rose once more. If I

had any doubts I was no longer at home, they were all being crushed by what stood before me. A towering mountain range took up my entire view, shooting up so far it pierced the river of color and continued straight through the clouds.

The one closest couldn't have been more than a mile away. The jagged stone stood over everything else like a sentry standing guard over its kingdom; which, in a way, it was. A large forest grew and spread out from its base, appearing to almost drip off the mountain. Towering oaks and beautiful flora bloomed everywhere I looked.

Where I expected the lush green of the trees and foliage, I saw a myriad of purples, blues, and pinks, some leaves so dark they looked black while others were delicate pastels; it was as if the very mountain itself breathed.

Second in size only to the mountain itself, was what could only be considered a palace. Built on top of the hillside, some of it disappearing into the mountain itself, the structure stood stoically over its domain.

"Beautiful isn't it?" Cashim stepped out onto the cobblestone path beside me.

"It's huge! Gorgeous, but huge."

His chuckle wrapped around me like a warm hug, with its contagious effect similar to how Geoff's always made me feel. "You think it's big now, but you're only seeing a small portion of it. The largest part is built inside the Crian Mountains, completely hidden from view."

There were openings high up on the mountain wall that could barely be seen from down below, windows or watch points that were bare pinpricks to my eyes. They must have only been accessible from inside, where I was sure the much greater structure lay.

Outcroppings in the rock had been turned into balconies or entrances, accessed from inside, or by what appeared to be open air staircases built straight into the side of the range. The dizzying height of some had my heart racing for the individuals brave enough to traverse the outside of the mountain.

I couldn't even see the whole thing from here. The forest billowed around it, framing its magnitude and blocking most of it from view; the tops of the palace walls were the only indication that it hadn't just popped out of the ground with the range.

Had it not been clear that it was well maintained from the shining windows to the faint gleam of the cream stone, I would have thought it abandoned due to the forest seemingly growing without care all around it. Trees lined the huge, terraced balconies, and vines blooming with white flowers hung off the windowsills of the small spires standing above the rest of the palace.

The most prominent part of all, though, was the colossal tower directly in the middle. Only the front half of it was visible, the rest hidden within. The top broke through the clouds, disappearing along with the peak of the mountain.

Large enough in height and width to best any thousand-year-old oak in size, it stood unmoving against the rock wall. Covered almost entirely by ivy on one side, it looked exactly like where princesses were rescued by their doting princes. A hundred feet below it, a structure jutted out from the mountain, the tower seemingly going right through it. The railing of a balcony and the glint of glass were the only things visible from the ground.

"Allasea has three major cities. Hassere and Ophineas are beautiful and just as rich in our people's culture and history. But our capital ..." He waved his hand to all that surrounded us. "Eskira is our jewel. It and the palace were built long before I was born. Life wanted enough space so that every single one of her people could reside within it, if they so wished. Our queen wanted everyone to feel as if they had a home." His voice carried an awe with it, a reverence for a long gone goddess as his ice-blue eyes stared intently into mine.

"You knew the Goddess of Beginnings?" I ask, stunned beyond belief. "That would make you thousands of years old."

"Yes, it would," he says with a small smile. "Maybe not as old as you think, though. My mother was one of the first Aetherian Descendents created by the queen and was her friend and advisor for thousands of years before she had me. Gradually, I grew up and went from being the toddler under their feet to a close friend and confidant of the king and queen."

That would explain the presence he gave off despite his appearance. Although he didn't look older than thirty, he had a timelessness about him that spoke to an inner knowledge and wisdom.

"The city built itself around the keep little by little until we got to where we are today," he said as he started walking down the cobblestone path, heading away from the palace and deeper into the heart of the bustling city.

Although it was impossible to see the entirety of it from here, the spread of the city fell across the hillsides like it was made to. The buildings blended with the wildness of the land-scape like they'd risen from the ground together. Trees of all shapes, sizes, and colors sprouted through ceilings without care, flowers bloomed in every window, hanging vines dangled from top floor nooks until they nearly touched the street, and vibrantly colored moss grew through cracked stones almost purposefully. A wide crystalline river ran directly through, cutting across the city diagonally before disappearing into the trees on either side, heading towards what I assumed was the Divinian Sea.

Large bridges criss-crossed the shimmering water that reflected the colors floating in the sky. I could pick out the boats, near pinpricks from up here, bobbing on the water. And out in the distance—which only served to show its size—was a huge, dark wall, wrapped protectively around the sparkling city.

Only so much was visible from our spot, but I couldn't even

imagine what it must have looked like from the terraces of the palace. While some of the buildings were simplistic in nature, obviously housing or stores of some kind, it all fell together naturally, like puzzle pieces. Every home was unique in its own way, yet it never deterred from the cohesiveness of the entirety of the ancient city. The flora that seemed to grow wherever it wanted—even if that meant a house had to be built around it—pulled everything together, the entire city holding a wild playfulness to it.

"Come. My niece lives at the palace with me, but she frequently spends time in town with the off-duty soldiers, being one herself. I think you'll both get along swimmingly, and she can probably explain your situation to you a lot better than I can. She went through her Awakening not too long ago." Looking back over his shoulder, he gave me a cheeky smile and a chuckle. "It has been quite a while since I went through it myself, and as my niece constantly points out, I'm not so relatable anymore."

I couldn't help but smile back, my wariness of the talkative man not lessening in the least, but his infectious joy hard to resist. "Oh, I don't know, something tells me that doesn't stop you from trying."

Laughing, he continued down the polished cobble street. We passed storefronts filled to the brim with breads or fabrics, and one stall even contained piles of spices in all different colors. People leaned out of windows from second stories, hanging clothes or talking to neighbors.

No two buildings looked exactly the same, no symmetrical or even lines, all of them with their own personalities. Several were three stories high, sitting on top of one another precariously, stacked almost without care. Each terraced area was used for more plants, and vibrantly colored birds swooped in and out of the connecting tree branches. It shouldn't have worked, and yet the beauty of the stone, the trees and plants growing around and through it, the love and laughter that seemed to emanate from the spaces around us, made every single part look seamless with the next.

They were all well kept; I couldn't see one decrepit, run-down home or business in dire straits, unlike my village. While there were drastic differences in the level of embellishments or the size of the structure itself, there wasn't one on the street that spoke of severe struggle. No chipped walls or leaking roofs. No broken windows covered over with blankets to keep the morning chills away. Every person we passed had shoes, some more worn than others, but none held any holes caused by years of walking on them without repair. We passed children who looked fat and happy, clean and dressed, playing a game of sorts in the streets with simple, leather balls.

Cashim must have noticed the look on my face, and gave me his widest smile yet. "Even though the king and queen have long been gone and the status quo has unfortunately changed quite a bit"—there was a grumble in his voice that hadn't been there before—"there are enough of us that still remember the days of their rule and wish to keep as much of it alive as possible. Basic rights to health and home being one example. No matter the circumstances, if a member of our society is struggling, we find a way to help, and that isn't limited to Eskira."

My respect for this man and his people grew. So many times back home I had passed the unfortunate, mostly the sick and the elderly who could no longer work, giving them what I could, healing them if possible. I watched, stepping in when I could, as others spat on them and treated them as if they were nothing. The idea of neighbor helping neighbor, the society picking up their weakest to help them stand again, was an idea that was mind-blowing in its simplicity, and yet, one the mortals had yet to realize. I remained silent, however, not yet knowing if that respect was deserved. Too many times I had seen evil and greed covered up by a pretty face.

Continuing on, we passed even more people, and besides a few curious looks and head nods sent our way, we were mostly ignored. Whether they informed the people beforehand or not about my presence here, no one seemed in a hurry to judge or examine me. Honestly, the more we passed, the more I understood that while I was flashy, I wasn't the most unusual of suspects.

If my eyes were to be believed, I was downright normal compared to some. A woman with dark-brown skin mottled in the pattern of tree bark, pink flowers in her black hair, strode by with her hand clasped around that of a little boy with the same markings.

A few had sharp claws protruding from their nail beds, others had scales crawling down their arms. A large man talking animatedly with a friend let out a big, boisterous laugh, and I saw the flash of fangs. There was a man with hair in a mix of oranges and reds so bright I thought it was on fire at first, and then as he turned, catching a beam of sunlight, I realized it actually was. The tips flickered with flames, although no one seemed concerned.

A blonde-haired man was riding a handsome palomino stallion that had swirling blue marks all along its body, with a distinct blue hue to his skin. A gorgeous opalescent horn shot out from the stallion's forelock. I must have stared for a second too long, the man catching my gaze, and instead of sneering in disgust like I might have expected back home, he gave me a harmless appreciative look and a charming grin in greeting before moving on.

My eyes crinkled in genuine pleasure at seeing such a wonderfully diverse world. No one was looked at weirdly, no matter their features or mannerisms. To them, this was a normal life. A young man around my age sneezed, a small stream of fire coming from his mouth, and instead of being looked at like a freak, his friends laughed teasingly as he blushed.

Sunrays broke through the branches and leaves, hitting my hair and scattering around me in an array of glittering light. People looked on, not with hate or jealousy, but with smiles on their faces. I couldn't decipher what those looks made me feel, a tight sensation in my chest loosening slightly.

Soft music reached my ears, a lilting song that felt almost physical with its touch, as if the notes brushed against your skin as they swirled through the air. The music became louder as we walked out from a side street and into a square where a bustling market was taking place. Wooden stalls filled to bursting with wares and goods lined the streets, and colored cloths hung from the buildings lining the square, shading the market as sellers yelled out prices to patrons.

And for the countless time that day, wonder raced through me. Not at the beautiful silks and fabrics being handed around by vendors, the sugary smell of sweet treats being passed into the tiny fists of children, or even the stall that held an array of powders and plants, some of which were glowing like nothing I had ever seen.

It was the energies that floated from the man and woman who were performing a dance to the music in the middle of the market. The couple glowed incandescently, a shine emitting from inside them becoming brighter as the dance brought them closer together. Their energies, a mix of pale pastel green and evening indigo, performed their own kind of dance. Twisting around each other in perfect synchronization until it rose up into the stream of magic above.

The dance, moving in time with the music, was almost too personal to watch. There was a spark, something I couldn't begin to understand, in the small smiles on their faces as they looked at each other. The partners so in tune with each other, they might as well have been one person. It was an intimate moment between two people who were so engrossed in each other it was as if the entire world had disappeared around them.

Other duos had joined in the dance, some with the same expressions on their faces, light pouring off them and joining in the music. Two men held each other tightly, foreheads pressed together, swaying to the song as their magic blended together, eyes unable to look away from each other.

Others, like a small group of young girls who jumped around laughing, were there for the pleasure of it, enjoying the moment with friends and family.

It was one of the most beautiful moments I had ever seen, as the light came together in a heavenly kaleidoscope. People joined together in a shared moment of life, some continuing to go about their errands, others enjoying the romantic display before joining in themselves.

I looked over at Cashim to confirm the stunning display in front of us, not even realizing tears had begun to pool in my eyes.

His eyes shined with joy as he looked down at me, the air infectious with feeling. "Come, my niece likes to frequent The Rapscallion." As we headed off to the other side of the square, I couldn't help but let my eyes linger on the embracing lovers still dancing to the soft tune.

CHAPTER EIGHT

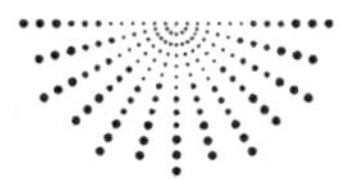

The Rapscallion was not what one would have expected of a bar frequented by tired, off-duty soldiers. At least not in looks. The cream stone was free from any dirt or grime that you would usually find outside an establishment like this; the tavern back home had been on the verge of collapse the last I saw of it.

There were no chips or cracks in the dark wooden beams that supported the small veranda overhead. Windows were clean and clear, flowers lined the sills in little wooden boxes. Other than the large oak that hung over the roof, dropping its pale blue leaves all over the shingles and ground, everything was in perfect order; and even that only seemed to add to the overall charm.

Honestly, the only old, worn-out part was the hanging sign. "The Rapscallion" was advertised in chipped, purple paint, and a cat, with its tail crossed politely over its paws, a suggestive grin on its face and a sly spark in its eyes, was painted underneath. The sign was a foil to its pristine, peacefully quiet outside.

"Definitely not what I was expecting," I said, taking it all in, not sure what I was about to get into.

"Oh, just you wait, it gets better." His dry sarcasm, thick with exasperation, had the hair on my neck standing at attention.

Pushing open the double doors, we stepped into a war zone. Pure chaos was more ordered than this. There were so many bodies going at each other, I could barely see anything. The perfect facade outside was completely smashed by the sounds of barbaric screaming as dozens wailed on each other with their fists—and magic, it seemed—as I watched one man go soaring past into a table, knocking it over and crushing a chair beneath him after being hit by a red ball of fire.

"Oh, this is definitely my kind of place," I said, chuckling, impressed as a man in front of us lifted a chair and smashed it over the back of another man's head, knocking him to the ground.

Cashim gave a weary sigh, rubbing a hand over his face. "Just the daily tavern fight."

"Daily?"

"Not every day, but Descendents are very primal creatures, so we tend to run a bit hot. One temper flares and a small argument turns into a brawl."

He wasn't wrong. Everyone was involved in the fight; even the barkeep and maids were lobbing tankards from behind the bar at anyone who got too close before ducking back behind it.

From the corner of my eye, I spotted a woman rushing towards us, swinging wildly with what looked to be a broken plate. Her eyes screamed crazy, obviously so into the fight she didn't care who was on the other side of her and her plate. Her mouth opened in a snarl, revealing sharp fangs descending from the top of her mouth. Just as she reached us, a plank of wood smacked her comically right in the face, throwing her off balance and onto her ass.

A stunning woman with black curly hair that shot out in every direction around her like a halo stood in front of me in defense, plank of wood in hand. "Sheesh, calm down, bitch.

There's plenty of people to cut up—you don't need to go after the one girl who looks like she doesn't know what the hell is going on." She shook her head, disappointed. "Damn, let's have some respect for ourselves—we're not complete barbarians."

I might have begged to differ, but I was just as likely to join in, so I couldn't judge too hard.

Turning away from her victim, the dark-skinned woman looked at me curiously. Her icy-blue eyes, lighter than the sky, were almost shocking in their depth, like staring into a frozen lake. They were framed by unfairly-long, black lashes and thick eyebrows that sat on a heart-shaped face. Full lips and a delicate nose completed the package.

She was beautiful, and also very tall, standing over me by at least five inches.

"Uncle, what are you doing here?" the woman asked, her accent the exact same as Cashim's—musical almost to the point of whimsy.

So this was his niece. Couldn't say I was disappointed. Any woman who kicked ass with a random piece of wood automatically rose to the top of my list of people I wanted to meet.

"Zanaya, how did I know I would find you in the middle of this mess?" he said. I almost would have thought he was angry with her, except for the small smile and proud look in his eyes.

"Middle," she scoffed loudly over the sounds of fighting. "I started it." Her wide grin spoke of how proud she was of herself. I choked back a laugh, enjoying her blunt attitude. She clearly gave zero shits about anyone's opinion of her.

"Of course you did."

"In my defense, some bear-shifting asshole decided to introduce his hand to my ass, so I decided to introduce my fist to his face. I really intended for it to end there, but he had some friends and I have some of the soldiers with me and you know, one thing led to another"—she didn't take her eyes off her uncle, not even flinching when two guys roughly brushed past her,

hurtling each other into the wall before crashing to the floor—
"and here we are."

Smiling despite myself at her depiction of the absolute anarchy going on, I found myself wanting to like the woman. I didn't let myself think on how maybe one day I could. Too much was up in the air, too many lies had been told for me to let my guard down. I hoped it wouldn't always be like that, but I wouldn't let the wool be drawn over my eyes again. Not by anyone.

As I went to introduce myself, an extremely large, extremely hairy man came out of nowhere with another plank of wood grasped in his hands, which were tipped in long black claws.

Where the hell was everyone getting the wood from? With speed shocking for someone so big, he reared back, aiming for the back of Zanaya's head, and swung.

Darting forward, far quicker than I had ever thought possible, I grasped the plank in one hand. Normally, I would have felt a hit from a man that size, even just a little bit, but barely a twinge ran down my arm. His eyes went wide in surprise as I yanked the plank from his grasp, his claws digging marks in the wood. Rearing back just like he had, a burning sensation built in my chest, spreading throughout my body like a raging storm. Remembering what happened the last time that feeling showed up, I tried to slow down my blow, but too soon the wood smashed against the man's overly large head.

It hit with a fierce crack, and his head whipped around, completely disorienting him. Using my chance, I leaned back and planted my leg through his chest with all my strength. Time slowed down as I watched the kick land, sending shockwaves through his body as he was lifted from his feet. He flew past people, all of whom had stopped fighting, and went straight through the side wall of the tavern.

The broken wall let in the outside light, which flooded the cozily lit place. Pursing my lips, wincing as a groan sounded from the pile of stone, I turned back to Zanaya and Cashim. "So … um … not exactly what I intended to do." Zanaya's look had me equal parts nervous and excited as she grinned from ear to ear. I pointed at the man-sized hole in the wall. "That was ass-grabber, I presume?"

Tipping her head back, she laughed boldly and without restraint. "Oh, I think you and I are going to have so much fun, Atallia."

Confused, I went to ask her how she knew my name, but Cashim interrupted, clapping his hands together. "Okay, everyone, time to cool off, I think. One hole in the wall is enough, don't you agree?"

And just like that, laughter filled the room as everyone started picking up unbroken chairs and tablewares. Backs were slapped and people were picked up by the same ones who had knocked them down.

The barkeep, whose locs I noticed had intertwined vines of violet ivy in them, stood up from behind his station. With a wave of his hands, wreathed in a purple light, suddenly broken tables were fixed, several planks of wood shuffling across the floor to their respective tables before fitting themselves back into place. The hole I created bricked itself over, no one going to check on the ass-grabber outside as the last of the stone filled in, cutting off the blinding light.

I guess it didn't matter if you joined in on the daily tavern fight if you could fix all the damage yourself.

Although all seemed to have been righted, and the people had become friends again, curious and measuring looks were sent my way. I must have broken an unspoken rule by sending someone through the wall. Into the wall was fine, but through it —oh no, how dare I stop a well-mannered plank to the head?

"Follow me. You both can come sit with me and the others." Zanaya tossed her head in the direction of the back corner, where loud laughter and bawdy songs were coming from.

"Unfortunately, I have other business to attend to, but I have no doubt I'm leaving Atallia in good hands," Cashim said to his niece with a smile, who returned it cheekily.

"Wait, what are we going to do about finding my adoptive parents and those things that attacked them? Maris and Geoff know how to fight, the majority of the village doesn't, so if they were taken out there's no way that those lazy bastards would survive."

I didn't even know why I cared; they had done nothing but cause hell in my life, making me just as miserable in my waking life as I was in my sleeping one. However, it would make me no better than them to leave them to their fate. I would be what they had always assumed me to be—a monster—if I let them die without trying to help.

Cashim walked up to me, putting his hands on my shoulders in comfort. "You either killed all the wraiths or scared them off. Zanaya and her soldiers made sure of it, and the Council has already sent trackers to your village to figure out where your parents are. They were able to follow your trace back to your home and started from there on figuring out what happened. They should be back soon with some news for us."

I felt relief for the first time in days. I still didn't know their intentions or why they would help me; all that mattered was that they would.

"I know this hasn't been the easiest time in your life, Atallia. You must be more confused than ever, but I promise we're going to do all we can to help you figure everything out and to find your parents."

Through his comforting words, I couldn't help but get caught on one thing. "You called them wraiths."

His brows drew together in confusion. "They've always been called that. Why do you ask?"

My expression must've matched his. How did I know to call them that?

He looked at me curiously, something indistinguishable sparking in his eyes. "Atallia?" he questioned quietly.

Confused more than ever, which seemed to be a recurring thing in my life, I shook my head with a smile. "Nothing."

Brows still furrowed, I feared he might argue it and ask for answers that even *I* didn't know, but he decided against it, giving a small nod back. "Zanaya, will you look after her and bring her back to the palace before nightfall?"

Zanaya, having caught our strange interaction, looked at us with interest. "Of course, Uncle. We won't be here much longer."

"Good." With one last nod, he disappeared back through the doors and out into the market.

I was more than a little unnerved by the exchange, by the whole day, but you couldn't survive by dwelling on things you couldn't yet control. But one day I would. Eventually. Maybe.

"Well, now that he's gone, you can come meet my soldiers; and maybe I can explain a few things that might be on your mind."

"Yeah, that would be nice." I gave her a quick and cautious smile as I looked around the once destroyed space.

The tavern was actually nice, when it wasn't in pieces of rubble. The whole place gave a warm, welcoming feel, with fires roaring in hearths and beneath pots of spiced stew. The circular bar stood in the middle of the room, the centerpiece of the whole place. The wood was rough and worn from countless hands and tankards being slammed on its counter. A cylindrical tube shot down from the middle of the ceiling, barrels of ale and colored liquids I couldn't identify hanging from it, spouts tapped and ready.

Long tables were piled with cups made of horn and wooden bowls of stew. Loaves of bread were passed from hand to hand, drinks were refilled, and laughter filled the air.

I followed Zanaya to the back of the tavern, where the

loudest of the noise was coming from. Sitting on benches and chairs were several soldiers; pieces of their armor were lined up against the back wall, gleaming in the firelight. Weapons were strapped to their bodies or thrown about on the table. They all seemed too preoccupied with harassing each other and downing the drinks in their cups to notice us coming toward them.

"Oi, you lazy lot, drunk off your asses already, I see." Zanaya walked up confidently, swinging her leg over a bench to straddle it.

"Oh, come on, Commander," said one soldier, a lean, muscular man with fox-red hair. "We've only just started, and besides, we were toasting to yet another battle won against your ever-present suitors."

Laughter erupted from the table again as others chimed in from the tables next to us. It was obvious by their good-natured pestering that these were more than just soldiers talking to their commander. They were her friends, the people she would fight beside not because she was ordered to, but because she chose to.

Jealousy lashed through me. I had never had anything like this. Friendship. Camaraderie. People to joke and tease with. Who accepted you for who you were and loved you even more because of it. People who supported you through every bad moment or horrible tragedy, who gave you a shoulder to lean on and leaned on you in return. I had only ever had Geoff and Maris, and now they were gone too.

"Yes, yes, laugh at my pain. How lovely of you all to find humor in my harassment." Zanaya sighed, put out by her friends' jokes. She turned to look at me, still standing back away from them. "Well, what are you waiting for?" She nodded her head toward the open seat next to her. "Get over here."

As I moved closer warily, all eyes came shooting toward me. Silence fell over the table as I took the seat next to Zanaya. I looked around at everyone. Letting my guard down with strangers was hard for me on a good day, let alone with everything going on now. There were four of them in total at our table, all shooting me a range of looks as Zanaya introduced them.

"This is Nala; she's our explosives expert. Don't let her cuteness fool you—she likes watching shit blow up and smiles while doing it." Zanaya pointed at the tiny, red-headed woman directly in front of me, giving me a warm, welcoming smile. Although she looked harmless, it was typically the ones you least expected that could do the most damage.

Her curly hair matched the blazing fire behind her almost perfectly, with its multi-colored strands. Small flickering embers dropped from the ends, winking out before they touched the floor. Her wild, and slightly crazy, yellow eyes held no fear, even as they widened when meeting my gaze and their own endless depths. After a few seconds, she dropped her gaze to my nose, but still faced me. Her smile never dropping an inch.

Pleasant surprise fluttered through my chest, a warm feeling spreading through my chest. It was definitely better than the flinches I had faced. Giving her a small smile in return, I looked at the lean, muscular auburn-haired man beside her; the one who had been teasing Zanaya.

Now that I was closer, I could see that his hair had a speckling of black throughout. His fox-like features, angular and pointy, gave him a severe look. His wide, boyish smile was almost canine in its openness, yet it lightened his presence. Something told me he could get up to trouble just by walking down the street.

"That's Zander, he's what we like to call our trickster. Oh, and don't let him get away with any of the flattery bullshit he's going to try with you. He's a massive flirt and a manwhore; has another man or woman in his bed every other day."

"I take offense to that," the fox-like man said, looking at

Zanaya in faux hurt, hand to his chest. "I am not a trickster; I am a mayhem specialist."

She scoffed, rolling her eyes. "Of course, that's what you decide to take offense to."

"I am not ashamed of my prowess. What can I say? I'm just too irresistible." A wicked smile played across his lips as he shot a wink my way.

I couldn't help the grin it drew out of me as the table laughed at his statement, drawing a pout to the vain man's face. A snort from the other side of Zanaya drew my attention. "Please, spare us your humbleness, Zander. How could we ever get by without your presence?"

The soft voice of the small woman was almost undetectable with the noise of the other patrons around us. Her short, pin-straight black hair was cut in an angular fashion, brushing her chin and framing high cheekbones and a strong brow that accentuated her features. Her warm, brown skin was near perfect except for the long, deep slash through her right eyebrow. Although most would have called it an ugly mark on such a woman, to me it only enhanced her innate, savage beauty.

With a neutral face that gave nothing away, she looked at me with green eyes more lively than spring grass; a calculating and sharp mind stared through them. "I am Saanvi. This is Orion." She nodded to the man across from her, who's too-large frame sat hunched in one of the tavern chairs.

Orion might have been the most unusual of the bunch. He was bald with a grayish hue to his skin and deep-set, black eyes. He sat seemingly relaxed in his chair, but his eyes kept shifting from person to person, and the large hunting knife he kept flipping back and forth between his heavily scarred hands did nothing to take away from his gargoyle-like appearance.

The big man gave a loud grunt in stoic greeting. I lifted an eyebrow slightly, my lips twitched, amused by his astounding communication skills. I gave a grunt of my own back with the obligatory head nod. I seemed to surprise the silent rock of a man, his pale lips lifting in the smallest of smirks.

"It's great to see you back on your feet," Nala said, bringing my attention back to her. "When we first found you, we worried you were dead. Although after that Awakening, we weren't quite sure what we would find."

"You found me? In the clearing?"

"Oh yeah," Zanaya chimed in. "I technically command a much larger group of soldiers, but for scouting missions, especially anything so close to Rhaelyth, our little group is sent. We went to scout out what the disturbance was, and we found you."

"How did you know where to look?" The Blackwood wasn't easy to traverse, and a lot of people could only go a hundred yards before getting lost.

Zander huffed out a laugh. "Darling, your Awakening was seen all the way from here. The Blackwood is a couple hundred miles south of us. You might as well have set off a beacon alerting anyone to your location. The implosion radius went in every direction for as far as we could see."

"Explosion, Zander. Explosion. How many times must I tell you? An explosion bursts outwards; an implosion collapses in on itself." Nala shook her head at him like he was an idiot. I mean, maybe he was, but I doubt most people were prickly about the differences between an implosion and an explosion. Unless you were Nala, it seemed. "Beautifully done, by the way, probably the best damage radius I've seen to date." Nala laughed maniacally to herself, the embers falling faster from the ends of her bright hair. "I wish I could have been there to see it."

I think back on the disintegrating trees and burnt ground, cosmic energy swirling around like a wrathful tornado, destruction and then recreation its only goal. I looked at her, straight-faced, as images of a happy Nala burning from within as my power caught up to her flashed across my mind. "No, you don't."

Her face sobered as silence fell across the table. The horrors that led me to that clearing played in my head, tormenting me once again. A sinking panic started to bloom, all the unknowns closing in around me like a cage. I shoved it all down inside me, forcing myself to not think about the memories creeping their way through. Otherwise I might just break down right here, and there was no way in hell I would do it in front of others.

"Ignore them," Zanaya said, shooting them a stern look. "But yes, we found you, perfectly intact. You had a whole flower circle growing a couple yards around you, and it was spreading even as we checked on you, trying to crawl over our boots and up our legs. We made sure it wasn't anything dangerous before we left and then Orion carried you home with us because we couldn't wake you. Speaking of which"—she moved to grab a bowl from the table—"you must be starving if you've been out this entire time."

I *was* starving, my stomach growling its displeasure as I reached out for the bowl of stew and crusty bread. I couldn't even remember the last time I had eaten, and if I had been out for at least a couple of days, it had been a while. My stomach gave an affirmative gurgle as the warm, spiced smell of the stew reached my nose. It reminded me of the one that Maris used to make during the really cold days of winter.

Throwing decorum out the window, I started shoveling the food into my mouth with the wooden spoon. I openly moaned at the taste, seasoned meat and vegetables hitting my tongue. They probably could have given me cold gruel and I would have loved it, but the stew instantly gave me the warm fuzzies. I only took a breath to dip the fresh, crunchy bread into the liquid, soaking up the delicious goodness. I popped that into my mouth and another moan left me. In mere minutes, I had scraped the bowl clean.

Peeking up from beneath my lashes, I paused, my tongue still on the back of the spoon licking it clean, to see everyone staring at me in amusement.

Clearing my throat, I sat straight up and dropped the spoon into the bowl. "Sorry, I can't remember the last time I ate. I fell asleep before I could eat anything, then I woke up to an absolute nightmare."

I had never enjoyed being looked at with pity. It always reminded me of my early days in the village, when the villagers had looked at me like I was some pathetic creature.

Somehow, within the span of a few minutes, the soldiers, who barely knew me, were able to give me more compassion than those who had known me my whole life, conveying their sympathies without making it feel as if they were sorry for me.

"I never thought I'd ever be aroused watching someone eat, but you just proved me wrong," Zander quipped, suddenly breaking the silence, staring at me intently with his head propped up on his fist.

A shocked laugh escaped me, his random comment taking me away from the negative thoughts. Zander smiled happily, obviously proud of his quip and ability to take my mind off of things.

"I tend to do that a lot with people."

"What? Prove them wrong or arouse them?"

I raised an eyebrow, a sly grin curling at my mouth, feeling more confident around the group. "Both."

He flashed me a wicked smile, canines flashing in the fire-light. "Marry me."

The table's silence broke as everyone laughed at his theatrics. Comfortable conversation picked up within the group again as they discussed the post on the eastern border wall, including me whenever they could. My face hurt from the smiling and my stomach cramped from the laughter.

I didn't know how much time passed, but soon I was yawning from exhaustion. I'd been unconscious for the past two days so I had no idea why, but from what the soldiers told me I was going to be eating and sleeping like a horse for days after my Awakening as my body got used to its new way of working.

Zanaya leaned over to me, knocking her shoulder against mine. "Are you ready to go? I'm telling you right now, if you fall over asleep I am not carrying your ass up to the palace."

I chuckled because something told me Zanaya would do just that for anyone, no matter how long she'd known them. "Yeah, let's get out of here."

CHAPTER NINE

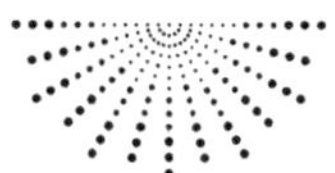

After saying our goodbyes, we headed out into the square. The market, which was full of life and laughter just a while ago, was packing up with the fading light. The sun was setting to the left of me, disappearing behind the mountain range, causing splashes of colors without words to describe them to brush across the sky like paint.

The market square wasn't too far from the edge of the city, and soon we were walking past the infirmary building. It was made of the same cream stone, a steepled roof topped with spires and carvings scrawled into the walls, making it look like an old temple.

Arched windows held a warm light, probably from the lit candles of those working late. Healers were constantly on the job, whether treating a patient or finding better ways to improve upon their skills. Many nights when I was younger, I would find Maris up at odd hours, working away in her apothecary. Geoff's snores, which could be heard from upstairs, were a sort of music to which she worked.

It was during those times, when late at night I was often awake more than I was asleep, that she'd taught me her trade until I could replicate her treatments nearly as well as she could.

The moss-covered cobblestone got wider as we began walking up the hill the palace sat upon, high above the northern half of the city and even higher above the southern.

The grassy, green hill was spotted with wildflowers, large commanding oaks, and fruit trees. Whistling birds flew in and out of the colorful canopy while buzzing bees were off to their hives. Roots had slowly crept out onto the road, weaving in and out of the stone and moss. Golden sunlight poured through the branches, rays breaking past the foliage, as the last moments of the day hung by a thread. I breathed in the last bit of warmth the air had to offer before the night chased it away.

"They really liked you, you know," Zanaya said from beside me, her keen blue eyes on me.

I wanted to trust her, I really did, but I had no idea how to. Friendship was a foreign concept to me, I wouldn't even know where to start. Unable to voice my thoughts, I shot her a quick smile. "Good, I really liked them too."

"You're more than welcome to join us anytime. We're on duty a lot and we split our time between the wall barracks and palace barracks, but I'm sure they would be happy to see you again."

"I appreciate that, but I'm not quite sure what's going to happen while I'm here. What your uncle and this Council will do with me."

"Well, I can promise you they won't do anything bad to you —at least my uncle will make sure of that," she said, shooting me a teasing smile. "They may ask you a lot of questions, but you're a Descendent and regardless of anything else going on, this is your home. By Divine Law, they can't deny you sanctuary or help."

Well, that was comforting at least, and I silently sent up a thank you to The Divine for that specific rule. I glanced up and saw our walk to the palace had slowly brought us closer to the Crian Mountains, their towering height standing watch over us.

"Do you think they'll help me find my parents?" I asked quietly, too afraid of the answer.

She looked at me with a sad twist of her lips. "I hope so, I really do. I'm sorry about all of that, by the way, I can't imagine how you must feel right now. Having to learn about all of this must be hard enough as it is without that added to your plate. As much as I would love to, I can't make any promises about your parents. You have the Council scared. Nearly all of Allasea saw your Awakening. The six Families converged on Eskira faster than I'd ever seen when they heard that you were actually a Descendent, and that you had been brought here."

"They came here for me?"

"There was already a meeting scheduled to take place in a week's time, what with wraiths attacking mortals and everything that's been going on here, but then you happened and it just sped everything up."

"Should I be worried?" I asked, hopefully not needing to be, but after everything that had happened, I was keeping my guard up.

She looked at me straight-faced. "Probably."

Grinning, I huffed at her blunt answer, preferring the fresh honesty over any bullshit. "Wonderful," I said, letting the sarcasm speak for me.

"Seriously, though …" Her face pulled tight with concern. "You've scared some of them. You're extremely powerful, probably far more than they are, judging by how you decided to announce yourself. Not only that, but you're a Descendent who was raised on the wrong side of the border, you know nothing of our world, and you had your Awakening in a way that possibly destroyed our secrecy with the humans." Her face tightened. "You're no small discussion, to put it plainly."

The gravity of my situation set in. I had caused a big problem for them, one I hadn't even known about.

"I'm not saying any of that was your fault, because it wasn't, but there are going to be those within the Council that are either threatened or intrigued by you, neither of which are good things. The Divine haven't sat on the throne in two thousand years, and the original Families took over a long time ago. Things have changed a lot from before the king and queen disappeared, and there have been whispers of possible changes to come."

"So essentially, I've gone from one battle to the next," I said.

She shrugged her shoulders with a sympathetic smile. "They'll call you to meet with them soon if I have to bet on it, and they'll question you on just about everything you can think of. Some of them will try to piss you off in hopes that you'll trip up and reveal something they can use against you, while others will show more compassion. They're the ones more concerned about keeping true to the old rules of The Divine then about power."

"It sounds like there's a big divide in this Council."

"It's been that way for a while. Two are playing neutral, two prefer the old way of things, and the other two want to capitalize on the opportunity for power. It's been a stalemate for decades. Before The Divine disappeared, the Council gave advice and helped discuss solutions for the people's problems. The Divine of course made the final decisions, but they took all opinions into account. Ever since their disappearance the six Families have been the ruling body, decision making has slowed to near nonexistence, which has caused increasing unrest amongst our kind."

I hummed noncommittally, not sure what to think. Reaching up, I brushed my fingers gently over the bright pink leaves of an overhanging tree; small apple-like buds having not yet flowered played against my skin.

Slight pinpricks shot through my hand at the velvet touch. A bolt of electricity moved its way through me until it reached the well of energy in my chest before bouncing back. The current was even stronger as it darted back the way it came. For a brief second, the veins in my hand burned gold, my fingertips glowing with an aura of light.

I went still as the light faded, watching in awe as the once barely-there buds flowered. The white and pale pink petals gently blew in the breeze before falling off, as it turned to fruit before my eyes, going from tiny, green pebbles to perfect, pink bulbs the size of my fist.

Reaching up, I grabbed one and twisted it off the branch. Its weight sat comfortably in my hand, none the wiser to its quickened state. Stunned, I looked at Zanaya in question.

Except she was looking up at the tree, her mouth hanging as she whispered, "Great Cosmos."

Turning, I watched as bud by bud, flower by flower, the entire tree's harvest matured in seconds. The pink fruit gleamed in the dying rays of sunlight shining through the branches.

If only it had stopped there, but as the last petal on the tree fell into the breeze, the next one over began turning too. Its own buds flowered, turning into fruit, and down the road it went, as each tree seemingly jumped forward several months to harvest time. The breeze picked up all of the dropped flowers on invisible waves and carried them along, swirling around us as if in thanks.

"Neat trick," Zanaya joked lightly, even as shock entered her pale, icy eyes. "I think we should get you to the palace before you accidentally turn spring to summer for the whole mountainside."

I gazed up at the tree, an almost imperceptible creak sounding as it looked to lean towards me, like a dog looking for pets. The winking fruit hung from the branches, now heavy and waiting to be picked.

"Yeah ... neat trick." My whisper was lighter than the petals on the wind.

If I had thought the palace was beautiful before, I was mistaken, because nothing could have prepared me for standing before it. I could see now the veins of gold that streaked the cream stone. Great walls protected the terraced sides of the palace, battlements and archers' windows placed accordingly. Anyone not looking would hardly notice, but large trebuchets and ballistas stood mounted to high walls, concealed well enough to not draw attention.

The palace wasn't just a pretty fixture for a god and goddess to rule from; it was a fortress—a last stronghold—for their people should they ever need it. The stores and homes down below weren't the city of Eskira. Eskira was the palace. The town and people just happened to live right outside of its walls.

It spread across the entire front of the largest mountain, the main body directly in the middle. Along the face stood scout stations and secret entrances that I wouldn't have even noticed had someone not walked through one. Hidden staircases traversed the outside of the mountain and circled some of the turrets, allowing entry into the elevated rooms above.

I had no idea the depths the actual structure went to, but there was no doubt it could easily hold and defend their entire population. The outside was fortified like nothing I had ever seen. I could see flashes of armor through boltholes, as warriors walked along the walls to reach their posts for the night.

The outermost wall stood at least a couple hundred feet high and the only entrance was a reflective black gate, so dark it appeared to suck in the last vestiges of light—the sun having gone down below the horizon. Carved into the gate was the most beautifully detailed dragon, every scale gleaming as its jaws opened wide, jagged fangs and blazing ruby eyes burning in defiance of anyone daring to breach its gate.

Colorful plants full of life flourished all around. Carefully cultivated ivy grew along the inner walls, trees topped with red and blue and purple leaves peeked out from the terraced courtyards and balconies, while flowers of all kinds—even those I'd never seen—bloomed in every sill and crack.

Zanaya walked up with confidence, bringing us to the gate, which gave a low groan as it was pulled inward.

"Why doesn't the entire city live here?" I asked as we walked through, passing guards on shift, dressed in everyday, leather armor. One had a claw-tipped hand acting as a knife, slicing a spiked orange-colored fruit in half. "It's obviously big enough to hold everyone."

She shrugged. "Some people do live and work here behind the lower walls, but not everyone wants to be under such watchful eyes all the time." She pointed out the guards as they passed by, lighting mounted torches as night fell over the sky. She took us up a flight of stairs to the left, leading up to the wall landing.

"And if I'm being totally honest, some of the more powerful, or should I say, power-hungry *elite*"—her face twisted in disgust over the word— "have made it so our weaker populations feel unwelcome here unless they're serving as maids or footmen."

Her clear disdain for these so-called *elite* was evident as storm clouds gathered in her eyes, rage pinching her beautiful face.

I looked out over the edge of the landing; the lights from the city dotted the ground below like stars in the night sky. The southern half across the wide river was more visible from here and covered the riverbank in light. The rolling, green hills had turned into a dark ocean, the river's luminescent depths cutting a path through the darkness.

After two more gates, smaller than the first, and countless

flights of stairs later, we reached an entrance. It was flat against the cliff wall where white marble, cream stone, and dark wood made up an arched doorway.

Two guards in full black armor, spears in hand and swords on hips, pulled on the door knockers held in the mouth of a dragon's head. Striding through into the mountain itself, we entered a dimly lit corridor carved through the stone.

"This is one of the side entrances; there are main ones on each level of the city, but I'm taking you to a room in the Residency Halls and this is the quickest way to them," she said, walking down the roughly cut hallway.

Eventually, the stone floor turned into wood and the gray mountain walls blended into the same ivory-colored stone from outside. Gold and black rugs covered the floors and colorful ceiling to floor tapestries hung from metal rods shaped like vines.

Light from the torches, the occasional window looking out onto a balcony or a hidden entrance, and the spacious halls kept it from feeling too oppressive.

Drawing to a stop in front of a door, Zanaya knocked once before walking in. An open room greeted us, decorated in off-white and pastel blue. Directly in front was a small sitting room with a cream chaise and dark wood furniture. Rugs detailed with intricate motifs covered the hardwood floors. Behind the seating area, windows showed off the star-filled sky and a miniature balcony overlooked the city down below.

Over to the left was a four-poster bed, covered in soft blue blankets and feather pillows. A trunk sat at the foot, just like my one back home. An open entryway, which must have led to the washroom, completed the room.

It was the nicest room I'd ever been in. Yet even as I stood in the opulence of this place, I couldn't help but wish I was back in my own home, with my twin bed and Maris and Geoff cracking jokes at each other in the kitchen.

"Do you like it?" Zanaya asked excitedly, moving to the balcony doors and pushing them open, letting the cool breeze enter the room.

I walked out onto the balcony before I spoke. "The room is amazing, and the view even more so."

The view of Eskira in its entirety was astonishing. Soft, pale light came from torches and houses all along the city side. There were different leveled walls, brightly lit by the watchmen who stood guard over the sleeping city. Even though we were barely halfway up the mountain, fluffy, white clouds passed by slowly underneath us.

A bright spot at the base of the mountain drew my eye. "What is that?" I pointed down toward it, right inside the outermost wall.

"The Pools of The Living. A natural hot spring right inside the base of the mountain. Everyone uses it from time to time, and legend says that it has some of the Goddess's healing magic flowing through the waters." She shrugged her shoulders. "According to some of the older Descendents though, the energy in it has decreased substantially since the Goddess Life disappeared. It can barely heal a cut now, but it still feels nice, so people use it."

"I can't imagine many people make it down there that often with how far it is."

"You'd be surprised. It's a lot of steps, but most everyone will tell you it's worth it." She walked over to the hallway door. "I'll let you get some sleep, and if you do decide you want to take a dip, the Residence Hall has a direct route." Pointing to the right, she said, "Just go all the way down the hall and take the last archway on the right. Follow the stairs and you're there."

"I doubt your uncle or the Council would appreciate me running around unguarded?" A sly grin quirked my lips. "I mean, that is why they had you watch me, correct?"

She smiled back. "You caught me. But between you and me"

—she leaned in with a fake whisper—"I've never been one to follow the rules. Just don't get caught if you go out." With a wink and a smirk, she sauntered away, closing the door behind her.

Alone for the first time all day, the silence was almost unbearable. I walked back out onto the balcony, sighing as the thoughts started to flow in. There were so many questions and so few answers, which seemed to be the motto of my life.

Something had been happening to me for months, years, if not my entire life. The thing inside me that had been waiting, ready to leap forward at any given moment, had gotten its chance and I didn't think I would ever be the same.

I had been trying to ignore it all day, but I felt its presence. Less and less in the background, even by the second I could feel it growing stronger, as if waking from a long sleep.

Tired beyond belief, the stress of it all catching up to me, I tilted my head back to look at the twinkling stars. Maybe they would hold the answers to all my questions.

Turning to head in for the night, I stopped as a dark wave sped by, blocking out the stars as it crossed through the sky overhead, its colossal shape, moving faster than anything I'd ever seen, out of view within seconds.

Pinching my eyes closed, I rubbed my face; the crazy was hitting a whole new level. Sighing, I whisked myself back inside. I didn't need more shit right now.

CHAPTER TEN

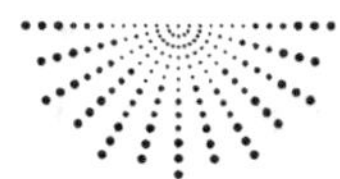

eat licked against my skin. My only savior was the cool sheet beneath me as I arched in pleasure. I tossed my head back in ecstasy, my arms held trapped above me as pure sensation was lashed upon me like a whip to skin.

A moan ripped free as his tongue brushed teasingly over my sensitive clit. I gasped loudly for more as he pulled back, enjoying the game of torment. Bucking my hips, I whimpered for more—more pleasure, more of him, more anything.

His dark, sensual chuckle sounded from between my thighs, spreading my legs wider over his broad shoulders. His strong fingers dug into my thighs with blatant possession, hard enough that I would probably find marks tomorrow.

My head thrashed to the side, my hands clenching at air as my body was wrecked and tormented. Placing one large hand against my stomach to hold me, his tongue slid inside. My fingers clenched tight, unable to move, as he feasted on me until I writhed, breathless and sobbing against him. His low, hungry groan only sent me closer to that precipice I so desperately craved. I cried out, near begging for more. Lifting my head to peer down at him—

I woke up with a jerk, panting wildly as my body struggled

to understand what was happening. My legs shook and my pussy clenched, aching for something that wasn't there. Squeezing my legs together, I pinched my eyes closed, trying to wring the memories of the dream from my head.

Rolling over onto my stomach with a groan, I turned my head on the soft pillows toward the wall of windows where the moons still hung high in the sky. I couldn't have been asleep for more than a few hours.

Keeping my eyes on the glowing orbs, my mind strayed to a story Maris used to tell me about them. How each was once a part of a family of great beings who were once stewards of the skies. One day, after washing in the nebulous rivers and walking across fields of stars, they found our world, a center in a vast expanse of wonder. These entities were so enamored that they could not resist staying, having fallen so in love that they turned themselves into stone and rock in order to watch over us.

For as long as I could remember, they had remained as they were. The blue, Heis, and the red, Ayu, were on the left. On the right in perfect symmetry to their siblings, was the white, Taipea, and the green, Sessa. Such simple words, colors, for such beautiful bodies. The swirls, markings, or rings that made up each of them were their own, each completely different and unique from the others.

The two largest—Heis and Taipea—could have been hidden behind a coin if I held it up to the sky, while Ayu and Sessa were barely the size of a marble. Together they stayed in the sky, circling around and around the planet, never sinking, never deviating from their paths. It was steadying, the routine of it. Even during the full light of day, their faded surfaces could be seen.

Only once a year did the path ever change. The Rising and Setting Eclipses was a day of celebration and time spent with family and friends. During the change between the warm and cold months, people all around Irropia spent the day outside, eating and dancing and being with loved ones as we all watched the moons make their way around the sun. During the rise, Teipea and Sessa cross behind the burning, white star, and travel together with their other siblings across the sky. By the time the sun begins its descent the four moons have made their path around the world, and Heis and Ayu make their pass behind the star, completing the journey.

As I watched the breeze rustle the leaves from the pink trees on the small balcony garden across the way, I couldn't help but wonder how Allasea and the Descendents spent the Eclipses. Did families gather on blankets in the fields, playing games and sharing old stories? Would I ever get to have that time with my family again?

And with that depressing thought, I sat up with a sigh, rubbing my hands over my tired face. I had never slept well, hadn't for a long damn time, too plagued by nightmares and dreams to ever be truly rested. Sometimes I was being held captive, starved and beaten, screams haunting me as they rang in my ears, other times I was given orgasms by strange men.

I wasn't complaining so much about that last one though.

The sleepwalking hadn't come until much later, when I got older. Just as the nightmares and dreams had worsened, so had my propensity to end up in the middle of the Blackwood, barefoot and in nothing but my nightshirt. Sometimes it took me hours to make my way back, finding Geoff and Maris already searching for me within the dark forest's depths.

Shoving off the bed sheets, I hopped down to the floor, my body too restless to go back to sleep. My skin immediately broke out into goosebumps as I walked into the small attached bathroom, the silk shorts and thin-strapped top I had changed into unable to protect me from the night air coming in through the open balcony doors.

A mirror hanging above the washbasin reflected the room around me. A copper tub sat off to the side, weird pipes hanging from the wall, which I learned earlier brought fresh water in. I had marveled at the invention and had almost taken a long soak, but exhaustion had made the choice between a bath and sleep easy. Soaps and salts lined the few shelves on the wall above the toilet.

My eyes stared back at me as I peered into the mirror. They had always been closer to gold, although they could have passed for a honeyed amber if you didn't look too closely; yet ever since I had Awakened, they were more gilded than gold coins. Now unmistakable in their color, they glowed with an iridescence that hadn't been there before. They now perfectly matched the softly spun curls that reached my hips.

I looked like a sculptor had carved me from alabaster and the rawest of metals. The soft sheen of my white skin was definitely new, as was the removal of all of my calluses from training. Nothing big had changed, but it was as if I had gotten a restart. No cuts and bruises, no damage—no nothing. Nothing to show that I had been ripped to pieces by the rotting carcasses of animals, or that an explosive power had broken from my body. No, I had just been dumped in a vat of glistening dust and proclaimed brand new.

If I had been shiny before, I was downright gleaming now, gods be damned. If I had ever thought I could get away with going unnoticed, that had been shot to hell and back.

Sighing my frustration, I yanked on the handle that brought water into the basin, watching in fascination as it went down the drain at the bottom. I splashed some on my face, the cold doing wonders to shock my systems back into place.

Heading out onto the open balcony, I stopped dead in my tracks because there, lying perfectly balanced on the railing, was the star-studded flower from the infirmary. It's white shimmering petals glowing in the night.

Walking out further, I glanced around, looking for whoever could have left it. There was no way they had come through my door, I would have heard them and I had locked it before falling asleep. The balcony garden was at least a hundred feet across from mine, and the open archways into the hall were empty. Picking up the long-stemmed flower, I peered over the edge at the plunging drop below. How the hell had it gotten here?

A tug in the center of my chest pulled me from my thoughts, my gaze shifting to the left. The bright entrance of the hot springs Zanaya had mentioned catching my gaze. Everything seemed to go out of focus as a rushing sound filled my ears. The energy which had been curled inside me all day unfurled, flowing through me like a tranquil stream. A fog hovered over my mind as I turned back into the room, the flower held loosely in my hand, intent on finding some clothes.

Zanaya hadn't been joking about the stairs. The path to the pools was a feat of construction all on its own. I had lost count after the first few hundred, but the building wave of heat I felt gave me hope I was almost to the end. I was already sweating in the brown trousers and navy blue top I had found in the trunk at the foot of the bed, that now conveniently held a glowing white flower.

With my small, bone knife shoved into my pocket, I made my way down into the underground staircase with surprisingly little hindrance. I was almost insulted by the lack of guards. I mean, I did hold someone at knifepoint. I could be a mass murderer for all they knew, going around slitting people's throats with my itty-bitty dagger.

Well, wasn't that charming to think about whilst walking down a dark, underground pathway to gods-knew-where probably hell if I had to guess because no angel had made these stairs.

I continued down the dark stone, the roughly cut outcroppings having been used over and over again until their faces were smooth and slightly curved from thousands and thousands of feet.

I was taking my time down them, having nearly slipped at the top. I had no desire to roll my ass down to the bottom and end up looking like a bruised apple for my troubles. The lit torches placed every few meters and my splayed arms gripping the jagged surfaces of the walls were my only safety measures.

Finally, I saw the barest hint of light, felt the pleasant heat seeping through my clothes and into my limbs. Picking up my pace, I jumped down from the last few steps and landed softly on the sandy bottom. The opening was a rough arch cut directly into the cave wall. I stepped in cautiously, going blind for a second as I exited the tunnel.

White candles lined the entrance along the black rocks, their wax having dripped down the sides from hours of burning. Billowing steam played through the room, misting my skin almost immediately and concealing the cave. The underground grotto had been left dim, allowing dark shadows to gather in the corners as the water seemingly disappeared into the back of the rough wall. Small shards of colorful crystals poked through the rock, glinting in the firelight. Flat rocks leading into the water acted as steps into the pool.

The water itself was serene and dark, a beautiful gloss on top so reflective it could have been a mirror. Yellow light swirled throughout the water, a lazy pattern starting near me before it disappeared into the darkness near the back, deep in the shadows.

I fought to see through the mist into the pitch-black shadows that seemed to move with a certain predatory grace, building up around the walls like a dark cloud. They almost seemed alive, reaching out from the back of the pool, crawling along the walls to reach me.

A cool, pleasant sensation wrapped around my leg. Looking

down, a few dark tendrils lightly licked at my skin. The buzz they sent through my leg shot up my body and tugged at something in my chest. It pulled me somewhere unknown–*somewhere I would happily follow*, I thought, as I watched them curl around my ankles–before reluctantly releasing me, holding on for as long as possible.

It left me reeling, the overwhelming feeling that seemed to radiate through me from such a simple touch. I swayed on the spot as my thoughts faded, a drum sounding in my head followed by a crackling hum. Blinking rapidly, I shook my head to clear the fuzz as a breath left my chest harshly.

I started stripping the clothes from my body, tossing them with the knife off the side. Beads of sweat built up on my skin in seconds, the warmth sinking into my bones and relaxing my muscles.

Stepping a foot into the inviting water, I let out a moan at the hot temperature. Step by step the water rose up, the candle-light playing across my naked body. A faint vibration floated through the pool, energy buzzing in the water—making it electrifying. As it pinged against my body I gasped, and the small gold stream rushed toward me. It was invigorating and calming all at the same time as it speared through my skin, quickly running through my body and back out.

The strange magic held a stronger glow now, the once faint stream more visible and brighter. Like it got an energy boost as well.

Back and forth it went, from the dark shadows in the corner back to me, once again rushing inside, bringing with it a shot of energy before coming out of me, stronger each time. Until after a few passes it stopped, going back to swirling around. The light was bright and wonderful in the dark, endless pool.

Smiling at the frisky water, I continued deeper. The water rose to just beneath my breasts, blanketing me as I soaked in its gentle current. Holding my breath, I ducked underneath the surface, feeling calm for the first time in days. As the hot spring cradled me within its heat, I could feel it willing me to heal from my emotional and physical battles—to surface only when I was ready to face those battles again, no longer the girl I once was, but as someone new.

Its caress encouraged and supported me all the same, neither pushing nor holding me back. The dark waters were pure peace, wanting nothing more than to nurture the life back into people, making them stronger so that they may continue whatever fight they faced.

I took my fill, collecting my thoughts and feelings so that I might finally begin to process them. So much had happened. So many new things had been revealed to me that I didn't know up from down. Left from right. I couldn't have found my own ass right now if I tried.

Everything inside me wanted to curl up in a ball and wait it all out, hoping my parents would come back and explain it all away as one big misunderstanding. As one bad dream. But as much as I wished that could happen, I was too practical to wait around for answers. I had been raised to fight my demons to the very end, and right now, figuring out what the hell was going on was one of them. An uphill battle that I had a feeling would knock me down at every turn.

Finding those answers may lead me to things that I don't want to know, like why Maris and Geoff lied to me my entire life. The truth was never easy though, and sometimes it took finding and accepting those hard truths to escape a prison of lies. I'd rather face a harsh reality and accept the freedom it would bring than be stuck in a cage of ignorance of my own making.

With that resounding thought and feeling more stable—for the minute at least—I pushed up from the bottom of the pool, breaking the pristine surface. Pushing my long hair back as rivulets of water ran down my skin, beads rolling between my breasts, I breathed in the humid air.

A prickling sensation all along my body froze me to my spot.

Opening my eyes, I locked gazes with a pair of glowing red orbs peering from the endless darkness.

I stood perfectly still, my heart beating fast in strange anticipation, as the shining eyes rose in the shadows. Growing taller and taller, they stood at least a foot above me, if not more. I couldn't see what the eyes belonged to, the shadows were too thick.

As if reading my thoughts, the darkness slowly parted, reluctantly letting go like one would a lover. Wisps of shadow floated in the air as a hulking body moved out of the sheer darkness and into the dim light.

For a second, my heart stopped beating before picking back up and nearly coming out of my chest. Every part of me burned, ached, as my power raced in time to the pounding in my ears. It rushed through my blood anxiously, unable to find a way out. I couldn't stop staring, stuck in a trance, barely containing myself as I stepped closer.

The largest man I had ever seen slowly waded through the water, shadows sliding across his shoulders, framing his muscular body, unwilling to let him go completely. He had to be six and a half feet at least, standing heads above me. His smooth, tanned skin looked warm and inviting, as if he spent every day in the sun, basking in its heat.

His broad shoulders and large chest took up my entire view as he came closer still, water slowly uncovering more of him. Every rippling muscle stood on display as droplets that I unnervingly wanted to trace with my tongue rolled between his abs.

I was incapable of stopping the arousal that built between my thighs, my entire body warming beneath his heated expression. Shaky breaths passed my parted lips as our gazes remained locked together. He had to be the most devastatingly handsome man I had ever seen. Which was saying something, since everyone in Eskira seemed to have been hit by the pretty stick.

But this man wasn't pretty. No, he was wild and uncontrolled in a way that could never be considered pretty, and the writhing shadows that played against his skin seemed to agree. He was everything delicious and masculine, and my reaction was proof of that.

His sharp jawline was hard enough to cut diamonds, and the neatly trimmed, dark stubble made me wonder what it would feel like between my thighs. His full lips almost begged someone to try and tame him, but what would be the point in that? That was exactly what made him so engrossing, the feral edge he carried all but had me rubbing up against him like some cat in heat.

The straight nose, sharp cheekbones, and furrowed, black brow all led to that piercing blood-red gaze. It was the gaze of a predator, burning even brighter the closer he stalked toward me. His dark hair was slicked back from his face, leaving nothing to hide his piercing stare, burning and filled with unimaginable heat, aflame from the inside.

My blood was scorching, my magic screaming at me to let it out. Not in defense against this beast—no, it wanted to brush against his skin, feel to see if he was as warm as he looked, to let loose and be as wild as him.

He stopped less than six inches from me, and I couldn't help but be disappointed that the water hit him just right, stopping anyone from seeing where those two angled lines of muscle on his hips led. I was in a daze, unable to look away.

I watched his expression, his nostrils flaring slightly, and for a split second his pupils, black holes against the glowing irises, constricted. The vertical, diamond-shaped eye reminding me of a snake, but that somehow didn't quite fit. It didn't match the energy he gave off, the monstrous beast that must have pulsed under his skin. Violence and death wrapped around him like a cloak, every raw and animalistic part of him on display.

I kept still as he began to encroach on my space, but I couldn't find it in me to care. Even as a part of me warned he was dangerous, that voice was drowned out by sheer, unadulterated need. Need for something inexplicable, a desperate, all-consuming hunger that shook me to my very core. It scared me with its intensity.

I waited with bated breath as he lifted one large hand and cupped my face. Later I would be embarrassed that a small whimper tried to escape my lips, but right now all I could focus on was the rough feel of his skin on mine as he leaned down from his towering height and brushed his nose against my neck.

The tension was almost visible, as if holding itself back in anticipation, the electricity bouncing back and forth between us pulsed throughout the cave. Shivers raced down my spine as his hot breath washed over me, the tip of his nose brushing against my skin as he slowly dragged it up, breathing me in. Helpless but to do the same, I took in his scent. Smoke, amber, and something deliciously smooth. My mouth watered at the heady smell, and if he weren't so close, I wouldn't have heard the deep groan that left the man's mouth as he took in mine.

As his thumb slowly stroked over my cheek, my breath caught. A loud rumble tore from his throat, booming throughout the entire cave, echoing off the stone walls, and sending ripples across the water.

The sound sent a bolt heat straight to my core and left me feeling concerned for my state of mind. A part of me was a little too excited at the idea of being caught, ready to be eaten.

The shadow man pulled back abruptly, yanking us out of our trance, and looked at me wildly as he clenched his fists, seeming to try to calm himself. Giving me one last heated, hungry look, he moved past me quickly, far faster than anyone his size had a right to.

I turned to watch him go, his back muscles rippling as he ignored the stairs and hauled himself out of the water. Every part of this man seemed to be made for battle, not an ounce of fat on him. He walked out of a hidden door—the ground entrance, most likely—that I hadn't noticed on my way in. Moving as quickly as a shadow, completely naked and unashamed, he vanished without a backwards glance.

I gaped at the door, trying to grasp what the fuck just happened. Groaning, I sank back underneath the water.

CHAPTER ELEVEN

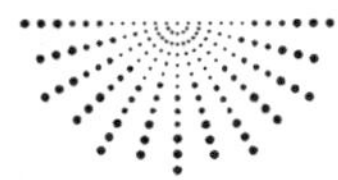

"Tell me again why I have to wear this thing?" I griped, pulling at the shimmery fabric of the dress Zanaya had all but shoved me into the minute she had stormed into my room. I'd barely been awake before she'd dropped me into the bath to get ready. I apparently smelled of sweat.

"Oh, quit your bitching. You look stunning and you know it," she said, looking over her shoulder to roll her eyes at me as she led us down a hall toward a copper door. "Besides, these things are typically very formal. Council meetings go back all the way to when The Divine ruled, and the Families like to bring out all the pomp and prestige whenever they can."

Great, I thought, looking at the dress again. It didn't have a corset, thank the Cosmos for that, my organs appreciated not being crushed together. The dress was, admittedly, very beautiful … and comfortable. It was annoying really, my pants-and-tunic-only conviction seemed very thin in the face of it.

The deep blue, tulle fabric draped down my body like water, falling to the floor in natural pleats. The gauzy material floated around me as we walked, giving me the air of some woodland creature. The v-shaped neckline, albeit plunging, was elegantly done. The cinching at the waist was held together by a wrapped golden metal belt shaped like starbursts. Simple gold-threaded edgings followed the neckline up to my shoulders, where more of the flowing fabric billowed behind me, falling off like a cape.

A high slit on either leg, deceptively hidden under the folds of the dress, gave me a surprising range of motion, and allowed me to carry a dagger as well. Zanaya had merely rolled her eyes, a small grin playing across her face, when she saw me tying the tiny letter opener tightly to my thigh with a piece of the bedsheet, before handing me a real dagger and sheath that she had brought along.

"I have a feeling you're more dangerous without a weapon than with one." She openly grinned. "Though I would be keen to see what dangers you would come up with if you were left defenseless."

I couldn't argue with that, I definitely had a cornered-cat mentality when I didn't feel comfortable in a situation.

I noticed our blades were completely different; her sword was made of a black glass, whereas mine was a simple, yet perfectly balanced, steel dagger.

After unceremoniously shoving me into the bath, Zanaya had sat me down on a stool, and began drying my loose hair with a gust of wind. To say it shocked me out of the last of my sleep-ridden haze was an understatement, as it left the metallic curls bouncing around my hips within seconds.

Without stopping to share in my awe, she put a rosy balm on my lips and called me done, claiming I had unfairly clear skin and she saw no reason to cover it up with the face paints that a lot of the highborns liked to wear. Which was ludicrous to me as she stood beside me in a stunning, form-hugging, blue dress of her own, the color matching her icy eyes. Her skin was as beautiful and smooth as polished ebony. Radiant in a completely natural and unaided way.

We reached the copper door, stylized with carvings of the

wind, and it opened without hesitation before us, fitting right into a slotted gap in the wall. Eyeing it, both in curiosity and wariness, I followed Zanaya as she stepped into the small box. It shook gently as we settled in, and the door slid out on its own, closing the box off. I couldn't help but send a wary and questioning glance over at my companion.

The wide grin which she was failing to hide only grew as a loud groan came from the tight walls around us. Jolting, feeling as if the floor was giving out beneath us, I steadied myself against the bronze wall. I looked around the compartment as the sensation of rising moved from my feet up my body.

Standing perfectly straight, completely at ease, chuckling, she said, "You didn't think we lived in this monstrosity of a city without coming up with a way to get around more easily, did you?"

"You're telling me we could have skipped all those stairs yesterday? That there is a way to get to the bottom without having to climb up and down a whole damn mountain? I went to those springs last night, do you realize how many fucking stairs there are … because if you do, let me know, I lost count and got bored after about four hundred."

Shaking in a fit of laughter, tears fell down her smiling face. "Oh, my gods"—she doubled over trying to catch her breath through her giggles—"you actually climbed that staircase, holy shit."

Shaking my head, I huffed out a chuckle of my own in reply, shaking my head. "You cheeky bitch."

That sent her into another fit of giggles before she replied, "Wind Aetherians figured out a way to use air to move these lifts up and down."

"Aetherians?" I asked, my curiosity piqued at the word I had heard Cashim use.

Wiping the tears from her face, she replied, "Cynthonians are of the God, they're the ones with an animal spirit. The really powerful ones—Primals—can sometimes control things like mind and shadow. Their creator is Death, after all. Aetherians are those who are of the Goddess. We're beings of energy, magic—whatever you want to call it—and typically have a specialty in one of the four elements." She leaned over, giving me a wink. "Unless you're special of course, then you're an Aether. There are also those who can bend light or heal, but you'll find that it's much more rare."

"So which do you control?" I asked, no doubt in my mind that she was one of the special ones.

"Mostly wind and water," she explained. "My family is known for their healing abilities, but I can only heal small wounds and cuts. My uncle is more proficient with water and healing, which is why in his spare time he helps run the infirmary."

The thought of such power was hard for me to grasp, and yet I remembered the storm of energy that had come out of me that night. I wasn't sure I had the luxury of ignorance anymore, because even amongst the Descendents, something told me that what happened that night wasn't normal.

The shiny box came to a harsh halt, knocking me off balance. Leading us off the lift, Zanaya walked out into a wide hallway covered in gold and black mosaics. "If it makes you feel any better, there's only a few of these lifts around. There isn't really one that goes all the way down. Most of the time you have to take a series of them to reach the bottom. It was designed that way for safety."

"Well, I'm sure it beats the fucking hike I had to do," I cursed back.

She laughed again, looking over at me appraisingly. "I think you'll do just fine here, Atallia. I've got a good feeling about you."

With that, she pushed through an arched doorway, and into

a large hall. The throne room was simple and classic in style, with an air of majesty to it.

The white marble, veined with gold, was a stunning contrast to the walls of dark stone, the rough cut of the mountain in which the room sat. Enormous spiraling black pillars stood evenly spaced throughout the room, shooting down from the rock ceiling and connecting to the floor. It was as if the room had been cut and formed around them, left supporting the curved, domed ceiling. The stone was amazingly crafted, stories carved around and around—from top to bottom they were a codex of history.

The ceiling shot upwards in height as we walked further in, and outcroppings jutted out on either side of the room, allowing an upper balcony to witness everything going on down below. Small, hidden staircases were expertly disguised along the back walls, allowing for discrete access to the upper levels. The delicately built, marble railing blocked most of the view of the higher room. Dark shadows gathered in the deep recesses of the arched areas, torches left cold with disuse. It was the only space that seemed to hold on to the darkness.

Large, stained-glass windows stretched from floor to ceiling, taking up the entire wall to the right, facing out toward the lower city. An iridescent white background shimmered in the light, and a black tree, with its spiraling trunk and twisted roots, stood proudly in the center. Golden leaves filled the branches, drops of deep maroon blood coated and dripped from the tips of the gilded, glass leaves.

An expansive balcony that shot out from the mountain, large enough to fit hundreds of people, could be seen on the other side of the glass. Clouds floated just below the railing, and the rising sun shone down upon it, fracturing through the glass and casting a shattering of light and color through the room. It was heavenly, with its dream-like haze.

A dark, wooden table, large enough to seat dozens, had eight chairs spaced around it. They all sat empty, still too early for the meeting to start. The council was made up of six representatives, one from each of the oldest Descendent Families. The two end chairs faced each other—one cast into a halo of light and the other seemingly in a shroud of darkness—perhaps left symbolically for the Descendents' missing leaders.

Six banners dropped from the overhanging balcony above, each flapping behind one of the chairs. On our side, in the middle, was the navy blue standard with the golden tree and white bird—Cashim and Zanaya's family crest—and on the left of it was the same green tapestry that also hung in the infirmary. The golden lotus was just as dazzling. The other banner was made with a yellow fabric, gold lightning shooting down from a tumultuous sky, hitting the ground in a blaze of flames.

The one directly across from Cashim's was red, a black insignia of feline jaws crushing a human skull with its massive incisors. The other two, one purple with black wings spread wide in flight, and the other gray with a fearsome depiction of a black sea serpent rising to strike, were just as formidable.

The most eye-catching things in the room, however, sitting on the raised dais off to the right, grabbed my attention like nothing else. I couldn't help but be stunned by the sight: sitting stoic and empty up on the platform were two thrones.

The one on the right was made entirely of black onyx, as roughly cut as the walls of the room, and polished to a dangerous gleam. The large piece of gemstone looked like it had broken right out of the floor, the white marble around it cracking apart with black streaks shooting in all directions. The jagged edges and savage look had been kept, like it had been pulled straight from the mountain in one piece. The base was carved with statues of animals, rubies used as their eyes, shadows and bone-white skulls twined throughout. A red velvet cushion sat affixed to the throne. The sculptor who had created the magnificent seat had obviously known who it was for. A throne made for the King of Animals—a throne for Death, the God of Endings.

Its counterpart on the left was equally beautiful, and terrifying in its own way. The white, opaque quartz was streaked through with veins of gold, and shaped to resemble a more traditional throne in comparison. The delicately hewn shapes of starbursts, the elements, and various plant life rose up around the backrest, framing where the queen would have sat. Solid, golden vines, thorns, sharp and threatening, erupted through the floor. They writhed and twisted up from the base, crawling up the chair before wrapping around the armrests. One would have to be careful lest they cut themselves on the thorns' sharp edges.

Similar to the king's, a golden cushion sat waiting for its ruler. It shone with a fierce beauty in the beaming sun, shimmering with an unseen light—perfect for the Queen of Elements, Lady of Light, the Goddess of Beginnings.

"Gorgeous, aren't they?" Zanaya said from my side, also looking upon the thrones with a deserved awe. They truly were something to marvel at. I couldn't even imagine the image they would paint if their rulers were sitting upon them.

"Very," I replied, giving the thrones their due reverence.

A loud echo reverberated around the empty hall as a secondary side entrance, opposite of our position, opened. A line of six people filed in, and were animatedly talking. Well, arguing, more like.

Their discussion was so heated I didn't think they had even spotted us, except for Zanaya's uncle, who walked over quickly.

Cashim was dressed to impress. Every silken thread was shining and on display. The dark blue velvet overcoat fit his firm shoulders nicely, wrapping across his body, with gleaming, gilded buttons on the left side of his chest. Gold edging, similar to the designs on mine and Zanaya's dresses, decorated the collar.

A polished scabbard, belted along the black trousers he wore, held a gold-handled cutlass. His polished, black boots finished off his aristocratic look.

I couldn't help but notice the similarities in the coloring and design of our clothing. All three of us wore various shades of blue and gold, whilst the other council members each sported their own specific colors.

"Niece, I hope I find you well," he greeted in his musical accent as he reached us, coming up to kiss Zanaya's cheek.

"You as well, Uncle." Her own accent was a lighter, more feminine version of his.

Turning to me with his icy eyes, a family trait no doubt, he gave me a fatherly smile before averting his gaze. Not quite a flinch, but an avoidance, nonetheless. I had to give him some credit, he held out longer than most. It was concerning the way he seemed to instantly put me at ease with his easy smile and comforting presence. I wasn't used to trusting anyone but Maris and Geoff, and now I couldn't even do that. There was also something else behind that warm gaze—something I couldn't quite put my finger on—that had me watching him carefully, making me want to look deeper.

"And you, my dear? I hope you slept well your first night here. I know after all the ordeals you've been through these past couple days you must be exhausted."

"Yes. Thank you, I did," I said, leaving out the part about my naked meeting with a man who made my blood simultaneously boil and sing. "Nice outfit," I said with a knowing smile, my eyes narrowed slightly as I looked him up and down appraisingly.

"Ah, I see you've caught my apparently not-so-subtle gesture." He smiled widely, a hint of his niece's wild cheekiness playing through his eyes. "You may not be a part of my family, but it can't hurt to send a message to the others."

I'd come to the conclusion that Cashim was a lot more like his niece than I'd thought. He just hid his non-conformity with a veneer of platitudes, politeness, and politics. I had a feeling I would come to like this little family of outlaws.

"And what message is that?"

Leaning forward conspiratorially, he said, "That while you may be on your own during this meeting, as we do make decisions regarding the safety of our people democratically, one of the six Families stands behind you; and that it might be in everyone's best interest to fall in line rather than risk discontentment amongst our ranks." He looked over his shoulder, the group of five still in a battle of wills of some kind. Shaking his head, he rolled his eyes in their direction. "Or more than there already is."

Zanaya nodded her head in support, and my heart couldn't help but fill with warmth and gratitude. These were people who barely knew me, yet would put their reputations and their family's reputation on the line for me. They might not be able to stand next to me during this meeting, but they were going to give me all the support they could.

I couldn't help the paranoia that I would be betrayed, that all of this was just some game they played to get me to lower my guard, but there was a part of me that really wanted to see what I could have here in this world of magic. They had given me kindness, something I had never really experienced outside of my own small family.

And it was a kindness I wouldn't ever forget. Smiling gratefully at them both, hoping I wouldn't later regret giving them the small inch behind my walls.

With a smile, he turned to look back at the gathered group once again, several pairs of eyes now looking our way. "We'll start the meeting very formally and then call you over to discuss all that has happened the last few days. If it goes well, we might be able to get them to agree that finding your parents would be beneficial. They obviously have some explaining to do in regards to you, and the

Council will want to know why you were raised in Rhaelyth."

"They won't be in trouble, right?" I asked, worry for them rising up inside me. I hoped I wasn't about to make a mistake that could get them jailed or worse. "I may be mad at them for lying to me, but they still cared for me."

With an understanding look, sympathy filling his eyes, he gave me a flat smile. "Honestly, my dear, it will all depend on why they kept you away from Allasea for so long. If they were aware of what you were, then there would have been signs of how powerful you would become. Your kind of Awakening, if it had been done in the wrong place, could have killed thousands." He sighed heavily. "We are very lucky that you weren't near any mortals at the time. As it stands, you've most likely piqued their interest, specifically their king's. Which is something we have been trying to avoid for two thousand years."

Dread settled in my stomach at his words, because Maris and Geoff absolutely knew what I was. Thinking back on the conversation I had walked in on, they were very aware that I was on the verge of Awakening, had even mentioned taking me home, leading me to believe that we all came from here.

I could feel the anger building quickly at the lies they told me and the danger they had put themselves and the entire village in. If they knew even half of what my Awakening would be like, then Cashim was right: they had known they were putting people in danger.

A telltale burn built behind my eyes as I went back through my entire life, questioning every little thing, every memory I had of them. My whole world was seemingly one big lie.

Reaching out a hand to grasp my shaky one in hers, Zanaya looked at me. "We'll figure this out, okay? Either way, we'll help you get through this." Strength was imbued in her words, and for that split second I believed everything would be alright.

Nodding my head back at her before looking at her uncle

and giving him the same, I blinked away the offending tears that were welling up.

"Alright!" he said with a nod, clapping his hands together with a reassuring grin. "Let's get this carnival show started." He walked over to join the group who were shooting me looks from the table.

Hushed conversation followed, the previous argument pushed to the side for now, as Cashim found his seat. My skin prickled in warning, an itch building in the back of my mind. Looking around, I couldn't see anything out of place.

I glanced up at the upper balcony, where darkness was over-taking the entire space. The gathering shadows in the right corner were thick and undulating with a sentience to them that wasn't normal.

Narrowing my eyes, suspicion clouded my mind as I whis-pered softly, "What is that?"

I glanced back up at the overhanging balcony, watching the shadows just as they watched me. The eerie darkness waiting patiently, moving slowly like a lazy cat around the dark corner of the veranda.

"What?" Zanaya's voice snapped me out of my thoughts. Her eyebrows were raised in question.

I shook my head. "Nothing, sorry, just talking to myself."

Smiling, she turned back to watch the proceedings. Following her lead, I tried to focus on the meeting even as my eyes kept straying to the corner.

"As we all know, this meeting was called to discuss the worrying reports we have received from our scouts in regards to the movements of the wraiths on either side of the Black-wood. But an incident occurred three nights past, of similar relevance, that also needs to be discussed here today. An unknown Descendent Awakened just inside the borders of Allasea with no knowledge of her power or our world."

Cashim's voice projected throughout the room, carrying with it a hint of authority that hadn't been there a moment ago.

Looking around the table at the six occupants, three on either side, I picked up on the subtle hints their clothing gave off. Cashim sat in the middle on one side with a woman in green and a man in yellow on his sides. All of their clothes, while stylistically different, were edged or patterned with golden thread.

The other side held two women and a man, their colored clothes decorated in black. The three families of the Goddess and God respectively, it seemed. Aetherians and Cynthonians.

However, it was the man in the middle on the God's side that pulled my attention. His black on red clothing drew a stark picture with his tanned skin and blue eyes. His dark brown curls were slicked back from a strong forehead and thunderous brow. He would have been handsome if it weren't for the sneer stuck on his twisted lips, mixed even more perversely with the plain desire in his eyes as he looked upon me.

I instantly disliked him; he reminded me of all the men back in my village. Openly hostile and dismissive of me in front of everyone else, and yet away from the prying eyes of society, they were the ones who would back me into corners or alleyways and try to force something that wasn't theirs to take.

After I had … let's say nicked … the first few, the rest left me alone for the most part, except for the occasional jeering comment that the only thing I was good for was a quick fuck, or a too-leisurely look that made me want to scrub my skin raw. Just the thought brought a bad taste to my mouth.

"Several weeks ago, wraiths began attacking the smaller cities and villages surrounding Vallenia. Subsequently, for the past few weeks we have been dealing with the same attacks on our own towns and villages. As it stands, we don't know how they are getting back and forth through the border and why they seem intent on making their way across the continent," Cashim explained, the councilors either focused on him or staring at me. "However, what we do know is that the attacks, mostly on our side of the barrier so far, have escalated from one or two in the night to full assaults over the past month. We need to discuss our next steps going forward and how best to proceed."

A hand banged down against the table, sending vibrations through the floor. "What we need is to get on top of this. All this talking gets us nowhere," the man in red yelled aggressively. "It has been months of this nonsense and we have still yet to move against these things."

"What would you have us do, Lars?" The woman in green spoke lightly, her voice drifting along an invisible wind. "We know nothing about them or their motivations."

"We could always try the Orama," the brown-skinned woman in purple spoke up from the end of the table.

Cashim was already shaking his head. "We have yet to pay back our debt for the last question we asked her. It's better if we leave her be on Corosa, and let the Eye Stones be our last option."

The aggressive lord—Lars—scoffed in derision, "That old bat is as cryptic as the day is long, and we don't need more riddles. As I've been saying for the past six months, give me control of the armies. I'll have them search far and wide until we find these creatures, and then we will eradicate them from the face of Irropia. We cannot continue to allow them to come after our people." The man in yellow nodded his head in agreement, but he was the only one to outwardly do so.

"And I'm sure the warlord would agree with that," the woman in gray snarked, rolling her eyes.

Lars's face pinched in displeasure before he continued. "The boy is still young, he took over way too early. He doesn't have the wartime experience that will be needed before this ordeal is over with."

The woman snorted in derision. "He properly challenged you and won years ago. *The boy,* as you like to call him, has made our military more competent than they have ever been since the rule of The Divine. Do not think us idiots, Lars. We all know you're trying to regain as much power as you can for whatever stupid coup you are planning."

"So much for your neutrality, Oakina." His words were spat in her direction.

"Neutrality does not mean I have to entertain idiots."

Lars sputtered unattractively, trying to come up with his defense, but the woman continued, glancing at Cashim, her voice as precise as a whip as she said, "Please continue before my mind explodes from this inane conversation."

Zanaya giggled at my side, enjoying the show as much as I was. I smiled at the woman's verbal beatdown, her scathing dismissal a masterclass in dealing with egotistical assholes. A flicker in my peripheral drew my attention, the darkness swelling in the corner, something flashing within it.

"Atallia." I snapped my eyes away from the balcony and towards Cashim, all eyes having turned toward me. He beckoned me with a wave of his hand, motioning for me to step forward. I walked towards the far end, the empty chair having been pulled away. Shoving away any nerves I had, I held my head high, the wall of windows at my back, the warmth of the sun giving me the strength I needed.

"Three nights ago, the wraiths made their way to young Atallia's village, and I think it best that she explain the following events." He looked to me to speak.

I swallowed down any brash comment I was inclined to make, not really one for the poshness of the whole situation. "I woke to find my parents gone, our house a mess, and a creature the likes of which I had never seen on our land. It was a thing of nightmares, and trust me, I would know."

As I told them about that night, I saw the shadows move closer, leaning in. I couldn't help shifting my eyes up there every few seconds, curious and almost certain I knew what hid behind them. "I ran to get them away from the village, and when they caught up that is when they started ripping into me." Memories flashed through my head of the bites, the feel of my arm ripping apart, my body being torn to shreds while I was conscious of every little thing. "I don't think I've known pain like that," I said, stuck in the memories of that night. "Where your skin pulls free and your muscles stretch to their breaking point before snapping."

My eyes glazed over as I stared up into the darkness once more, willing the shadows to come closer. For a split second they rippled, and I could see a glowing red flash.

"But that pain was nothing compared to the agony that had been building before that. The raging storm that I had been dealing with my entire life finally decided it had enough of being kept locked up. And by that point, nearly dead, and lying in a pool of my own blood—I didn't care what happened." I looked each and every councilor in the eye, forcing them to listen to my story. "So I just let go, and ... it ... just ..." I shook my head at the memory of the funnel of power destroying everything in its path, the beacon of light shooting back into me, "... ravaged."

The entire hall was silent, nobody moving, not a single sound. The dark shadows writhed, having grown larger and more frenetic in their movements.

"Well, I for one don't think a Little Miss Nobody from some backwater village, not even within the borders of Allasea, could have caused such damage. Has anyone even checked her power since she's been here?" Lars, the pompous dick, was doing an excellent job of proving me right about him. What a fucking asshole.

Looking at him innocently, a huge fake smile plastered to my face, I asked, "When shit comes out of your mouth, can you smell it or are you blind to it by now?" I shrugged my shoulders. "Inquiring minds and all that."

The auburn-haired man wearing the yellow suit jacket on the other side of Cashim choked back his laughter. The stunningly beautiful woman in green and gold, with her long hair and black, almond-shaped eyes, giggled gently, her voice as musical and ethereal as singing bells. "Delightful, darling. Just delightful."

Lars, however, did not seem to find it funny at all, and gasped at me in outrage. "How dare you, you little bitch. You should be on your knees before me." The shadows were angry—murderous—whipping around and lashing out in the air. "Begging me, us, to give you asylum."

"For your information, Lars, several healers from the city infirmary can confirm her power level. Considering the fact that it left many of them blind and injured after the numerous attempts to compromise with it when Atallia was asleep, to the point we had all but evacuated the building, she is in fact powerful enough to cause such damage."

I ignored Lars's heated reply, barely hearing the words spoken by the other members as the swirling vortex of darkness built and built upon itself until I was shocked that no one else was concerned. More flashes of red came from the funnel of shadows, the same piercing, red eyes staring into mine just as they had the night before.

Those eyes shot through the darkness, fury making them burn bright, so bright that not even the darkness of the recess he hid in could hide the glow. I waited, wished, for the shadows to peel back and reveal the rest of him, just as they had last night.

"Do we bore you, young one?" The quiet question came from the beautiful blonde woman in gray, Oakina.

I waited, watching the man in the inky darkness, refusing to let go of his gaze for fear he might disappear into shadowy depths not even I could see into.

Narrowing my gaze, our eyes still locked, I swore I saw a wicked smirk peeking out from the pitch-black fog.

"Do you plan to come down here any time soon, or do you just like to watch?" My voice echoed loudly across the space, my question impertinently digging at his behavior in the spring. Everyone turned to look, their eyes unsuccessfully searching for who I was talking to.

I thought he might not step forward, but just as I was about to call out again, the cloud of darkness moved to the railing and into the light. The sentient shadow seemed to grip the rail before tossing itself down the several story height. The council members gasped in surprise.

What should have been a hard fall and loud boom against the marble was instead as light and soundless as a floating feather. As he hit the floor, the shadows fell away, exploding outward and dashing back to their corners. A man was left standing there, head bowed. The hulking predator from last night looked formidable in front of the thrones.

Slowly, he lifted his head of curls so thick and dark they seemed to suck in the light, staring me down with a gaze that pierced straight through to my soul.

A heated look crossed his face as that sinful smirk lifted his full lips, showing off four sharp canines, and in a voice as smooth and deep as his smoky scent, he drawled, "You called?"

CHAPTER TWELVE

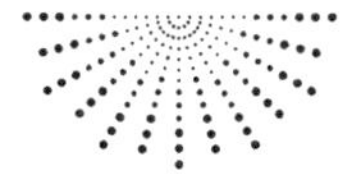

Seeing him in the full light of day was shocking. He seemed too much a creature of the night to ever set foot in the day, and yet here he stood, his massive frame on display in the sunlight, silhouetted by the two thrones behind him.

While I still thought he belonged to the darkness, I couldn't help but appreciate the advantage the light gave me—allowing me to look my fill.

He was wearing a black leather tunic, gold buckles and chains holding light armor to his shoulders, the material straining against their breadth. The warm, tanned skin of his arms was bare of all but the leather gauntlets which held small daggers. A magnificent broadsword was strapped to his back, crossing over his shoulder. The black metal pommel was shaped to look like the head of a red-eyed dragon, the detail so fine I could see the individual scales and horns from where I stood.

I wasn't sure which version I liked best, the naked one or the clothed one. I'd always been very open with my sexuality and never hid from my desires or needs, yet I couldn't remember a time in which a man had held my attention so intently. Granted, the men I had lain with before were the sons of traveling merchants, handsome and charming enough, but they were nothing compared to the man in front of me. The air around him vibrated with a primal ferocity that set me ablaze.

I met his eyes, ones that refused to back down, to turn away. No flinch or wince, but that wasn't what had me frozen in place, staring into the red depths. It was the other thing in his eyes. An intensity so deep I might as well have been on the other end of a wolf's jaws. I was locked in the sights of a dangerous man, a predator; something that probably shouldn't exist and yet here he stood.

His piercing, ruby gaze sent chills down my spine. I couldn't tell if it was because I wanted to run, to get away from an animal on the hunt, or for the simple fact that he would chase me and that I might like it.

If I had any doubts about whether I was stuck in a dream, surrounded by the magic of my imagination, he tore through that theory like it was wet parchment. No way in hell was he in any way human. The mask he wore was very good—he might even have been able to draw normal people in, too distracted by what was on the outside to notice how close they were to death.

But the thing was, predators recognized other predators. I may not know what I was capable of, but I sure as shit knew I wasn't prey. Not even to this beast in front of me.

"What are you?" I asked him bluntly, no reason to beat around the bush. I had had enough with people doing it to me in my life—in general, people seemed to dance around the truth rather than be honest with each other—and I had no intention of being part of the problem.

A sensual grin, bringing thoughts of whispered secrets in the dark, grew on his face, small dimples making what I presumed was a rare appearance. "I am Kanan."

I tilted my head, peering into his eyes, trying to figure out what about that name seemed familiar, but just as I was about to grasp it, it eluded me.

I shook my head free of the runaway memories, chalking them up to having met him before the meeting. "Good for you, but that's not what I asked."

His smile slowly faded away, and a darkness, completely different from his shadowy companions, entered his expression. His eyes shuttered for a second, before completely closing off.

"Kanan is the warlord of our army. Although I wasn't aware we asked him to be here." The woman dressed in a plunging purple and black dress spoke up.

"I did." Cashim looked at me grimly, giving me an apologetic smile. "To ascertain your threat level. Please join us, Kanan." He waved him closer.

Honestly, I couldn't blame them for the lack of trust, could I? I was doing the same thing to them. On one hand, they didn't know me, I could be here to lure them into a sense of false security before killing them all, and on the other hand, I did end up destroying entire swathes of forest with little to no control over myself.

I couldn't help the part of me that was satisfied they saw me as a big enough threat to call in their warlord. At least I was being taken seriously. Hopefully that would be enough.

"Thank you, Councilor," he said pleasantly. His shrewd gaze tracing over those sitting, stopping shortly on Lars, lips twitching slightly. "Don't mind if I do," he said, pulling out the chair on the end all while he stared Lars down with a bored, calculating look I had seen on the faces of barn cats when they were deciding whether to kill or play with their prey. Settling in, the massive chair fitting his frame, Kanan turned his focus back to me.

I lifted my chin and raised an eyebrow challengingly. "And? Am I to be considered a threat?"

"Most definitely." His face was serious as he said the words.

"I find myself very keen on seeing what happens when you truly understand what you can do."

I could feel the simmering power in my veins, pulsing in my very soul; every cell vibrated with it. A never-ending well of strength and potential. I had a feeling I could do a lot worse than destroy a clearing if I wanted.

I had no intention of adding fuel to the already flaming fire of mistrust between all of us, so I kept quiet. The human pustule, however, saw fit to interject once again.

"So, my boy," he said patronizingly to Kanan, attempting to give off the fatherly air Cashim did so naturally. As if he hadn't just been attempting to undermine him. Kanan just stared blankly as Lars continued. "You've basically confirmed for us that she can't be left uncontrolled lest she cause irreparable damage."

"Who are you again?" I asked impertinently, enjoying watching his face turn red.

"Oh, my sincerest apologies, Atallia." Cashim spoke up, trying to hide his own amusement.

"This is Elaric Pyke, Head Aether of House Pyke." He indicated the man on his left in the yellow and gold, his blonde hair falling down his back in a pleat. His vibrant green eyes, while pretty, held no real spark in them, nothing that made me think that this man should be overseeing an entire people.

"Pleasure." I dipped my head shallowly to him in greeting and received one back.

"This lovely woman next to me is Lilyi Jai, Head Aether of House Jai." The woman was stunningly beautiful in the green and gold wrap dress that hugged her figure in a simple yet classic way. Her keen, unfathomably black eyes were sharper than any blade.

"Flatterer," she said, turning to Cashim with a friendly smile, which he returned. They were obviously close allies and friends, possibly something more guessing by the way they held each other's gazes for a second longer than was necessary. I filed that piece of information away for later.

"Yeva Ikaria, Head Primal of House Ikaria, and Oakina Vyn, Head Primal of House Vyn." I looked toward the two women, who wore purple and black and gray and black respectively, on either side of Lars. Yeva Ikaria with her warm, brown skin and eyes, and sharp nose looked almost dreamy in comparison to the other woman.

In contrast, dressed in light gray, Oakina Vyn had the look of a predator. Wary, alert eyes of silver bounced back and forth between me and Kanan, as if she didn't know who the bigger threat in the room was. However, I could see something lurking behind those eyes, ready to put up a big fight if needed.

Something about the way she seemed prepared to jump into action at any moment made me like her. Or maybe it was that she was in trousers and a tunic, properly made and just as fine as the rest of the council's clothing, but trousers, nonetheless. Apparently, my practicality-over-fashion approach was shared, which only made me more annoyed with the beautiful, gauzy thing I wore.

"And you, sir?" I asked, turning towards Lars. I kept a placid expression on my face, refusing to give him any kind of reaction.

"Lars Braxix, Head Primal of House Braxix, and former Warlord of the Descendent Army." His snooty nose was stuck so high in the air I half expected him to be talking to the ceiling.

"Former … huh," I said, giving him a sympathetic smile. "What a shame."

Even as I turned my attention back to the rest of the Council, I saw a snarl twist Lars's face. I guess I wasn't going to be making any friends there.

"Now that we've been properly introduced, perhaps I can share my story with you." I looked pointedly at the ass-boil, who's face was as red as his suit jacket. "Uninterrupted this time, of course."

"I was found, abandoned, on the edge of my village by my two adoptive parents, Maris and Geoff. They raised me as their own and taught me everything I know, from fighting to medicinal practices." Emotions tried to clog my throat as I remembered my earliest memories with them, happy and filled with unrestrained joy.

"They were kind to me in a place filled with people that only seemed to hate and despise me. You see, the mortal world has been losing its magic, something you're probably aware of if you've had scouts going across the border." Their nods of affirmation told me as much, but no one offered an explanation. It made me wonder if they even knew why it was disappearing.

"On top of the disappearance of magic, whatever is left, whether it be artifacts and objects—even children who show a hint of power—it's all being taken by King Starga. It has left a lot of people bitter and angry. The villagers could sense what I was or at the very least knew I wasn't like them. While they refused to turn me over to the king's guards, they hated me for it. Hated that I had what they never could, even if I never asked for any of it."

The council shifted uncomfortably, whether from my treatment or the idea that the mortal King was stealing what magic the humans had left; either way the information did not sit well with them. Cashim was frowning in dismay, Zanaya's brows had puckered in anger, and Lady Oakina looked ready to go to war.

It was…touching, in a way, to be validated by strangers who knew so little about me, yet were ready to defend the young girl I used to be. It was unnecessary though. It took me a long time, too long, to figure out that the people of my village simply needed an outlet for their anger, and I happened to be a shiny target. I was a reminder of everything they had lost, and part of me understood their hatred towards me, even though I knew I didn't deserve it.

I couldn't imagine losing a child like so many had over the years, thinking of sweet Ms. Banks down the road who had smiled at me and given me chocolates. She even let her son play with me after his studies, while the other mothers had shielded their children from view when I walked by. Then her little boy showed the smallest bit of magic, making a leaf morph into a rock before our eyes. The wrong person saw and the next thing I knew, he was gone. I had never forgotten his name—Oliver Banks—or how kind he'd been to me. My one and only friend.

He was my only playmate, and after he was taken—the woman hadn't been unkind, but she no longer stepped in when the other children tried to bully me, their mothers turning the other cheek as they yanked my hair or pushed me to the ground. They only stopped after I bloodied the oldest and meanest of the boys.

Meeting Kanan's eyes, I could see the bloody depths swirling with fury. I was surprised to see that anger reflected in everyone's eyes; the thought of what had been happening for years in Rhaelyth was upsetting enough to be visceral for everyone.

"My adoptive mother was tracking the wraith attacks," I added, hoping to incentivize them more into finding them. "There was a pattern forming and I think she might have figured out what it was. She had a map in our shed that showed all the attacks from the surrounding villages, and even some from the capital. She also had notes on the infection as well. We had been treating the patients that were close enough to reach us, and I read through them."

That seemed to catch the interest of everyone; even Zanaya stepped forward to hear better. "What did she have to say about it?" Cashim asked intently, making it obvious that they seemed to be in the dark about all of this as well.

"Mostly she spoke of an energy spark within our patients,

and even mentioned how it seemed to be dying out; but she was very confused about that part." Quick, worried looks were shared by those at the table. "She also made note that there wasn't much left of one for her to help heal our patients."

"Then your mother was almost certainly a Descendent. There would be no other way for her to be able to guide a spark into healing its body." Lilyi's musical voice spoke up, turning to me. "An energy spark lives inside of every living thing, this planet included, and it is what makes us who and what we are. For those of us with magic, our spark is what stores it. It is our soul in the simplest of terms."

Cashim nodded along in agreement. "House Jai and House Zuberi have been leading a joint effort in trying to stop the spread of infection in the mortals. So far it hasn't affected the Descendents, but that's because we haven't yet seen a Descendent who has been bitten."

"You said you worked on your mother's patients with her?" Lilyi asked thoughtfully.

"Yes, my father taught me combat and my mother taught me healing. I was proficient in both, so I had a well-rounded education on top of my other studies growing up."

Nodding at Cashim before looking back at me, she replied, "Perhaps then you might be willing to come down to the infirmary and share what you and your mother have found. We'll send people to retrieve the map and notes from her study, but it might be worth having you explain everything you've picked up since treating the patients. Being so closed off as we are, we haven't had the opportunity to study it up close, so at the moment, we have no way of knowing if we can do anything to help."

The daughter in me only wanted to find my parents, not wishing to waste time on most certainly useless pursuits. However, the healer in me knew I possibly could have what they needed to help the mortals. After seeing Brendon and the others we had treated, there was no part of me that could refuse, unwilling to be complacent in letting anyone else die in such a way.

"Of course," I said seriously. "It would be my pleasure, although I don't know how much help I will be. She wasn't forthcoming with what she knew, I only stumbled upon them the day before the attack."

"At this point, dear"—her voice was both sad and angry—"we will take whatever you can give us."

Nodding in understanding, I gave them the sliver of information that I hoped would never come to pass: "She was preparing for a plague, a mass spread of it throughout the entire region."

"We feared as much as well."

"You said your father taught you to fight?" asked Zanaya, who, up to this point, had stayed out of sight and off to the side.

I turned towards her, answering, "Yes, he used to tell me that he was a retired guard from some lord's service in Vallenia, but knowing what I know now, it is very possible that was just what they told me over the years to keep me from prying."

I knew eventually I would have to come to terms with everything that had happened. To how I felt about it all, the betrayal, the feeling of maybe finally belonging somewhere. It was all too much for me to ignore forever.

"Thinking back on it now, I'm almost certain he was a Descendent. Not the same as Maris, but like you," I said, looking over toward Oakina and Lars. "He gave off a different kind of energy, one I don't think I could have put into words until now—very animalistic in nature."

"When you sparred, did you ever see him bleed?" Kanan asked, pulling my attention back to him as he finally spoke in his rich tone. The sound sent shivers down my spine.

"Yes, but it would heal very quickly. I brushed it off as a healthy body and Maris's help, but now I'm not so sure."

"If he was a Descendent and you were able to cut him, you would have needed to use heartsglass," Zanaya added.

"Heartsglass?" I felt ignorant, asking questions left and right, but saw no other way to rectify that mistake.

"It's a long story, but it's the only material that can affect those of us with magic running through our veins. White heartsglass injures and simultaneously inhibits our powers for varying degrees of time and intensity. And black ..." she said, pulling out her blade, the dark crystal sucking in the light. "Black heartsglass can kill us. There are a few cases of damage so extreme it forces us to use our power to stay alive, and has even led to death, like explosions and such, but it's rare. Cynthonians are able to kill using their claws and fangs, Primals with power over shadows do some pretty interesting things, and Aetherians can deal death blows with their magic. Other than that we're a pretty hardy people."

Narrowing my eyes, I reached my hand into the slit of my dress, pulling out the blade she had given me earlier. It was light and well oiled, sharp and balanced, but its silver metal was completely plain and normal in comparison to the deadly, black crystal of her blade. And apparently it would do absolutely nothing against them.

I looked back up at her with an unamused look on my face, a smirk on her own. "You couldn't have really expected us to give you something you could hurt us with, did you?" I rolled my eyes at her, not holding a grudge against something I would have done as well. I had thought it stupid of them to arm me, but now I knew they had just placated me. Like a kitten who thought it was a tiger.

"So, wait," I said, pointing at Cashim with the tip of the dagger. "When I held you at knifepoint yesterday, you weren't the least bit nervous?" I remembered thinking he was too calm for someone under the edge of a blade.

Giving me a pitying smile, his eyes laughing, he shrugged. "I was, but not for the reasons you're thinking."

I chuckled at the ridiculousness of the situation. "Well, shit," I said, tossing the blade on to the table, the useless metal bouncing on the wood. "That's embarrassing."

The table chuckled, even the serious Oakina cracked a smile, with the exception of Lars. He still sat pouting, angrily switching between boring a hole into the side of my head and staring at Kanan calculatingly.

Alarm bells went off in my head at those long stares he was shooting at Kanan, who's gaze hadn't moved from me the entire time. I honestly didn't know if he had even blinked, his eyes following my every move. My reaction to it was almost as unnerving as the man himself.

"We sent scouts to your village a day ago," he said reassuringly, shadows twining through his hair. "They couldn't find any trace of your parents, but they did pick up a blood trail leading away from your house, so it is possible they were trying to lure the wraiths away from you."

I don't know why the news hit so hard. I knew it was a long shot that they would be at the cottage waiting for me to return, and yet it took everything I had not to break down right there.

I thought I saw Kanan's eyes soften with emotion, but in a blink his face was as closed off as it was before. "They were asked to collect some of your things, which they were instructed to drop off at your room," he said, his voice only slightly less rough. "They were also persistently followed by, and I quote, *some sort of goose creature in the body of an abnormally large donkey and his parade of farmyard animals.* Apparently, the chickens rode him like a horse all the way to the border."

I let out a bellyaching laugh, needing that little slice of home. His eyes danced with a hidden gleam. "They were brought to the stables and are being well taken care of. I am sure Commander Zuberi"—he looked towards Zanaya, who nodded back—"can point you in the right direction if you wish to see them."

I couldn't help it as I gave him the most sincere smile, open and wide, a slight ray of sunshine breaking through the dreary darkness that had settled over me. "Thank you."

Inclining his head to me with all the seriousness of a knight accepting his vows, his eyes caught mine once again, refusing to let them go—refusing to back down from my gaze.

"We have hunting parties and scouts out now searching for your adoptive parents. Don't worry, Atallia." My name sounded like a prayer on his lips. "We will help you in any way we can." And with that, he stood from his chair and walked away, uncaring of the fact that the Council were the ones to make the final decisions. He faded into the shadows and left me with even more conflicting feelings than when we started.

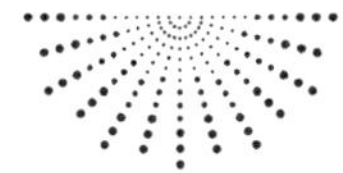

Rushing into my room, Zanaya hard on my heels, I scanned the space, quickly finding what I was looking for. I strode over to the wooden chest at the foot of the bed where Kanan's soldiers had left my things, my attention on the two daggers laying on top of the pile.

Grabbing them, I ran into the bathroom, ripping a cloth from the small stack next to the basin. Dunking it under the water, I scrubbed aggressively on the flat of one of the blades, careful not to cut myself on its sharp edge.

I heard Zanaya step into the room, but I didn't take my focus from my task. Just as I was about to give up, silver streaks marked the white cloth, a transparent white glass left underneath. My arm froze as my stomach dropped. I stared down at the daggers, a reminder that my life had been a fake—nothing, not even the weapons they had given me, had been real.

"I'm sorry, Atallia," Zanaya said, placing her hand on my arm. "I can't imagine how all this must be for you."

"I trained with these every day," I whispered hoarsely, swallowing hard. "Every day."

"Did the paint never wear away?" Confusion was thick in her voice. "Eventually it would have, right?"

"I used them enough, scuffed them up with countless sparring, that I always brushed off the spots that sometimes peeked through." I peered at her over my shoulder as it finally hit me, the answer coming out painfully. "Those tended to be the days that Geoff offered to resharpen them for me."

That must have been when he repainted them, allowing me to go on thinking nothing was out of place, tricking me into believing the false world they had built up around me. Zanaya's flat, pursed smile told me she thought the same.

Dropping the blade, the metal ringing against the counter, I rubbed my hands over my face. Too much had happened. Too much had been a lie. How had they gone through every day knowing they had to hide the truth about every little thing— even my godsdamn daggers?

"Let me grab you some clothes to change into. You'll feel better once you're out of that dress."

"Thank you," I said softly.

She came back in with my folded clothes and my old boots, handing them to me. Compassion radiated from her, thick enough for me to feel. "For what it's worth, the way you speak of them tells me they must have loved you. I don't know why they did all this, but it had to be for a reason, a really important one." A sadness came over her as she continued. "I lost my parents when I was really young, but had I ever known them, I can only hope I would have talked about them the same as you do. We'll figure this out, okay?"

"Thank you, truly. You don't know how much that means to me." She smiled, the dark expression slipping away in her gaze.

"I'll let you dress and then maybe we can head down to the dining hall and grab something to eat." She left the invitation hanging.

Smiling, a slight warmth in my chest, I replied, "That sounds amazing."

"Perfect. I'm going to go and change myself, but I'll be back to pick you up."

She left, leaving me to figure out how to undo the straps of the dress. Finally, I stepped out of the gauzy material, freed from the confines of the skirt. I grabbed my black leather trousers and brown bodice and shimmied into everything, enjoying the sensation of the supple leather against my skin.

I let out a sigh, trying to shake off the useless disappointment as I stepped out into the room. The sun shone through the windows, the curtains having been pulled back while we were away. I had never had someone to clean up after me, so it was a shock to see that the bed had been pulled down and remade from where I had done it before we left.

I was trying to distract myself from the reality of everything, which was very healthy of me, but I wasn't yet ready to deal with the repercussions that this would bring to my family. I couldn't even find it in me any more to feel angry. I was numb, which was infinitely worse.

It was my naivety, I realized, that made me the most furious. Several times I had questioned the things they told me, knowing it was not the full story, and yet I never brought up my concerns, thinking all was right in our little world.

Soon, a knock pulled me from my turmoil. I opened the door, and Zanaya stood on the other side dressed very similarly to me in sparring leathers and worn boots. The preferred form of clothing for the both of us, it seemed.

Leading the way down the hall towards the lift, I couldn't help but ask, "So what was all that at the beginning of the meeting?"

"That was you witnessing a political battle that has been going on for years," she responded as we stepped into the bronze box.

"The Council is in the middle of a dispute that has been going on for centuries, since The Divine disappeared two thousand years ago. Each generation typically has its moment when the topic is brought up again," she explained as the floor seemed to fall beneath us. "It just so happens that this might be the year that the opposing side finally wins."

"And what is this big dispute over?" Genuine curiosity made me ask; the tension between the group of councilors was palpable.

Looking over at me, her expression dead serious. "To name new rulers. Not a Council, but a new king and queen."

I raised my brows at that, not quite understanding, but even I could understand the importance of such a topic.

"You see, Descendents do better with a power hierarchy. We are primal beings at our core. Too many of us have too much power or too dominant a personality for there to not be someone at the top of the food chain, so to speak." We exited the lift into a much wider hallway, busy with people coming and going about their morning.

"And when the God and Goddess ruled, their place at the top kept us all at peace; no one could dispute who the alphas were. We didn't need any other leaders. But over time, as they've been gone, there have been power struggles. More powerful people being kept under those with less simply because they don't have influential families, causing dissension and infighting. Some with too much power and not enough structure are getting away with abusing their position against the weaker Descendents."

About halfway down the expansive hall, we came upon two arched doors as tall as the ceiling. Pushing against one of them, leaning her shoulder into it, Zanaya led us in. Noise assaulted my ears as we walked into a great hall, dozens of long tables filling the space. Trays of delicious smelling food lined the middle of each, people passing them through the air on a gust of wind or with a simple thought. One girl pulled water from a man's cup, the stream following her commands, before she flung it onto her friend. He growled, fangs flashing, as the water soaked his shirt. Conversation flowed and buzzed until all I could pick up was the overall noise of the place.

Dark wood surrounded us, one wall covered in gorgeous stained glass nooks where people could look out at the view while they enjoyed their meal. Two doors on the far side opened and closed every few minutes, bringing with it the banging of metal pots, the shouting from the kitchen crew barely perceptible.

Making our way down the rows until we found an empty spot, we sat and began filling our plates. "So, some of the Council think crowning new leaders will settle the power structure," I said, catching up to where this was going, as I filled our glasses with some sort of red fluid. Taking a sip, a pleasant fruity richness hit my tongue, tasting like a mix between a cherry and something else entirely.

I could see the wisdom in wanting to try to stop the fighting, to keep a peace within the people, but I could also see where those who wished for more power would try to take advantage —thinking themselves the best fit for king or queen.

She nodded, "Exactly, and for the most part, those of us still rooted in tradition, and who believe that the God and Goddess will return to us one day, see it as a betrayal to our creators. There is a reason no one has sat on those thrones in two thousand years, and it is not just symbolic sentiment."

Seeing her side of things as well, I couldn't help but ask, "What is the reason, then?"

"There's just no one powerful enough to keep us all in line. Not like they could." Her face grew sad. "As much as the idea of it is great, eventually it would send us into a civil war, and I'm not sure the world could handle that."

I stared at her for a few seconds, really taking in what she had to say, and understanding that she was most likely right. The night I had Awakened was enough proof for me to agree that a world in which the Descendents fought was a world doomed to be decimated.

"What do the people want?" I asked, curious to know the opinion of the people who would actually be ruled.

"Well, see, that's where it gets a little tricky," she said, raising her eyebrows in thought. "They're just as divided as the Council, if not more so. At least with the Council you either want to continue with the old ways, stay neutral, or wish to crown new rulers; but the people all want or believe different things."

I listened to her talk, picking up a small pink fruit, the same as the ones on the trees I had turned. I wonder if they had to be harvested early, like I thought. Biting into one, I wasn't expecting the bright purple center, the flavor unlike anything I had ever tasted. My confusion must have been apparent because Zanya chuckled before saying, "Those are paku, they're like apples, but they taste a lot different."

Nodding in appreciation, I bit into it again—intrigued by the odd fruit—before asking, "Why do they all have different opinions on the idea?"

She sighed. "It really has to do with whether they believe The Divine will return or not, and then, on top of that, there are a whole slew of beliefs regarding how that will come about. Some believe they're still amongst us, others believe they became pure energy again like they were before they came to Irropia, certain groups think they'll reincarnate at some point, and even more think they've passed their powers on to a chosen one that will come and herald in a new era for our kind."

"So no one can agree on one idea or another," I said, finally understanding. "And I guess that means that even if they were to bring their wishes to the Council, no one course of action could be achieved."

She pursed her lips, poking at the food on her plate. "So you see, it's not just the Council, it's our entire people that are at a stalemate, and unless The Divine suddenly decide to show back up, I think we'll be this way for the rest of our time here on this world. Unless Lars has his way," she added, rolling her eyes.

The frustration she felt for her people was more than justified. "That sounds exhausting. I'm not sure how your uncle deals with it all."

She chuckled. "When I was younger and lived with him, I used to hear him up at all times of the night just pacing and muttering to himself about all this. It used to drive me nuts that he wasn't getting enough sleep, so much so that it often woke me up in the middle of the night; he'd end up setting me up in his chair and would tell me a story until I fell back asleep." She shook her head, a smile on her face. "He'd keep on working until dawn, and I can't imagine much has changed there."

The way she talked about him, love filling every word, reminded me of how I was with Maris and Geoff. How our little mismatched family had come together and carved a little life out in this world that was just our own. "Sounds like you were lucky to have each other." My voice came out quietly, the slightest wobble hooking on the end.

"I was, and everyday I remind myself how lucky I was to have someone there for me when my parents died. Someone who loved me and cared for me like I was his own." We shared a small smile, joined together for a split second in our similar upbringings, the love we had for the people who took a chance on us.

"It must have been fun having an uncle who knew the God and Goddess personally," I say, moving on quickly from the moment of vulnerability, still unsure how to begin to trust. "He must have had the best stories to tell."

"He did. I got to hear all about that golden era for our people, when The Divine walked amongst us, before we hid ourselves away."

"I can't even imagine what that must have been like, let alone knowing them. What were their names?" I asked, curious who the people behind such power had been.

She tilted her head confused. "Whose names?"

My brow scrunched before I clarified, "The God and Goddess. I know they often go by Life and Death, but I assumed they had real names as well. Surely people didn't go around calling them the God of Endings and the Goddess of Beginnings all the time. If it were me that would have gotten old."

"Oh …" She paused, her eyes clouding over as she thought about it, her eyebrows scrunching together. Almost immediately, however, her gaze cleared and the confusion smoothed away. Smiling, her troubled expression wiped clean, she said, "He must have told me at some point, but I can't seem to remember."

I couldn't help but be baffled by that statement. The two most powerful entities in history, outside of the Cosmos himself, and she couldn't remember their names. I would have called her on it, but she truly seemed not to remember. The muddled expression on her face was too real to be faked. Even still, all I could muster in response was a skeptical, "Huh."

She shrugged her shoulders, her face free of any noticeable deceit. "Are you almost done? I figured we could go see your farmyard friends down at the barrack stables."

Shaking my head clear of any questions I would have otherwise asked, I nodded in response. I needed the small bit of normalcy that would be seeing Gideon and his gang of feathered and furred companions.

***

We walked for what felt like only a few minutes before exiting through a tunnel and out onto a large outcropping of mountain.

Built into the side of the rock face were large structures—the barracks.

The grounds had been separated into multiple open areas that were being used as sparring rings, archery ranges, and what appeared to be spots for training magic. A tall, lean man stood in one of the squares, a ball of fire held in his hand that refused to burn him. Chucking it at a straw dummy thirty yards away, the red flames hurtled through the air before hitting the target, sending an explosion of smoking straw through the air.

Racks of weapons were left out for everyone to choose from; most I could name, and others I had never even seen before. They all varied in make, however, some were constructed of black heartsglass and others just plain steel, which I guessed were used for more cautious training matches.

Several bouts were going on, drawing crowds from the other rings. The clang of weapons filled the air, their exquisite echo ringing in my ears. The blood in my veins began to pump harder, matching the sounds of battle. I felt the warmth rushing through my muscles, as if preparing themselves for a fight. The hot core in my chest, which I had realized was where my energy pooled the most, flared and crackled.

"Well …" Zanaya said quietly, ice-blue eyes fastened to a match going on to our left, where the largest crowd gathered around the ring cheering on the fighters. "Maybe there is one who could lead us."

Glancing over, I saw what had caught her attention, my own being snagged as well by the sight. Standing there, seven men surrounding him, in nothing but trousers and a thin layer of sweat glistening on his muscles, was Kanan.

"What are they doing?" I asked incredulously, distracted by the eight sweaty, mostly naked men putting on a show for everyone around.

Zanaya giggled. "This is how our warriors, mostly the males, work out any frustration. If you ask me, they just like to show off their pretty muscles. Not that the crowd minds all that much."

Kanan's long, tan legs flexed in anticipation, rivulets of sweat rolling between hard-earned muscle. I admired how his body moved as it struck out, his muscles honed like a well-oiled machine. Although I found him dreadfully beautiful, I could also look at him from a combative stance. He was magnificent, every part of his body ready to go at a moment's notice. He was a predator, a hunter in the darkness, a man built for war. One that was never unprepared or caught unaware.

He stood at least a head taller than any of the other men out there. They were impressive themselves, but they stood no chance against Kanan as his body flexed and relaxed, ready to move.

Snapping out with a closed fist, quicker than a viper, he slammed it against the jaw of one of the other men. A crack broke through the air as it landed, making the entire crowd wince in pain as the man slammed to the ground. He was pulled off to the side, next to several other unconscious bodies. A pile of Kanan's victims, the bruises already starting to show all over their forms.

Unable to help myself, I moved closer, slipping through the throngs of people who had gathered, more and more walking over by the second; everyone wanted to catch a glimpse of this fight it seemed. I made it to the front, the crowd catching sight of my shiny hair and then my eyes, which immediately had them parting for me as I walked through.

Sometimes it wasn't all bad.

Reaching the edge of the sparring ring, I looked up and accidentally caught his eyes. As his sights locked on to me, the intensity that was once focused on his opponents settled on my form like a several-ton weight. The tug in my chest ignited, trying to pull me in his direction. As I moved to step into the ring, his head was whipped to the side by a vicious cross.

Taking advantage of the brutal punch, another of his opponents stepped in with long claws held high before bringing them down across Kanan's back. His back arched away from the pain as he threw his head back, roaring out as they sliced through. The bone-chilling sound was loud and paralyzing. The crowd backed up several feet before freezing completely in their spots, leaving me standing alone at the edge.

Those red eyes began to glow, their swirling depths edged in fury at the cheap shot. Long, thick claws of his own shot from his nail beds, the rich black gleaming in the sunlight. Turning his head, he growled at the other man, the rumble shaking his chest, the barest hint of dark scales peppering his skin.

A chuffed laugh left his mouth as he bared his teeth. The two sets of sharp canines on top were terrifying enough, having witnessed their gleaming edge during the meeting, but it was the bottom row that shocked me now. They were all razor sharp and ready to tear through flesh.

He seemed to grow in size, his chest huffing as he launched himself at the six men who backpedaled, regret clear on their faces. They knew what was coming next.

He moved like a savage beast, incapacitating one after the other, a dark blur the only thing visible to the naked eye. Never in my life had I seen a fight over so quickly. The six males laid on the sand, injured so badly they couldn't move or were lost to oblivion. Nobody stepped in to help them this time, not wanting to draw the attention of the pissed off male.

He stood unfazed, in control of himself as if nothing had happened, barely looking my way before heading off towards the barracks. With a wave of his hand his neatly folded tunic flew into his waiting hand. As he turned to go, I noticed something I hadn't been able to see in the grove—scars. Hundreds of them, lining his back like some maze of abuse. The ones the man had given him had already healed, leaving the patchwork clear for all to see. The crowd parted for him, taking him from my sight as the whispers followed in his wake.

"Champion of Death."

"Champion of Death."

"Champion of Death."

Over and over the words were repeated, awe and fear in equal parts threaded through their voices.

"He's one of the reasons some are calling for change." I jumped, not having heard Zanaya come up behind me. Looking at me, she lifted her chin in the direction of where Kanan had disappeared. "He's the most powerful Descendent in recorded history. If there is anyone who could possibly lead us and keep the peace, it would be him."

The revelation wasn't a shock, the man seemed to be a force of nature. "What do they mean? Champion of Death?"

She stared at me with a confused tilt to her head. "How much do you know about Descendents? About our history?"

"Not much, to be honest," I said, shrugging my shoulders. "Really, just the basics that Maris taught me. The God Death and the Goddess Life were once cosmic energies, still are technically, but the Cosmos gave them form after the creation of the universe to watch over the planet. They eventually created the Descendents, and ruled for thousands of years."

"You're not far off, but she left out a few of the important points."

"Color me shocked," I said dryly, resisting the urge to roll my eyes. Next thing I knew, I was going to be questioning whether my name was real or not.

We started walking across the training fields, as Zanaya continued, "The Goddess was a being of complete life-giving energy. She was *the* Aether. We can do extraordinary things—heal the dying, control the elements, manipulate light—but we are just a watered-down version of her. Yes, we control the magic that flows through our bodies, and can access the energy of the world around us, but the Goddess was pure and uncorrupted creation magic. She was the part of the Cosmos that was used to help create the structure of the universe."

There was a heaviness in her voice that spoke of the importance the queen had held, not just to her people, but to the world and worlds at large.

"The God of Death was her pair. In every way possible, he was her perfect fit. An absolute ending to her resounding beginning, and together they created a balance across existence. The God appeared on these lands first in his original form, followed secondly by the form he's known best for."

She tugged me over to a flag waving softly in the air above one of the many barracks, the red material offset by the crest of a fearsome black dragon on it. The same dragon I saw on the guards' chest plates. The same one who guarded the gates so fiercely.

"He was a dragon," I said, awe coloring my voice.

Nodding at me, she pulled me past to continue on our way. "I told you about some who believe that The Divine gifted their powers to one of their creations in order for them to lead us once again. He's the reason for those beliefs—that's why they call him the Champion of Death." She turned to face me as we reached the stables. "They call him that because he shifts into a dragon, Atallia. A dragon that matches exactly how our histories depict our king's second form."

CHAPTER FOURTEEN

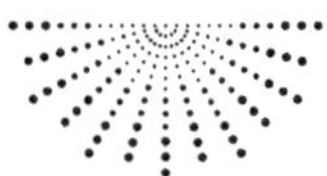

I stared, slack-jawed, as I tried to comprehend what she was saying. "As in wings and claws and scales?"

"The very one. You think he's terrifying now? Wait until you see him in full form. It's something I will never forget, and a shadow I hope to never see coming over me."

"Well, damn, and here I was thinking it was just one big tug on his ego," I said, my lips fighting not to smile.

She let out a laugh, shaking her head at me. "Oh gods no, I wish, but unfortunately he deserves the name and the respect that comes with it. As much as I'm against the idea, if anyone is going to lead us, I hope it's him. At least he has honor and integrity, unlike Lars Braxix."

"Is that what that was all about? All the sly comments and weird looks he kept giving him?" The greedy way Braxix had eyed Kanan didn't sit right with me, having seen it too many times in the faces of the selfish.

"That man has been after the throne since he sat in on his first Council meeting. And once Kanan shifted for the first time and took over as warlord not too long after that, Lars has been after a way to control him and his power. His latest attempt is trying to force a pairing between his daughter and Kanan." She scoffed, her disgust plain and visible on her normally jovial face.

Before I could ask what she meant, someone shouted her name from the direction of the archery ranges. She walked backwards away from me, nodding towards the barn. "You'll find all of them in there. You know how to get back, right?"

I nodded, and she turned and broke into a run, leaving me at the doors to the stable. The sounds of shuffling shavings and hay, the random cluck from a chicken or horse, were comforts I didn't know I missed. My chores around the cottage typically involved taking care of the few animals we kept on the property.

Walking through the open doors, I took in the sights and smells around me. The stable was large, each stall big enough to hold three horses, with runs that led out into vast green pastures.

Several heads poked out, taking in the newcomer who had walked into their home. I smiled at them, having never seen horses such as these.

Their coats glistened, every color in existence represented by one of the majestic creatures. Their long manes were just as vibrant and hung gracefully down their necks. Swirling marks climbed up their legs, and down their necks and backs. Their eyes held secrets and unknowns, something I was becoming increasingly familiar with myself.

However, it was the long horn pushing through each of their forelocks that grabbed my attention the most. Each was as unique as the horse itself, long and spiraling, but different in every other way. Some were shorter or more curved, others were long enough to be daggers, while some gleamed with an inner light.

I reached out with my hand, allowing the closest one—a light green mare with stunning blue markings that looked like she had the wind crawling across her sides—to breathe in my scent. Her horn was of the purest ivory, long and slender, and every part of it sparkled in the sunlight. Her hot breath washed over the back of my hand before she lipped at me, obviously finding me worthy of her attention.

Smiling, I stepped closer, running my hand down the bridge of her nose as I admired her beautiful blue eyes. They stared back at me, a gaze that spoke of an intelligence far beyond my own, as whispers brushed against my ears.

Crashing waves breaking against the shore during a raging tempest—ebbing away only to come back stronger. An ethereal song cutting through the storm. Teeth chattering against the cold lick of a frozen wasteland. The last sigh of someone entering the afterlife. The shifting of sands whistling in the wind. The clinking of glass and bone. A woman giggling, the very sound made of menace, the sounds of war beating in the background as a man roared my name. Most of all, drowning out everything else, the cries of thousands screaming in pain.

I broke eye contact and the whispers abated, slowly fading away into nothingness. I looked back at the mare, who kept nudging against me for more pets. I let out a shallow, nervous laugh. "Well, aren't you a special girl?"

"Cheeky things, aren't they?" a small voice asked from behind me, making me jump. I hadn't heard them come up behind me.

Turning around, I was met with open air. I looked around in confusion, knowing I heard someone speak.

A pointed cough has me looking down to find a very small man staring up at me. "Oh!" I said in shocked surprise. "Hello."

He couldn't have been more than a foot tall, his legs covered in the tiniest pink tulle skirt I had ever seen, but his chest had been left bare, the dark brown of his skin on full display. I didn't know why I was surprised, but his tiny body was shredded with muscle.

I found out why a second later, as two pearlescent wings unfurled behind him. Their sheer membrane was stretched so tightly as to appear nearly translucent. His short, white hair matched his wings and stood out starkly against his dark skin and eyes. He flittered up from the floor to sit on the edge of the stall next to the mare.

"You're the new girl, right? The one who has everyone in a commotion?" he asked, patting the mare's nose with his small hand.

"Uhm … yes, I think so."

"You think so? You don't sound confident about that answer. You do know who you are, right? You don't have a concussion or anything do you, because that would be very bad and I don't know plant stuff." His tiny eyebrows rose on his forehead as he started wringing his hands, a look of genuine concern on his face. He was the cutest damn thing I had ever seen.

Smiling back at him, I laughed a little, guessing plant stuff meant healing. "Yes, I'm the new girl, and no, I don't have a concussion; although I didn't mean to cause a problem for anyone, at least not this time."

"Oh, good." His wings drooped slightly in relief before immediately perking back up again. "I don't know how I would explain that it wasn't my fault this time if you had passed out. That would have looked bad for me." He gave a little indignant shake of his head.

I let out a full laugh. "I'm Atallia." I reached out my hand for him to shake.

"Yeah, I kind of guessed that one," he said, grasping two of my fingers with both hands in a surprisingly tight grip, shaking it up and down. "My name is Wrynn."

"Nice to meet you, Wrynn."

He smiled back, a shine to his eyes that I couldn't quite place.

Just as I was going to ask what he was doing here, the mare nudged me with her nose, deciding she didn't appreciate the attention being taken away from her.

"What are they? They're the most beautiful horses I've ever seen."

"We call them the whispers," Wrynn said, floating up to straddle the mare's horn, sitting between her two fluffy ears. "A little on the nose if you ask me, which no one ever does for some reason, but I guess it fits."

"Is that what I just heard?" I glanced back at the mare to find her blue eyes were still looking at me, but she seemed more concerned about whether I had a treat to give her than letting me hear the sounds again.

"She must really like you if she let you hear them." He looked at the other whispers, who all stared looking at me. The whispers built again, *crashing waves, chattering teeth, shifting sands,* coming from all directions before I forced myself to look away. "They're normally very selective about who they allow to hear them."

"What are they, the sounds I hear?"

He looked back at me, his tiny wings flying him up close to my face. "It's the noise of the future. The whispers see things that we can't; their eyes are attuned to a different level of this world. If they like you, they might let you listen in to what they see when they look into your future."

I wasn't comforted by that at all. I'd already been living my life stuck in nightmares I couldn't remember; now magical horses were telling me that my future would be full of them.

Spectacular.

I half expected Wrynn to budge in and ask what I heard, but he stared at my eyes for as long as he could. "You have really pretty eyes," he said spontaneously, apparently not giving it a second thought as he headed over to pet the other whispers.

While it seemed insignificant to him, I think it might have been the first time anyone had complimented my eyes. The swirling, golden depths were usually too terrifying for anyone to ever actually appreciate them.

"Thank you," I said quietly, almost overcome by emotion. I found myself immediately liking Wrynn, which was unusual for me. He gave off an innocence that I couldn't help but fall for. His cherub face and anxious fluttering were too charming to be wary of.

"Wrynn, do you happen to know where an overly friendly, very loud donkey might be? He probably has two chickens on his back."

"Of course I do!" Happy to help, he shot off down the aisle with me following behind, chuckling at his enthusiastic response. "We've gotten close, him and I, although he's quite dramatic. Don't tell him I said that or he'll just say the same about me. I'm not dramatic, I'm flamboyant, there's a difference."

Wrynn zoomed past most of the whispers' stalls, talking the whole way. Taking a left turn down a side aisle that led into an adjacent hall of the stables, open sections were filled with hay and grain and various pieces of tack hung organized on the walls.

One of the few stalls in the back had a makeshift gate built in front, made with several crates stacked on top of each other to block the entrance. The actual door had been left open, and I only had one guess as to why.

Two brown, fluffy ears popped up above the crates before the rest of his head followed. His coat had been washed and brushed out, judging by its shine. His short, stubby mane and tail had been detangled, an impossible feat that I had never been able to accomplish.

As he lifted his head, hay sticking out of his mouth in every direction, he chomped away with little care in the world. He had obviously been enjoying himself here, being pampered like the prince he thought he was.

The moment he noticed me was almost comical, had it not been for the fact that he was my little piece of home, something

I badly needed right now. Perking his ears towards us, his big, brown eyes locked on me as he stopped chewing, dropping all the hay from his mouth to let out a happy honk. Trotting up to the gate, he tried his hardest to push through the wall of boxes as he stretched his neck out towards me and nipped at the air to get me over to him.

I let out a choked laugh, swallowing a sob as relief hit me hard, just now realizing how worried I had been about him. I hadn't seen him out in the pasture with his friends when the wraith had attacked, and I had all but given up hope that they had survived.

Running over, hopping up onto the crates with my new and improved agility, I grabbed his big furry head and gave it a big hug. I could feel him lipping at my pants, looking for treats hidden in the pockets. For him, this had probably been one big adventure, whereas for me it had been a nightmare straight from the bowels of hell.

"Great Cosmos, I never thought he would stop talking about you," Wrynn said, fluttering his hands about in exasperation. "And people think *I'm* talkative."

Laughing at the … I actually didn't know what he was, and I couldn't help but ask, "Wrynn, what are you exactly?"

With a dramatic gasp, hands on his chest, he exclaimed, "I am a sprite, madam. One of Allasea's greatest, in fact, and as your new friend, I suggest you live and learn the motto, 'Wrynn is the bestest of the sprites and should be revered for his intelligence, power, and wisdom.'"

I stared at him, eyebrows raised. He stared back, frozen. "You know, in case someone asks," he said, shrugging his tiny, muscular shoulders.

"That's quite a long motto," I said, trying my best not to laugh at the indignant sprite.

"Well … there's quite a lot to praise about my amazingness, so it has to be long," he said as explanation.

"Anyway, I have to get back, so I'll leave you to it. Bye-bye, new friend Atallia." He stopped only to give me a wave, and off the winged man went. With the attention span of a squirrel, his departure wasn't very fast, a new thing catching his eye every ten feet as he flew.

Apparently I had a new friend: a tutu-wearing, hyperactive, anxious sprite. Chuckling once more, I turned back to Gideon, rubbing his fluffy cheeks before hopping down into the stall. I was careful not to knock over the makeshift gate someone must have constructed once they realized Gideon's escapist tendencies.

Landing in the soft straw someone had thrown down, I saw two black and white chickens, a hen and rooster, sitting perched regally on Gideon's back. I smiled at seeing Henrietta and Frank, still amused by their roost of choice.

I felt something nibble on the back of my tunic and I turned to find both Clementine and Mabel, our two goats, safe as well. I let out another sigh of relief, comforted by one thing in my life not changing, and gave everyone the scratches they were looking for.

Walking over to sit on the far wall, I let my legs stretch out and leaned my head back against the wooden siding. I knew I should have taken the time before now, as everything from the past couple of days rushed me finally caught up to me. I honestly had wondered how long I could hold it back. Eventually I knew it would break through the walls I had erected, but I had held out hope that the roaring wave of emotions wouldn't drown me under its weight.

There was so much conflict inside me that I didn't even know where to start unraveling it. The first shining tear of frustration came with the low rumble of thunder outside. I reached out to pet Clementine as she came to lie next to me, more tears falling shortly after the first.

And that's when the wave crashed, pulling me under as it hit a crescendo with the crack of lightning in the sky, pulling me deep into the tangled mess of emotions that I had been shoving down inside of me for days. I let out a choked sob that wouldn't stay buried any longer.

My parents. Both my source of worry and anger. Of dread and mistrust. How could I have been so stupid, never questioning anything? That wasn't who I was. I was the paranoid one, the one always looking for a reason not to trust someone. I had spent too many years being outcast and shunned, spit on and hissed at. It had turned me jaded and cynical. I always expected the worst, and yet I hadn't seen the betrayal, the lies, from those closest to me.

I hadn't even once questioned the validity of their stories, expecting everything they said to be true simply because they loved me. And that's where my anger smashed against an immovable wall—because I did believe they loved me. I didn't know if I could handle it if that had been a lie as well.

And now they could be anywhere, lying dead in some field in the Blackwood, torn to pieces by those wraiths just like they tried to do to me. Or they could be alive and facing much worse than death. At least death was peaceful—permanent. Some things made death look merciful.

I was openly crying now, heaving sobs were wrenched from my throat as I hid my face in my hands. It was pouring rain and thunder rumbled, shaking the structure as the droplets hit the roof. The once-sunny day had turned tumultuous in seconds. I gasped for air, hardly breathing through the sound of my heart breaking—whether for or because of my adoptive parents, I wasn't sure.

Gideon, his sweet, brown eyes confused and sympathetic, lipped at the sole of my shoe as more sobs shook free of my chest. Reaching out, I brushed my fingers over the donkey's soft nose, trying to reassure him even as I needed someone to reassure me.

The most confusing part of it was that a piece of me, the piece that I had always been the tiniest bit afraid of, was excited and happy to be here. To finally have a place to belong. The power had finally opened its eyes, and it had been wondrous to watch, but also terrifying as I realized that power was me. Was who I truly was.

The storm of energy, so thick and commanding that it turned flesh and blood and bone to ash within seconds. It ... I destroyed thousand-year-old trees without so much as wavering. That was what I truly was. It had been the thing I had kept suppressed as much as possible for fear of exactly what had happened.

When I finally let go, my restraint destroyed by the pain, I felt liberated. Finally free to be who and what I was. It was scary, frightening, actually, but it was also beautiful. Like some cosmic maelstrom, not evil or monstrous, but wondrously unrestrained—free for the first time in my life.

I couldn't hide from that joy. Of being let out of my cage. A cage I had built around myself, but one I had built out of trepidation of further rejection. That once everyone saw what I was, what hid behind my golden eyes, that even Maris and Geoff would abandon me. That they would finally understand why the villagers could never accept me, not because of the bigoted hate and anger, but because of the thing that caused such pervasive, overwhelming terror.

I now understood it better, those feelings they held because of me, having seen firsthand what I could have unleashed upon them. But I couldn't force myself to let go of that feeling of being released from my shackles. I was finally melding with the energy that had sat inside me, watching and waiting, becoming such a part of my daily life that most of the time I had forgotten it was there.

So many things had happened, I thought as I wiped the tears from my eyes, that it felt like I had been through years rather than a few days. But that was the thing about devastating trauma, no matter its vessel it didn't matter if it was years or hours—it made a lasting impression.

And that might have been the hardest thing to grasp, I realized as more fucking tears rolled down. They had betrayed me, betrayed my love, and worst of all betrayed my trust. Even if we found them, I wasn't sure if I would ever be okay getting over what they had done. Reasons or no, they had lied to me about everything that could have allowed me to understand what I was. They had kept me away from the one place that could have shown me acceptance.

I could have had friends, like Zanaya and the others. Friends like Wrynn. I could have had a relationship. One that didn't only last for a quick tumble in the hay to satisfy an itch; one with someone besides a merchant who was only there because I was unique and different, not because I was worth courting or even getting to know.

My differences would have meant nothing here, and I could have lived my life just as I saw fit without the lingering doubt and fear that a group of people would burst into my room to set my bed on fire with me in it at any moment.

They had threatened it on multiple occasions, and no matter how much I tried to not let them affect me, some days I could see it in their eyes. The conviction that today was the day, that if they rushed me, they could take me down and I wouldn't be able to stop them. A few of the men had brought up that maybe they could have some fun with me first before they got to it, so at the very least, according to them, I would have been of some use.

As if they hadn't tried that before. I thought back to that night, lightning cracking in the distance. A group of teenage boys had tried to drag me into the woods, to *teach me a lesson,* they said when I fought back. And fought back I did. They hadn't been able to find the bodies even after the snow had melted in the spring.

To say my standing hadn't improved after that night would have been an understatement. I got nasty looks for weeks, months, but I remembered that cold night all too well. Remembered passing by a few windows with faces in them, faces that turned away as I was dragged past. Some had been other women.

All the pain and suffering, the humiliation, could have been stopped, and yet they let me go through all of that. For what?

I have every intention of finding out, I thought angrily, as I swiped away the last of my tears, wiping the golden residue on my pants. As soon as I found them, I was going to find out what made all of that worth it.

I stood, brushing the shavings and straw from my pants, and gave everyone one last pat before jumping back over the crates. Straightening my back and wiping my face one more time, I headed out into the rain. There was only so much one person could handle, and I had reached my limit, but now was the time to rebuild.

It was time to get back on my feet just like I had been taught and to keep fighting another day. I let the rain drench me, and it covered up what was left of my tears as it washed away all the bad thoughts until I was left only with steely determination.

There was a certain kind of power that came with that kind of resolve, not like the power that now stormed in my body, ready and waiting for my command. No, it was the kind of power that left you feeling like you could burn the fucking world down if you needed to.

And what the hell, maybe I needed to do just that. Burning the world down to find the truth, hidden amongst all the lies, didn't seem like such a bad plan. A smile sprung to life on my lips. The magic in my blood heated in response, more than happy to remake the world if need be.

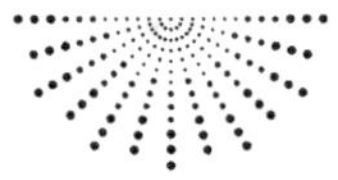

The dark clouds blocked out any sunlight. Only the faintest hints of the colorful wind that was so part of the Allasean sky poked through the gloom.

The rain had turned into bullets, hitting fast and hard against my skin, and I was thankful I could no longer die by mortal means because the temperature had quickly dropped to dangerous levels. A chilly breeze rolled through the air, carrying with it the scent of rot and decay.

Knowing that smell all too well, I took off at a run, soldiers sprinting for their posts all around me. I reached the sparring pits much faster than I ever could have before and sent up a silent prayer of thanks to the Cosmos and the Goddess for the speed I was given. I wasn't one to pray often, but it seemed like as good of a time as any, taking in the organized chaos of the barracks.

Soldiers were armoring up with battle-ready efficiency, helping each other when necessary. Others were making quick adjustments to their weapons and sheathing even more. Cythonians were either in partial or full shift, large animals standing off to the side. Huge birds of prey circled the air, some coming to land but shifting mid-air back into their human forms to report back to their commanders.

I spotted Zanaya standing around a makeshift war table, water being held off the maps by an invisible force. More and more started to surround her and the other commanders, listening in to the battle plans. I made my way over at a run.

"They've hit us hard on the eastern wall. The border patrols are already out there fighting, and the north barracks are seconds away from joining. All other groups have been alerted, and they'll be keeping watch on their side of the wall unless otherwise called in for reinforcements. The last thing we want is to be hit unaware on all sides."

The soldiers around her nodded in agreement, barely noticing the pounding rain and rolling thunder, following her lead and accepting her command without fault. I saw Nala, Zander, and Orion amongst the crowd. I shoved my way over to them; Zander saw me coming and shifted over, giving me a roguish smile.

"What the hell is going on? I smelled wraiths on the wind."

"A group of about a hundred, from the last count, hit the north wall a couple minutes ago out of the blue." He nodded to our left towards the large stone wall off in the distance. "The patrol on duty reported that they just showed up out of nowhere, and as far as we know, they're trying to get through."

"Shit."

"Yeah, no kidding." He turned back towards the meeting, listening in to Zanaya, that dimpled smile of his vanishing completely. The severity of his angular face took on an even deadlier sharpness.

Dread settled in my chest. If Zander was getting serious, then something bad was happening. The clicks of the wraiths' bones still wrung in my ears whenever I thought of them, the way their emaciated bodies seemed to be on autopilot, searching for whatever meal they could get. The smell of their decaying tissue hung in the air even from miles away.

"What about the warlord, Commander?" one of the soldiers in the back spoke up, having to shout over the pounding rain and blowing wind as a gust came through, pulling at my hair and nearly knocking me off balance.

A thread of nervousness thrummed through the crowd, wondering where their leader was; I could feel it coming in from all around me, and the reason came to me with sudden clarity. They were an untested army, at least most of them were. If they had been behind their barrier and walls since The Divine disappeared, it was likely most of them hadn't known real combat.

But it was their determined faces, the set of their shoulders, that let me know they were ready. Ready and willing to fight for their people, the mothers and fathers, brothers and sisters, all of whom were in the city below.

"The warlord left on Council business an hour before the report came in. We've sent some of the airborne after him, but we can't hope he can be caught in time. It's on us to hold the wall, and I'll be damned if we won't."

The cheers of all the soldiers ricocheted off the face of the mountain, the pounding call of battle clear in their voices.

"That's too much of a coincidence for my liking," I said to Zander, Nala and Orion peering around to listen. "How is it that just as the Descendents' biggest and most powerful weapon flies off, an attack happens?"

This attack was way more planned than just some herd of wraiths making it to the wall without detection.

Zanaya walked up to us as the soldiers all headed out for the eastern wall, the clank of glass blades a song in the air mixing with the roars of blood-hungry predators.

"You all ready?" she asked, the authority in her voice bleeding out as she came in close to her friends. Strength turned into worry for those she considered family, her eyes praying that this didn't go horribly wrong.

"Are you kidding, Commander?" Nala piped up, shaking with anticipation, a wildness in her eyes. "This is the most fun we're gonna get to have since that time we set those smoke bombs off in basic maneuvers."

"Where can I grab some blades that will actually do some damage?" I asked Zanaya, fully prepared to throw myself into the fun as well.

She turned to me, shaking her head. "I can't just toss you into a battle untested and untrained. You're a ticking time bomb waiting to go off. An unknown that I can't have out on the field."

"I am a ticking time bomb that's a damn good fighter—I blasted those things that came after me. Not to mention it seems like a good portion of your army is untested, and if I'm an unknown," I said, raising an eyebrow, "don't you want to see what I can do?"

"I say we let her come," Nala cut in.

"You just want to see what shit she can blow up."

The cute and fiery redhead, with her multi-colored flaming curls pulled back into a tight braid, was near jumping for joy at the thought. Her love of all things that went boom was only slightly concerning since she was on our side.

I pointed at Nala, smiling at the psychotic pyro before locking eyes with Zanaya. "Besides, if you leave me here I'll just come anyway. At least this way you can keep an eye on me."

Glaring at me, she sniffed, clearly not used to having her authority challenged. Too bad she met me, I thought, smiling my shit-eating grin.

"Fine, but you stay with us at all times. I won't have this coming back to bite me in the ass."

Raising my arm, I saluted her. "Sure thing, Commander, whatever you say."

By the annoyed, yet amused, look in her eye, she thought I

would do the exact opposite of that. She probably wasn't wrong, but I would make sure whatever happened wouldn't come back to be a pain for her—I was starting to like her too much.

"Alright, let's move out. Atallia, there's heartsglass over on the racks—pick what works for you and meet us over at the edge." She nodded towards the cliff; the width of the outcropping was much smaller there than anywhere else.

Nodding, I ran over to the racks of weapons I saw earlier, a mix of black and steel blades just waiting for their chance to be blooded. The water glistened on the steel, the droplets pinging off. The black heartsglass, however, continued to suck all light from around it until I could barely see the rain falling on the blades. A slight sheen on the hilts was the only indication that they were getting wet.

I picked up the first daggers I saw, the two blades long and sharp, slightly longer than my forearm. They were perfectly balanced, unsurprisingly, and the hilts, while better suited for a larger grip, would do just fine.

Looking underneath the racks, I found twin woven baskets of extra sheaths. The familiarity of it hit me; it was similar to Geoff's setup next to our ring back home. I buckled on a pair and shoved the blades in before grabbing an arm sheath for the tiny knives held on the bottom. I slid one in, a backup, in case I needed a last resort or something to throw.

Running, I reached the group in seconds. Zanaya nodded at me, checking over my weapons, before stepping out into open air. I gasped, lunging forward to grab her. Except she didn't fall. She stood there, smirking in the rain, over the drop that was at least several hundred feet down.

An invisible platform of air was holding her up, and the others quickly stepped off too.

Walking up to the edge, I glanced down, the rocky bottom that could shatter bone lay far below. With a shrug of my shoulders, and a smile tinged with just a hint of crazy, I stepped off. I wasn't sure what to expect, but as my foot came down, it met a hard surface.

Giggling like a madwoman as I stepped off the cliffside, I looked at the others. "This is fucking amazing."

They chuckled at me, and the air below us started to move. Quickly, it built speed until we were hurtling toward the large, walled structure in the distance, flying over the city below. I saw several other groups of soldiers using a similar method around us. We must have been a sight for the people below, a flock of very strange birds, perhaps. Except they were probably used to it and had maybe done it themselves a couple of times.

We couldn't have been in the air but a minute, covering miles in seconds, before we were arriving at the wall. The blocks were bigger than some of the houses in the city. Archers lined the top, covering their arrows in colorful energy or flames before firing them down below. Watchtowers held large glass structures that Aetherians were using to shine light down onto the forest's edge, allowing the soldiers and archers to see through the darkness that was overtaking the sky and illuminating the crawling surge of wraiths.

The horrifying creatures were as nightmarish as they had been the night they attacked me. Their chittering bones made a raucous sound that grated on my nerves.

Click. Clack. Click. Clack.

The static, humming that I'd begun to associate with my power built in my ears in response, doing its best to drown out the sounds of slicing flesh and the hungry chattering of the wraiths. There were definitely more than a hundred of them down there, some falling to the onslaught of the Descendents while others were in the midst of digging into the open chest cavity of a fallen soldier.

I watched in horror as the beast tore through muscle and tendon until a small glow showed from within the soldier's ribs. As the wraith swallowed the glowing orb, pieces of its flesh began knitting together. Its hair, once patchy and covered in greasy blood, now started to come through the skin shiny and full. Bone shards began to patch themselves back through the holes they had ripped out of, the skin healing over the open wound.

The transformation stopped before fully turning the creature back into its former self, bald spots and an open rib cage still peeked through, but what was once a walking corpse now could pass for a semi-normal animal.

"Oh my gods," Zanaya whispered next to me, having witnessed the same thing. "They're eating the sparks. Stealing our energy is how they stay alive." We turned towards each other, distress in both our eyes.

Several others had noticed the event as well, doing their best to stay in groups, working together to rescue those that had been taken down. The barbarity of it all was nearly mind-numbing, and the thrumming rang louder in my ears.

The platform of air began to drop as Zanaya gave the signal for her warriors to join in. The power in my veins ignited as I prepared to fight. I could feel the burn, no longer painful, but full of a warm anticipation. As if every cell in my body yearned to be set free as it had when I Awakened.

Doing what I did then, now knowing what it meant, I fell into the deep bottomless well, allowing it to engulf me and fill me with pure power. The world around me heightened, my hearing and sight sharpening. I could feel every particle of wind and rain against my skin. The smell of rotting flesh became almost unbearable.

My gaze shifted, the golden sheen falling over my eyes, but unlike when it normally came along, I was still me. I could see my veins glowing gold, shining through my skin as an aura built around me.

I could feel the eyes of the others on me, watching as I let myself off my leash. We all prepared to jump for it, only about ten feet separating us from the battlefield. People began leaping from their platforms, rolling on the ground before popping up and running into the fight. Pushing against the hard air below, I shot into the sky, a miniature sun burning against the hazy darkness of the storm.

Coming down, I landed in the middle of a large group of wraiths, and without thinking, I pushed against the power lashing under my skin, forcing it outward. In a shockwave of golden, fiery light, my energy tore through the pack of wraiths. I watched as fire and air ripped twenty of them to shreds before my eyes, some exploding from the pressure building inside of them.

However, as the shockwave left my body, so too did the cosmic power. The metallic sheen over my eyes, the golden aura, the cracking skin with the lava core—all were gone in a flash; leaving me the center of attention for every being on the field.

While I still felt stronger and faster than I had ever been, I couldn't seem to call the magic back to my veins. The well of power was cut off from me by something, like a wall had been erected between it and me. I could still feel it, but no prompting got it to rise to the surface.

Low, hungry growls froze me to my spot. Looking up, I was met with the rabid stares of the surrounding wraiths. More were coming in by the second, their bodies twitching and jerking as they prowled towards me. Some even left their downed prey to turn their sights towards me, blood and magic dripping from their exposed jaws. Of course, this was when my trump card would get performance anxiety and disappear on me.

"Fuck me." I mean, if I thought it couldn't get any worse from my dealings with the wraiths the first time, I was very wrong. They all slowly stalked closer, eyes intent on their prey.

"Atallia, what are you doing? Use your magic again."

Zanaya's voice shouted over the sounds of rolling thunder and steel on flesh. A gust of wind came from the direction of her voice on my left, barreling through the ranks of wraiths, carrying shards of ice that slashed through their putrid skin.

"I would if I could, but I can't reach it." I yelled back, my eyes locked on the wraiths as I pulled my blades from their sheaths.

"What do you mean, you can't reach it?" she yelled over the sounds of the screeching and chittering creatures. Peeking over, I could barely see her fighting her way through the crowd of wraiths; cutting them down by sword or by ice blue magic. It didn't matter which, as they all fell to her artful precision.

"I mean, I can't reach it. It's blocked or something."

Slicing out with one of my black blades, a badger creature that had gotten too close shrieked at me in rage as I cut it across the cheek. "At the worst godsdamned time too," I whispered to myself.

A boom shook the ground, a wave of fire bursting into the air right in front of me. Nala's giggles followed the screams of the melting wraiths and the smell of burning flesh. A streak of red and orange hair dove into the fray of dying enemies, cackling all the way. *Got to love crazy*, I thought with a smile even as I turned back to my own battle.

"Hold on, Atallia, we're coming." Zander's red hair flashed in my peripheral, the glint of black claws flashing in the combined light of the towers and Nala's fire.

"Not much else I can fucking do."

The badger creature darted back towards me, its spine poking out of its hunched back, patchy fur and skin sloughing off behind it as it ran. Crouching, holding one blade in hand, I waited—preparing for the impact—as the wraith leaped, barreling straight into my chest and knocking me to the ground.

Landing hard, I grappled the beast's jaws away from my throat as its claws dug into my chest. Quickly throwing it off me, I rolled across the muddy ground. Leaping onto the badger, I dug my knees into the mud on either side of its body as it writhed against the ground trying to fight me off. I lifted my dagger high before bringing it down hard straight through the wraith's skull.

It went limp, my blade lodged deep, the spark of crazy—the only piece remaining—went dark. Breathing hard, I stared down at the body below me, recognizing that I had killed something.

I stood, mud dripping down my clothes and caked in my hair, and took in the herd. They had watched their packmate die by my hand and were now circling me warily. Most still had their eyes on me, unnaturally focused and uncaring as those behind them continued to be slaughtered by the soldiers working their way closer.

One of the big cats roared angrily, letting its bloodlust get the better of it, preparing itself to charge and riling up the rest of them. It pawed at the ground, big, huffing breaths caused the black spittle in its mouth to fly out and speckle the ground.

Adrenaline rushed through my body, letting me drop into that focused space I did when I fought. The sounds around me cut away, letting me hear my own breathing paired with my beating heart. Pulling the second blade from its sheath, I did something incredibly stupid. I charged the group of wraiths, diving to the left, to where Zanaya and the soldiers were still fighting through the mass of rotted bodies.

The smaller group I picked out snarled as I approached, their breath puffing out in the cold air. With a quick movement, I replaced one of my knives in its sheaths using the free hand to pull the small blade on my forearm out, throwing it with precision. The small, dark blade, no bigger than the size of my hand, flew through the air before piercing through the eye of the panther whose entire skull shone brightly under the light of the battlement towers.

Falling to the ground in a heap, my tiny knife sticking from its socket, I darted for the small space between the wraiths' ranks. Zanaya and Zander fought side by side just thirty yards away, Orion, Nala, and Saanvi not far behind them. Ice and claws, earth and fire and speed took down wraith after wraith.

Making my way toward them, slicing and cutting at anything that approached, I couldn't help but feel dread as two more replaced every one that fell. The smaller corrupted would come in behind their bigger counterparts dragging the fallen corpses away into the dark, chilling forest, leaving nothing behind.

Just as it all seemed to be turning in favor of the wraiths, a boom cracked through the air. Louder than the rumbling thunder, a roar that shook the world and sent a wave of chills down my body. The wraiths crouched in fear, eyes on the sky; the army of Descendents yelled out in triumph.

I looked up, blinking through the falling rain, into the dark clouds above as lightning illuminated the sky. A dark shadow, bigger than anything I had ever seen, blocked out my view as it came down closer and closer.

Breaking through the clouds, a beast of nightmares—of legend—shot like an arrow toward the battlefield. The face of a dragon would be burned into my mind forever. Immediately, I knew who it was. I would have even if Zanaya hadn't told me; those burning blood-red eyes filled with rage. The vertical slits promised pain and destruction.

He came in close, opening his massive jaws, showing the daggers that were his teeth, white and sharp. The back of his throat lit up, glowing from within, before a rush of fire bellowed out. The bright flame lit up the forestline, throwing everything into light and shadow.

I crouched, covering my face with my arm when the wave of heat hit me as Kanan turned the battle into a bonfire. Their screeching echoed across the land, and they writhed as the skin started melting from their bodies. I watched as blast after blast was thrown down upon the wraiths by the colossal dragon.

He flew high into the air, his wings brushing the ground as he drifted upwards. He circled high above before diving back down, his frame blocking out the sky. Soldiers rushed out of the way as the beast came to land. The earth shook, the vibrations nearly knocking me off my feet, as his heavy weight settled atop the ring of fire.

He stared down at me, his gaze just as piercing in this form. A crown of horns framed the reptilian face. His black scales shone with the reflection of his fire, the water turning each of them into miniature mirrors. The field, the city—the world—stood silent in his presence.

Standing beneath him, I must have looked like an ant in comparison, larger than any creature I had ever seen he rivaled the wall in height. A low rumble rolled in his chest as he brought his head, eyes level with mine. I could see the anger in those eyes even before he opened his maw and let out an ear-shattering roar in my face. I had never known what death sounded like, but now I felt I had a pretty good idea.

I stood unflinching in the opening of his jaws, his dagger-like teeth mere inches from my face, as his hot breath pushed my hair back. Closing his mouth, staring me down, he blew out a puff of air in my face. Someone was feeling testy, but so was I.

"OHHHH! *You're* mad?" I yelled at him, shouting up at his big dumb head, "Do you know how much shit I've had to deal with the past couple days? I've been lied to, attacked by these fucking corpses—TWICE—I fucking exploded, I'm wet and covered in this godsdamned mud. AND YOU'RE MAD?"

I just let it all out, screaming my problems at the pretentious lizard; smacking my hand against his hard, scaled nose.

He jerked his head back, surprise lighting his eyes at my outburst, before narrowing those swirling blood irises. Another rumble shook in the big cavern of his chest. Dark webs began to crawl across his form, shadows pulling themselves from the recesses of the forest, climbing through the air to cover all of him, until he turned into a giant cloud of undulating darkness.

They pulled back from him, Kanan's human form stepping from within the darkness, the shadows licking at his skin one last time as the raced back to their spots.

Still large and impressive, his eyes were hard, face thunderous as he stalked up to me. He stopped barely six inches from my face, I could feel the heat radiating from his body.

I couldn't stop the sway that almost sent me into his chest, the tether in my chest yanking me towards. The closer he got, the more insistent it became. Even my flaky magic pulled itself from the recesses of the cage it locked itself within to get closer to him, buzzing beneath my skin and making my hair stand on end.

"What the fuck do you think you're doing out here?"

Before giving me time to answer, he turned, yelling at Zanaya, who had walked closer with the other warriors. "What the fuck is she doing out here, Commander?"

She opened her mouth, but I snapped my fingers in his face, drawing his feral attention back toward me. "Hey, asshole! I don't know who the fuck you think you are, thinking you can get in my face and yell at me for trying to help, but you better back the fuck up."

Of course, the piece of shit just got closer, bumping into me with his chest. "Who am I? I'm the warlord of this army, and by the looks of it you were nothing but a problem. Needing saving like some damn damsel in distress."

Oh no, he didn't. "Fuck you, I was doing just fine on my own." I definitely wasn't. "I know how to handle myself." Mostly. I mostly knew how to handle myself. "I certainly didn't need some overgrown lizard to save my ass, thank you very much." Okay, maybe I kind of did, but I sure as shit wasn't going to tell him that.

His nostrils flared, his burning red eyes glowing in the darkness. We were so close our chests brushed as we breathed, and steam curled between us. Looking down, I saw that although the rain had finally abated, the water drops clinging to his abdomen were drying, the blazing fire that lay inside of him evaporating them. His black claws clenched, tendrils of shadow curling in between the digits and climbing up his arms. He was angry, too angry to just be mad at me for coming out here. Fury rose like a wave in his eyes.

A very sick part of me wondered how those claws felt scraping over my skin or the strength of his arms around me. A very, *very* sick part of me indeed. I certainly had no plans of getting close enough to this prickly asshole to find out. The heathen in my head pouted at the thought.

"Atallia, why didn't you release your magic like you did before?" Zanaya stepped closer, her eyes darting between the two of us, trying to deescalate the situation.

Taking the out, I gave Kanan one last look before stepping away. "I couldn't. I tried, but the second I released it, it locked itself away."

Zanaya looked over at Kanan, confusion written across her face alongside worry.

"I take it that isn't normal?"

"No, not at all."

"Fabulous." When had anything in my life been normal?

"I have someone that can tell us what is going on," Kanan said, hands on his hips. The deep anger still flickered in his eyes, but I could see him shoving it down.

"Why don't you just do it, sir?" Saanvi asked, coming out of nowhere, black blood spattered across her face and leathers. She must have already been here, or somewhere close by. Looking me up and down, those viper-green eyes missed nothing. "Looks like the golden girl got a little dirty. Who knew that shine could be covered up?"

I flipped the finger at her teasing words, my blade glinting menacingly in the light still dripping with the tar of the wraith I had killed, and a nearly invisible smirk danced across her lips as she seemingly found me acceptable. *I feel so honored*, I thought sarcastically.

"Bron is more accurate, and has more practice with picking through someone's mind," he said, face still as dark and thunderous as the clouds above. He took me in, covered in mud and the thick blood of the wraiths, my spine straight and eyes sharp. "Take her in and get her cleaned." He looked me up and down once more. "She's a mess."

He walked off before I could throw swears at him that would make a sailor proud; I wasn't that dirty. I still couldn't help flipping him off as his delicious backside walked away.

"Fucker," I grumbled to myself, glaring as the soldiers all give him respectful bows as he checked on the wounded.

Nala giggled, and Zanaya stared at me like I had two heads. Zander stood behind her, barely able to cover his laughter, shoulders shaking from the strength of it.

I shrugged my shoulders. "What? He is."

Letting out a world-weary sigh, Zanaya waved me forward as she started heading back towards the wall. "Just come on, I don't have the patience to explain to you all the ways in which you just disrespected one of the most important leaders of our people."

"Important leader or not, you don't get to act like an overbearing ass," I said, with a scoff. "If you're gonna be a fucking asshole, get treated like a fucking asshole; that's what I was always taught."

She blinked her eyes at me, obviously not seeing it as humorously as I did, before turning back around, shaking her head and mumbling under her breath. Laughing a little, I followed behind, mud squishing between my toes.

CHAPTER SIXTEEN

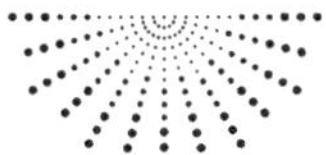

Okay, so maybe I had been that dirty—the water had run off in a stream of brown and black. The wraith's blood had turned it a putrid color—and smell. Thankfully, the east barracks had fully stocked bathing rooms, and I was able to get it all out in a wash. Or two.

Still, I stepped out of the wide chamber that allowed water to free fall from a spout in the wall. The hot water had chased away the chill from my bones and revived me from that place where I detached myself from reality, if just a tiny bit.

Zanaya had fetched me a new pair of leathers, well-worn from countless uses and as soft as the cotton socks she handed me after. After buckling my sheaths back to my thighs and forearm, we moved along the interior structure of the wall.

Once outside, we were met by a sea of red tents. A war camp for all intents and purposes. The extra soldiers who had come to fight needed a place to rest their heads for the night while still being close enough to jump into action should it be needed.

We passed guards and soldiers on the move—everyone was needed to make repairs and get the wounded moved off the battlefield and into the makeshift infirmary for the healers to see.

The healers wore blue or green tunics edged in gold, the insignia of the healers' guild stitched to their chest, and they moved as fast and efficiently as the warriors. Some even more so, carrying supplies back and forth, holding down screaming patients, and altogether keeping their shit together in the face of half-eaten people whose intestines were spilling out.

Even my own iron stomach was tested as I witnessed the sight. The poor man was barely coherent through the pain, moaning and begging for death—yet Death did not take him.

The healer inside me wanted to rush over and see if I could help, but I had learned from Maris that too many hands and opinions typically had a way of getting between the wounded and the best care they could receive.

Besides, the healers moved together like a well-oiled machine, working as one to give the man the best shot he had, and I had no intention of getting in the way of that. No matter how much my blood sang with power, having come out of its self-exile in its need to fix everything.

I was shocked to see Kanan there, grasping the man's hand and speaking to him, and even more surprisingly, the man responded.

Speaking to his warlord, to Kanan, seemed to give him something to focus on other than the pain and the fast hands of the healers. Even as he was choked up, blood spurting from his lips, he tried to talk back.

It wasn't until one of the healers poured a colorful liquid into the man's mouth, his eyes quickly falling back into his head as a deep sleep was forced upon him, that Kanan let go of the man's hand. Gently setting it back down, he spoke with one of the many menders, their voices lost amongst the loud sounds of the camp.

Moving away, he headed straight for us, person after person

running up to him to ask questions, everything from resource inventory, to a list of the dead, to orders for the rest of the army. He was the focal point through which everything flowed. He may have been their Lord of War, but it was clear that to them he was much more than that.

He was their rock in a stormy, tumultuous sea. The mountain that stood tall over the city below, watching, guarding against the evils that may come for them. They had a healthy amount of fear for him, but not because of who he was. No, regardless of the position he held, they knew that he would be the fiery, swift death that would come down upon anyone who dared hurt his people.

He was still an asshole.

A smirk danced across my face at that thought, one that he caught if his narrowed eyes were anything to go by. I stood strong under the force of that gaze. His eyes told stories just as mine did, deep and endless, full of secrets that I yearned to know.

I couldn't help but wonder if that was why only he could hold my gaze, if on some level we were the same. If maybe the things that lived within us, although different in manner, were of the same cloth. Two pieces of the same fabric, two halves of the same whole. Powers of such force that only we could stand to look it in the eye and not flinch in the face of it.

He came to stand in front of me, looking me up and down. "Well, this is certainly an improvement from before." The backhanded compliment came out as a purr, the sound rubbing up against my skin.

I went to answer with my usual snark, but Zanaya cut in, attempting to stop the fire before it began. "We're ready whenever you are, sir."

Nodding his head at her, he led us over to one of the many tents around the barracks. This one was twice the size of the rest, the black material flapping gently in the breeze. The army's dragon insignia flew high above it, as well as The Divine crest, the blood dripping from the tree more prominent today than it had seemed before.

Pushing through the front flaps, I was met with warmth and a wave of Kanan's masculine scent. The amber and smoke mixed with something dark and sensual filled my nose.

I could feel my response to the overwhelming amount of it, felt my body heat up, like a physical touch along my senses. It was a hand stroking up the inside of my thigh, getting closer and closer to my aching center, only to teasingly move away at the last second. A whisper of breath on my ear, or the drag of sharp fangs against my neck. The sound of his low rumble—a purr—in the darkness.

Letting out a shaky breath, trying to calm my now racing heart, I took in the space. The tent itself held a nest of sorts in the far corner, low to the ground on a pallet and piled high with furs. A makeshift bed for the lord to sleep in, nowhere near what someone of his station would have normally demanded, but Kanan seemed to have zero complaints about it. A dark wooden table had been pushed into the middle of the room, maps and paper strewn about on top.

A mixed tray of cold cuts, fruits, and cheeses had been brought in alongside a board of crusty bread. A pitcher of what I assumed to be ale sat right next to it, white horn cups waiting to be filled. Picking at the offerings was a man I don't think I would soon forget.

He had stark white hair, straight as an arrow down his back —half of it pulled up into a bun—and eyes of the purest, unmatched silver. If Kanan was beautiful in a feral, primal kind of way, this man was striking. Someone who maybe didn't have the most perfect of features, with a slight crook to his nose and twin parallel scars running up on both sides of his neck to the bottom of his jaw, and yet he still drew your eye all the same with the sheer magnitude of his presence.

He looked like the kind of man who could tell you about his life for hours on end and barely scratch the surface of all he had seen and been through.

His pale white skin was somehow warm and full of life. Somehow even without doing so he appeared to be smiling, a light shining from within that could not be dulled.

The dual swords crossed across his back marked him as a warrior. His dark brown leathers were flecked in black blood, making it likely that he had been in the battle.

Out of the corner of my eye, I could see I was not the only one appreciating the view. Zanaya was caught in the man's magnetic spell herself, looking him up and down appreciatively.

"I see you're already helping yourself to the food, then. You're worse than a stray dog." Kanan shook his head in faux irritation, a small smile gracing his lips. I was sure the sun broke through the clouds at the miraculous appearance, his gloom and anger dissipating slowly in the face of his friend.

The man, Bron, I assumed, looked up with a cheeky smile. "Woof." Popping more foodstuffs in his mouth, he continued. "If you're going to leave me by myself for hours on end, the least you can do is feed me." His voice held a brogue to it, a lilt that made him sound as if he was singing as he spoke.

Kanan huffed out a breath, chuckling in his own deep voice. "You know Commander Zuberi," he said as he walked over to a trunk sitting against the back flap of the spacious tent, looking over his shoulder at me with something unknown in his gaze, indicating toward me with a nod. "And this is Atallia."

"Of course," he said, coming around the table, looking at Zanaya intently. "Commander, a pleasure, as always." He reached out to grasp her forearm in a warrior's greeting, both holding on longer than necessary, before turning to me with a bright, wide smile. "And you. You, I've been wanting to meet ever since I heard you smacked this bastard"—he nodded toward Kanan—"on the nose and then proceeded to call him out on his overbearingness. I'm Bron."

Smiling, my brow wrinkled. "That was only a couple hours ago."

"Yes, it's the only thing people have been thinking of—they're shouting it, really—and I've been laughing my ass off ever since. I am sorry to have missed that show; it would have made my year." He chuckled again, two dimples appearing at the corners of his mouth.

I could see Kanan roll his eyes, but there was still a curl to his lips. It was obvious the two had known each other a long time, their friendship on open display between them.

"I bet it was even better than when yo—"

"Okay, why don't you actually get on with why you're here," Kanan said, shooting him a look that shut Bron up. The two looked at each other, a silent conversation being held between them.

Bron turned to me, his smile back in place. "Yes. Alright, come here and sit down and we'll see if we can't figure out what sort of mess you've gotten yourself into."

Pulling out one of the chairs, I sat myself down before asking, "What exactly are you going to do to me?"

"Oh, nothing too bad. I'm just going to play around in your mind for a bit." I leaned back slightly, eyes narrowed. He laughed at my expression, which was probably a mix of wariness and horror. "Don't worry, it's harmless so long as I want it to be. Certain Cynthonians are gifted with limited mental abilities, coming from the God of Death, of course, able to do party tricks at best. Typically, mild telepathy of some kind. However, I am considered to be the oldest of our kind and a little something on top of that, so that makes me extra special."

"How old are you?"

He gasped dramatically, "You should know better than to ask

a man his age, beautiful. We can get sensitive about that kind of thing."

I rolled my eyes and couldn't help but grin at his theatrics. It was hard to imagine him any older than me, his body showing no signs of aging. He looked thirty at most, and with his playful spirit, I just couldn't picture him being one of the oldest Descendents in the world.

And yet his gaze told a different story. I had always found that the eyes held the truth of us. They played the story of our lives across their colored irises for all to see if they looked hard enough. Bron's eyes, while playful and happy, held a lot inside their reflective depths. A long tale of life by the looks of them, filled with pain and sadness, happiness and joy.

I asked him once again, my tone serious. "How old are you?"

He smiled gently, looking me in the eyes, the thousands of years he'd seen flashing by in seconds. "I have memories of the day Death first appeared, the darkness that hung over the world those few days. Not malicious, he was just curious. I could feel it." His eyes glazed over, remembering those days so long ago, a smile still on his lips. "I have memories of the day he took his third form, that of a male. I remember the Time of Nightmares, when he unwillingly lost control over his powers and nearly killed the planet." His face grew solemn at that, looking over at Kanan, whose face had gone stone cold. "I also have memories of when the Goddess came, how she helped him; unable to leave her pair to suffer such madness."

"You knew the Goddess?"

He smiled, open and wide, his two canines just slightly longer than the rest of his teeth. Chuckling a bit, his eyes shone bright like liquid starlight as he looked at me. "Yes, I did, and she was more magnificent than even the stories say. I have never met someone quite like her and I don't believe I ever will. She was one of the most beautiful creatures to grace this world, both inside and out."

I could hardly believe he had been on this planet longer than Death and Life, that he had known them. One part of his story caught my attention even more, though. "You were an animal. Before I mean," I said, not realizing until after I had said it that it might be considered rude to call him such.

Thankfully he laughed, not offended by my unthoughtful comment. "Yes, I was. The original Cynthonian, the first one made by Death. You see, I was his first friend. When he was alone he had me, and I had him." His wide shoulders shrugged. "Death had already extended my kind's already long life, so when The Divine pair decided to create the Descendents, I had no problem being the first."

He had to be thousands of years old, older than Cashim, who seemed to hold the world on his shoulders. He was the first Descendent, friend to Death, and here he sat. In front of me smiling like some new youth. The thought of all the years behind him, all the stories he could tell, I couldn't even begin to grasp it. To understand all he had been through.

"You said you were different though, that you were also something else?"

"Ahhh, yes," he said, leaning back. "You see, I wasn't just any animal—I was more sentient than the others. My mother was a saberthor," he waved flippantly when I went to ask. "You'll know one when you see it, and my father was what we call an Anima, a type of animal spirit that has mental abilities to make up for its lack of physical ones. He is where I got my washed-out coloring from, as well as my hypersensitivity to people's minds."

"And this will help you find out why I couldn't reach my power during the fight? It seems to have come back, but I can still feel the barrier, like it is keeping part of itself from me."

"He should be able to tell us what is keeping you from reaching it, and why it seems to let you access it only to a certain degree." Kanan came closer, pulling out a chair. "Hopefully, that will allow us to stop it from happening again."

I nodded along, even though most of what they were saying made no sense to me. Once again, my life of ignorance hindered me, showed me how my life was never truly my own. The lies I was told sat coldly in my stomach, like heavy rocks that had been tied to my ankles and were now dragging me down beneath the surface into a sea of anger and mistrust.

A hand rested against mine, larger and warmer than my own. Turning, I saw Kanan staring at me, an understanding compassion clear in those unflinching eyes, something I'm sure he was as unused to as I. I tried not to analyze the way that look made me feel or how every point of contact from his hand lit my body on fire. Swallowing hard, I forced myself to look away.

"Alright, tell me what to do," I told Bron, who had a weird expression on his face, lost in thought.

Jolting, he came to, looking at me calmly. "Just try not to fight it when you feel me in your head. It's not a painful process, but if you fight against me, it won't be a comfortable feeling. And if what I heard you did to the healers was true, I'm not sure I want to be on the receiving end of your power should it decide not to like me intruding upon its space."

I nodded my understanding, and he reached up with hands I just now noticed were scarred. The white lines were jagged and uneven, like glass had been slashed over and over again against the delicate skin. They disappeared into the sleeves of his leathers, but I was almost certain they continued up his arms, and something told me it wasn't just a bad accident that caused them.

He caught me staring, giving me a wane smile. "Seventeen thousand years is a long life, not all good, not all bad." He shrugged his shoulders as if waving off seventeen thousand years was natural.

"Yeah, I'm sure it is," I whispered softly. Those scars said more than any words could.

He cupped my head between those damaged hands, closing eyes of liquid metal. Shutting my own, I waited, and within seconds I felt it. At first, it was like a thought that was not the same as the rest. A nudge at the back of my mind, a knock on the door, in a sense.

Remembering what he said about not fighting him, I did my best to open my mind, allowing him entry inside by cracking that door open slightly. And then I saw him, glowing within my mind, vibrant and calm as my own power surged, rushing to meet the intruder.

Gold met silver, and for a split second, I could feel the burn, the need to force it out, to not allow it further. The silver took a step further in and the golden force, all-encompassing in my mind, stood tall and ready to attack at any moment. I clenched my teeth and felt myself grip Kanan's hand tighter, felt it grip me back.

"Easy, love." Kanan's sensual voice, barely a whisper on the wind, rubbed across my skin like velvet. "Let him in. He isn't going to hurt you."

I froze a little at the softly spoken name, chills making me shudder with some unknown emotion. He cleared his throat, his hand tensing in mine, almost like he hadn't meant to say the word. I shook off the weird sensation and instead used the words to reassure myself and the wary power inside me, taking everything I had to pull back on the golden nebula that was nearly smothering the silver cloud. I could feel Bron moving slowly so as to not startle the instinctive magic. As he worked his way through, he left a cold, unsettling feeling.

I ignored it, trying my best to not fight against him. I could feel the walls of my mind trying to close in around his, like the mouth of a trap trying to shut behind a pest. Even as I pushed to keep that door open, the magical side of me, the one that stared back at me through the mirror, fought to shut it—to trap him inside—and remove the threat.

Following his signature, I saw the endless well of energy in my mind's eye, the glow so bright it was almost a physical sensation. Peeking at it, I saw the core of myself, the bright sun that burned beneath my skin whenever it cracked apart, the thing that bled through.

Except, unlike how it normally looked, a shimmering wall was erected around it, keeping the tumultuous energy within; only the barest hint of that power leaked out from a small crack, a trickling stream compared to the expansive ocean.

Appearing next to the barrier, the silver form of Bron's mind stood looking at the small crack that slowly spilled my magic. A small tendril of the silver reached out tentatively, and with the barest touch against the barrier, a pulse shot through it.

Like a golden arrow, it headed straight for Bron, who raced back out of my mind the way he came in as I forced the door open for him. Just as he raced through the opening in my mind, a searing pain had me crying out. Falling from my seat and to the floor, I grasped my head, my skull split in searing agony. Squeezing my eyes shut, an explosion of angry gold light flooded my mind, burning everything up like a wildfire.

"Wait outside. Now!" I heard Kanan order as a sharp stabbing pierced my brain, like glass was being shoved into my eyes, and I was being bludgeoned all at once.

I barely felt the strong arms wrap around me as I was lifted from the floor and carried off somewhere. Seconds later, I felt a pleasant touch against my lower back as a warm hand gently brushed my cheek. I let myself melt into the hard chest I was sitting up against, my head falling to rest against hot skin. A warm, smoke smell filled my nose and pulled me slowly out of the haze, my head still pounding in pain.

Too tired—and comfortable—to move, I peeked out of my eyelids, barely lifting them. Sitting in the nest of furs, Kanan had us up against the mound of goose feather pillows. With his knees bent and his arms caging me in, I waited for my fight or flight to kick in, but all I did was relax into him further. The atmosphere somehow softened as a low purr shook free from his chest.

Slowly lifting my eyes, blinking away the haze, I spotted tendrils of inky black shadows, so dark they were visible even in the dimly lit corner, crawling up from the ground and across the makeshift bed. They moved freely, winding around his muscled calves before twining between my legs. More curved down from behind us, over his wide shoulders, before wrapping around me like a blanket of darkness.

"How am I supposed to deal with all of this?" I croaked, my voice dry from screaming. I focused on his hands, the warmth of them traveling through my leathers as he drew them down my arms. Part of me balked at sharing something so vulnerable with a stranger, with a man who could no doubt use it against me if he so wished; but the other part of me needed someone— anyone—to listen. To help me.

It was one punch after the other, knocking me down each time I tried to stand back up again. I was doing my best to move forward, to keep fighting, but it felt as if the world wanted me to fail, as if it was watching and laughing at my pain, my frustration. I had walked out of that barn intent on solving all my problems, and yet more were piled on by the minute and eventually I would break from the weight of them all, unable to get back up again.

I felt him shift, tightening those heavy arms around me, comforting me in whatever way he could. A gesture he probably wasn't quite sure of, if his stiff muscles had anything to say about it. "One day at a time. One day at a time is all you can do."

Leaning my head back slightly, I peered up at him through gritty, painful eyes. His sharp jaw was clenched, a muscle spasmed as I watched, and his bright red eyes were hard. He looked like he wanted to break something apart with his bare hands, rip it to shreds because at the very least, that would give him something that he could do.

It was an extreme contrast to the gentle way he held me, firm and reassuring. His eyes were full of shadows and memories, ones that I'm not sure had anything to do with our situation. Those eyes met mine now, staring intently, sharing his own pain with me.

"We just have to take it one day at a time. Sometimes the bad days feel overwhelming, like they're just waiting to swallow you whole and drown you under their crushing weight. You just can't ever let them win. At some point, you have to decide that no matter how many times something or someone tries to knock you down, you're going to get back up. No matter what."

His voice was low and hesitant, like it was not regularly used, and yet it held waves of emotion that I could not quite understand, too much going unsaid even as his glowing stare tried to convey it all.

"What if sometimes I don't feel like I can keep fighting? What if those bad days just become unbearable? Sometimes I get tired and think it might just be easier to give up, to let them win," I whispered softly, memories flashing through my bruised mind of the worst moments of my life. All the days I felt worthless because I couldn't fit in, because I was different. The night I was attacked and had to kill for the first time. It had been in self-defense, and yet part of me still couldn't help but feel guilty because of it. And even more recently, with all that had gone on in just the past few days, it was a wonder to me that I was still on my feet.

His soft lips brushed the shell of my ear, shivers racing down my spine. "It's okay to have bad days, Atallia, because they make the good ones all the brighter. You just have to remember that the good days will come." His thumb gently brushed away a shimmering tear I hadn't known had fallen, and I couldn't help but sink into those red depths. He stared down at my lips before tearing them away to catch my gaze. "And it would be a damn shame if you weren't there to see them."

There was so much that I wanted to say, even as my words caught in my throat. Trust was a hard thing for me, had always been that way, but for a second I wished it weren't. Wished it so that I could explain to this confusing, contradicting man that he was right, and that maybe those were the exact words I had needed to hear; but it was the darkness hidden in his gaze, secrets of his own that kept me from opening up. But gods did I wish.

"Sir, I don't mean to interrupt, but you might want to get out here." Zanaya's lyrical voice was heavy with worry, and the muffled sounds of people shouting outside had us quickly separating.

Pulling away, I stood up, the pounding in my head having lessened to a manageable level. Turning to look at him, I straightened my leathers, his eyes not leaving me as he yelled out a response to Zanaya. I tried not to notice how I could feel his stare as it traced a trail of heat down my side, the sensation of being physically touched too strong to be imaginary.

I moved quickly towards the exit, trying to escape the urge to stay with him, next to him. Looking over my shoulder, I gave him a small grateful smile. "Thank you." I paused, clearing my throat. "For everything."

He nodded his head, looking down at the ground, hands clenched into fists before flexing by his sides. I escaped out into the open where hopefully the fresh air would help clear my head and make me sane again.

CHAPTER SEVENTEEN

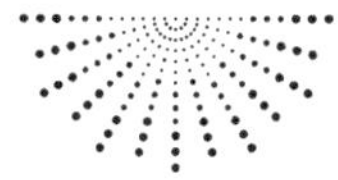

The storm had thankfully moved on, leaving sad, gray clouds in its wake, but rays of sunlight were breaking through, hitting the streams of magic that had finally penetrated the storm's haze. A shower of rainbow beams shot down, a mirage of light similar to the wall of stained-glass in the throne room.

One of the medic tents off to the side had a sizable crowd growing around it, more people running over from the surrounding areas. The flap behind me was pushed open as Kanan stepped through, swiftly moving towards the crowd. I followed closely behind with Zanaya.

"What the hell is going on?" I asked her, both of us having to jog to keep up with Kanan's long strides.

Her expression, hard and solemn as tears welled in her eyes, said enough. Reaching them first, Kanan shouldered people out of the way until they realized who he was and made a path for him into the heart of the tent.

A wailing scream reached our ears, the agony clear in the voice. I had heard the sobs of family members over their dead, and the tortuous cries of those in pain. The sounds of my own bones breaking still rang in my ears, my scream afterwards something I would never forget. And still, the weeping sobs of the man currently on his knees, grasping the body of a dead soldier, were the most horrifically hopeless noises I had ever heard.

They were filled with anguish, heartache, and misery all the same. Tears rolled down his face, sorrow a living, breathing thing that radiated from him. I could feel it perfuming the air, pulling everyone around into its orbit, forcing them to feel the crushing sense of hope that was pouring out of the man.

The warrior on the low cot was cold and lifeless. What probably was once a beautiful man, full of life and hope, was now a bloody, mutilated mess. His ash skin was covered in both black and red blood, gashes cutting into his entire body. The most gruesome wound, however, was the gaping hole in his chest, bloody and jagged—the wraith that had done it only caring about reaching the power that was once held inside. His face was a frozen mask of horror, his last view before dying was that of his chest being torn into, his spark being stolen from him.

The man on the ground, lean and strong and alive, was mumbling incoherently. Tortoiseshell-colored claws punched out of his nails, beige and brown fur growing up his arms. His screams started turning into growls of pain and rage. Someone from the crowd tried to reach for him, whispering soothing sounds, but the inconsolable man swiped out, nearly amputating the helping hand.

Several healers tried to calm him, their hands wreathed in magic. An angry roar was the only response; insanity creeping into the man's eyes, slowly overtaking the grief. Kanan moved forward, blocking the healers from the claws that swept out to cut them. They sliced through his skin, blood puckering from the deep wounds before healing back over within seconds. The skin knitted together without fault until only his tan skin and the line of blood were left. Having barely flinched, Kanan growled quietly, a low roll that might as well have been a boom. The sound wasn't one of anger, but of command.

The man, who had slowly been turning into a leopard-like creature, judging by the rosettes now peppering his skin, bowed his head and lowered his eyes, letting out a low whine. Shifting back, skin replacing fur, he let out another gasping sob, throwing himself over the dead man once again.

Touching my face, I felt wetness on my cheeks, tears having welled without my knowledge, sharing the poor man's pain.

"I can't imagine losing your pair." Someone behind me spoke quietly, sadness in their voice.

I turned to Zanaya, who stared on with a dark, pain-filled look on her face, gaze focused on something that wasn't there, tears running down her own cheeks. "What is that? A *pair*. It's not the first time I've heard it."

She jolted, as if she hadn't been entirely here, coming back to the present. Swallowing harshly, several more tears dropping as she stepped away from whatever memory she had been stuck in. "When the God of Endings, when Death, lost himself to madness during the Time of Nightmares, The Divine later realized that the Cosmos had made a mistake."

My head whipped towards her, surprise hitting me at her blatant disrespect. The Outskirts's priest would have gasped in horror at the blasphemy, shouting prayers to ward off the bad omens her words would bring.

The Cosmos was the most revered figure in the history of Irropia, even Rhaelyth, who had all but forgotten The Divine, still worshiped the Cosmos.

The Outskirts had only had one priest for as long as I could remember, and he traveled year-round throughout the three villages. The gnarled old man had always given me the creeps, and I purposefully avoided the center of town when he came around. He had a tendency to follow me through the village, his beady black eyes looking at me like I was a ten course meal.

Zanaya shrugged her shoulders, similar disbelief on her face, "I know it sounds unreal, believe me it's one of the craziest things we learn in school when we're little, but even the Cosmos is capable of missteps. He created The Divine from his power over life and death, never realizing himself that it was one power, not two. They weren't ever meant to be separated. They were never suppose to be Life and Death, two completely separate entities, but instead were meant to be Existence. They were so tightly connected that when the Cosmos created Death, he accidentally separated him from Life. So, when the Goddess heard Death calling, she initiated a bond that reconnected them."

She nodded toward the grieving man. "When they created us, we inherited that same imbalance. So now when a Descendent Awakens, we spend our whole life looking for our pair because the longer we go unbalanced, whether we are a Cynthonian without an Aetherian or an Aetherian without a Cyntonian, the more likely we'll lose ourselves to the same madness that nearly took our king."

I glanced toward the fallen man, who was mumbling to himself as he stared down at the face of the dead warrior. "He lost the only thing keeping him sane."

"He lost more than that. Those two, Harrison and Josiah, have been together for the past two hundred years. We used to joke around the barracks about how sickeningly sweet they were around each other." Her eyes glistened as she watched the grieving man. "Harrison had a hard life growing up, was always stuck in some dark place in his mind, and then he met Josiah and it was like the sun came out for the first time.

"Losing your pair is like losing a piece of yourself, not just because they keep your energy balanced, but because they become a part of your soul when you bond. Pairs can be anything to each other; it's a bond that becomes what the two need it to be. Partners, best friends, lovers, siblings, it doesn't matter. Regardless of the type of relationship, they become a piece of you, and to lose them, I have been told, is akin to having your soul ripped out. That madness the bond keeps at bay comes rushing forward all at once." Her voice choked off, a sob catching in her throat as that darkness reappeared in her eyes. "Most don't survive the loss."

Harrison released another wail, a cry of pain, for everything he once had and now lost. For his partner, but also for the part of him that went with Josiah when he died. The cry reverberated inside me, and my magic came crashing through the barrier that had blocking it from me. It flooded through me, filling every corner and cell of my body with one purpose in mind.

His pain became my pain, his grief was my grief. Without thinking, I moved forward. Both Zanaya and Kanan reached for me to keep me away from the volatile Cynth, but I pulled away and out of their reach, going down on my knees next to Harrison and Josiah.

He lunged towards me, intent on keeping the body of his lover safe. I was ready, though, prepared for the instinctive reaction. Reaching up faster than him, I grasped his face between my hands and released the magic that was at the ready, just like I had at the cottage with Brendon. Moving through me and into him, Harrison stopped, letting out a sigh of relief as my energy connected with his.

As my power touched his, the crushing grief and sorrow overwhelmed me, trying to drag me into the pit of despair Harrison now found himself. Pushing back against it carefully, not wanting to hurt him anymore than he already was, I offered whatever moment of peace I could, doing my best to protect him—even for a second—from the brutal storm of emotions he was stuck inside.

His eyes cleared slightly, the crazed expression backing off. It waited in the corners of his mind; I could feel it like a weight, prepared to crush his sanity beneath it. Only the golden force that was my magic held it at bay, barely, my energy a patch job at best for the hole that was left behind by his mate.

Tears were falling like rain as he stared at me, his voice a cracked whisper, the screaming having damaged his vocal cords. "He's gone"—another sob—"He's gone and I can't feel him anymore."

I pulled him to me, wrapping my arms around his shaking shoulders and laying his head against my neck as I ran my hands down his back. I whispered calming nonsense, trying to keep his emotions from breaking me along with him.

"I know. He's gone, and I am so sorry. I am so, so sorry." I kept repeating the words over and over; nothing I could say could possibly make the gaping hole in his heart better. I offered him whatever I could, though, comfort and a moment out from underneath the thumb of the madness that would inevitably take him.

Connected to him like I was, even the tiniest bit, I could feel the hardships he had been through. How Josiah had been the stars in his night sky, the sun on a rainy day. Every moment of happiness in his life was because Josiah had made it possible for him to see the light again. He had lived in a dark cave, a never ending tunnel of destruction, one of which I couldn't completely catch from the flashes of memories and emotions.

Even after he had gotten out of whatever situation had put him in that place hopelessness, he struggled to free himself from his own thoughts. The memories strangled him of any joy or happiness. With the utmost sadness, I could feel that he had thought about ending his own life on more than one occasion. And then Josiah, bit by bit, had brought him out of it. They had been friends long before they had ever bonded, and when they had, Harrison finally knew what it meant to know love.

Calming him, rocking gently side to side as he sobbed, I

noticed two healers come close. Locking eyes with me, I shook my head, conveying all they needed to know, and with a nod they let me know they understood what had to be done. I grasped him tighter, squeezing my eyes shut as I tried with all my heart to give him every last drop of peace I could muster; refusing to let him feel anything else with what was about to happen.

He mumbled quietly, hopelessly, into my ear, "Thank you." I only held him tighter as his body jerked, not in pain, as a black blade was shoved through his heart.

I couldn't stop the gold-flecked tears that soaked into his tunic, as I gently took the hilt from the healer, and pulled the blade out. Leaning him back onto the ground, I looked into his eyes, unable to help myself as I tried to put pressure on the wound. His blood seeping between my fingers, warm and slippery.

His head flopped to the side as he looked at me, catching my gaze. Blood spurted from between his lips, a plea in his eyes as the words came out rough and gurgled. "Don't. Please don't, I'm begging you. Let me be with him. Please, just let me be with him."

I stared down at him, the healer in me bucking at the idea of allowing someone to die without trying to stop it, even though I knew this was his only chance at peace. As I looked into his eyes and knew that even if we did save him, he wouldn't truly be alive anymore. Reaching down, I grabbed his hand with mine, not caring as his blood dripped down my fingers, and Kanan—who at some point had come up beside me—grabbed his other, making it look small within his large grip. As we held him, I willed him to know that he wasn't alone, that he was never alone and never would be.

Meeting my eyes, he smiled brightly, even as blood dribbled from his cracked lips, even as his skin went pale, even as his blood flowed so quickly from his body and across the ground that I was kneeling in a pool of it within seconds. He smiled in spite of it all.

And finally, looking up towards the sky, with a smile still on his face, he said on his last sigh of breath, "I can see him."

And then I felt his life force leave his body. His chest didn't rise again, remaining still forevermore. Like the world had released a breath, I felt as his spark left his physical form, felt it like a living pain in my own body.

A moment of silence followed, only interrupted by the quiet sounds of weeping from the gathered crowd. A numb feeling settled over me as I gently lay his hand on his chest before reaching to close his eyes so that he could rest, small streaks of red painting his skin where my hand touched him.

Standing, I ignored the stares as I walked out of the tent and into the open air, his blood covering my hands like paint, dripping down to the ground. Lifting my head to the sky, I closed my eyes as I tried to settle my own emotions. So quickly I had attached to his feelings, to his grief, that it had almost become my own.

Releasing a breath, I raised my hand to wipe my face free of tears, only to be stopped by the dark blood covering it. Dropping it, I stared up into the array of light, my eyes sore and the salt tightening my skin.

I was so lost in thought I didn't hear Zanaya come up behind me until she put her hand on my shoulder, squeezing it gently. Her voice was soft and full of grief. "I know it must not have been easy, letting him go like that, but what you did was a mercy for him. Trust me, I've seen first hand what someone can become when they lose their other half." She didn't fill in the question that rose between us at that statement, only whispering, "So thank you, for giving him that peace."

We stood together in silence for I don't know how long, but eventually two stretchers came out from the tent. Black cloths draped over the bodies, honor guards carrying them away. It wasn't long after that before Kanan stepped out, his face harsh in the light, his eyes hard. I could almost see the fire building inside of him, ready to explode forth and destroy all those who dared harm his people.

As he made his way towards us, his steps heavy against the ground, the earth shake a little with each step, as if his power—the dragon within him—had to release its anger somehow. He paused in front of me, expression unreadable save for the storming ferocity that was building.

His typically dark and sensual voice was now filled with rage and sadness. "Thank you. I know you owe us nothing; we haven't yet done anything to deserve your trust or loyalty, but I hope we can one day repay you for today. You showed him a great kindness, a mercy that I know as a healer and fellow warrior could not have been easy."

Continuing, he looked away from me, his eyes not holding mine for the first time. "I also want to apologize for earlier. You couldn't have known your powers would react in that way, and I had no right to admonish you for trying to help. As the Lord of this army, I should have shown better decorum and respect to an ally and hopeful friend of our people. With my utmost sincerity, I hope you accept my apology for my appalling behavior."

A little mystified, wondering where the formal address had come from, I inclined my head nonetheless. "Apology accepted, Warlord. I was raised by a soldier, so I would like to offer my own apology for not thinking of the repercussions an unknown combatant could have had on your strategy and commanders." Looking towards Zanaya with that last comment, her nod of acceptance was all I needed.

Even though it hurt my pride to admit, I meant every word. I should have known better—I did know better—than to put myself into a battle untrained in the ways of the group in which I was fighting with. Geoff had taught me much more than just combat, battle strategy had made up a huge part of my education. He would smack me on the back of the head for getting so caught up with the fight that I inexplicably put others at risk by being an unknown.

Zanaya had even said as much. I had acted foolishly and more like an untrained child than someone who had a blade in their hand even before they could walk. Thankfully, Kanan inclined his head in acceptance as well.

Zanaya spoke up, "What are we going to do, sir? This is the first real fight we've seen in hundreds of years. The wraiths are getting more daring, openly attacking our borders goes outside of their normal behavior."

"With the missing people and the attacks in Rhaelyth, something is brewing." He ran his hand through his head of thick hair, the midnight strands sucking in the light.

Would it be as soft as it looked when I ran my hands through it? I swallowed at the intrusive thought, before focusing my attention on something he said. "You have missing people?"

He nodded, jaw clenching in frustration. "Dozens in the past few months, even more in the last couple of weeks. They all line up with wraith attacks, but we've never seen who or what is grabbing them. It's mostly been civilians living off on their own, some low-level guards assigned to the smaller towns. This was the first attack on one of the bigger cities."

"What do you think brought it on? I mean, by the sound of it, they're picking those off at the edges. Why all of a sudden start going after the bigger fish?"

"What if it's not bigger that they want, just more?" Zanaya mused. "It could be that there are just too many of them now. The attacks we have had before were just one-offs, a single wraith here or there. Typically, the bodies of their victims were too mutilated by the time help got to them for us to realize that they were feeding off of their sparks. If that is their food source and what keeps them from degenerating into lifeless skeletons, with a group as big as today, a small town with only a few people wouldn't be able to sustain them."

"And I'm guessing the civilians that live outside the bigger cities aren't as powerful," I assumed, trying to understand why the creatures were attacking. "So they would need to feed on more of them to survive. Whereas here in Eskira, we're surrounded by powerful people."

"That would make sense, but then why are they attacking humans? They don't have magic."

"It's possible that they're all so hungry in Rhaelyth, with there not being much magic left there, that they're attacking anything that could possibly house a spark—small as it may be," Kanan, deep in thought, said almost to himself. "But that wouldn't necessarily explain the pattern on the map you said your adoptive mother had."

"When will the scouts be back with the papers?" I asked. If we could get a look at the map, we might be able to figure out what the wraiths goal was on the other side.

"Not for another day or so." He said, jaw ticking. "It's a long journey, despite sending airborne, and once they're in Rhaelyth they have to be careful not to get caught. We can't have our secrecy being revealed on top of everything else going on." He lifted an impertinent eyebrow at me.

I narrowed my eyes at him, understanding what he didn't have to say. "How the hell was I suppose to know that was going to happen. It's not like I wanted to turn into a beam of light."

He lifted his hands placatingly, his lips turning up at the corners. "Just saying."

I rolled my eyes, ignoring Zanaya's look at our exchange. "Moving on, do we even know what they are?"

"No, even when we've successfully killed one, there are others in the wings waiting to distract us so that they can pull it away and disappear with it."

The intelligence that they would have to possess to know to remove their dead gave me chills.

"That's calculated. Way too calculated a movement for rabid, blood-frenzied creatures to make on their own."

Kanan grunted, small coils of smoke puffing from his flared nose. The sound reminding me of a grumpy animal—a fifty ton fire-breathing animal. Something crossed over his gaze, as he seemed to fade in and out of the present. "Yes, and that is what we are worried about."

The words were soft, but the tone was as sharp as a freshly forged blade. His eyes heated, the red burning bright until I swear actual flames flickered in his gaze. Darkness crawled between his fingers, crawling along his arms. A shadow seemed to grow behind him, forming arching deadly wings, yet nothing was actually there.

My blood boiled at the feral look, my energy responding to his unspoken command for war. As he walked away, people who had been waiting in the wings once again rushed to him with questions, and I had the sneaking suspicion that this was just the beginning of things.

CHAPTER EIGHTEEN

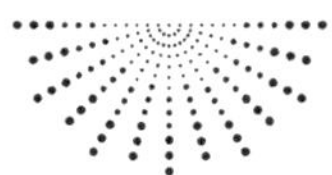

I had just lain down to sleep when a thump right outside the door had me jolting upright in bed. I slowly slipped my hand beneath my pillow. Keeping my eyes locked on the door, I gripped the dagger I kept there. Pulling the blankets back, I made sure to avoid the squeaky floorboard as I stood.

The room was dark, save for the few beams of moonlight that shot through the balcony windows. I had left the curtains open, letting in the night sky and stars, reveling in the freedom of the mountain air and magic.

Moving quietly to the door, I listened for any movement on the other side. Hearing nothing, I eased it open, looking for where the sound came from. An empty hallway greeted me, the dark shadows only interrupted by the dim light of the sconces.

Stepping forward, my foot hit something, sending it sliding across the polished floor. Puzzled, I looked around again, both sides of the hall dark and empty. Moving towards it, I bent down, picking up the object.

It was a book, no bigger than the size of my hand and covered in a white leather. Embossed on the front was the twisting black trunk of The Divine crest. Its golden leaves were as detailed as the ones on the stained-glass window in the throne room, the dark red blood dripping from the gleaming tips.

With one last look, I turned back inside, shutting the door quietly behind me. Padding over to the chaise, the moonlight more than sufficient to see in, I propped myself up on the plush pillows. Only the word Xotin marred the surface of the cover, scrawled across the bottom underneath the crest.

Flipping to the first page, the words were tiny and written with a certain flourish. I could barely read it, even in the bright moonlight. Turning to the wooden table on my side, I looked for the box of matches I had been using to light the glass oil lamp.

Had my magic not been a useless jerk, I might have had the power to light it with a flick of my finger. As it was, the fickle magic only came to me when it wanted to, filling my veins with a rush seemingly incapable of helping itself, before disappearing without a trace not five minutes later.

Just as I took out one of the small wooden sticks, positioning it to strike, a subtle glow caused me to pause. The book's pages had illuminated. Setting the matches down, I picked up the hand-sized tome.

Each individual word on the pages had lit up from an unknown source, the lettering now easily legible. Whoever had written the book, or maybe whoever had left it for me, must have known the small words would be difficult to see. Settling in, the blue-gray parchment soft and worn beneath my fingers, I started at the beginning.

***

Part One
Xotin

The War of Three was not thrust upon us with abandon, nor without warning; it crept up like a snake in the grass. A venom that swept through the bloodstream and corrupted all it touched. It cut away at a person from the inside, cut and cut, until nothing was left the same. It was a disease, one that most fell to at some point.

Jealousy.

An emotion that could turn good into evil, love into hate, and twist the best of a person into the worst. Just like an ugly illness, it could spread through hearts and minds, eating away at everything in its path until all that remained was a twisted creature of greed and envy.

The God of Chaos, brother to the king in every sense but the literal, fell prey to these emotions; or maybe he had always held such feelings and simply waited for the right moment to enact his plan.

That moment came, within days perhaps, of the Time of Nightmares coming to an end. When Life came to Irropia and paired with Death for the first time since their creation.

In an attempt to save her mate from insanity, she gave up her solitude and isolation to repair the bond that had been irrevocably changed during the divergence.

Maybe it was her beauty and kindness, or perhaps her skilled mind and warrior heart that called to Chaos. Or was it her power that drew him in?

For who could resist Life herself, a being of pure energy? A planet-bringer, the life-giver, the very essence of which the Cosmos used to construct the foundations of the universe. Irropia's heart beat with its queen's, for she was who sparked it into existence. Who couldn't help but be entranced by her magnificence? Chaos and Death were no exception.

But it was Death that was her other half. The part of herself that she had been missing. They were each other's everything, able to fill the gaps that were left behind after their separation. They were lovers, partners, equals ... mates in every sense of the word.

Perfect is something unachievable, but in their presence, basking in the love that radiated from them, perfect didn't feel so unreachable.

And in the shadows of such love, Chaos lived, watching year after year. Jealousy slowly ate at him, tearing away at his mind and heart. An evil whispered in his ear, spoke to him of ways to achieve all he ever wished for. Power. Respect. Greatness. Love. All things that had seemingly been given to Death, but not to Chaos.

Most of all, he craved the bond Life had with Death. Fate had cheated him, in his eyes, of all that should have been his. A dark greed rose through him as the decades went on, watching how powerful The Divine Pairing had become.

We are unsure when Chaos's plans began, but we know the event that triggered the beginning of the end of this golden era. That event was the creation of the Descendents.

Furthering their greatness, we suppose in the eyes of Chaos, their people were full of the magic that made up Irropia's atmosphere, its soil and seas.

Seeing fit to add his own mark to the planet, Chaos attempted to do the same, and was left severely disappointed. Not only were his people few in number, but they lacked any real ability to hold magic.

This was the last snub Chaos could handle, and thus the War of Three began. A war that would lead to the disappearance of Life and Death, and to the near destruction of the planet.

CHAPTER NINETEEN

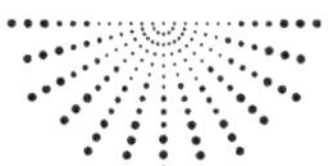

For the second time in less than a few hours, a sound at the door roused me from sleep. Only this time I knew who it was banging away on the door, being loud and obnoxious.

"You better not be naked because we're coming in, you have ten seconds." Zanaya's lyrical voice broke through the sleepy fog that hung over me. I jumped up from the chaise, where I had passed out reading into the early hours of morning.

"Oh, please be naked." An excited Zander laughed behind the door, which meant that—

"I second that." And there was Nala. I was unable to help the small smile that graced my lips at the two trouble makers' laughs.

Quickly padding over to the trunk at the foot of the bed, I unceremoniously shoved the book under the stacks of folded clothes and blankets. The star dusted flower still shimmered at the bottom, having yet to wilt. My trove of gifted treasures was slowly getting bigger, if only I could find out who had left them. Closing the top just as the door to the room opened, I turned to greet my early visitors.

Zanaya, looking more than put out by the two redheads following her, was dressed in fancy leathers, the dragon insignia pressed into the chest plate she wore, a blood red cape cutting across her shoulders. Zander and Nala were dressed similarly, although maybe not as grandly.

"Now this, this might be even better," Zander said wickedly, looking me up and down playfully.

Peering down at myself, I saw the cream silk shorts and bandeau did little to cover my skin. The cool morning air that burst in from the hallway didn't help either. My nipples pebbled against the material, and with my undoubtedly mussed hair I must have been quite the sight. Looking up at him with a scowl, eyes rolling, I flipped him off. The sly fox's devilish grin only seemed to raise more at my gesture.

"You don't happen to be into women, do you?" Nala asked, giving me an appreciative look of her own.

"Unfortunately not," I chuckled, shooting the redhead a wink. Nala's upfront attitude and ability to never let anything ruin her good mood, made it very easy to like her. It didn't hurt that her being slightly nuts made her all the more interesting.

She tsked in disappointment, pointing a finger at me, "Let me know if that changes."

Zanaya pinched the bridge of her nose, looking like she was either going to laugh or scream. Or both. "If you two are done flirting with her, we have things to do."

"I mean," Nala paused, pursing her lips at Zander who shrugged his shoulders, throwing his hands up in defeat, "we weren't, but go on."

Zanaya closed her eyes, tilting her head back to the ceiling, and started counting to ten under her breath. I pressed my lips together to stop the laugh that was shaking my chest. She opened her eyes, expression just as vexed as it had been, narrowing in on me. "Don't encourage them."

With an impish curve to my mouth, I asked, "What's going on?"

"My uncle and Lady Jai were hoping you would come down to the city infirmary. They want to compare any notes you and your adoptive mother may have on the wraith disease, since we now have Descendents who have been bitten," Zanaya said, moving over to the wall of windows looking down on the city below.

Nala and Zander spread out on the chaise lounge, right where I had been not too long ago reading the weird book. I kept an eye on them even still. They would have to look in the trunk to find the book and star-crusted flower, and as much as I wanted to ask them about the two objects, I couldn't quite figure out the opening up thing. Trusting anyone was going to be a work in progress after everything.

"We're on our way to meet up with Orion and Saanvi at the eastern wall and they asked us to escort you."

"Oh, of course." I reached into the trunk, careful not to open it all the way, quickly pulling out some clothes. I was just as eager to see the sick warriors, curious to know if the illness that was plaguing the mortals was the same. "Let me just get dressed."

Walking into the bathroom, I called out, "I thought you were mostly stationed at the palace barracks."

"We typically are, but my soldiers were reallocated there to help bolster our forces on the east side until we're able to fully assess the damage done from the attack."

The palace barracks were mostly used as the last line of defense, if the Descendents were ever pushed back into their mountain they would still have a force capable of protecting their back until they all made it inside; so it made sense that they would also be the pool of warriors called upon to help at the walls if needed, especially if they didn't want to risk putting the other sides at risk.

Making quick work of slipping on the dark leather trousers and plain white tunic, braiding my tousled gold hair, I walked back out to the main area to slip on my daggers.

"What do we know so far?" I questioned, moving with the group out into the hallway, making sure to close the door behind me.

"Well, despite them being unsuccessful, the horde was definitely attempting to reach the inner city. We found scratch marks from where they tried to climb over the wall, and holes where they attempted to dig under." She shook her head, scoffing. "It wouldn't have worked either way—the wall is too high and sheer, and it goes underground—but it's worrying that they didn't seem to care. Which means they're likely desperate, and will probably attack again."

Dread coursed through me. The attack on the eastern wall had been the creatures' first assault on one of the major cities. The fact that they had come for the capital first, and dealt heavy damage in the first few minutes before the alarm went up, had everyone worried what another offense might look like. The war camp had been abuzz with nervous energy, tightly wound and ready to blow, by the time I left.

"Do you think it could lead us to war again?" I probed, wondering what mess I had walked into.

All three of them blinked at me, their brows wrinkling. "Again?" Nala questioned.

My voice was unsure as I answered, "The War of Three." I studied them, waiting to see the confusion turn to understanding. From what I had been able to read before I fell asleep, the war had led to The Divine's eventually disappearance.

As possibly the most important time of war in the history of their people, I found it hard to believe that three warriors, all of them respected members of the army, wouldn't know about it; and yet they were regarding me with a glazed expression, bewilderment on their faces.

"Where did you hear that theory?" Zanaya asked, laughing strangely. "There's never been a war. The most our armies have faced, even when the God and Goddess ruled, is a few battles if you can even call them that."

"Man, they keep coming up with crazier and crazier theories," Zander voiced, chuckling with Nala.

"And you wonder why I said we'll never come to a decision on whether or not to have new rulers. There are more and more opinions by the day." Zanaya laughed, knocking her shoulder into mine as we walked. "Who told you about that one?"

It was obvious by the way they spoke they had no idea what I was talking about. I was baffled. If the War of Three was some untrue story, why had someone written it down in a book? More importantly, why had someone left it at my door?

I gave her a wan smile, my thoughts too clouded to do much else, I murmured back, "I must have heard it in passing somewhere."

It didn't take us long to reach the infirmary, as we chose to go by air rather than on foot. Within minutes, I was saying goodbye as they dropped me off, rushing away on the wind towards the eastern wall.

I walked under the grand structure's veranda, its sculpted pillars teaming with blush-pink ivy and cream flowers, and through the mahogany doors. Beneath the vaulted ceilings I felt small in comparison, the tapestries hanging down reminding me of who the infirmary's patrons were.

The golden starburst exploded with light against the iridescent material the crest was stitched upon. The Queen of Light's crest, if I had to guess. She was a healer, which was fitting, seeing how she carried pure life within her. If you could spark the hearts of planets, then a wound or two should be no problem.

Moving past the grand staircase and down the blue hallway,

I made my way to the back of the building, following the path I took during my escape attempt.

The halls were more alive today, the once-quiet building now a hub of noise. Healers rushed back and forth between rooms filled to the brim with books and medicinal stock, others seemed to gather together in laboratory-like rooms huddled over steaming pots and mortars.

I was given brief glances and smiles by those passing by, barely more than a look or two, before they headed to wherever they were needed.

While they didn't seem phased by my presence, I definitely was by theirs. It didn't matter how many I passed, the unique and decisively different aspects of each Descendent were truly eye-catching.

One woman I passed had short thorns poking out of her arms, laying flat against her skin. Peach-colored roses made a crown around her head, seamlessly growing from the strands of her brown hair. It was the soft petals that made up her eyelashes, however, that really had me staring.

At that moment, an extremely large hawk, bigger than any I had ever seen in Rhaelyth, flew in through an open window. Mid-flight, a vibrant orange mist covered the bird, growing significantly until a man stepped through the haze. He walked on without hesitation, the transition complete within seconds.

All I could do was blink, taking in the sight, my jaw dropped in wonder. No one but me was gawking, so snapping it shut with a click, I made my way to the infirmary. The large double doors came into view, both having been pushed in, allowing light into the hallway.

Healers dressed in blues and greens, the queen's star insignia on the corner of their tunics, were dashing across the room, checking in on patients, or sitting huddled around one of the many workbenches down the center.

Looking around, many of the beds were filled, unlike the

first time. Standing at the foot of one were Cashim and Lady Lilyi, the curtains separating each bay having been pulled shut.

Making my way over to them, stepping into the bay, my heart stumbled. Standing next to the woman in the bed, fury pouring from him in waves even as his expression was calm, was Kanan.

Blood rushed through me, my energy perking its traitorous head up, as all my focus centered on him. His dark presence hung over me just like the shadows did him. Shadows which were drifting down his shoulders, swirling around his hands, and even sifting through his messily curling hair.

He didn't seem to notice them, or the fact that a stab of jealousy ran through me at their ability to touch him as they pleased. His glittering red eyes took me in, blatantly looking me over from top to bottom. Catching my gaze, forcing the breath in my lungs to catch, a hunger formed in those swirling depths.

Not one to be outdone, I took my fill. All six and a half feet of him were covered in raven leather, both shoulders capped in dark, gleaming metal that resembled the scales of a dragon. His tunic, in his color of choice—of course—was fitted to every dip and angle of his body.

Equipped with that astonishing broadsword, the glaring red gems in the hilt's dragon eyes were the same startling shade as its owner's. The large sword was perhaps the most notable weapon on his body, but the numerous others did not go unnoticed. Every available space was covered in them. No surprise the warlord was ready for battle.

With our gazes locked, it was hard to focus on anything else, and it was a testament to my distraction that I barely noticed Bron standing right next to him.

A striking and terrifying man in his own right, Bron was hard to miss, especially next to the cloud of darkness that was his friend. His clever grin, however, was very noticeable, lips curling in an overly feline way. His pale skin was nearly the same color as the sharp, white canines, and the silver armor he wore turned his eyes molten.

"Atallia, there you are, dear. Thank you so much for coming," Cashim greeted, his fatherly smile making it hard for me to not confide in him. His gentle manner and open kindness were all but begging me to trust him.

Lady Jai stood next to him, as beautiful as the lotus on her crest. The woman's grace was undefinable, even whilst standing, seeming to float above the floor, never making a sound. Her impossibly dark eyes seemed to hold the universe within them, sparking and reflecting the light.

"Of course, I'm happy to help in any way I can, although I'm not sure if there will be much I can do. As I told you before, I had only just stumbled upon Maris's notes when everything went to hell."

He nodded in understanding, moving closer to the sickbed. "Yes, however, you are the only one here who has had any exposure to the disease the wraiths seem to carry within them, and while it may affect our kind differently, we desperately need any information you can give us."

"It could also tell us about the wraiths. Their origins. Their purpose." Kanan spoke softly, immediately drawing my attention back to him. He locked on to me, a flash of something flittering across his face before returning to his normal stoicism. "We would appreciate anything you could tell us."

Swallowing hard, I glanced away, trying my damndest to ignore whatever the hell his voice did to my body. Looking at the woman in the bed, two things became blatantly apparent. Moving closer to the woman's side, I pulled down the sheet covering her body, exposing her midriff.

Several bites and scratches marred her dark skin, oozing the same black and green puss that had seeped from the wounds on the humans. However, unlike those two, the wounds weren't scattered. They weren't done without care as if some rabid beast had just been biting at any limb it could reach; the fresh marks were centered around the woman's chest, her breasts covered by white gauze, but I could see even more gouges in her skin peeking over the top of the material.

"Well, I can tell you two things from just looking at her. One is that the wraith or wraiths that attacked her took a more rational approach to eating away at her. Obviously, these are not the attacks of sane animals, but unlike the two mortals I treated, her wounds are more centered," I explained, circling my hand around her chest. I nod my chin toward her unmarred limbs. "Knowing what I do now, I'd wager they were trying to get at her spark. Why waste time on the parts of her that don't possess the energy they so desperately need?"

"That takes thought," said Lady Jai, her voice ringing like bells.

I shook my head at her. "No, it takes direction. I don't know if any of you have been face to face with one, close enough to look it in the eyes?" I asked. Only Kanan and Bron nodded in assent. "But there isn't much behind those eyes other than hunger and insanity. Whatever they are now, what they were before is dead. I don't believe they are capable of much thought, let alone calculated planning, but maybe there's enough left for them to listen. To obey."

They all shared a troubled look, knowing what it meant if the wraiths actually were taking orders from someone. It was one thing for them to be infecting humans in such a way, but if they could spread the illness through the Descendents, then there was someone out there who possibly had an army that could kill immortals.

"What's the second thing?" Bron asked, his silver eyes hard and cold.

Shrugging, I looked down at the poor unconscious woman and her ample body. "She's not emaciated. The humans were mere skeletons when they reached us, and according to those who knew them, they were perfectly healthy right up until they disappeared. I'm not sure if this is just the way it affects Descendents," I said, peering around the sheet that separated the beds and into the next bay where a man lay unconscious in a similar state. "Or if it's just this group of warriors. There are too many variables for me to make any sort of guess as to why it's affecting them differently."

Glancing over at Cashim and Lilyi, I couldn't help but feel guilty that there wasn't more to offer. "I'm really sorry, but that's about all I really know." Frustration boiled me alive inside. The thought that there were more and more people being affected by whatever this was and I was unable to help, had me in shreds.

Cashim moved closer to me, putting his hand on my shoulder. "Do not worry, my dear, you gave us more than what we had gathered." His words were comforting, but he was doing a terrible job hiding the distress and anxiety he was feeling.

"Do you know how the infection spreads?" Lilyi questioned, her tone indecipherable, I could only surmise she was just as worried.

"Just that it spreads fast, but again, that was with the humans and they most likely died from whatever starvation-like state they were in rather than the actual infection. I don't know if your soldiers have made it back or not," I inquired, glancing at Kanan. "But Maris had dozens of parchments on the disease, some even from other healers across Rhaelyth. She had been gathering them for at least a month before I found them."

"They're not back yet," Kanan grumbled, the room darkened around him for a split second before returning to normal. "As soon as they land I'll make sure to have them brought to you and the other healers."

We talked for a while longer, with them asking questions and me doing a pitiful job answering them. I had never felt so inept as a healer. After nearly two decades of experience—at least with mortal ailments—I wasn't accustomed to feeling unhelpful when it came to the medicine. However, it seemed we were all in the dark with this one, and part of me felt at least a tiny bit better that the powerful, immortal people were just as clueless as I was.

I moved away to check in on the other sick warriors, all unconscious, once the conversation had turned to a different topic. I found the same wounds on each of them, some more deep and putrid than the others, but for the most part, each one of them bore the same purpose. To devour their souls, consume who they were as people. The slow-crawling veins of disease would spread through their bodies, eventually leaving nothing behind.

Feeling a tug behind me, I turned, my vision blocked by a wide chest. Kanan's chest to be exact, his body close enough for me to take in his smokey, warm scent, the deliciously dark undercurrent doing its best to draw me into its depths. How I had not heard him I wasn't sure; a man with his commandeering presence and size shouldn't have been quieter than a feather on the wind; it just wasn't fair.

Gazing up at him, my heart beat so hard I could hear it in my ears and feel it against my breast. Swallowing, I cleared my throat before stepping back slightly. "How can I help you, Warlord?"

"I know the two of us may not have gotten off on the right foot, and I know that I'm probably to blame for that." He spoke softly in his low, rumbling voice, the sound running down my back like a caress.

Trying to claw back some of the ground I was losing to insanity. I interrupted him. "Do you mean by watching me undress at the Pools of The Living, or when you were particularly ..." I paused, moving my eyes across his wide shoulders, remembering how his sun-kissed skin had looked dripping with water, "... draconian after the battle?"

An almost imperceptible grin lifted the corners of his mouth, the smug dragon completely unembarrased by his complete lack of decorum at the hot springs. Here I was expecting a blush or for him to at least glance away in chagrin, but I should have known better. No man like him cared about social propriety, and he certainly did not apologize for bucking against it.

His wicked look sat firmly in place as his shadows writhed and twisted around his fingers. "I know it has been quite the hectic few days for you, so I was hoping that you would allow me the chance to show you Eskira and all of her finer sides."

I was tempted to say no, just to wipe the arrogance from his face, but it was the genuine look in his eyes that had me pausing. He was reaching out, passing me an olive branch, so to speak, and I would be a bitch not to see that and take it. I mean, I normally was anyway, but not an outright rude one. Besides, I had yet to come down from the mountain fortress to see the lower city as a whole, and it would be nice to see what everyone was fighting for.

"Aren't you kind of important?" I asked with a teasing smirk. "I'm sure you have many other duties you could be doing besides walking around the city with me."

Now, with a true smile, he chuckled. "Yes, I'm sure there are, but I find myself irritated by the idea of them today. I've done my job well enough that the city won't fall apart if I go for a walk with a beautiful, snarky woman." He said it with such certainty that I had no choice but to believe him. I steadfastly ignored the beautiful comment, the things it did to my body not at all understandable.

"Please." The word was whispered, but it broke between us like a crack of thunder.

Surprise flickered through, more than a little shocked by the plea, so much so that I nodded in agreement without even thinking. His eyes sparked, a pulse going through them, as the round pupils constricted into the dragon's diamond shaped ones. They pierced through me before returning to normal, an emotion I couldn't place dancing within them.

My breath stumbled, and my heart raced as red and gold clashed, our gazes locked. The reaction those eyes brought out in me had me worried about just what kind of hold this man had over me, and whether it would come back to bite me in the ass.

CHAPTER TWENTY

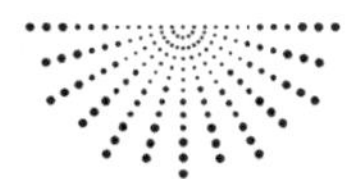

"You know, it's been a good long while since I've seen Kanan all twisted up over something," Bron said, his deep brogue breaking through my thoughts.

Twisting around from where I had been leaning against the wall, waiting for Kanan to finish discussing something with Cashim, I saw the pale man making his way towards me. His silver eyes twinkled in amusement, a smug, carefree grin on his face.

"What do you mean by that?" I asked, trying to hide my curiosity. Reading Kanan was like reading a book upside down in the dark—you couldn't even see the words let alone make out what they said.

By his smile, I was doing a poor job of concealing my interest. "You don't really think he *asks* someone for something often, do you? Kanan is many things, subtle or courteous are not either of them. He *commands* something to be done, Atallia," he said, looking dead serious. "And then people jump over themselves to do it. There's not a gentle bone in his body, and there hasn't been for quite some time, but you have him in knots."

I quirked an eyebrow, my skepticism rearing its doubt-filled head. "What's so special about me?"

He huffed out a laugh, looking over his shoulder to where Kanan stood talking with Cashim and Lilyi, before meeting my eyes, "So many things beautiful," he said cryptically. Sighing, his eyes lost focus as they stared through me, looking for something only he could see. "So many things," he murmured, almost too quietly for me to hear.

Bron hadn't done anything to warrant it, but annoyance and anger flooded me. His non-answer reminding me all too much of the other problems that refused to resolve, namely the secrets that seemed to stick to me like threads of spider silk.

"Did you need something?" I demanded rather impatiently. I knew that my reaction to such a small thing was irrational, yet I couldn't help but feel like I was in a room of complete darkness, walking around blind with no way to escape.

A white eyebrow quirked, seeming to catch my rather quick change in mood, and possibly the reason behind it if his apologetic gaze meant anything. Clearing his throat, he moved in closer, lowering his voice, "We didn't get a chance to talk after I checked the block on your magic, but I wanted to let you know what I saw."

"And?" The anxiousness was clear in my voice as I waited with bated breath for what he had to say. Maybe if I could figure out the origin of the block, I could figure out how to break through it.

"I'm sorry, but it looks like both blocks were put on you by someone else."

I swallowed, everything around me seeming to stand still, as I forgot how to breathe. "Both?"

Pressing his lips together, he looked anywhere but at me,

closing his eyes before releasing a big breath. "I hate to say it, beautiful, but when I was inside your head, I got a glimpse of another block. One on your memories, to be exact. I wasn't able to get a good look at it because your energy reacted so poorly to me testing the one on your magic, but I have to assume they were both placed by the same person. They had a similar energy."

I blinked up at him as my thoughts raced with the information. If someone had purposefully put a block on my magic and my memories, what were they trying to keep from me? How had they done it? It must have been when I was a child, possibly why I had been left in the mortal lands for Maris and Geoff to find. But then that brought up why Maris and Geoff, who were most certainly Descendents, would be there in the first place. Did they know what had been done to me, and if so, did they know why? Or had they just been pawns in the game being played by whoever the hell had put the blocks on me in the first place?

"Wha-What does this mean?" I stammered, needing to know what I could do to fix this. If it could even be fixed. Great Cosmos, the idea made me sick to even think about. Knowing I had been violated in such a way, that my memories and power— two things so intrinsically bound to me—had been taken from me, and I was none the wiser.

"It means that someone didn't want you to be able to use your powers, and they wanted some memory or memories hidden from you. Possibly something you saw or heard." He shook his head, his frustration clear. "As much as I would love to, I don't think I'll be able to remove them, either. Not only were they incredibly powerful blocks, but they were extremely defensive. One brush against it and it attempted to use your power to trap me inside your mind, which very well could have killed us both. The one on your magic didn't feel malicious, but it was placed with strong intentions, ones that I'm not sure I could break through even if I was able to."

A rising panic was building inside me, causing my hands to shake. Clenching them together, I forced that inner calm I felt when I fought to overtake the fear, focusing on the cold fury that simmered underneath. "So, what can I do about it? There must be something."

"Well, for a start, your power is still *yours*," he explained with narrowed eyes, the wheels of his mind visibly turning. "There isn't anything someone else could do to make it stop being yours, not even tricking it into staying within the block. It's just a thought, but if you keep reaching for it, force it to recognize you as its master, show that it's fighting against itself, then I'm confident that you could slowly chip away at the barrier until it eventually breaks."

"And my mind?" As much as unlocking my power was important, my memories were even more so. I had lived a long time, at least as a human, without magic being present in my daily-life, but my memories … those were mine and mine alone. That they had been taken from me wasn't something I could handle. I needed something to rely on, even if that was just my own mind, and now that it had possibly been taken from me…I didn't know what I was going to do.

"You'll have to let me look into it some more," he said thoughtfully. "There's nothing I can do about it right now, nothing that won't hurt the both of us, but I'm looking into a few options that might be able to help keep your magic's defenses at bay so that I can get a better look at the block."

I gave him a genuine smile, thankful for any help I could get. "Thank you Bron, I really appreciate it."

He smiled, looking over as Kanan began to walk in our direction, before clasping my arm and giving it a comforting squeeze. "Just remember, beautiful," he whispered, giving me a wink, "I'm on your side." Giving a two-finger salute to the tall, dark, and deadly who stopped next to me, he shot one last grin over his shoulder before prowling off.

"What did he want?" Kanan asked expectantly. It didn't matter how many times I was around him, each felt like a blow to my lungs. The dominant air that permeated any space he entered rolled across my skin like a caress of violence, a perfectly balanced blade just waiting to tip over, singing for blood. He left me feeling raw, and whether he knew it or not, he didn't seem to care.

"I don't see how that's any of your business," I teased. Poking the bear—well, dragon—was never a good idea, but some dangerously addicted part of me wanted to see how far I could push that blade before I got cut.

The air wavered, shadows licking at the strong lines of his neck as his eyes burned blood-red. "I'm the warlord, which makes the safety of all Descendents my business. As that now includes you, I think it best you fill me in on any problems you may be having."

Tilting my head, pretending to think it over, I smiled teasingly, "No."

The space around him seemed to darken, even as his lips twitched. "No?" he puzzled, bemused. "Just no?"

Shrugging a shoulder, fighting off the laughter that wanted to escape, I answered, "Just no."

There was too much mystery surrounding the hulking man. Too much that he seemed to intrinsically know about me for me to easily trust him, even though a deep part of me so badly wanted to.

I had no idea who would put blocks on me, and I had zero clue where to start to find those answers; but I still didn't know these people all too well, and the idea of giving them such personal information almost sent me into hives.

A deep seated hunger stared back at me, one that said much more than the devilish grin formed on his face. His voice was coaxing, running down my spine, seducing me to answer. "Is there anything I can do to change your mind?"

I knew what he was doing, but it didn't change the fact that he was the most sinfully beautiful man I had ever seen, and his voice was made from the heavens. My body responded whether I liked it or not, all he had to do was walk into the room. *I was not prepared for this today.*

I smirked tauntingly through the fire he ignited in my blood, looking him up and down, "No."

Licking his lips, fangs biting into the lower, he let out a small chuckle. Dipping his head, something unfamiliar sparkling in his eyes, he replied, "Alright then. I guess we'll head out, and I can ponder whether you should be punished for your insolence."

I couldn't stop the husky voice that came out as we started to walk. "The only men that get to punish me are the ones I ask to." My smile turned downright wicked as he seemed to freeze. A deep, guttural laugh, one full of promise, escaped him, sounding more like a low growl than anything.

***

Walking through the city with Kanan was like walking next to a black hole, constantly drawing everything and anything into its orbit. I don't think it would have mattered if a building burst into flames at any minute, the attention would still be on the dragon in sheep's clothing walking beside me.

It wasn't even his fault, which made it all the more fascinating. If anything, he seemed oblivious to the reverent and covetous looks the city dwellers gave him.

Maris had taught me to people watch as a form of entertainment during the long days at the market when I was younger. We would sit and craft stories about the travelers and merchants who were making their way through the Outskirts. It made those hot summer days around the villagers bearable, so the way we were being treated didn't escape my notice.

Not the way both men and women were smoothing out their clothes or gently touching their hair. Not how the warriors, off-duty or on post, straightened up before giving respectful nods to their warlord as we passed. Even the children who were playing a game stopped to watch, staring up in wonder at the giant before them.

As we passed by the blue-moss-covered alley they were playing in, one of the leather balls came flying towards me. No bigger than my fist, it wouldn't have hurt had it hit me, but as I raised my arm to deflect it, the toy froze inches from my face.

Kanan grabbed it from the air, the small projectile looked no bigger than a skipping stone in his palm. He walked over to the group of children, the tallest barely coming up to his knee. Squatting down, he held the ball out, and his face seemed to soften slightly from this angle as he looked at their nervous faces. "Careful," he warned gently. "You wouldn't want to lose it."

The youngest of the group reached up with both hands to take it from him, giving him a toothy grin. "Thank you."

Lifting his chin towards the back of the alley, where several rings were hanging at different heights, he waved them off. "Go on, looks like someone is winning."

As he made his way back, I raised my eyebrows as I muttered teasingly, "Big, bad dragon."

"Shut up," he replied, rolling his eyes at me before walking on, steadfastly ignoring my giggling behind him.

Leading me down the shaded street, royal purple leaves fell down on us from the trees above. We moved through the city with ease, people parting from our path without thought, only having to meet the piercing, red gaze of their warlord for them to treat him like a king.

Several vendors had offered us drinks and street foods to take on our walk. We had declined everything, but they had persisted until finally Kanan handed me a stick that held a spiced, honeyed fruit of some kind. I moaned my appreciation with every bite, as the vendor looked on with happiness and Kanan with something else entirely, those inhuman eyes burning away.

When he went to leave payment, the vendor—an aquatic Cynth of some kind, blue scales nearly invisible on his arms—had all but fainted. It wasn't until Kanan forced the coins into the man's hand that the refusals stopped. Giving us grateful smiles, he sent us on our way with well wishes.

"What do you think about some of the Council members' plans to possibly place new rulers on the throne?" I asked off-handedly as we neared one of the bridges that connected the northern and southern halves of the city.

"You mean what do I think about Lars's plan to place himself on the throne?" He snorted in derision, the annoyance thick in his voice.

We came up to the bridge, the wide marble expanse crossed the Falla River's reflective surface. When I first saw it I thought the river only reflected the colors in the sky, but up close it was just as magical as the rest of Allasea. Through the crystalline water I could see the bottom of the deep crevice, streaks of magic flowed beneath, darting like fish. Magentas and blossom pink. Teal and sea blue. With the magic, the occasional shine of fish scales, and the large chunks of quartz that rose from the bottom made the whole river sparkle like a diamond.

The bridge itself was just as mesmerizing, with its hand-carved stone. Coming to a stop midway, I leaned up against the railing looking out towards the south where inevitably the river would hit the Strait of Laos. Or so I'd been told.

"Well yes, but also what some of the people are calling for," I continued, tipping my head up at him as he leaned next to me, looking out over the rippling water. "You're not an oblivious man, nor a dumb one, you have to be aware that some think you should be king."

"Well, Lars has had a chip on his shoulder toward me ever since I became warlord. He both hates me for my power and separately wants it for himself."

"What happened there between you and him? He seemed sour about you taking over." To be fair, I think the man had been born sucking on a lemon, but he seemed to be especially bitter toward Kanan.

He shrugged his massive shoulders. "I thought he was doing a bad job as warlord. I challenged him for it." He looked at me matter-of-factly. "I won."

He was so candid and upfront about it that I had no doubt that it had played out exactly as he explained it. He saw someone doing poorly, thought he could do a better, so he fought for the position. It was as simple as that for him.

"So he's had a hard-on for you ever since," I joke, trying to replace the dark look that had flickered across his face.

He grinned, his four canines on display, as he shifted to the side and faced me. "Lars has been desperate for power since the day he was born," he voiced, before clearing his throat. "Or so I'm told. It doesn't matter that he's a Primal, one of the God's elite Cynthonians. He wants the most of everything, to be powerful and respected. Feared even."

His eyes turned tumultuous, a brewing red storm. "I took away some of that power, and ever since, he's wanted to find some way to climb the hierarchical ladder until he once again rests firmly above me, but I'm too powerful for him to take head-on so he's tried to bring me to heel."

"Ah yes, I've heard about the daughter." I taunt, even as a flash of irritation flares within me, for gods knew what reason.

He groaned, rubbing his hand over his face in agitation, as he grumbled, "Don't remind me."

Snickering, I look back out across the water, watching the glimmer of a school of fish zip by. Boats of all sizes paddled about as the river gently lapped at the riverbank. One of the only ways into Eskira was up the Falla River, so the ports were a place of heavy traffic.

A moment of silence passed between us as we enjoyed the view. *And possibly the company,* I thought begrudgingly.

"And the people's opinion?" I probed, finding myself intrigued by the multifaceted man beside me. How different he could have turned out to be had he not been born a power in a world that worshiped it.

"The people see me and they see their long-lost king. I don't begrudge them that, but I'm not so sure I am what the people need in a king. At least not without certain things falling into place first." His eyes were on the surrounding forest as he spoke, but I could almost feel his attention tuned into every move I made.

"Are you going to tell me what those certain things are?" I needled, knowing the answer before he even turned towards me.

"No."

Snorting, I replied mockingly, "No? Just no?"

A genuine, broad smile curved over his lips, the wildness only making it more intoxicating. "Just no."

Swallowing hard, I committed it to memory, not understanding how he could become even more addictive. Because he was, that smile was proof. It was embarrassing to realize I would do just about anything to see that smile again.

Leaning closer turned out to be a deadly and disastrous thing for my libido as his smoky scent hit my nose and his sensually dark air drew me in. My words came out more carnal than I liked as I murmured, "Is there anything I can do to persuade you?"

His eyes brightened as they studied my face, settling on my lips when I bit the lower one. Shooting back up to my eyes, red met gold, and everything stopped. The gentle breeze fell away, the soft sounds of the river pulling at the bank ceased, the very planet seemed to hold its breath.

Breaking through the hold between us somehow, he sighed heavily as he quietly muttered, "Probably."

I was left speechless, gaping like one of the fish below, unable to breathe as he cleared his throat. "Let's get you back to the palace."

As we moved through the city streets, standing closer than before, I fought myself the entire way to keep from leaning into his fire-warmed body. The silence as we walked spoke more volumes than any words, neither of us willing to break the taut tension between us.

It was like we were on a knife's edge, precariously balancing on a ravine, where one strong gust of wind could knock us off. What we'd find at the bottom was anyone's guess.

CHAPTER TWENTY-ONE

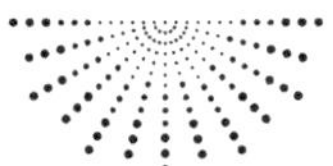

Spring gave way to summer, and days turned into weeks. Weeks of waiting for something, anything, to break through; and yet, nothing. More attacks were reported every day from the outer reaches of Allasea, the warriors always one step behind. It didn't matter how far or close they were to the brutality, they never got there in time, missing it by mere minutes in some cases.

The map had been recovered, along with Maris's notes, but it only proved that the attacks in Rhaelyth weren't as random as we thought. Which only served to confuse us more, random we understood, but a pattern meant something more, we just didn't know what.

People had taken to avoiding Kanan at all costs—his mood was beastly to say the least. His snarls could be heard throughout Eskira every time another report was brought in, more and more Descendents having gone missing—having been taken or killed. He tried to hide it, to not take it out on his warriors, but I could see the murder in his eyes.

We hadn't spoken about the day at the bridge, acting like it had never happened, but I had caught his eyes, an unmistakable desire growing in them by the day.

I knew he had to have felt mine on him, unspoken words passing between us that not even we could understand. It was insanity, the thing between us, something that shouldn't have been. The icy, hardened walls I had built around myself after years of torment cracked and fell around him for no reason I could fully comprehend.

Whatever it was inside me that recognized the same in him tugged at my soul in a way that had begun a war with my mistrusting and cynical mind.

I shouldn't have been dropping my guard around someone so dangerous; a man who wore violence like a cloak, blood dripping from each of his onyx scales. He was brutal in his command of the army, not letting up for even a second, and yet I let him.

Even if I hadn't, he somehow saw past every barrier I had constructed. It was unnerving to say the least, and yet I found myself unable to say no whenever the opportunity to be around him came up.

Which was how I often found myself having breakfast with him on one of the many outcroppings the Crian range had to offer, letting our feet dangle into the abyss.

We listened to the birds beginning to sing their first songs and watched the mountain mist fall into the valley. We talked about everything and nothing, and for a moment in time, the world felt right.

Our meetings had an annoying tendency of making my day better, as if I had started it off right, and I could only now get on with my plans. Plans that often had me feeling useless and frustrated.

I had been down to the infirmary a number of times with Cashim and Lady Jai, hoping to be of some help in figuring out how to stop the infectious wounds the wraiths left on those left alive. We had read and combed through every note Maris had made on it, but they all pertained to humans, and no matter how hard we tried to understand why, it was affecting the Descendents differently.

All the warriors who were bitten at the eastern wall were comatose, not dead or dying like the mortals I had treated, but not alive either. As if they had gone into some kind of hibernation. A dormancy of sorts. The infection had spread outward from their wounds in the same way, black and green streaking across their bodies and faces. Nothing the healers did could wake them.

Some part of me knew I could help them, none of them too far gone to be hopeless, but my power continued to be sporadic at best. It flickered in and out at random, sometimes powerful and far-reaching like with Harrison, and others not even a trickle got out of that small crack in the shield.

Bron had no solutions for me even after weeks of sifting through old texts, and while I was fighting against the block on my power, my mind was just as sealed as before. If only I knew what was hidden in my memories, maybe then I could figure everything else out.

Like the weird book that had been left for me, filled to the brim with story after story of the time right before The Divine disappeared.

Soon after reading it for the first time, the story took a dark turn. Chaos, in his jealousy, tried for hundreds of years to experiment with the bond between pairs, attempting to force the connection between people.

He had spread his evil to the susceptible minds of his weak and greedy people. It had become an epidemic in its own way, an assault on the Descendent population. It wasn't until he kidnapped the Goddess Life, outing himself as the puppeteer behind the sadistic crimes, that the War of Three began.

There was no record of Life's time while in captivity, only

that she was held for a year. During that time, not only was Death on the verge of madness once more, but her presence was missed across the world. Flowers refused to bloom, rivers dried up, hearths would not light, the magic wind would not gust.

Irropia could not breathe, standing deathly still in grief. The Year of Sorrow it was called, for the very planet had mourned the loss of its queen.

And yet no one remembered any of this. Not a single person I had asked could tell me a thing about it, thinking it a work of fiction. No warrior could recount the tales of the war. No high-born lord or lady could think of their king and queen's names. Healers and historians alike did not recall a time in which Irropia nearly died of heartache.

It had occurred to me that the book filled with wild stories was possibly just that, a storybook. That someone left it for me to simply enjoy some light reading, but it was not lost on me that the more I read, the more intense my dreams—my night-mares—became.

Where I struggled to remember the most basic of details before, now I struggled to not remember. The once hazy recol-lection of torment and screaming had turned into memories that plagued my thoughts during the day.

They had only been spurred on by the horrific details, connected to history in some way I couldn't yet see. More often than not, I was locked behind those white bars as monsters bit into my flesh and pain lashed through my body. And I had to wonder if it was the past, clashing with my overactive imagina-tion, or my future.

My sleeping had taken a nose dive right off a cliff, so I started splitting my time to keep busy. Sitting in the barn loft with Wrynn during the night, reading more on the forgotten history, and visiting Zanaya and the other soldiers during the day. They had all but forcefully adopted me into their pack. *Not that I fought them on it all that much.*

They all had their duties, but there was usually someone around for me to join. I knew they could see how the lack of action was chafing at me, and found myself falling into an ease with them, what with the way they tried to include me in anything they could.

Zander had taken to being my unofficial guide to all things social within the city. He brought me to any taverns and parties he could find whenever he had a night off. Nala typically joined, which always made the night more interesting.

I begrudgingly went every time, purely because I didn't think I could bear to see that boyish grin fall in disappointment. I found, shockingly, that not all people were as close-minded and hateful as the people I grew up with.

Of course, Zander took this as an opportunity to point out that my own unwillingness to open up to people, expecting the same reactions I had gotten my entire life, was a kind of closed-mindedness of my own.

Cheeky bastard.

Nala, of course, being Nala, spent her time helping me work through my pent-up rage. The pyro had found ways around my twitchy magic by having us throw shattershells—tiny, red stones that, on impact, broke open into anything from small, localized explosives to full-scale incendiaries. Something that, to no one's surprise, she had invented herself with the help of Orion.

I made sure to add it to my list of reasons why I was glad that she was on our side. It really was a great way to work out some issues. Nothing said 'I'm dealing with my problems in a healthy and productive way' quite like blowing shit up.

Orion and Saanvi were unarguably the most closed-off of the group, but they showed their support in different ways. In ways that mattered to me more than anything else.

I had set myself up in the loft with Wrynn, determined to read every inch of the crested book. The smell of hay and saddle oil reminded me of home. Of the days I would help Geoff hook Gideon up to the plow, or how every morning the animals would squawk for their food until they finally roused me from bed.

The company didn't hurt either. Between Gideon, his cohorts, and Wrynn I could always count on a good laugh. The little sprite had a bad habit of getting into trouble. Never on purpose, but disorder and havoc tended to be left in his wake.

That's where Orion and Saanvi found me. Consoling a distraught Wrynn, who had found himself on the wrong side of a snarling Cynth. He thought the old, grumpy wolf needed some cheering up and decided that painting the warrior's leathers pink, yellow daisies dotting the chosen canvas with a childlike glee, would do the trick.

"I-I just thought it would be pretty." The tiny wobble in his voice nearly cracked my heart in two. His head hung low as he wrung his hands, pink and yellow paint still streaked across his skin, blatant evidence of his crime.

I wanted to hit the surly warrior over the head for making the poor sprite upset, his disappointment and rejection clear on his face. I could see the self-doubt creeping into his gaze.

"I thought it looked beautiful," I said quickly. The child in me that had dealt with her own self-doubt about being different was desperate to protect the untouched and pure joy he held within his small body.

He lifted his head, dark eyes shining with unshed tears. "You really think so?"

The uncertainty in his voice was heavy and dark, which probably had something else to blame for than him getting yelled at by some asshole. I knew a few cruel words could break his heart, crush his big spirit that was so full of life and energy. The light he carried inside would flicker out forever. The thought made me sick to my stomach.

"Absolutely!" I said, as if it were obvious, trying not to draw attention to the crippling insecurity that he seemed to carry. "You know what I think? I think he just doesn't have good taste. I mean, did you see the way those leathers looked before?"

His big eyes grew wide as his shimmering, white wings flung him up, where he stopped a few inches from my face. Relief worked it way through me, the chasm of anxiety avoided for now. The shadows in his eyes were wiped away as if they had never been there, replaced quickly by emphatic indignation.

"That's what I thought. How dare I try to help spice up the lives around here, but oh no, I'm just a sprite. I should stick to cleaning up after the dumb animals." I watched wide-eyed as he waved his hands down at the whispers. His rant included multiple hand gestures of unknown meaning—probably not good—and shouted curses. "I mean, do they even know what they are? Those 'dumb animals' are more intelligent than most beings on this planet. They're lucky that the few still around haven't abandoned us to join The Silence yet."

His cherub cheeks grew red with anger, going from one extreme to the next. Emotions that, if I had to guess, originated from a far more toxic source. I did the one thing I wished someone had done for me when I'd been left reeling.

I hugged him.

Reaching out with my hand, gently hauling the manic mess of a sprite into my arms, I just held him. He went silent, and I could feel his ragged breaths against my hands until he finally let out an audible release of tension and sank into me.

I don't know how long we were like that, but a cough eventually interrupted. I looked down over the edge of the loft, one leg dangling over the lip. Below, Saanvi and Orion stared up at us expectantly.

Turning back to Wrynn, I straightened the yellow tunic he had made for himself, dusting off the hay that clung to it. "Are you going to be alright?"

"Oh yes, you go. I was overreacting. I tend to do that from

time to time." He smiled sincerely, waving off his feelings like they were nonsense, his wings flapping behind him rapidly.

"Hey, you weren't overreacting. You have the right to feel upset, and you shouldn't feel like you need to apologize for needing to talk it out. I'm always willing to listen. That's what friends are for, right?"

His big eyes stared at me like I hung the moons and the stars, biting his lip to keep it from wobbling as he nodded his head, whispering quietly, "Thank you, I'll keep that in mind." He flew over to the edge, getting down on his hands and knees, before peering over. "I think your big friends need you."

The corners of my mouth curved as I turned and stepped my way down the wooden rungs of the ladder. Hopping down onto the floor, I took in their appearance: slightly disheveled with mud on their boots. It was the look in their eyes, though, that made me pause.

My eyebrows drew down, immediately put on high alert. "What is it?"

They glanced at each other and then back at me. These two were usually as open as clam shells, so I was already on edge even before they spoke.

"We—"

"He." Saanvi's low voice cut Orion off.

He glared at her, his black eyes boring a hole into her head as he spoke, "We." She rolled her eyes, making his narrow further before he turned towards me. "We went to the warlord and asked to go back to your house in Rhaelyth to see if there was anything the scouts didn't pick up on that we could."

My interest was piqued instantly, hoping to grasp at any straws of information I could. I knew they had been gone for a couple of days, but no one knew where, just that it had been approved by command. They wouldn't have come to me if they hadn't found something worth mentioning. As much as the both of them liked to hide it, they were good people. Kind people.

Who had seen and been through enough, I figured, to not want to cause unnecessary pain to someone else.

Orion shuffled his large feet, the dust and dirt grinding against the stone. "I was able to pick up on remnant vibrations that happened the night your parents and you were attacked, and Sani was able to scent the wraith blood that must have dripped off them." He wrinkled his nose, "Even after all these weeks the blood was still rancid enough for her to pick up on."

"It was faint, but enough for me to notice," she calmly interjected.

I swallowed, my throat tight, feeling as if my air was being cut off. I didn't know what would be worse, if they were dead or if they were infected, which means they might as well be anyway.

"They were alive, Atallia. They were alive when they were taken from your home."

A shuddered breath escaped my lips as I bent over my knees, as I tried to process what they had said. They were alive. At least they were the night of the attack.

Relief. Terror. Anger. They all stormed inside of me like a tornado, unable to discern one from the other as they scrambled together.

A large hand rested on my back, cool to the touch and rough. Looking up, still bent over my knees, I kept the welling tears at bay. "You said *when they were taken*." I sniffed, trying to keep contain my emotions.

Orion's sad eyes locked on mine, sympathy plain across his stone gray face. Looking away, he nodded his head. "Yes, I was able to follow the ground vibrations and the shifts in the dirt, but Sani was the one who followed their scents when the vibrations stopped. It looked like they struggled for quite awhile around your home, probably fighting off the wraiths, before something or someone made them stop."

I straightened, trying to hide my fear at the thought of what had to have happened to get them to stop fighting. "You tracked them, though, right? By the scent?"

"Yes, it was so faint I'm not surprised the warlord's scouts couldn't pick up on them, but I was able to follow them after they were subdued. They entered the Blackwood, with whoever or whatever took them out. I couldn't pick up on anything else, so I can't tell you who they're with, but I can tell you that they are in Allasea. They made it all the way across the border before the scent dropped off the face of the planet. They were there one second and gone the next."

Her pupils switched to a vertical diamond slit for half a second before returning to their usual state. The viper green stared at me, a hard look like a frozen mask on her face. She may not have been the most emotional person, but I could see she was deeply disturbed to have lost the trail.

I nodded, lips pressed tight as I held back the scream I wanted to let loose. How could they be so close, and yet so far? I didn't know what was worse, the anxiety that came with wondering what was being done to them or the anger that they were in the same place I was, but still lost to me.

"I am sorry that we couldn't do more." Her soft whisper had me snapping my head up to stare at her. For once, I wasn't worried about scaring someone with my eyes, needing her to see I believed every word I spoke.

"How could you be sorry?" I exclaimed, baffled by her apology. "You"—I huffed out a breath, shoulders dropping as the tension I had been holding on to left me—"You just gave me the first real hope I've had since this whole thing started."

I implored her with my gaze to understand the magnitude of the gift she had just given me. "Thank you." I faced Orion, giving his big, solid hand a squeeze. "Both of you."

It was that conversation that had me waiting eagerly every day for news. Waiting to hear any sliver of information that might point towards the cause of these attacks, adamant that my parents' disappearance was connected.

But three days later, I couldn't handle it anymore. I was done waiting. We weren't ever going to find them by doing nothing; it was time to act, and there was only one person who could make that happen.

CHAPTER TWENTY-TWO

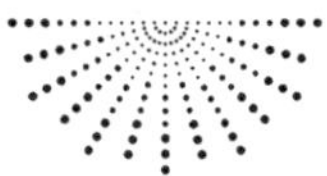

You would think finding a six and a half foot tall man would be easy. Wrong. As I stomped through the palace, he was nowhere to be found. I was tired of waiting for answers to show up on our doorstep, and he seemed like the only one willing to help me bend the rules a little bit. I knew the Council didn't know what to do with me, but I was tired of sitting on my ass while I could be out there looking for Maris and Geoff.

Unfortunately, the shadowy bastard couldn't be found. I checked with Zanaya and no one had seen him all day.

I started my hunt for him, completely bypassing the barracks and heading deep into the mountain fortress. I found myself taking turns at random, following whatever felt right. I figured at this rate I would find him within a year.

I swore the deeper I went, the bigger the palace grew. If I hadn't known magic was involved in its making, I would have been concerned about the lack of actual rock in the mountain.

So many rooms and hallways, all interconnected in some unknown pattern that I couldn't understand. Hell, part of me wanted to think it was random chaos, but there were intricate patterns in the floors, ceilings, and walls that somehow mapped it all out.

It had taken me several days—and Zanaya pointing it out on one of our many walks—for me to notice the tiny details. Inscriptions or delicately drawn images that supposedly told you what level you were on. If I was honest, I still hadn't quite figured it out; there were so many floors to the massive structure.

Thankfully, most of the used rooms, dining halls, and meeting places were on the middle levels. The top was reserved for the throne room and the bottom for all the extra living spaces that the queen had made, so that everyone could live inside the mountain should they need it.

I had been warned that past that were the dungeons, where I thought I heard guttural grumbles and bone-chilling screams coming from. Needless to say, I avoided it at all costs. Taking care not to get too close to the sloping hall that led down, down, down into pure darkness.

I eventually found myself following the soft sounds of a piano. The drifting notes reached my ears, louder and louder the closer I got, pulling me in like a siren.

Walking through an open doorway, I entered what appeared to be a sunroom. I hadn't realized I had made it to the outside of the mountainous structure, but there were large floor to ceiling windows that spanned from wall to wall at the back of the room. The beautiful, blue day shined through. We were high enough above the clouds that it was almost like I could walk across the sky.

Chaise lounges and overstuffed reading chairs dotted the small sitting area. Cherrywood floors and a gold chandelier burning with magic fire gave the room a cozy warmth. The walls were beautifully decorated, paintings of dragon scales and sunbursts scattered about the space.

Standing grandly in front of the windows, the white sun

shining through and creating a halo, was the piano that drew me to the room—silent now—and sitting on its bench, was Kanan.

Hands resting on top of the beautiful instrument, he sat staring out into the distance. As if he could see far beyond the horizon, and well beyond our reach.

Lost in thought as he was, I was able to take all of him in. How his long, lean fingers must have looked playing across the keys. His muscled frame on display for all to see, covered only in the thinnest of undershirts. The white material was nearly see-through in the light of day, his suntanned skin peeking through in tease. His rolled-up sleeves showed off his powerful forearms, corded and strong.

The barely-there shirt was tucked into his trousers, the black leather worn soft and supple, sitting against his thick thighs like they had been painted on. Bare feet poked out from beneath the bench, tan and smooth. With his head turned, I could see the individual curls of his hair, a few inches above the tops of his shoulder. The black was all-encompassing, no light able to penetrate the inky strands.

He appeared to be an artist's muse, escaped from his painting. A fallen angel set free from the stone of his sculptor. Yet no angel could hold a candle to his magnitude, no painter or sculptor would ever be able to render the edge he carried. The feeling that radiated from him spoke of things done in the shadows, as well as the fierce burn his enemies would feel. The rough feeling of tree bark biting into your back, small beads of blood pooling, as you panted with ecstasy.

I could feel my body heat just at the thought, more than happy to test the theory, as I was left wondering if that was just who he truly was—a beautifully savage contradiction. Death's shadow had never seemed more alluring.

"You know, when I was young, I used to think that there could never be anything more beautiful than this." His rich voice ran its velvety hands across my skin, doing nothing to help the ache his presence seemed to cause within me.

Stepping further into the room, I moved to stand in front of the windows, looking out towards the horizon. "And now?"

"Now I know better."

Looking over my shoulder, I caught his eyes, the sunlight making the red gleam like shining rubies.

He went to rise, and I spoke teasingly before I could help it, a mischievous smile gracing my lips as I watched him. "Are you going to hide from your duties today?"

He rose to his full height, my breath still taken away by his size—I barely came up to his collarbone—as he narrowed his eyes. A wicked smirk of his own lifted the corners of his mouth. Coming to stand next to me, he gazed out the window, appearing unaffected.

"I haven't been hiding," he rumbled.

A snort escaped me before I could smother it. "Certainly looks like you were."

He glanced down, his eyes flickering over every aspect of me. His smirk widened, a small chuckle left him as his eyes ignited with a deep, fiery passion, and he spoke softly. "I don't hide, love. Ever."

I hummed my disbelief. "Big claims."

He shrugged those mighty shoulders, his lips twisting into a cocky grin. "Just the truth."

I chuckled, shaking my head at his arrogance, because, to be honest, I did believe him. Nothing about this male spoke of someone who would hide, who would run away from a fight, from what he believed in.

Beneath the clouds, a forest of magic, just as wild and untamed as the man beside me, spread out far and wide. It was beautiful, the purple and indigo leaves nestled on their branches of oak. A quiet river snaked through the trees, cutting a path all the way to where I could see the faintest glint of the sea. It was truly a beautiful sight.

The most striking was the curling trunk of a black tree right in the middle of it all. Standing alone amongst a clearing, it towered above the others. Unlike the rest of the mountain forest, full and flourishing, this one was bare of any leaves. The roots coiled and stretched all around; the large, twisting trunk needing the support. It was stunning and yet somehow melancholic, like it grieved.

I mentioned this to Kanan, turning to ask and finding him already watching me, something he seemed to do a lot.

"The Eskalla Arboritos. The Tree of Balance. It's the spot where Life and Death met, where they became pairs, became whole again for the first time since their separation. The story goes that the tree—the whole of Eskira, really—the mountains, forests, rivers formed when they joined."

"That's the spot?" I looked back at it incredulously, not entirely convinced. The tree was beautiful, no doubt, but it seemed to lack something that spoke of such a momentous moment in time.

He smirked, hearing my disbelief. "It doesn't look how it's supposed to right now. The moment the Goddess left this world, the leaves fell and withered away."

"Oh," I said stupidly, saddened by the thought. Trying to imagine it with leaves, the resemblance dawned on me. It was the same tree as the one on The Divine crest, but whereas this one was bare of its golden leaves, the crest had a full crown of them.

He looked at me from the corner of his eye, the smile still firmly on his face. I had amused the dragon, apparently. *Yippee.*

"How have I not seen this part of Eskira, yet?" Zanaya and Zander had made it their job to take me to every part of the city. We spent many nights exploring the different roads and shops that we found.

"We're on the other side of the mountain. The rooms that face this way were used by The Divine and nothing else. They have been left relatively untouched since their vanishing so as to not disturb their space. So, for the most part no one gets to see the view."

It was such a shame because it was breathtaking. I gazed up at him with an expectant look. "Then how come you get to be here?"

His gaze flickered to my mouth, before meeting my eyes again, leaning in close. "I'm just special like that."

I leaned in as well, whispering conspiratorially, "You're a rule breaker, you mean."

He let out a huffed laugh, stepping closer. He brought his face near mine, mere inches separating our bodies. "Well, if I'm a rule breaker, what does that make you?"

"An accomplice, probably." I felt myself brush against him, the contact scattering my thoughts.

I saw his nose flare, the dragon taking in my scent, as he shook his head slightly. "We should be ashamed of ourselves."

I barely felt myself say, my voice distracted, "So ashamed."

The tug to move into him was strong. Stronger than anything I had ever felt, like I was tied at one end of a rope and him on the other, pulling me closer and closer.

Just as I moved forward, lost in that haze of something unknown, he pulled back slightly. I looked up, wondering what had stopped him.

"Do I frighten you?" His quiet voice held a note of indecision in it, that feral, hungry look still burning hot, yet held back as he waited for my answer.

I furrowed my brow in shock, my answer immediate. "No. Why would you?"

He tilted his head, pupils shifting to diamond slits for a second before speaking in a low grumble, the ferocious dragon that lived inside him rising to show its fangs. "Most sane people are frightened of me. Even my own people fear me, and right-fully so. I could kill every person on this planet, and nothing could stop me." He stated it so simply that I would been lying if I said chills hadn't run down my back. "I've done things that make mothers warn their children to behave for fear that one day when they grow up, I'll be the one coming for them. They're not wrong. I can, I will, and I have."

Without hesitation I stepped into him, reaching up with my hand, tiny in comparison, to cup the side of his face. He exhaled, turning into it as his eyes closed in relief. I gently brushed my thumb down his lips, snagging his bottom one.

He stared down at me through his lashes, half closed in ecstasy, like my very touch brought him all the pleasure in the world.

"Let me explain something to you, Warlord. I spent the past twenty-one years being treated like a monster, an outcast—the thing that hid under the beds of the village children—all because those people saw something different inside me. Saw something that they couldn't possibly understand, even if they had wanted to. A thing to fear. And now that I know what I'm capable of, magical blocks aside, they were right to."

I tilted my head up. "You say you've done things, killed people; well so have I, and something tells me I'll have to do a lot more of it before this is all over."

He leaned his forehead against mine, swallowing harshly as he closed his eyes again tightly, large hands coming to grasp my hips tightly, possessively. His fingers dug in slightly, then released, and tightened again; almost like he was fighting with himself.

Refusing to lose him to his own thoughts, I pressed up onto my toes, rubbing myself up against him as I went, pulling a groan from him. "Maybe I can hold your gaze because some-thing in you recognizes something in me. Maybe I'm just as monstrous as you."

His eyes snapped open, hands settled on gripping me tight as he yanked me into him. "That could never be possible—there's nothing monstrous about you." And then he kissed me, and everything was right in the world.

We both groaned as we came together, grappling at whatever part of each other we could reach. Need raced down my spine as he wrapped my hair around his fist, and I could do nothing but hold on as I yielded to him, allowing him entry.

Pulling on my hair, he tilted my head back as he spun us around, pushing me up against the glass. He bit down on my lower lip with his fangs, licking away the hurt. The kiss was heady and desperate and completely out of control. Both of us lost to the feeling of the other as his wicked tongue stroked mine like he owned it.

Reaching down, he gripped my thighs, easily lifting me. Locking my legs around his hips instinctively, he pressed his cock into me, grinding against my clit through my thin, leather pants.

I let out a whimper as pure pleasure shot down my spine, heat flowing through me like a raging river. Snarling in satisfaction, he kissed me again, the caress of his mouth letting me know that any woman would be lucky to have him between her legs. My core throbbed in response, more than willing to be a participant in that game.

We broke apart, and my eyes met his, both of us pawns to the unseen connection between us. The two of us were stuck in an uncontrollable frenzy, without the ability to stop. The sea of attraction was drowning us both beneath its crashing waves.

He leaned his forehead against mine, our noses brushing, his mouth hovering over mine. "Tell me to stop," he breathed out, a plea in his voice.

"Gods, don't stop," I panted, claiming his lips. I almost sobbed at the thought of stopping, the uncomfortable level of need turning me ravenous for him. Letting out a moan, I moved my hands to his shirt, pulling it free from his trousers.

Moving my hands underneath, I ran them over the dips and valleys of his muscled body. I dug my nails into his skin as he rubbed up between my thighs. Letting out an animalistic, near painful groan, he started nipping down the side of my throat. He dragged his fangs down to the soft spot where my neck met my shoulder, and I closed my eyes, gasping breaths coming out of me as I tilted my head to the side to grant him further access.

That seemed to be the right thing to do, because another rumble of satisfaction rolled through him as he bit down gently with those sharp fangs. I moaned, writhing against him as he lingered on the sensitive spot, unable to pull away from it with his grip so tight, keeping me exactly where he wanted me.

Each tug of his mouth sent a pulse through my body. My core clenched in response, but only gained slight relief from the mindlessly slow rubs from his cock. I scored my nails down his back, no doubt hard enough to leave puckered marks on his bronze skin, helpless to do anything but take the pleasure he was giving me. My neck had always been sensitive, but nothing had ever compared to this.

Even though I knew it would leave a mark, I whimpered for more, causing him to growl against my skin. Of course, the teasing bastard gave me no such relief, continuing his nips and sucks and licks. The too gentle grinding only seemed to keep me enthralled, right on the precipice, but never pushing me over.

Recapturing my mouth with his in an all out assault on my senses, the kiss was carnal and possessive. Each stroke of his tongue only pushing us further into starvation. Wanting, need-ing, more of each other.

One large hand, big enough to span my entire stomach, slipped under my tunic. The roughness from his calluses, defying the Descendents' healing abilities, slid across the skin of my breast. He swallowed my cry as he ran those pianist's fingers over my nipple, and I arched into his touch, rolling my hips into his hardness.

He let out a hiss, pinching the tortured nipple in punishment. I gasped at the feeling, and my breathy response only seemed to spur him on. It was like he knew every button to push, every touch to make, to have me in a puddle, completely at his mercy.

I reached down between us and undid the front lacings of his pants, my breath harsh and jagged. But he stopped, grabbing my hand as he froze. I could almost feel the indecision battling inside him. Lowering me back to the ground, he removed his hand from beneath my tunic and stepped back. His heavy breathing and ferocious eyes were the only indicator that he was as affected as I was by the gut-wrenching attraction between us.

"I'm sorry," he said, before I could even ask what was wrong, already backing away to the door. "We shouldn't have done that. Commander Zuberi will be by later to get you prepared for the ball." The man of shadow moved like one, out the door and into the darkness within seconds.

I stood there, stuck on the precipice of an orgasm, left gasping, horny, confused, and just the slightest bit rejected. He was well within his rights to stop at any time, but I had no idea what I could have done to make him want to.

Did he say ball?

CHAPTER TWENTY-THREE

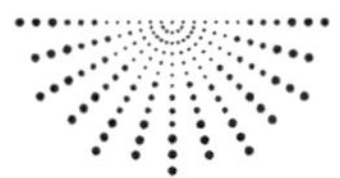

The ball turned out to be even worse than I thought. I had already been dreading it when Zanaya came to get ready, and proceeded to look like she would rather be wraith fodder than attend. It hadn't gotten any better the closer we got to the hall it was being held in. If I hadn't known any better, I would have said she was looking for the nearest cliff to jump off of.

Normal parties, in my opinion, were already something out of the realm of hell, used to torture you with mindless chatter and passive aggressive gossip. Where supposed friends talked behind each other's backs simply to make themselves seem better than the other. To raise their own standing amongst some invisible ranking system that they all graded each other on.

I had always found the idea of them tedious. Even the small ones I had attended very rarely when Maris forced me out of the house for the evening had been boring at best, and a downright massacre of humanity at worst.

Some of my most hated memories consisted of the times when simpering ladies had cornered me in the many alcoves of the town hall that I would hide myself away in for the duration of the dance. They would conceal their vile insults and passively snide comments behind their heavily decorated feather fans. Like aggressive peacocks, they flashed their pretty colors at each other, all the while looking for a way to peck each other's eyes out.

Maybe I was a bit biased, but no social event I had ever been to had gone smoothly. So, I guess I couldn't really say I didn't have a strong opinion on balls. They were fucking awful. That was my opinion. And after seeing Zanaya's reaction, I didn't hold out any hope for Descendent parties to be any different— full of mind-numbing gossip and pretentious people.

As it so happened, it was filled with both. But it was also completely different from any I had ever been to, which wasn't saying much, but I knew that not even the parties held in Vallenia could compete with what was playing out.

The hall was deep inside the city palace, buried under a couple thousand tons of rock, and yet it couldn't have been more open or filled with light. The ovular shaped room was roughly cut into the stone, as most of the rooms in the mountain were.

Vibrant green and gold ivy hung heavy with blooming, spring flowers, that crawled up the supporting pillars before spilling across the stone ceiling. The gilded vines hung down from the rock, and large, waxy leaves glistened with a curious dew that dropped down softly onto the people below.

Orbs of glowing light floated all over the hall, sticking close to the ceiling and out of the way as they illuminated the space. The shimmering balls of energy flickered like miniature suns, no bigger than my fist. The white quartz floor, veined with copper streaks, reflected the hazy yellow color, as if a gold fog had moved in.

The most amazing feature of the room, however, were the large shards of crystal, in every color of the rainbow, that shot out from all directions. They were larger and thicker than trees in some cases, and strong enough that they could hold the Descendents who used them as benches.

The beautiful gemstones showered rays of color down upon the floor whenever one of the glowing orbs got close enough to hit it just right.

And that was just the room.

Fabrics were made of the richest materials, sparkling gemstones that shined like the stars hung from wrists and necks and ears. Some were directly applied to the skin like crystalline body art. The women, and even some men, showed off decorative face paints. Hair was artfully coiffed, ornamental pieces gracing the crowns of many heads.

The peacocking fans of Rhaelyth were replaced by open displays of magic from the Aetherians. Cynths bared their fangs or measured claw length—there had to be a joke in there somewhere—wings of all shapes and sizes, leathered or feathered, were flared on the backs of human forms.

Somehow, I could tell that most of the people present were younger, which for Descendents was probably more relative than anything. Young could be anywhere from decades to hundreds of years old. Maybe it was because of the naïve, youthful air most of them carried; or maybe it was the annoyed and hopeless looks being shot at them by those that had a bit more … sophistication.

Either way, regardless of the collective laughter and the beautifully sensual atmosphere, there was an overall sense of reluctance and exasperation present in the room. From what I could tell, these were not well received parties.

Maybe it was the overlooking Council members sitting at the head table at the front of the hall, raised high above them on a dais. Their watchful gazes were locked in consideration of the amassed people. Their hawk-like eyes making note of every interaction between the two species as if their lives depended on it. Or maybe it was the guards that lined the walls, there to protect or to make sure no one left before the event was over?

"Tell me what the point of this is again?" I asked Zanaya as I watched two Aetherians, the skin of their forearms looking to hold actual flames underneath, toss a ball of fire between them.

She let out a disgruntled sigh. "A couple of centuries ago, the majority of the Council decided that the younger population needed help finding their pairs. According to them, too many of us were losing ourselves to the madness far earlier than those before us." She had an annoyed expression on her face. "They're not wrong; we've gone from having centuries, even millennia, to find our pair before we lose the battle to the madness to now only having decades in some cases. Not everyone has been affected in the same way, obviously." She indicated those that I had marked as being older. "But enough to worry the Council. Much to the annoyance of the rest of us. It's basically a way for them to set up arranged partnerships and maneuver us like pawns in their political game."

"Do you know why the younger generations are having such problems?"

She shrugged her shoulders. "There are just as many theories about it as there are about what happened to the king and queen. The one that makes the most sense to me is that The Divine have been gone for too long. As our king and queen, as well as our creators, they balanced us out in a way not even our pairs can. Merely by existing they kept us together, gave us a longer, more stable life. Being in their presence, I've been told, was to face the powers of the universe, a true balance of all parts of ourselves. I think we have just reached a point where the newest generations have never been exposed to their energy, their power, and it's finally affecting us. Their loss has been felt on many different levels, I don't think we'll ever truly understand the full consequences of it."

I hummed my interest, finding it curious the connection

between the Descendents and their creators went so deep. However, on a foundational level, it made sense. These were people of energy and power. Of planetary elements and worldly animals. Of light and dark.

They were the children, creations, of cosmic beings—they needed that connection to keep them grounded to this plane. So much of each of them—of us—was volatile and unstable, that without the God and Goddess it made sense that the powers within would start destroying each other, and ourselves.

Glancing toward the table of Councilors, I noticed all of them but Cashim were there. I brought my question up to Zanaya.

"Oh, he despises these things as much as the rest of us do, but he gets outvoted every time it is brought up. Even those who try to stay neutral think this is the solution to our bonding problems. My uncle believes that pairings should be formed on their own time, not semi-forced like they are here. He's not wrong; while it may have taken longer, what the Council is doing here is not in any way natural. It skirts the line of being forced, which for pairings can end disastrously."

We started wading our way into the crowd, the hall full of people. "How so?"

Waving to a few people, she smiled at the friendly faces. All the while, I was given curious looks. They weren't hostile, thankfully, most just taking me in before giving me a warm greeting as well. I may have acted like a bitch sometimes, but Maris raised me with manners, so I made sure to not bare my teeth as I smiled back.

"Well, the only real way for pairs to form their bond is for their energy to connect outside of their body, so unless you just walk around with your spark on full display—touching other people's as you go—which is considered very rude, by the way," she warned me, pointing a serious finger in my direction. "Unless you are doing that, then finding your pair can take a long time as there are only certain situations where energies connect like that."

"And the Council is trying to manufacture those types of situations," I guessed, catching on to the idea.

"Exactly, although the way they do is considered by many to be coercive," she said with disdain. Looking up at the ceiling where the golden vines dripped down upon us. "The liquid the vines are creating is called nagexo. In high concentrations, it can be a powerful compulsive drug. In low doses like this it *opens the mind*, as the Councilors like to put it. Basically, it'll make you feed on the energy of your surroundings, so if everyone is having fun and showing off their energies you may be more inclined to do so as well. To me, and to a lot of other people, it feels like they're forcing us into situations where our energies can brush up against each other, which is highly dangerous if the energies decide they really don't like the other."

"What about forced bonds?" I asked out of curiosity, remembering what Chaos had done in the book left for me.

"No one has tried to or successfully forced a bond, thank The Divine." She shivered in horror at the thought. "It would be akin to an assault as a pair bond reaches all aspects of your soul."

But someone had tried, for years, to do just that. If my book was to be believed, Chaos had experimented on Descendents in his quest for power, and he didn't stop until his plans were discovered. How did no one seem to know what I was talking about? How come no one remembered anything?

"Why do people come then?" I questioned, confused as to why the entire population of young Descendents came together every month.

She sighed heavily as we finally got through the crowd. Zander's wild laughter reached us before we could even see him. "Because as much as we hate it, we hate the idea of losing our sanity more." There was a lot packed into that one sentence, resignation the most present.

As we came up on them, it was hard not to stare at the two redheads of the group. Zander and Nala were dressed to impress in their matching red overcoats. Both of them, however, wore no undershirt.

Zander's tan skin was shimmering with some sort of body paint and red gems, the silvery flecks making him sparkle as they hit the light. Nala had a bandeau of crystals across her breasts; unsurprisingly, they had been attached to her skin with nothing else underneath.

They seemed to be the only two who appreciated the opportunity to dress up—the rest still wore their leathers from earlier. Orion, the big, tough mountain of a man, looked downright ridiculous in his gray tailcoats over a silken shirt. He appeared positively ill as he tugged at the collar, his ash grey skin turning a pale white.

All of them were there except for the quiet snake woman, who was an odd piece to the lively group, and yet integral all the same. "Where's Saanvi?"

Zanaya grunted. "Lucky bitch is already paired; happened six years ago when she had barely Awakened. She lucks out every month and gets a night off with her pair and two lovers while we're all stuck in this farce of an event."

The others murmured their agreement, even Zander, the butterfly of the group, as they started up light conversation. I took measure of the room, taking notice of the ones who wanted to be here and the ones that didn't. A dividing line of willingness spoke loudly to the reasons behind such events. Politics. Pairs weren't forced, but they could be strongly encouraged, it seemed.

A shiver worked its way down my spine, like fingers lightly following the curve of my back. My blood began to heat, shocking me as that unfaithful power of mine burst free from its cage, releasing only part of my magic into my bloodstream. I could feel the scorching energy, the well of it inside me responding to something.

The tether in my chest pulled tight, drawing my attention behind me. Like a beating heart, it pulsed steadily, alive and strong. I knew who it was even before my eyes landed on the top step—no one else caused such a physical reaction in me. There was only one person capable of making me feel his presence even before I saw him—the same man who had left me panting and on the edge of finding my release mere hours ago.

Kanan.

The clit-tease in all his glory stood atop the staircase like some king surveying his dominion. The entire floor had gone silent, everyone feeling the energy that shifted when he entered the room, turning to watch the feral predator amongst them pretend that he wasn't a wild storm barely contained. Like he wasn't a beast of shadow and death that could rain a fiery hell upon them if he wished.

Draped in black velvet, his fitted jacket struggling to contain his wide shoulders, the dragon was dressed to the nines. Etched in gold thread, his collar shone in the orb lighting, bringing attention to that irritatingly perfect face. The fallen angel had indeed come out to play tonight, his expression downright sinful.

The slow smirk that appeared on his face was one of sheer confidence; he knew he was the most wanted man in the room —in any room—and he used that to his advantage. He approached everything as if it was a battle to be won, strategy his main ally; if it meant utilizing the physique he had been blessed with, I knew without a doubt he would do it.

Those striking red eyes took in the crowd with a slowness that said he was in no rush, allowing everyone to drink their fill of him, that he was the alpha in the situation, and he would do as he pleased. His eyes ran over the different people, some shifting on their feet or patting their hair, all in hopes of grabbing his attention. That look soon found me like a beacon of a lighthouse, pulling in lost ships at sea.

Taking his time, he walked casually down the steps, hands in his pockets. The crowd parted for him as he walked, some people calling out for his attention, and yet he spared them no glance, his gaze burning intently into me, almost begging me to run. Run away like he had. I could see the dragon beneath egging me on, wanting me to bolt so that he could chase.

I refused, unwilling to give the stupid lizard the satisfaction. I stood straight, spine as stiff as steel as he walked up, stopping directly in front of me, barely acknowledging the bowed heads and respectful nods from my friends.

He slowly looked me up and down, taking his sweet-ass time until I narrowed my eyes and cleared my throat. His gaze met mine, those dark lashes of his casting shadows across his cheeks. His smirk widened into a smile.

"You look divine, Lady Atallia." I forced my body not to erupt in goosebumps at the sound of my name on his lips.

Instead, I raised a taunting brow at the formality. "I feel like a mare brought to auction."

He chuckled, finding my contempt at having to dress up amusing. I truly did dislike it, but I also hadn't stopped myself from admiring the dress Zanaya had brought me to wear.

The entire floor-length gown was made of a nearly sheer, white-gold fabric. The thin straps hung off my shoulders, encircling my upper arms. The sweetheart neckline dipped, showing off my ample cleavage. The bodice cinched at my waist and was held to my body only by small ribbons of fabric that crisscrossed my back. My hip-length golden curls were on full display, and a small circlet of gold-painted leaves and roses made of quartz sat atop them.

The silken fabric slid over my hips like water, hugging every curve I had in a lover's embrace. Deep slits on the front, all the way up to the tops of my thighs, showed off the toned legs that had spent countless hours in a training pit with every step I took.

Despite its form-hugging nature, I found it remarkably easy to move in and, much to my irritation, was so comfortable I probably could have slept in it.

I hated that I loved it.

That didn't stop what I said from being true. I did feel like livestock at a buyout, waiting to be picked from the lineup. I hadn't missed the appraising looks by some of the more interested patrons of the ball, their agenda of finding a potential pair clear in their gazes; or by the Council members whose wariness hadn't changed much from our meeting several weeks ago.

"Regardless, you're more radiant than the sun." I heated under his gaze, both loving and hating my reaction to it. I wasn't one to beg for scraps off the table, and if he wanted to run away from whatever the hell seemed to keep forcing us together, then fine, but I sure as hell wasn't going to simper for compliments.

Conversation gently picked back up, but I could see out of the corner of my eyes how our entire interaction was being analyzed. Some probably wondered why their warlord would ever stoop so low as to interact with me. Others were calculating how they could use me to their advantage if I had Kanan's attention. I could see it in the way they mentally put me in a different group than I had been before, my worth to them increasing with every word Kanan spoke to me.

"Thank you for the kind words, Lord Kanan, but if you'll excuse me, I was in the middle of a conversation with my friends."

I watched his eyes darken with emotion before it was hidden away behind his walls. His smile grew in spite of my rejection, not taking it as one at all, it seemed, as he quickly reached his hand out. "I was actually hoping to ask for a dance from you."

I stared up into his eyes, the music changing as if on cue to a soft melody that spoke of passion and enchantment. He kept his hand out, patiently waiting for my answer. His eyes dared me to take it. They spoke without words. Whispering in my ear to not turn away from him.

"I'm not a very good dancer," I told him, fully expecting to make a fool of myself.

The corners of his lips lifted further. "I'm sure that's not true; you just have to follow my lead."

I narrowed my eyes at him as I placed my hand in his, already expecting the warm grip, the rough calluses that I had become so familiar with but a few hours ago. I found it hard to focus on anything but how those hands felt on my body, how his strong grip had only made me want more. The bites and nips down my throat, that did indeed leave a mark. How every second of the encounter had been playing in my head on repeat all day.

The snarls, the moans, my nails scraping down his chest like some wild animal leaving their mark. Done in a feral haze of pure passion, dealt by a connection neither of us understood. Every gasp, every groan of pleasure, the feeling of his cock grinding into me all floated through my head as we walked through the parting crowd to the dance floor.

I couldn't help but feel his commanding grip on my hair, my leg, as he gripped me now, getting us into position. The naked need in his eyes, bare and unashamed, had me by the throat.

My only savior was the reminder that he had run from me, leaving me to finish myself off. The panic that crossed his face for a fleeting moment as he backed away was an emotion I never thought I would see on a man so in control of himself.

"You are annoyed with me; I can see it in your face." He spoke softly as we began to dance together, his hands tight around my hips as he led me in the first steps.

"I don't know what you're talking about," I replied as we

separated, our hands coming up between us, palms facing each other but not touching—barely an inch between them—as we circled each other. Our eyes stayed locked, even as those around us mimicked our motion, a test of wills that neither of us seemed willing to lose.

He smirked at my icy reply, stepping in close to me as we switched directions, leaning down to whisper in my ear, "Oh, I think you do, or did I mistake your moans and whimpers for something else?"

I refused to give him the satisfaction of seeing me blush, so instead I replied, "Really, because the way I remember it, you up and ran before you could get the job done."

My smirk was a little evil as I peered into his face. Our bodies molded together as we swung into the middle of the floor, while the dancers all around did their best to look as if they weren't trying to overhear our conversation.

"Easy there, love. You could bruise a man's ego with a tongue like that," his easy timbre rumbled next to my ear.

"Just telling the truth. If you can't handle it … well, I guess you know what they say about overcompensating. Truly, if you were intimidated by me, you could have just said so and saved us both the time. There was no need to run away."

He stopped us dead in the middle of the floor, hands gripping me tightly to his chest. Tight enough for me to feel his heart beating through his jacket. He bent his head down, his thunderous brow creased in emotion I couldn't understand.

"I didn't run away, I—"

"Hastily retreated," I cut him off, not able to help myself as I lifted my chin, refusing to bow down to the commanding glare he sent my way.

"I didn't run," he ground out, his jaw clenched tight, fingers digging into my skin, the strength behind them only making me wish that he would grip harder.

"Gods, if you knew the will it took to force myself out of that room …" He scoffed, shaking his head. "You wouldn't be teasing me right now; you would be the one running from me. Because when I look at you, all I can think of is how easy it would be to carry you off to some remote area, somewhere no one could find us, and tie you up until I've had my fill of you."

I swallowed hard, the image burning itself into my mind so that I could never forget it. My stomach clenched in response, my entire body pulsing with the fire he seemed to fan inside me.

He lowered his head, his nose brushing against mine. "I assure you, love, it wouldn't be quick. No, I think I would quite enjoy the sight of you tied up and at my mercy. I would want to take my time."

My breath came out ragged and shaky. "Then why did you leave?"

I watched in confusion as a mask fell into place. His mouth flattened, nostrils flaring wide as his eyes almost shuttered with how quickly he closed down.

Looking away, he opened his mouth before closing it again, the words getting stuck in his throat. Shaking his head, he released a big sigh. "I wish I could explain. I really do, but there are some things that you just wouldn't understand right now."

"You know, I'm really tired of not *understanding* anything about my own life." I huffed out a chuckle, frustration making me want to tear my hair out. "You're not even lying to me, and yet I still can't get a straight answer."

He winced but said nothing, continuing to keep his omissions to himself. The same old shit, just from a different person. I tried not to think about the sharp sting in my chest, nor the part of me that had hoped he wouldn't be like the rest. I should have known better; nothing in my life had been easy, had ever gone smoothly. Why would this?

I had always been a physical creature. It wasn't an easy thing being surrounded by people that hated me, but I found ways around it. Brief dalliances with the occasional traveler. Never anything that would amount to a true relationship, one of feelings and companionship, but it was enough to satisfy the itch that demanded to be scratched.

And now here I was, standing with a man to whom I was irrevocably connected to in some way, whose very touch made my blood boil and my heart race, and yet not even he was immune to the plague of lies that followed me.

I could see the indecision in his eyes, the war that seemed to tear him apart from the inside, and still he said nothing. Lies were like the sun, a constant in a world of chaos, unperturbed by such a thing as truth.

Pain and sympathy radiated from him as he reached out for me. "Atal—"

I felt the shockwave first, rolling through the room like thunder. Then a force smashed into me, pushing into my chest until I was flying through the air. A loud, cacophonous boom shook the mountain palace as the entire side wall exploded.

CHAPTER TWENTY-FOUR

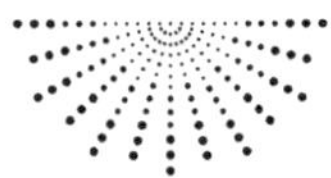

There had been many things in my life that had brought me to the realization that pain and suffering were just as much a part of life as pleasure and joy. That it was the natural order of it to be filled with all forms of emotions. Just like death, it was neither good nor bad, it just was.

That doesn't mean when bad shit happened we didn't curse our creators for putting us in such a situation; even if they had no part in it. We needed someone to blame, so why not them? Why not the very beings who emanated these universal forces? Weren't they the ones who put us in this mess?

In actuality, I believed they were just as stuck as the rest of us, doomed to watch the cycle of existence over and over again. The joy, the pain, forever etched in their memories. Just as I knew this moment would be in mine.

The ringing in my ears brought me back, gasping for breath as I pushed up onto my knees. I choked on the dust in the air, my vision blurring, as drowned out screams and cries came from all around me.

Looking around, all I saw was rubble, chunks of rock, and the large beautiful crystals littering the entire hall. A huge chunk of the stone wall had fallen right where I had been standing. I tried not to look at the blood smeared across the floor, leaking out from underneath. I guess this was one of those times Zanaya was talking about, where Descendents could sustain injury from massive trauma.

It was sheer chaos in the hall, people panicking and pulling at those stuck beneath the rubble. Most weren't soldiers, but even the ones that were seemed completely bewildered. But it quickly became apparent what to do as shapes appeared in the giant hole in the wall. They streamed in, silent as Death himself, wielding blades of black and white.

I expected wraiths, but no, they were humanoid; infection ran across their mostly naked bodies, black and green with disease. I watched in horror as they rushed the confused Descendents stabbing out with their blades, some dropping dead the minute the daggers pierced their bodies.

Others fell unconscious and were dragged off through the gaping hole, everyone too distracted to notice. I stood, my legs shaking with effort. Pulverized stone fell from where I had been covered in debris. Looking around, I rushed over to the first fallen person I saw, a young woman whose leg was caught underneath a slab of rock.

I was nearly there when a corrupted attacker charged me, eyes empty and soulless; yet it came for me with a determination that was unnatural.

The woman's formerly blonde hair was lank and greasy, sweat-drenched and patchy. Her skin was pale and had a sickly tint to it, covered in lesions with black tar oozing out from beneath her blood-soaked bandeau.

I pulled the black heartsglass dagger I had hidden on the inside of my thigh, and even dazed, it was not hard to deflect her attack, body weak and decaying like the wraiths'. Dodging her reaching grasp, I spun around her before punching my dagger up between her ribs, straight into her heart. The creature, no longer a woman, made a gasping croak before falling over dead.

Another took its place, teeth bared in a snarl, ink black blood dripping from it mouth. It, he, charged me. Swiping out with a clawed hand, I ducked to avoid it before I could be eviscerated.

Darting in close, I punched my fist into his sternum, knocking him back a few feet. The creature stumbled, losing its footing on a chunk of crystal. Taking the opening, I jumped on top of the writhing man-beast, showing my dagger down into its throat.

Blood spurted onto my face as I yanked the blade out, the thick substance warm and smelling of rot.

I didn't allow myself to dwell, rushing over to the young girl, her pink feathered dress covered in dust and blood. She whimpered in pain even as she tried to lift the rock off her trapped legs. It barely budged, all her strength and energy zapped from the trauma. She looked up at me as I neared, pleading with her eyes for me not to leave her to be picked off like a wounded deer by a pack of wolves.

"Help me," she gasped, breathing hard like she was struggling, blood spurting out of her lips. "Please, help me."

Her labored breathing worried me as I noticed bruising already forming on her bare chest. So close to the wall she must have been pelted by rock after rock, possibly shattering some of her ribs. Even Descendents had a limit. They may be immortal, but they could still get injured; they just couldn't die from it. Which, in some cases, was more a curse than a gift.

Major trauma forced them to utilize all their energy to keep themselves alive. The girl couldn't lift the rock because had she been mortal, her heart and lungs would have collapsed, pierced by her ribs. Only her magic was keeping her alive and breathing.

Looking over my shoulder, making sure nothing was

creeping up behind us, I saw terror in the flesh. More bodies seemed to be lying on the floor than not, and the ones still standing were fighting to escape. I saw a flash of long, red hair before another small explosion sent corrupted bodies flying. I breathed out a silent sigh of relief that Nala was fighting, giving me hope that the rest of them were still alive.

I tried not to think about where Kanan was, knowing he would be fighting if he could, which only served to worry me even more. Shaking myself, I turned back, holding my dagger clenched between my teeth as I squatted down, thankful for the slits on my dress as I fit my hands underneath the large chunk of stone, hoping that my newfound strength wouldn't be as flaky as my magic.

I breathed out, air rushing out the sides of my mouth, before I lifted up with all my strength. I felt it as it happened, the strain disappearing as my body burst alive with energy, my cells soaking up the power like a plant did the sun. My muscles flexed, filled to the brim with a new vigor that had me lifting the stone like it was a piece of paper.

I held it up as the woman dragged her body out from beneath, her face pinched in utter agony. I was impressed by her will as she pulled herself from the wreckage far enough for me to set the thousand-pound rock down.

I dropped down next to the girl, her breathing easing only slightly. Her eyes fluttered as her brain tried to turn her body off to rest. She locked gazes with me briefly, a small, relieved smile lifting her blood spattered lips as she breathed out a whispered, "Than—Thank you."

Her head lolled to the side as she fell unconscious finally. Checking her pulse, I looked around, finding more and more of the corrupted filing in through the hole. The civilians had been pushed behind the fighters, shooting what magic they had when they could; those that could help others who had fallen or been crushed were doing so.

Sheathing my blade, I picked the girl up, not even feeling her weight as I ran her over to the far side of the hall, hiding her in a dark alcove. As I set her down, I felt hands grasp me by the shoulders, nails digging into my skin before jerking me back.

Losing my footing, I dropped to the ground as I was dragged across the hall. Kicking out, twisting and turning, I fought the grip on the back of my dress. The assailant lost their grip, but as I went to stand, another came out of nowhere to pin my arms, wrestling me onto my stomach, the grit digging into my face.

I grunted and swore as the two tried to pick me up. I writhed and kicked and screamed, knowing that in the chaos no one was coming to help, too busy with the wave of attackers pinning them against the opposite wall. Another set of hands grabbed my bucking legs. I kicked out, landing a blow to the chest, I thought, but just as they were free, a weight settled on top of them, like a body laying across me. My strength seemed to barely phase them, power of their own flowing through their veins.

"Gods dammit, just hold her still!" a male voice yelled above me and shock froze me in place for a split second.

Wraiths, the corrupted, didn't talk. I could smell the decay wafting from the things around me, knew the creatures had a hold of me, but there was someone else. Someone who was still alive, sentient enough to talk, and who was attempting to kidnap me of their own free will.

I couldn't even register the surprise that rushed through me because the person had taken advantage of my disbelief, and even with the bodies weighing me down, I could feel us moving across the floor, getting us closer and closer to the blown-out wall.

With a renewed fervor, I fought against the hands on me, trying to wrestle my arms free from the tight grip they were held in. The futile struggling only made me more frustrated; my anger rose like a serpent of fury. Focusing inwards, I beat against the shimmering wall that kept my power blocked. All my attention fell on the one weak spot, leaking the smallest hint of my actual power.

I shouted and screamed, my rage, my anger, my fury, a hammer against the barrier. All my hate and shame and guilt acted as a spear to pierce the obstacle in my path. Anxiety, helplessness, and fear wormed their way through the fissures.

And with a mighty scream, the wall cracked underneath the force, a shockwave of energy bursting out of me. The surge of power knocked all the hands away, lifting the weight of the limp bodies from me, before slipping back behind the wall. The shimmering barrier was nearly perfect if not for the fracture, now significantly bigger, marring its face.

I wasn't even mad about it, taking the relief I was given without complaint. Pushing up onto my feet, I pulled my dagger free. Breathing hard, adrenaline flooding my body as my eyesight became sharper and my hearing more acute.

A groan had me looking over to my right to see a man getting to his feet. His dark brown hair was dusty, rock and glass stuck in the strands. His wide set shoulders were covered in a nondescript, black tunic, an emblem of some kind on the breast, his legs clad in worn leather.

He was impressively plain, and then he wasn't, and then he was abnormally normal in a way that had the hair on the back of my neck standing to attention. His features were both handsome and not, completely stunning and average at the same time. Was his nose flat or crooked? Were his eyes blue or green? Hazel, maybe? Was he tan or pale? It felt like every second his face shifted features, never seeming the same.

He locked eyes with me, a sentience that I knew no corrupted wraith, or whatever possessed the infected people, was capable of. His eyes glinted with sharp intelligence, his full —thin—lips lifting in a sneer. He took one step toward me and then the entire world went dark as a roar promising death filled the cavernous room.

I braced myself, blind in a way I'd never experienced. A darkness that was born from the shadows of the world. The night itself wasn't this dark, wasn't this overwhelming. This was the color of death.

I flinched as the screams of creatures and people alike filled my ears. My muscles were tense, my eyes trying their hardest to find any light, failing miserably.

Sheer agony, croaks of the dying, was the only noise. I heard the splatter of blood, the crunch of bone and flesh. I tasted the fear in the air. The cool touch of Death's Champion curled around my ankles even as sounds of muscle being ripped, torn apart beneath claws of onyx continued.

I had always loved the dark; a shadowy caress across my pale skin, my golden hair. The beauty in it could be found in its versatility, the ability to bring about things of wonder, but also of fear. To terrorize one and fascinate another.

And then it went quiet, a silence I had only heard in the wake of a massacre, my nightmares haunting me even now. Not a single soul dared to draw the attention of the primal creature who walked with Death.

Then I heard it. The gurgling, a slow drip falling to the floor. A choked sound, a gasp for breath as the darkness pulled back. I covered my eyes; even the dim light from the few glowing orbs still left was too much after the jet black emptiness.

Blinking away the glare, I saw the creator of the inky haze; the absence of light not able to pull back all the way, wrapping around him like a cloak of slithering snakes, whipping out into the air in furious agitation.

The crowd of partygoers, the ones still alive and present, stood behind the warriors, who had their weapons drawn. They were exhausted and dust covered, shock on every face in the bloodied group—much smaller than it was to begin with.

Several people were digging others out of the rubble, able to do so without worry now that Kanan had killed … everyone.

Amidst the fear was a bloodthirsty hunger. Anger pulsed through the crowd, feeding off of their true leader even as Council members could be seen among the crowd, several of them holding weapons of their own.

Cashim stood next to Zanaya, and I let out a breath I didn't realize I was holding, relief filling my lungs once more. The rest of my new friends were behind them, looking on at the scene unfolding before them.

Kanan's chest heaved with harsh breaths, his chest bare, scraps of fabric hanging off his muscled body, and covered in pulverized rock and blood. The pile that would have crushed me, where the blood had been leaking, was nothing but a few small bits of rock and crystal. Completely disintegrated.

He had pushed me out of the way, I realized, allowing the brunt of the explosion to pulverize him beneath. I couldn't even tell if the blood was his or not, despite the sheer amount covering him. And in his clenched hand, claws digging in as red flowed over, was the man with the shifting face.

The bodies of the attackers lay dead at his feet, offerings to his unimaginable power. The man's features would have been unrecognizable regardless of his powers, so beaten and bloody he would have looked dead were it not for his hands tearing at Kanan's grip, the kick of his feet trying to meet the ground once again.

His loud rumble was all dragon, fury too tame a word for what rode the waves of that sound. His gaze was locked in on the man who, to his credit, did his best not to piss himself in front of the dragon. With a roar, Kanan threw the man across the room, the weight of a full-grown person nothing in comparison to his strength.

He flew through the air like a rag doll before smacking against rock and metal. A crunching sound followed him as he rolled to a stop a few feet in front of me, unmoving except for a hacking cough.

Kanan turned with a predatory grace, eyes focused on his prey, as he slowly stalked toward the fallen man. Every step, every breath he took, made him look bigger than before. His foot fell silently on the floor and the mountain shook in response. The vibrations rattled the ground, glass and crystal ringing. The great mountain structure trembled in fear of this male, a beast living in his skin that could shake the universe.

One of the corrupted soldiers, lying half dismembered on the floor, moaned quietly. Using the one arm it had left, it tried pulling itself out of the way of the oncoming danger.

Kanan watched it, a mixture of boredom and annoyance on his savage face. As if attached to a hook, the creature was lifted into the air before him, body hanging limply even as it shook in pain.

The dragon tilted his head, shadows writhing around him, the darkness around the room seeming to move forward. With the barest twitch of his clawed hand, the creatures neck snapped from an invisible force. It dropped to the ground with little care, crumbling into a heap before Kanan.

His blood eyes shot back up, the animal inside him once again locked on his prey. He stalked forward, the dead sack of skin and blood sliding out of his way.

A manic laughter bubbled up from the man in front of me, shaky and broken as blood splattered the floor. It got louder and louder, more crazed even as Kanan continued toward him, unperturbed. "You'll never keep her safe. He saw her Awakening, and he's coming for her."

Kanan only growled in response, low and rough, the sound of a hunter before he pounced. However, I looked at the man, picking up on what he just said.

"Kanan!"

The fiery red eyes only burned brighter, the diamond slits dilating. His strong gait did not pause.

Running past the broken man, I moved in front of the angry dragon, stopping in his path. I ignored the cackle from behind me, focusing all my attention on the embodiment of death. "Kanan, you can't kill him—we need to find out what he knows."

His eyes didn't even glance in my direction, lost to his own rage. Walking straight up to him, stopping him in his tracts, I grabbed his face. My hands looked almost childlike compared to his size. He flinched at my touch, and the haze cleared slightly across his eyes.

Forcing his gaze to meet mine, I stared into the fire and heat trapped inside. Actual flames dancing in those irises. "You can't kill him, however much fun that might be …" I peered over my shoulder at the sneering smile, nose scrunching in distaste. "We need him, unfortunately."

He let out a low grunt before saying roughly, "He tried to take you."

"Yes, but we'll never figure out why unless he's alive," I replied reasonably, even though all I wished was to let Kanan finish him off.

He looked at me for a long moment without saying anything, and then he pulled out of my grip. He walked around me, over to the man crumpled on the floor, and grabbed his tunic in his fist.

Pulling him up off the floor slightly, Kanan gazed down at the man, a battle being fought inside him; and then the man just stopped moving, eyes rolling to the back of his head.

Dropping the unconscious man, Kanan casually walked away from the broken body. He strode towards me intently, his eyes wholly fixated on me. "Are you alright?"

I stared at him, mouth gaping, his entire body bloodied. A fine layer of dust covered his rich, black curls, even more blood ran from his mouth, turning his pearly white canines red. I started looking for injuries, staring at the crazy male in concern. "Are you?"

He shouldn't be walking. No one, not even the Descendents, should have been able to walk away from being buried alive underneath several tons of stone. He should have been in worse condition than the woman in the pink dress, but here he was looking half dead and asking me if I was okay.

He didn't answer my question, his glowing gaze insistent. I realized he had no intention of moving on to deal with other things, his body as still as a statue on a quiet night. Even as extra guards who, too late, started arriving in the destroyed hall and began calling his name. Stretchers were carried in and decisions needed to be made, but he didn't move. Waiting.

I looked him over once more before nodding, quietly whispering, "I'm alright, but Kanan, those warriors." I nodded to some of the corrupted lying dead on the floor, their faces familiar. "Those were the comatose soldiers from the battle. They need to go to Cashim and Lilyi. We need to know what we missed."

He came to life, nodding once before moving like a man possessed, shouting out orders left and right. His usual smooth and sensual voice boomed with a powerful compulsion behind it. Within a second, he had grabbed everyone's attention and forced them to listen—an alpha calling them all to heel.

"Take him to the cells," he said, pointing to the broken man lying unconscious on the destroyed floor. "Bring the dead corrupted to Lord Cashim. Do not deviate from your task. If he does not receive them in the next hour, you will have to answer to me. Do you understand?" The commanding voice demanded obedience, and threatened punishment for those that did not listen. "Now."

The guards were quick to shout their acceptance of their tasks, the warlord taking over, already on the move again as dozens of voices came together as one. "YES SIR!"

CHAPTER TWENTY-FIVE

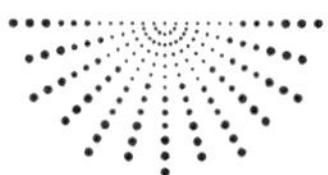

The mountainside was covered in a thick fog, respectfully quiet in honor of the mourning. The sun did not dare shine brightly on such a day. The gray clouds above reflected the feelings below; grief a potent element among the gathered crowd. A cool breeze worked its way across the cliff-side, brushing against the tear-stained cheeks in sympathy.

No birds rode the wind—all wings of flight had been driven to the ground by the heavy weight of sorrow. The sky was bare of its colors, a pale canvas blank of any inspiration except for the cries of its painters. Wails wrapped around me like the black shrouds that covered the dead.

No one slept the previous night. Everyone worked through the dark hours to collect the bodies and treat the wounded. A census of the party showed that several more had been kidnapped and taken back out through the exploded wall. The guards who had been standing sentry over the side entrance, which happened to lead in from the city, had been found dead.

They had been killed by the sick warriors who had stayed dormant until something had awoken them. Cashim had confirmed that they were all from the infirmary and had killed several healers on their way out. No one knew until it was too late. We had let corruption into our stronghold, riding in on the wounds of our own people, and learned the hard way exactly what the disease had in store for the Descendents.

Morale was nearly nonexistent as the procession made its slow march through the solemn halls of the breached palace, through the empty streets of the lower city, and out to a far cliff that overlooked the gulf. Mist rose from the forest all around, clouds hanging low in reverence of the too many pyres that sat atop the rocky face.

Lanterns had been carried on carved poles, lighting our way through the darkness, so as to not get carried into death alongside the lost. A woman's voice rang over the silent cliff, overflowing with sadness, singing the songs of passing. Guiding the souls into the afterlife, into the embrace of their God.

The shrouded bodies had been set upon their pyres with respect and gentle hands, carried to their resting place by friends and loved ones. Tears wet the eyes of all, the deep pain felt by thousands.

The flat ground was covered in green grass and vibrant blooms that lined the edges of the clearing. They brought an unexpected beauty to a place filled with such agony. A large, jutting stone split the space in half, standing sentry over the victims. The crowd gathered on either side, waiting as families said their last goodbyes. The ground beneath the pyres was charred black, burned and cracked all the way to the rock beneath.

How many pyres had to have been lit, how many wails had to shatter the skies, to scorch stone? The bedrock marked with the grief of this place.

I stood next to Zanaya, off to the right of the large stone, watching the proceedings with overwhelming heartache. It wasn't hard to pick out those that had been affected by such an atrocious attack, even though all of us were dressed in mourning black—the heaviness of their shoulders set them apart.

Some, who I suspected had lost their pairs, appeared to be lifeless. Hope had drained from their eyes the same as Harrison's had after the attack on the eastern wall. They stood, held up by those around them, with the expression of someone who had just lost their will to live and had yet to gather the courage to end it all. Zanaya told me some would survive the torment.

Most wouldn't.

The cost of bonding to your pair it seemed. A wound so deep, an anguish so inexplicably painful, you might as well have been killed yourself.

Salty streaks lined Zanaya's beautiful face, her heavy gaze looking out across the field. We were lucky, our friends and family made it through the horrible attack nearly unscathed, and yet the crushing pain coming from her spoke differently.

As if she could feel my question, she turned to look at me, a deep sadness in her eyes. "My mother was killed when I was four. She and my father were pairs, and when she died my father fell into madness."

"Zanaya," I started, not wishing to make her relive such painful memories.

"It's okay," she choked out, shaking her head, a wan smile on her lips. I quieted, letting her finish.

"They were beautiful together." She smiled, happiness in her every word. "So beautiful. I still remember how they would dance in the living room together, or how my mom would sing me lullabies until I fell asleep, my father looking on from the doorway. She was his everything."

A tear dripped down her face. "Before she met him, she had a lover, but once she knew who my father was, it didn't take long before it was over between them. She tried to do it right, tried to not let the bond mold into one of love. She never wanted to hurt anyone, my mom," she said, her memories, words, so full of love.

"But she couldn't help falling for him anyway, and so she ended things with her lover. He didn't take it well, to say the least. Even years later he was still bitter."

Her brow wrinkled, "I don't know what did it, if maybe he finally snapped, or if it was because he saw how happy they were with me, but one night he snuck into our home and stabbed her with black heartsglass."

Her voice held the pain and confusion of a young girl, who didn't fully understand why her life had been changed forever. "My father went mad within a day, and nearly killed half a dozen people."

I closed my eyes, shining tears streaking down my cheeks, unable to comprehend the horror she faced at such a young age.

"And so I lost my mother and father, and my uncle had to kill his brother." She let out a heavy sigh, "That's why I don't do well with these kinds of things, it just reminds me of them."

I didn't know what to say. No words could help, could fix, what had happened to her and her uncle. Doing the only thing I could think of, I reached over and grasped her hand tight, giving her the silent support I wished I could have given her as a child. Silently thanking her for sharing her memories, both good and bad.

She looked over at me, icy blue eyes bright with tears. Giving me a grateful, watery, smile, she squeezed my hand before turning back to the procession.

Once everyone had fallen back into the crowd, some grief-stricken people having to be carried as their tears stained the ash-colored ground, the red-robed flame bearers set their poles all around the clearing. Stepping one foot back, they crossed their arms over their chests in an X, bowing their heads.

Cashim and the Council members stepped out of the group and came to stand beneath the jutting rock. They were dressed, for once, not in their house colors and crests, but in the same black as everyone else. Their shoulders were straight even as their faces held the pinched sadness that flowed like a river through the people.

I, however, did not miss the slight flash of annoyance on Lars's face as Cashim stepped forward from their little group, probably irritated that he wasn't the one presiding over the ceremony.

"Today is a day of great sadness, a day that will be marked in our histories forever. Not because of triumph or magnificent joy, but because of an aching grief that will haunt us for centuries to come." Cashim's lyrical voice, music in its own sort of way, was subdued even as the words reached far and wide. He had no need to shout, for no one was able to mumble a word past their own misery.

"I've always said that being one of us, being of The Divine, is a great gift that was given to us. One we could never repay even if we tried. And yet it is days like today that make me rethink my own words, my own beliefs. For maybe if we weren't so intrinsically part of the magic in this world, if maybe we were as mundane as mortals, then this pain would not follow us through the millennia."

His voice held steady even as it dropped slightly, his own memories of pain and loss seemingly pulled up through the void by the suffering of others. "I wish I could tell you that it won't, that your time here on this planet, extended beyond belief, will be filled with anything but sorrow and pain. That each new day will be brighter than the day before … but I can't tell you that."

Tears welled in the crowd's eyes, falling freely without shame. Today everyone felt their cool, salty touch.

"I have been alive only two millennia, a blink of time in the eyes of the Cosmos, but I can tell you that in such time I have felt more than maybe one person should be allowed to feel. The grief and pain of loss, the happiness and joy of gain." His icy gaze slips over to Zanaya, a small smile briefly lifting his lips at the sight of his niece. "Pain. Happiness. Grief. Joy. Maybe this is the curse that we are bound to suffer, by feeling everything Life has to offer us without the peaceful embrace of Death"—he paused, taking in a deep breath—"but we do feel that embrace. However immortal we may be, we are still at the mercy of existence, and every beginning has its ending. No matter how long it takes, how many years we may see, we will eventually pass through the same gates as everyone and everything else."

"Many fear Death. His darkness and great power. They see and fear it as the last of who they are, and in a sense that is true, for our time as we are when we pass has come to its end. However, as Descendents we know better. We know that stepping into Death is not just an end, it's the beginning of something new. Possibly something better."

"So, I will leave you with this," he said, looking around at the people. "Do not fear what our mothers and fathers, our sons and daughters, our brothers and sisters have to face, for they are on a new path. One that we may not be able to see or follow behind, but one we can believe is better than the one they walked before. Guided by our God, consoled and comforted by our Goddess, they are where they are meant to be. So grieve, but do not mourn the lives they've lost. Look on with hope at what they may discover next."

He stepped back, and Lady Lilyi reached out to grasp his hand, giving it a squeeze. He looked down at her with a small smile as he wiped the salt from his face.

His words echoed in my head, the beautiful speech making it hard not to feel the current of the hope he spoke of. The gathering felt it as well, spines straightening and faces being wiped clean. Tears still flowed, and sadness still beat its painful song, but a new melody was carried with it. One that spoke of a horizon, of the sun rising above it the next day and the day after that.

Women dressed in white slip dresses, golden chains hanging down from their belts, moved out of the thick fog. Their voices were carried across the wind as they began to sing as one. The sound rang across the valley, hauntingly beautiful. Down past the silent forest, across the sorrowful sky, it wove a tale of new hope. Though it was made up of no actual words, I could still hear the message, the high arching notes hinting at reverence and passing, urging on the souls of the lost, helping guide them into the realm of Death.

Men with fiddles joined in, stirring emotions and forcing you to move with the sounds, the strings only adding to the alluring call. Pulling you into the music, guiding the living souls as well as the dead.

I felt the breeze pick up, blowing my curls across my face, before I heard the gentle flapping. Looking up, I saw Kanan descending from the sky in his magnificent form. Onyx scales glinted even without the sun shining down, each as reflective as a mirror. His two arcing horns pierced the sky, and his giant wings sent a shadow across the gathering.

The song of sorrow and hope continued as he landed gently on the jutting outcrop in the middle. Settling on his four legs, bigger than the Blackwood trunks, his wings folded inward gracefully. The long tail, edged in black spines, ended in one sharp point, as deadly as any one of his claws or fangs. He curled it off to the side, hanging over the edge of the rock that he barely fit on.

I had the distinct urge to race over and run my hand down one of those scales, needing to see if they were as smooth and hot as they looked; like freshly polished lava stones. Those burning eyes, alight with flames, swept over the crowd. The ancient power that was held within the breast of such a creature was barely contained. The anger, fury, and grief that held everyone within its grasp poured off him in waves.

He turned my way, and the stunning crown of horns never

ceased to amaze me. I looked into those endless eyes, that gaze that held years well beyond his actual age. The swirling maroon was a whirlpool, pulling me deeper and deeper in. A pulse of red flashed outward from the diamond pupils, dilating as a glow began to build.

Shifting his gaze to the funeral pyres, the rock creaking underneath him, he pulled back to his full height. Towering over all of us by several hundred feet, he flared his wings wide, the black membrane semi-transparent.

Rearing back, he opened his maw, the bright orange-red light building, before thrusting his head forward and releasing a mighty breath of flame that completely engulfed the pyres. The fire crackled as we watched, the wood logs snapping in half before being reduced to nothing. Within seconds everything was ash—the pyres, the bodies, gone—and new char marked the ground. Smoke rose from the cracks in the rock, ash still burning with the last few embers.

Shadows began pouring out from his scales, curling from underneath his claws. They raced from the hidden depths of rocky crevices, covering his massive form in a giant, ebony cloud. Swirling up and up, it was so thick and dark I couldn't see anything beyond it. An absence of space. A hole in the world.

Until they fell to the ground, exploding out and dissipating into the air. Standing where the dragon was, Kanan's human form walked out of the darkness. The shadows that popped from his skin, living parts of his body, flicked and tightened around his biceps like bands of dark metal.

His hard, toned body was bare from the waist up, leaving his chest on display. Black markings had been painted onto his chest and crawled up his neck, caressing his jaw—hard, angular lines and patterns that only added to his feral edge. He was as deadly and awe-inspiring in human form as he was in dragon. The pulse of the wild beat beneath his skin, the slightly faded outline of dark scales patterned across his arms, the dragon sitting just beneath the surface.

The crowd stared, enraptured by his presence, by the markings, hanging onto his very breath. The air around him wavered with his power. His footsteps were silent, though I could feel every step shaking my bones.

"I am not a man of many words, as you all know," his voice boomed with that unnatural quality once again, carrying a weight it normally didn't. "I find that actions hold more meaning. Words can lie—they can omit—and they can make false promises. So, know that my words here today are only spoken to prepare you for my actions."

He stood stoically upon the rock, meeting the wet eyes of the crowds, the weakened bodies of the grieving. His face tightened almost imperceptibly in anger and grief, his rich voice reverberating with force against the mountainside, in a way that the universe, the Cosmos himself, could hear his intentions.

"I have failed you all. Our enemies were allowed to take something precious from us today that can never be given back. Something that *I* cannot give back. It is a shame that will stay with me forever. I will not give you pretty words of hope, nor tell you that there won't be more days like today, because I would be lying. But know this ..." He paused, his face twisting with righteous fury. "I will hunt our attackers down, and I will take from them what they have taken from us. I will not stop until their heads are mounted upon spikes and their blood spilling across this ground. I made the mistake of thinking that our isolation and solitude would protect us from outside forces, and that mistake has cost us dearly."

His chest heaved, bringing more attention to the markings running down his body. His hands clenched into fists, and his eyes hardened to lead. "Never again will I allow us to be caught off guard and unprepared. I will never again allow such a heedless slaughter." His voice grew quiet, apologetic. "It should have never been allowed in the first place. Starting today, retribution will begin its hunt, vengeance will taste the blood of its prey, and justice will be served."

His four fangs were bared as three-inch jet claws slowly curled out from his fingers, shadows weaving between them. Flames grew higher in the shine of his eyes, and as he turned his back, heading off towards the palace, I could see the outline of large membranous wings underneath the layers of scars on his back.

War had just been called by the Champion of Death, and I feared for anyone who stood in his way.

CHAPTER TWENTY-SIX

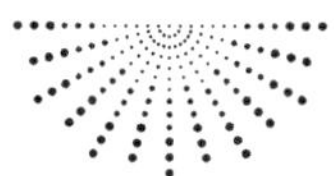

I don't know what possessed me to go deep into the heart of the mountain after the ceremony had concluded. Well…I did, I just didn't want to admit it.

I had hastily said my goodbyes before following the brooding shoulders of the warlord. Marked with paint and heavy with the duties he bore, he proceeded down into the deepest parts of the palace.

I stayed far enough back to hopefully not draw his attention. I had gotten lucky as most of the guards that lined the halls had been present at the funeral or on the new strict patrols that were being run outside—and inside—the walls.

My curiosity was piqued the deeper down we went, as I suspected he was going to the cells. I had just as many questions for the man with the shifting features as Kanan did, if not more.

Starting with what he knew about the wraiths and the attacks on the villages, and how he was connected to it all. I'd probably throw in why the hell he was trying to kidnap me just for shits and giggles.

In my weeks here in Allasea, I had never come across abilities like the strange man's. The Cynthonians were able to change shape, even localizing it to one part of their body, but I had never seen it be so unstable. The man's features were like shifting sands, never staying in one place for long, never looking the same way twice.

The floor sloped gently the farther down we went. The wooden floors and pleasant cream walls slowly turned into jagged gray and black rock. The floor was mostly smooth, the wear made by hundreds of feet walking over it again and again, but it was still rugged in comparison to the rest of the palace.

There was no light, not even a torch, in the dark tunnel, and yet Kanan walked unhindered, his back turning around a corner and out of sight.

Following behind quietly, I turned only to pull up short, nearly bumping into Lady Jai. I jumped slightly, having not heard a single footstep from her.

"Oh, my dear, you scared me half to death," the delicate woman said, putting her hand to her chest.

"Lady Jai, my apologies. I was just on my way to—" I fumbled to come up with an excuse to be this deep within the mountain stronghold.

"To watch the warlord interrogate the prisoner? Yes, I would assume so."

I looked at her sheepishly, like a child who had gotten caught with their hand in the cookie jar.

She giggled girlishly, and her impossibly dark eyes—so black I couldn't see her pupils even in full daylight—shone with amusement. "Oh, my dear, I would have been disappointed in you had you not been curious."

I gave her a small smile, relieved that I hadn't been caught by someone else. "I'm just sick of not having any answers. I can't keep going on like this, being blind at every turn, allowing others to pacify me with half truths, only to be confronted by more lies."

She nodded her head along to my ranting, something like

sympathy flashing across her half obscured face; the shadows kept us rather hidden despite being out in the open.

"It is understandable, young one. You are a child of Cosmos. The vast universe was a part of your making, a great power at your fingertips. Yet you might as well be powerless without the knowledge of who you truly are. Honestly, my dear, I am quite impressed with your fortitude. Any one being would have cracked by now, and here you stand. Asking only the bare minimum from anyone. Standing tall and strong, determined beyond belief." There was something in her voice that I couldn't decipher, but it was her calm and parental smile that put me at ease.

I sent her a grateful smile, even as my stomach twisted itself into knots, the words ringing in my head for some reason. I had been through some fucked up stuff in the past few weeks, and I had a tendency to be too hard on those around me. Of never asking for help because I didn't think there was anyone to trust, or because by this point, I just expected no one to help me. So, I ended up putting it all on myself, and I would smile as I struggled beneath the weight.

Coming to Eskira had shown me a different side of things, people holding out their hands to neighbors who were struggling. They helped each other without being asked or expecting anything from it. The same had instantly been applied to me, even though none of them knew me. I thought of Zanaya and Cashim, who had instantly welcomed me into their small circle of trust.

Or the other warriors, Nala and Zander, who had made it their mission to distract me from all the things plaguing my life right now; Orion and Saanvi trekking all the way back to my village to find proof that my parents were alive. Then there was Wrynn, who filled my life with laughter just by being himself.

For the first time in my life, I had friends who wanted to help, who were willing to stand by me. To say I was still adjusting to the overwhelming sense of belonging was an understatement.

Which was why I was down here in the dark by myself, the need to do everything on my own still ingrained in my mind. I was too stubborn, not wanting to allow the chance that this was all a dream, that the acceptance and friendship would all disappear in a puff of smoke. A part of me wished to open up to the small group who had worked their way into my life, to ask for their help in all of this.

I was working on it, but I just wasn't there yet.

"Small word of advice, dear one." Her musical voice rang despite her quiet tone. "Take the stairs on the right up to the second floor. You'll get a better view of the show, and the dragon won't be able to see you as easily."

With that, she walked away, almost gliding down the hall like her feet wouldn't touch the stone. Her gauzy gown flowed in an unseen breeze behind her. Shaking my head at the interesting conversation, I turned back to my task at hand.

Turning the corner, I crouched down as I came to an open arched doorway, wide enough to fit two full-grown men side by side. Walking through it, I came into a curved hallway that disappeared in a crescent on either side. Another open doorway in front of me led into a ginormous circular room.

Ignoring the doorway, I turned right, jogging quietly down the curved hallway. The barest hint of light came from a dim sconce, the flame inside nearly flickering out with every breath. I chased off the shiver that wanted to work its way down my spine; the whole area was freezing cold and smelled of blood.

I came upon a crude staircase, steps jutting out of the stone wall with no railing to guard from falling, and climbed up the steep incline. Stepping up onto the floor, curving around the circular room, the arched windows gave a perfect view below.

Empty jail cells lined the back wall, matching up perfectly to the open windows, no railings in sight. The small rooms held singular cots that sat on top of a straw-covered floor, a pail in the corner for the prisoners to do their business in, but nothing else graced the room.

The bars were made of glowing white crystal. Heartsglass. I could feel their power pulling at me from where I stood, sensing my own—however self-contained—and wishing to capture its shining light.

Ducking to the side of one of the open windows, I peered up to see at least five more floors, likely filled with more cells. The design of the prison was both masterful and poorly crafted. Each cell had an uninterrupted view of the floor below—which you could conveniently throw someone out of—yet there were no precautions put into place in case of escape. I would have called it arrogance or stupidity, but I knew they would have never confined prisoners down here without some kind of guard. But where was it?

The soft, nearly imperceptible steps of boots had me turning back down to the pit below. The space was open and flat except for the steel chains hanging from the wall. Racks of ... tools stood off to the side. In pristine condition, the black heartsglass gleamed in the dim lighting that was coming from somewhere above me, but I couldn't see where.

Off to the far right, a large gate stood rooted into the stone. The iron bars were thicker than my wrists and it was one of the only cells not barred by heartsglass. The space behind went deep, the soft rattling of bones could be heard from within. A chill, a brush from death, seemed to emanate from it. Terrified of what could be behind those bars, I turned away from it.

A man kneeled in the center of the wide room, pitifully small compared to the size of the prison structure. My attacker—the man without a true face—was restrained on the floor. Chains of silver steel wrapped around his wrists and ankles, shooting up from the cold gray stone. It was the white heartsglass collar around his neck that held my attention, though, seemingly freezing his abilities.

His chestnut hair glittered with reds and golds, while his pale green eyes were incredible in their color, the same shade as a new sapling. The slightly crooked nose didn't take away from the fact that he was extremely handsome, but the half crazed, half psychotic grin on his face did. I was clueless to whether they were his actual features or just what they had stopped on when he had been chained.

He had been stripped of his clothing; a simple cloth tied around his waist covered his cock and not much else. His pale skin was washed out and bloodied, the shadows of the prison only highlighting the already growing bruises. His lean chest was almost entirely blue and black, which made me think had he not had magic of some sort, he would have hemorrhaged out hours ago, the swollen areas resulting from fluid build-up.

In complete contrast to his crazed and beaten appearance, his hardened, intelligent eyes told me he had a vague idea of what was in store for him.

I had a feeling he really didn't.

Sympathy tried to creep in, only to be squashed by the memories of the shrouded bodies on their pyres—so many pyres—that had to be burned today.

He jerked his head up as Kanan walked into the pit carrying a chair in one clawed hand. He was still shirtless, and the painted marks seemed to come to life in the dark shadows of the pit. Each harsh stroke completely hid his bronzed skin beneath. They seemed to suck in all light, nothing peeking through the pitch black, curling around and cutting across his body.

They were fearsome, and they told you exactly who you were dealing with. Darkness. You were dealing with a being made of shadow and death. His very blood was created from the shades that made fathers double check the locks and had children hiding beneath their covers.

His glowing red eyes swirled with fire, muscles bunching as he sat down gracefully in front of the man, stretching out his legs, as relaxed as a cat lazily sunning itself on a warm day.

I watched the man swallow harshly, sweat already building on his temples, as his reality finally hit him. I saw it in his eyes—the glimpse of fear he tried to hide behind his fake confidence, but I saw it. Which means Kanan definitely did; I could tell even from here by the slightest lift in the corner of his mouth. He was enjoying watching his prey squirm.

"What is your name?" he asked softly, his voice made of velvet and shadows, intertwined with something feral, something that would make anyone quake in their boots. The deep rumble worked its way through my bones, vibrating within me. The dragon was speaking.

The chained man stayed silent, probably thinking that saying nothing would save him from the pain coming his way. He was dead wrong.

I never knew a chuckle could sound like a threat, but Kanan's did. It spoke of unending agony, sliding over your skin, the promising slash of pain. I could almost feel it rippling over me, an echo that had the hair on my arms standing on end.

"A quiet one," he purred, sounding nothing like a house cat and every bit the fire-breathing beast that lived inside him. "The quiet ones are always the most fun, you see. They scream the loudest."

The man swallowed again. I could see the wheels in his head turning, the silence ringing in my ears. Finally, he broke, "You can call me Jasco."

"Tell me, Jasco, do you know why this prison was built?" The question was spoken so calmly and yet I could feel its sharp edge even from up here; and now I understood why the prison had been built the way it was. It gave a clear view from every cell of the scene below. Showing those held behind the bars just what was in store for them, growing their fear.

Jasco stayed quiet, knowing that it wasn't an actual question, keenly aware that he was seconds away from death at any given moment. One wrong move, one wrong word, and Kanan would kill him. He might even do it solely because he was bored with the lack of conversation. Jasco's life was being thrown up into the air like a coin at any given moment. The result—survival or death—was just as unknown.

He had to know his only card in this deadly game was his knowledge. Knowledge that only he had, and that we wanted. The only way he survived this, and even then, it was a maybe, was if he played his hand right. He had to offer something that was worth Kanan's time, but not too much so that he became useless. Even then, Kanan could decide that the information wasn't worth the trouble of dealing with him.

The dragon looked around the large space, his face serene and calm, as if he was merely contemplating something of casual interest instead of interrogating someone who had set about a mass murder and kidnapping. "It was built for prisoners, of course, but the original purpose was to hold the God of Death himself. Obviously, it wouldn't have lasted long, but maybe it would have given those fleeing a few minutes' headstart. After he nearly lost his mind to the madness, he had it constructed to contain himself. Just in case he ever lost hold on his power again."

My ears perked up at that tidbit, not having read it anywhere in my book, but then again, the strange tome seemed to gloss over the unnecessary parts of history, mostly depicting the horrible war. The size of it made sense, though; if the king decided to change into his second form, it was large enough to hold a dragon.

Barely.

"That never happened, so it's mostly been used to hold traitors, criminals, and cowardly attackers such as yourself." A muscle twitched in Jasco's cheek. "To await their punishment."

The man's green eyes flashed with a hidden light, a righteous anger coming to the forefront, burning through any self-preservation he may have had. "Quite the tactic you have going here. I mean, really a splendid job, but you're under the impression that I'm not exactly where I want to be." Kanan's eyebrow rose a hair, but otherwise he wore that mask of calm boredom.

Jasco, on the other hand, continued with his blustering act. "However, I will say I am a little disappointed. I honestly expected the great Champion of Death, the Warlord of the Descendent Army, to have a little more …" He paused, tilting his head. "Oomph. I thought the world's greatest nightmare was going to appear before me from all the stories I had heard about you, but you're just a pretty boy."

The pit darkened slightly, which made it hard to make out any details. A pleasantly cool sensation brushed over my ankle. Looking down, I saw the shadows had pulled themselves off the walls and were now crawling across the floor, covering it like a fine mist. It slowly began to pour over the sides of the openings and into the pit below. A waterfall of darkness fell from above, the upper levels leaking shadows as well.

The shadows of the prison were being taken from the walls, from the cracks and recesses, yanked away from their corners, heeding their master's call. It was the strangest sight to witness, neither darkness nor light, nothing filling the space that the shadows had occupied.

The midnight mist pooled at the bottom like a jet-black lake, and yet Jasco didn't even seem to notice. He was so focused on trying to belittle a man incapable of caring about his opinion that he couldn't even tell death was close enough to curl around his ankle. Kanan hadn't moved an inch, but I knew he was calling the cold shroud of shadows to him.

"I guess it's just a mask you put on, huh? This mantle of

badassery that's as fake as those tattoos. I bet the ladies love them." He chuckled impertinently. "Great Cosmos, if only I could go back and tell myself that I wouldn't have to worry about your pansy ass. You walk around shirtless for gods' sake."

He wanted to die.

That was the only explanation I could think of that would explain his blatant disregard for his own personal safety. He was hoping that he could anger Kanan enough that he would just kill him and get it over with, skip the pain and torture and just go straight to the finale, taking his information to the grave with him.

That or he was just incredibly stupid.

Kanan stared at him, not even deigning to give him a response. I watched in fascination as the painted markings started to smoke. No, not smoke. They came away from his skin, licking the air, before wrapping themselves tight around his muscles again. They were bands of darkness, stuck to his body like chains that had been tightened to keep him restrained.

"I didn't feel like washing your blood from my shirt," he said matter-of-factly, like that was the exact reason he had chosen to not wear anything. He simply couldn't be bothered with the mess that Jasco would make after he was through with him. A bone-deep chill worked its way through me at the apathy.

I saw Jasco come to the same conclusion. That a shirt was more important than he was in this moment, that he only registered as something to be cleaned off in the bath afterwards. He breathed in harshly, preparing himself.

"I hope you know that I will enjoy every second of this," Kanan's voice was inhuman, something straight out of the nightmares that made hell look like paradise. Not even the dragon made that noise. I could feel my breath catch, something deep inside me recognizing that this was the voice of death, of sheer annihilation.

The black gloom that he created crested around him, silhouetting his shape in a halo of deadly blight. I could see them sliding down his chest, over his lap, tendrils reaching out and locking themselves tight around Jasco's body, holding him down.

All his muscles clenched, fighting against the unbreakable hold, the chair jerking as he tried to break free. The crystal collar pulsed with light, restraining any power that may have wanted to come out. The darkness swelled within the room, rising up like a wave ready to crash down and drag you under.

I didn't see what happened, but blood started rushing out of Jasco's eyes, running down his face like tears. He threw his head back, his mouth open in a silent scream, as his face contorted into a frozen image of agony. The twin streams of blood trailed down his neck as even more began to bead all over his body, as if it was coming straight from his pores.

I couldn't help but feel a sick sense of satisfaction watching him writhe in pain, knowing that he had caused so much more to the people of Allasea. Part of me thought I should be revolted, disgusted by such a horrifying sight, but vengeance came in all forms.

How could I stand in front of the thousands who had lost those they loved to these baseless attacks and then pity the man who might very well have orchestrated them?

"The problem with your little plan was that you expected to be able to outlast me. You had come prepared for the possibility that I would torture you. Somewhere in that brain of yours, you came to the understanding that capture meant physical pain, and on some level, you could respect that." Kanan's calm voice, layered with that fear inducing quality, was more chilling than any rage he could have shown.

"But you didn't come prepared for me to attack your mind, for the fact that I don't care to break your skin when breaking your mind is so much more satisfying. I've torn the information from your mind. I have all I need to know, the rest"—he paused, looking at the few drops of blood that speckled his chest with a savage, inhuman curiosity—"well, now this is just for fun."

I cursed silently. Any hope of overhearing anything had just been lost. If Kanan was able to reach inside his mind and find what he wanted, there was no way I would be able to figure out what he knew about these attacks and the reason behind them. With how cagey Kanan was, I highly doubted he would be willing to share his insights.

Jasco gasped for air, slumping in his restraints, as some unseen force let him go. Drenched in sweat and blood, he looked as if he had been through a years-long war. The white cloth around his hips had been stained red. The pale, washed-out color of his skin had become splattered with the red ichor like some artistic tapestry.

"Stay the fuck out of my head, you shadow Cynth bastard," he cursed back, breathing hard and wincing as he spoke.

"Now, why would I do that?" Kanan asked, a sardonic grin curving his lips. "We were just getting to know each other."

"Fuck you," he spat out just as his body locked up again, fists clenching as pain twisted his face into a gruesome snarl.

Over much quicker than the first time, Kanan released his mental grip on Jasco, who looked ready to fall unconscious to the floor. The slow drip of his blood leaked onto the floor, disappearing beneath the black fog covering the floor.

Kanan rose, his large form looming over Jasco's as he peered down at his handiwork with vague interest, an animalistic tilt to his head. The harsh angular marks all across his body pulsed once, their grip tightening even further around him.

That seemed to snap him out of it as he turned away silently. The dark shadows slowly started to dissipate, melding into his body or returning to their rightful places within the empty corners of the prison.

A weak chuckle followed him. "That's all you got? You're

never going to be able to keep her safe if that's all the fight you're going to give."

The dragon stopped mid-step, his back tensing as did mine.

"You didn't truly think that we wouldn't come for her, did you? That she would be safe as long as you kept her behind these walls? Hell, half the world saw her Awakening; how did you see this playing out?" Jasco asked, genuine curiosity in his tone.

"He wanted you to know personally that no matter where you try to keep her safe, he's always going to come for her."

CHAPTER TWENTY-SEVEN

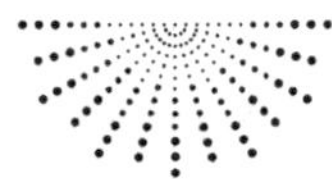

nless there was another *she* that had come into this world with such a crazy entrance, he was talking about me; and had just made it clear that he wasn't the leader of this operation. There was someone else behind this malicious scheme and for some reason, he wanted me.

Kanan reeled around, storming over with powerful steps. The prison darkened in response to his thunderous approach. With a quickness that was near invisible, he reached out, onyx claws gleaming sharply, clenching Jasco's throat in his hand.

A growl broke through his clenched teeth, jaw as sharp as glass. The rumble shook the pit, rattling the chains bolted into the stone walls. The glow of the heartsglass collar burned brighter, trying to weaken the power that was the warlord.

He didn't even flinch, even though I knew that being in such close proximity to the glass must have been draining on his power.

He picked him up from the floor, only stopped by the short length of the chains, and leaned down to the man's ear. Jasco's mouth gaped open and closed as he fought for air. I couldn't hear what was whispered, too far away to pick it up, but I could see Jasco's eyes going wide in fear.

"My Lord," Cashim's distinctive lyrical voice echoed across the lower pit. I could just barely make out his form in the entrance.

Kanan stared into Jasco's pale, fear-filled eyes for what felt like forever until he abruptly dropped him. The chains clanged as he folded over, coughing as his lungs tried to fill with air. With a last snarl, Kanan turned and made his way over to Cashim.

"What?" he snapped in agitation.

Cashim cleared his throat. "Apologies, but I was hoping you might have some information I could share with the Council. Tensions are running high and we are all anxiously waiting for some news."

"I got glimpses of Rhaera from his memories, images of wraiths lined up outside the town's borders." Kanan sighed heavily, running a hand down his face. "Cashim … the wraiths, they're Descendents; not all of them, but enough. Corrupted beyond belief, neither alive nor dead, but they're Descendents."

Horror grew within me at the implication that the very things that were attacking us were our own people. The infected soldiers were one thing, but the wraiths had been attacking in beast form for months. The same horror was mirrored on Cashim's face as he spoke. "So our worst fears are confirmed true, then. Someone is infecting Descendents and using them as an army."

"It appears so." Kanan placed his hands on his hips, the shadow markings pulsing once again. "I saw flashes of a few infected humans, who might as well have been dead for all the use they appeared to be, and some animals; but for the most part, he only interacted with the wraiths who mostly seem to be Cynths in their second form."

Cashim ran his hand down the bottom of his face, deep in

thought. "Were you able to find out why they attacked, aside from wanting to kidnap more of us for whoever is controlling them?"

"Why do you think?" he asked dryly, a deep-seated anger riding the undercurrents of his voice.

"I guess Lady Atallia's Awakening was noticed by more than just us. Do you think—"

Kanan held his hand up, interrupting Cashim before he could continue. Frustration roared within me, hoping to over-hear what they would say about me. I was in the middle of some game, and I didn't yet know the rules, and trying to figure them out was like wading through quicksand—pointless and frus-trating.

"Do you want to come down here?" Kanan turned in my direction, looking up at the opening I stood hidden behind, and locked eyes with me. He took a step toward me, a teasing glint in his fiery eyes to match the grin on his face. "Or do you just like to watch?"

I narrowed my eyes at him, not missing the remark I had made to him not so long ago. I stepped out from behind the arch's pillar, peeking over at a wide-eyed Cashim. "I don't know, I'm sort of comfortable up here."

His smile grew wicked in its intensity as he took another threatening step towards me. "Don't make me come up there and get you myself, love. You won't enjoy it if I do." He tilted his head mockingly, raising an eyebrow. "Or maybe you will."

Staring him down, I walked off the ledge of the opening, bending my knees to absorb the shock of the impact. A few weeks ago, a drop like that would have most likely broken my legs, but thankfully with my stronger bones and muscles I barely felt it now.

I walked straight past him, barely sparing him a glance. "Not even in your dreams."

"Oh, I wouldn't bet on that," he mumbled quietly from behind me, making my heart skip a beat.

I moved over to Jasco, half unconscious against the floor, careful not to get too close. Blood covered him from head to toe, dripping off him and staining the stone. I maneuvered around the puddles of blood as I squatted down in front of him.

He slowly picked his head up, those light green eyes muted with pain. Despite that, he met my gaze for a moment, a wall shuttering down over his eyes. His glass collar pulsed and then dimmed before burning with light again.

Grasping his chin in my hand, I tilted his head into that light. I couldn't help but feel a sense of familiarity as I stared at his features. Something about them struck me as odd; but then again, how would I ever be able to tell if this was his real face or not?

"He worked you over good, didn't he?" I mused, peering down at the rest of him, his body still bearing the brunt of Kanan's anger.

"Tell me, healer, how can you stand by a male so intent on violence? It seems to me it goes against everything your kind stands for."

A violence of my own whipped through me at his condescending tone. Gripping his face tighter, to the point that he tried to fight it, I leaned in closer with my teeth bared in a savage smile. "So you know about me. Unfortunately, whatever information you may have gathered left out the important details of who the fuck I actually am."

Anger and rage rose inside me, stoking the fire that was my power. I burned inside as it battered the walls of its confines, the weight of it layered throughout my voice as I spoke. "Those people you attacked last night, most of them wouldn't know what to do with a sword even if they saw one; and I can't heal them because your actions got them killed. So, you'll have to excuse me if I feel no sympathy for the absolute ass kicking you received."

I dug my fingernails into his skin and watched as tiny beads of blood cascaded down his cheeks. "And to answer your question, I find it very easy to stand next to him as he reaps the justice that is deserved. I only wish I was the one doing it."

I shoved his head away, standing up with one last sneer of disgust down at the cowardly bastard. Meeting Kanan's gaze as I turned, I saw pride and hunger shining in those eyes that were more red than Ayu.

"Where is Rhaera?" I asked, looking at Cashim, who stood awkwardly off to the side.

He immediately started shaking his head, guessing my intentions. "My dear, that would not be a wise idea. You overheard everything. You are being targeted; leaving the safety of Eskira would most certainly lead to your capture."

He didn't need to point out that without my newfound powers, almost completely unreachable, all the wraiths would need to do is outnumber me. No matter how hard I fought, without my powers I would be a sitting duck.

I refused to be stopped by such a simple obstacle in my path. I had lived twenty-one years without magic—I saw no reason to rely on it now. Too much rode on me finding out the truth. Wheeling around to Kanan, I asked bluntly, "Are you going to Rhaera?"

I could see it in his face that he didn't want to answer, but even as he sighed heavily through his nose—tendrils of smoke blowing out gently—he nodded his head.

"Good, you're taking me with you," I said decisively.

"No, I'm absolutely not." His tone was dead serious, his entire body tensing at the thought.

Cashim reached out, squeezing my arm gently, whispering so as to not be overheard. "Atallia, listen to us, dearest. You wouldn't be able to protect yourself; these creatures are no longer our friends and families. They're vessels of corruption that would seek to steal your spark. A very powerful spark, if you remember, regardless of whether you can reach it at the moment or not."

"But I wouldn't have to worry about that, now would I?" I say smartly, looking at a decisively grumpy Kanan. "I would have him. Unless, of course, you don't think you could keep me safe. I mean if the great Champion of Death can't keep me safe, then nothing will."

His arrogant smirk shone bright, his dagger-like canines only slightly menacing. His eyes danced with silent laughter, even as his jaw ticked. "That's not going to work, but nice try."

I smiled back, raising my eyebrow. "I think it's working a little bit. But either way, I've had enough of sitting around and waiting for someone to bring me news. Of my parents. Of me. Now I find out that I'm being targeted by the same things that have haunted my dreams for years."

I snapped my mouth closed, not meaning to share that about myself. At first, I'd convinced myself that the coincidences were just that; but the more my dreams lined up with my reality, the more I couldn't ignore the similarities.

The rotting guards with the green and black infection, the heartsglass, all of it lined up. If only I could remember more.

"What dreams?" Kanan's stern voice demanded an answer. Tough shit, he would have to get in line.

"What dreams, Atallia?!"

Any other time I would have kept quiet just to be stubborn, but this might have been my only chance to convince them that I would be of some use on the mission.

Glancing over my shoulder at Jasco, who looked unconscious, but the stiffening of his shoulders and the slight tilt of his head made me suspicious. Waving them to follow, I moved over to one of the shadowed alcoves that marked the lower level of the prison.

"I've had them for years, dreams that didn't always feel like dreams. I could never recall much of them once I woke up, but they've started becoming more clear since I've been here."

"What do you remember?" Cashim whispered, something brewing behind those ice-blue eyes, his dark skin nearly blending in with the surrounding shadows.

"A guard of some kind, infected just like the comatose soldiers, attacking a person," I muttered quietly, leaving out that the person had been me, as flashes of my nightmares came racing to the forefront of my mind.

Kanan and Cashim shared a look. "What else?" Kanan asked.

"A war." I looked at both of them, trying to catch any glimpse of familiarity. Kanan stepped closer, the shadows bending around him. I always said he was beautiful in the light, but in the dark he was stunning. Bronze skin and red eyes striking through the darkness looking like some creature of the flesh, sin and sensuality his only trade.

"Was this before or after you arrived in Eskira?" he asked.

"Both."

Another cryptic look passed between them, an unspoken conversation happening within seconds. I narrowed my eyes, not appreciating even more secrets being kept from me. "Listen, I understand the risks and fully accept them, but there's no way in hell that I'm being left behind. If the past twenty-four hours have shown anything, it is that I'm not much safer here than anywhere else. Getting answers is my only hope of figuring any of this out, and only my parents know why I was kept out of Allasea. If this trip in any way leads us to them, I want to be there."

"My dear, I don't know—"

"Was there anything else? Anyone or anything that stood out

to you?" Kanan asked forcefully, causing me to feel a little defensive.

"No. I mean, yes, there have been people in them, but they were mostly fuzzy and I can never pick out their faces once I wake up," I said with caution. It wasn't until recently that I had begun to remember more about the people I interacted with in my dreams, but I needed to keep some cards close to my chest.

Kanan narrowed his eyes at me, picking up on my wariness, his whisper still somehow sounding like a shout. "I still don't think it would be a good idea."

I scoffed. "Then I'll get kidnapped. At least then I might actually be able to learn what all this is about. I'll go with or without you; either way, I'm going to figure out what the hell is happening. I can't sit here anymore and do nothing."

Looking at the huffing and puffing dragon, Cashim looked beaten. "She would be the safest with you, Lord Kanan. At the very least she will be on the move and less of a target inside these walls." He rubbed his face wearily. "Unfortunately, it has been proven that our defenses aren't as foolproof as we would like them to be."

I could practically see Kanan grinding his teeth together, his stare downright lethal.

"Fine," he ground out, "but you will do everything I tell you to. Do you understand?"

I raised my hands up with a big smile. "I'll be on my best behavior."

He sighed, running his hands over his head, his dark curls appearing blue in the cold light. "I doubt that very much," he grumbled.

A dark chuckle mixed with hacking sounds came from behind us. Turning, I saw Jasco lifting his head up, peering through the messy, chestnut curls that had fallen in his face. "Is your little meeting over with? Because I am getting fucking bored over here waiting for you to be done. Don't you want to ask me about Rhaelyth?"

It was all a façade, I decided, realizing that this was his only defense mechanism. Sheer arrogance wasn't going to keep him alive forever, but it just might keep him alive for now, and that was all he cared about. It was his only playing card besides any information that Kanan was able to pick out of his mind. If he pretended that he knew more than he was letting on, more than we knew about, then there was a good chance we would keep him alive.

Crossing my arms as I stared at him, I asked Kanan, "What did you get from him? Besides Rhaera, I mean."

"Not much. Someone has taught him how to properly guard his mind. If I were to break through it, I'd run the risk of shattering his entire personality and memory in the process," he said, coming to stand next to me.

"Would that be such a bad thing?" I asked teasingly, a perverse part of me enjoying the slight color loss in Jasco's cheeks as he listened to us.

Kanan chuckled, the corners of his mouth lifting into something resembling a smile, but not quite there yet. "I figured we should see what else we could get out of him before resorting to such measures, but I'll keep your idea in mind."

Something confused me, though. "I thought you couldn't do the mental thing like Bron does?"

"Oh, I can do it alright, but picture Bron as a sharp-edged scalpel, and me as a battering ram. I can be meticulous when I want to be, but for the most part, I would prefer to crack someone's mind open and get what I need from them. Saves more time that way." He looked at me straight-faced. "I figured you would prefer it if I didn't do that."

I nodded back, eyes wide. "Good choice."

"Hey, asshole." We looked over to the kneeling, bloodied

man. "Are you ever going to let me up? My knees are going numb and these chains are starting to chafe."

"We need to go soon. Who knows how long ago he saw those wraiths at Rhaera. How soon can you be ready?"

We started walking back towards the entrance, ignoring the swearing coming from behind us. Cashim joined us as I said, "I'm not sure. I'll need some provisions and a change of clothes. I'll have to see if Zanaya can help me."

"Don't worry about that. I'll get her to get you a pack and some rations for the trip," the healer said, his tall, lean form towering over me as we walked through the wide, arched entrance.

"Give me a few hours then. We can leave right after sunset."

"Alright, after sunset. Meet me by the barracks. We'll head out from there."

"What are you going to do to him?" I asked, turning to look at Jasco still kneeling in the middle of the floor. He was pitifully small compared to the large prison.

"You'll never keep her safe. Do you hear me, asshole? You'll never keep her safe," he yelled crazily, his eyes shining with a madness that sent shivers along my skin.

Taking a final glance over his shoulder, Kanan let out a decisively evil chuckle. "I hope you enjoy Helmina. She gets lonely without anyone to keep her company down here."

Waving his hand in an arc, a mix of steel and heartsglass bars shot down from all the openings. Slamming down in front of me and into the small holes on the floor, the crystal and iron bars blocked the way back in. Or out.

Quickly, the entire pit was sealed off as the large gate at the back of the open space slowly lifted, and an interested grunt sounded from the dark emptiness. A bone-chilling scream, animalistic in nature—like some demented fox—came from the deep cell. Jasco whipped his head around as the clicking of claws on stone started coming closer and closer.

My curiosity egged me on to stay and watch, but Kanan and Cashim were already walking off. In spite of my curiosity, I wouldn't put it past Kanan to leave me behind if I was even a second late. I turned, despite wanting to see whatever the hell was in that cell, and made my way down the corridor, catching up to the two men.

Screams, echoing loudly against the stone tunnel, followed us as we walked away.

CHAPTER TWENTY-EIGHT

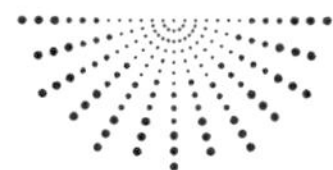

"What do you mean I can't come with you?" Wrynn pouted. He was attempting to look serious, but the white wrap dress he made from some poor soldier's stolen bed sheet and the sparkly, pink boots that covered his feet, really ruined it. He confessed he had indeed painted baby booties that he had—once again—stolen from somewhere in town.

Put that together with his adorable bedhead that included straw sticking up from every angle in his shiny white hair and his cute, silvery wings that kept fluttering in agitation, and I was a goner. I had come to say goodbye, not wanting the sweet sprite to think I had abandoned him, and now I was two seconds from a full-blown argument with a paint-happy, kleptomaniac.

"Wrynn, it'll be dangerous. You could get seriously hurt or captured, and who knows what they could do to a sprite." Did I feel a little bit like a hypocrite reciting what Cashim had told me? Yes, I did. Was that going to stop me from making sure Wrynn stayed safe in his little barnyard paradise? No, no, it wasn't. "Anyway, who would take care of the whispers while you were gone? You can't seriously tell me that someone else would do a better job than you."

His pink-booted feet shuffled in the straw of the loft, I had gotten him there. He looked up at me with those wide doe eyes and my heart melted. Somehow he always had a way of making me feel guilty for trying to do the right thing.

"Bu-But friends stick together, that's what you always tell me. What kind of friend would I be if I didn't go with you?" he asked in a small voice.

I sighed because he had me there. "Oh, Wrynn, just because you can't come with me doesn't mean you're a bad friend. I barely get to go, if I suggest you come, Kanan might actually explode. I mean that literally, he's already made of fire, I don't think it would take much."

"You're going with the warlord?" His already big eyes seemed to double in size, their shiny, dark depths glowing brightly. His silvery white wings began to glow and flutter like crazy, dragging him up into the air, bouncing him up and down in the slight breeze.

"Yeah, I got him to agree to let me go, and, Wrynn," I say seriously, emotion thick in my voice, "I really need this. It could lead us to my parents. To figuring out who I am and why they took me away from here."

Crossing his arms, he frowned. "Fine, but if you're not back in a few days I'm calling in the cavalry."

"Who's the cavalry?" I teased, a smile lighting up my face. No one could get me out of a mood like Wrynn could.

"Well, me, of course," he said matter-of-factly.

"Ahhh, of course, my apologies." I nodded formally, how dare I not know that.

I looked at him, reaching out with my arms and pulling him to my chest. "Come here. I'll be fine, you don't have to worry, okay. Maybe I'll finally get the answers I need."

"Okay," he mumbled quietly into my shoulder.

Letting him go, I started climbing down the ladder, to the barn floor. Picking up my pack that Zanaya had dropped off at my room, I tightened the straps before heading out.

"Atallia," Wrynn called out.

I turned around to look at him. "Yeah?"

He shuffled his feet again, looking down at them before shaking his head. "Nothing, just be careful okay, I don't have many friends like you."

He looked like he wanted to tell me something, but I left it, knowing he would tell me in time. Giving him a wide smile, I said, "I definitely don't have many friends like you, Wrynn. I'll be fine, don't worry."

His little wings fluttered fast and a pink blush stained his dark skin as a goofy grin took over his face. Waving, I headed out into the night breeze, the moons big and bright in the star-filled sky. Nebulas and galaxies far away were out in full force, the sky so filled there was hardly any darkness.

The magical streams of color, flowing like rivers made of blues and teals and silvers, only enhanced the beauty. I found myself unable to take my eyes off of it. The majestic vastness of it all spoke of wonders and worlds well beyond our own. It made me curious if there were people on those worlds, if they too were looking up and glimpsing the same sky I was.

"It takes my breath away every time."

I spun around, jumping at the low voice, not having heard anyone approach. Kanan had come dressed in all-black leathers, like I had. I found him looking at me instead of the sky, though, causing a blush to stain my cheeks.

"Is there anything I can say or do to get you to stay here?" he asked softly, his voice riding the gentle breeze. "Anything at all, because I'll do it without hesitation."

"I can't do it anymore, Kanan," I implored, stepping closer, begging him to understand. "I can't sit by and wait any longer. I need answers, real answers, and this might be the only way for me to get them."

He sighed heavily, jaw tensing as he looked me straight in the eye, red meeting gold, his fists clenched in frustration. "Fine, but you do everything I tell you, and unless I say otherwise, you stay close. I don't care if it's for five seconds—you stay within arms reach."

I smiled impishly, "Got it, glue myself to your ass."

His straight face did nothing to help the rising giggles in my chest. "I mean it, Atallia. I know you know how to fight, but that all means nothing when you're battling against magic. Especially without access to your power."

I could see it now, through the barest crack in his walls. Worry. He was scared for me and struggling to deal with it. Stepping closer to him, I grabbed his fisted hand and gently unclenched his fingers, holding on tightly. The heat from his body radiated around him, sinking into me even through the cool breeze.

Peering up at him through my eyelashes, I leaned in close. "I'll be okay, I promise. I'll listen to your orders and stay close. No jokes. I will do whatever you tell me to, I just need to see this through, okay?"

He reached up with his other hand, rubbing his thumb lightly over my cheek. Breathing out through his nose, he shook his head in resignation "How do you always seem to get your way, love? It's baffling."

I smiled up at him, my heart tripping slightly over the name. "It's one of my many talents."

"It's something alright," he muttered, releasing me as he checked the straps of my pack. "Keep this strapped to you. I don't want it falling off during the flight."

"Flight?"

Now he was the one with the wicked smile. "I hope you

know how to hold on tight." He laughed with wild abandon as he turned and took a running leap off the cliff face.

Gasping, I rushed over, coming down to my knees, hoping he hadn't just inadvertently killed himself with stupidity. Just as I peeked over the ledge a huge body shot up through the air. Falling back onto my ass, I watched as the obsidian dragon swooped through the air, blotting out the starlight.

Every color of the night was reflected in his onyx scales, turning him luminescent. Coming down to land, his wingspan was nearly wider than the entire barrack's grounds. With giant sweeping motions, his bat-like wings stirred up a wind that had my hair whipping around my head.

His hind legs touched down first before his front, his gentle landing almost knocking me back to the ground. Sitting down, he neatly folded his wings and tucked his tail over his front claws. *What a polite dragon,* I thought as I stared up in awe.

Bending down from his towering height, claws digging into the loose dirt, he stuck his neck out. Tilting his ginormous head, which stood over me by tens of feet, he gave me a long sniff. The red irises pulsed with light, and his diamond pupils constricting.

Stretching out my hand, I brushed my fingers lightly down his nose, the small scales warm beneath my touch. He pushed gently into my hand, asking for more. I let out a breathy laugh, running over the small points that framed his nostrils.

He let out a small purr, closing his eyes, before nudging me again and pointing with his head to his front leg. Walking over, dragging my hand along the underside of his thick neck, I stared up.

His back was at least a hundred feet above me if not more. Looking around, I saw thick spikes on the back of his leg. Grabbing the one above me, I stepped up, climbing the matte black barbs like a ladder.

If I had access to my power, I could have floated up onto his back like Zanaya and other air Aetherians, but unfortunately, no matter what I did, my magic was still locked behind the opalescent barrier. The crack, which hadn't grown anymore since the attack at the ball, barely allowed me extra strength and speed.

The thin trickle of power only seemed to keep me healthy and strong. Cuts from sparring were healing in minutes; but even with the extra boost from the attack, it wasn't anything substantial. I couldn't say I blamed Cashim and Kanan for their worry; neither had seen something like this after a full Awakening.

I reached the halfway point, still far below his back, before I could go no farther. I looked around, trying to figure out how to reach the rest of the way. Kanan watched me, his eyes laughing, as he opened his wing, lowering it to my level.

The webbed membrane was thin enough to see the hard, bony structure underneath. Jumping the small distance, I landed on the bone beneath, bracing myself as he lifted me up. As it started to go vertical, I began to slide. Putting my hands down, I slowed myself enough to push off, jumping the distance to his back and grabbing one of the spinal barbs.

It was long and sharp enough to impale someone like a spear, and I held on to it for dear life as I got my footing. I let out a harsh laugh as I stood straight, the scales smooth underneath my feet. I weaved in and out of the spikes until I reached his neck.

At the base, where his neck and shoulders met, was a bare spot free of barbs. Straddling him, I grabbed on to the many smaller spines that decorated his neck in rows. Looking down, I laughed in nervous excitement. The ground was so far below me everything looked child-sized in comparison.

"You better not drop me," I joked, patting his scales.

He let out a warble that sounded remarkably like laughter before shaking his long body, nearly unseating me. He unfurled his magnificent wings, and with mighty bounds that had me squeezing his sides for dear life, he ran straight for the cliff edge before diving right off it.

We flew straight towards the ground, the forest rushing up towards us at an alarming rate. "Fuck!" I screamed, my voice getting lost in the rush of wind as gold strands whipped back away from my face.

I squeezed my legs together, my knuckles turned white from their grip on the spines. I started spitting out prayers to the Cosmos that would have made Maris proud. At the last second, a breath away from the treetops—so close I could almost reach out and touch the leaves—he pulled up, sweeping us into the air. The ground disappeared below us as we shot into the night sky.

I hit my hand against his shoulder, my heart racing. "You bastard, you nearly gave me a heart attack."

I felt his chuff before I heard it, the noise vibrating between my legs. I peered between his crown of horns—the two giant ones arching high above my head—as we headed east toward Rhaera. The four moons rose high in the sky, lighting our path.

As Kanan leveled out, wings beating a steady rhythm, I felt a presence in my mind. It was a trick that Bron had taught me on one of the many mornings he had invited himself to breakfast with Kanan and I. He wanted me to be able to sense people's presence in my head, hoping it might better help hold my magic at bay if we ever needed to go back inside my mind.

It was a warm stroke against my mental barriers, like smoke and the sensual brush of fingers against skin. The cool touch of darkness and all the promises it held. Kanan.

Picturing a door in my mind, I cracked it open, allowing him a small entry. It was another trick that Bron taught me in order to control the flow of power that guarded each person's mind. Unlike Bron, Kanan didn't step inside, instead his mental presence stood right at the doorway to my mind; one proverbial step and he would cross the threshold. However, he seemed content to whisper through the entryway.

"Look up."

His smooth voice purred within my head, a grumble to it that was reminiscent of his dragon form. I felt him gently trace the edges of the doorway before he stepped back, disappearing completely from my mind.

Tilting my head back, I gasped in wonder. Reaching up with my hand, I dragged it through the stream of magic that ran through the sky. The river parted around my hand, twirling in between my fingers. Some strands curled about my wrist playfully before continuing on.

I giggled at the sensation, tiny pricks tingling my skin. Throwing my arms out wide, I closed my eyes, embracing the bite of the wind against my skin. In spite of that, the heat from Kanan's fire-filled body was more than enough to warm me. His smooth, glass-like scales were each a miniature furnace, full of the fire that filled his eyes and chest with a blistering power.

With slow, sweeping beats of his wings, he carried us through the celestial sky. As he drifted to the right, I lurched, grabbing onto his spines quickly. I couldn't help but laugh again, my heart beating in time with his. The massive thumps in his chest flowing through every inch of my body.

I don't know how long we flew, time slipped by without thought. I wasn't sure of the distance between Rhaera and Eskira, but something told me that flying dragon-back got you places a lot quicker. In what felt like minutes, we were circling high above a small town, only a few hutches and buildings built around a wide clearing.

We looped around, scouting ahead before we went in. The small village was dark, not surprising considering the late hour, but there was a silence in the air that could be felt even from our height. A chill that crept into your skin, sunk down to your bones, and filled you with a lasting fear.

There wasn't a single candle lit. No late-night conversations, or children reading under their bedsheets afraid of being chastised by their parents. A shadow hung over the clearing, and not in the way Kanan's tended to wrap around his arms and shoulders. No, this spoke of an evil that sought to seep into the very ground the village sat on.

Something in my gut twisted, a bad feeling that itched at the back of my mind. I gave Kanan's scales a soft pat, and he seemed to read my nerves, quickly beating a retreat. I looked over my shoulder; and although nothing appeared to be wrong with it, the dark clearing looked rotten in comparison to the rest of the surrounding forest.

We flew on for another few minutes, covering ground faster than I could have imagined. Soon we were circling above the edge of the forest, right behind a large, stone building that stood just off the main road. The glowing light within gave me hope that the corrupted feeling we'd felt hadn't made it much farther than the little town.

Coming down with strong wingbeats, the blowback throwing my hair all around, making me regret not braiding it, we landed with a jolt. Standing from my spot, my thighs screamed despite their new strength. I guessed riding a dragon was hard even for a Descendent.

I walked down his back, and with a little maneuvering, I got to the ground. I had to hang off his wing like a monkey until he decided to plop me on the ground, causing me to fall on my ass, but I got down. I'd take it. I was still brushing off the dirt and grass when the shadows billowed around him and he appeared from the darkness, trying his hardest not to laugh and failing miserably.

"Yeah, yeah. Laugh it up, but I'll have you know that you've never had to ride you, so you can't say shit. Ride a dragon and get back to me, and we'll see who's laughing then."

That only seemed to make him laugh harder. Shaking my head, trying to keep from smiling, I started walking toward the shining light coming through the sparse trees.

I had only gotten a few feet before strong, muscular arms wrapped around my waist and pulled me back into a hard chest. The man was a walking furnace. He burned so hot I would have been worried about a fever had I not known what he was.

Soft lips brushed lightly over my ear. "You rode me just fine, love, but I do think we'll have to work on your mounting."

A surprising pulse of heat struck my core, a blush heating my cheeks at his words. My attention was locked in on the feel of his hands holding me, the soft skin of his lips against the shell of my ear.

Every point of contact ignited my blood, like striking a match and letting it burn you all the way to the ground. A single match could light a candle or start a forest fire, and that was what Kanan was doing to me. Setting me ablaze completely, waiting for me to burn and rise from the ashes.

The thought brought me back to the blaze that lit the pyres, the souls that were on their last journey. Clearing my throat begrudgingly, I stepped out of his arms, remembering why we were here in the first place.

He seemed to come to the same realization, tipping his chin toward the golden glow coming from between the trees. "There's an inn that the soldiers use as a resting spot when they travel this far out. We'll stay there for the night and go into town at daybreak. I didn't like the feel of the place, and I want to get a better look before we go barging in."

Nodding in agreement, we headed off into the trees, using a well-worn path to cross the short distance to the inn. The stone siding was rough cut and well built. The wooden roofing was new and taken care of. A small garden all along the back of the inn was tended to and held a beautiful variety of plants that Maris would have loved.

I itched to see what there was to work with, but an over-whelming fatigue was settling deep into my muscles. The stress of the past few hours—hell, days—was finally catching up to me.

I had learned very quickly that just because magic now ran through my veins didn't mean I was completely indestructible. I still needed to eat and drink. Still needed to sleep.

As much as I wanted to rush into Rhaera and start demanding answers, I knew I would crash sooner rather than later, and I had no intention of walking into danger without being at my best.

The inn seemed to be the perfect place to do so. The whole place spoke of the love and care that went into it every day. The clean windows, a fresh coat of paint on the door; even the brass doorknob shined in the lamp light above the entryway.

Kanan pushed open the heavy, wooden door, letting me enter first as I ducked under his arm. The cozy sitting area was warm and well kept. Although no one was sitting by the tended fire or playing cards at the little tables set up by the windows, this late at night everyone had most likely retired to their rooms.

There were couches that all but called my name, their plush softness visible from here. The room was situated in a sort of organized chaos. Throw pillows in all colors were puffed and fur blankets lay over the backs.

The whole place reminded me of home, with its warm friendliness that welcomed everyone through its doors, and an abundance of all things comfort. I loved it immediately. Kanan looked pleased as well, his normally stoic face only slightly less so; there was an easiness to his mouth that wasn't normally there.

Quiet footsteps came from our left, padding across the dark wood floors. A voluptuous woman entered through the hallway off to the side. Her curly, brown hair was pulled up in a messy bun, tendrils framing her beautiful face. With soft brown eyes—still hazy from sleep—and plump lips, her white nightshift flattered every curve. Laugh lines that few Descendents seemed to have spoke of a life full of happiness.

She approached with a welcoming smile, bowing her head respectfully. "My Lord, you honor us."

Stepping forward, he grabbed one of her hands, bending over it to place a kiss on the back of it. I ignored the twinge of irrational jealousy I felt. He smiled up at her cheekily. "The pleasure, as always, is mine, Ellenia. I apologize for our late intrusion."

"No, not at all," she replied warmly before turning to look at me with a smile. "And I see you brought a beautiful friend with you."

Something about her sunny disposition immediately set me at ease, her smile infectious. I chuckled shyly, not used to such warm praise. "Thank you, I was just thinking the same of you."

Grasping my hand in her own, she gave it a squeeze. "Oh, well, that is mighty kind of you. Now, My Lord, you know the rules. Everyone is always welcome, and we won't ask questions as long as you guarantee any trouble will be taken outside of our little inn."

"Trouble? Me?" He gave her a wink that caused a pink blush to appear on her cheeks, and I couldn't really blame the woman. Losing the cheeky, playful attitude, his eyes went serious as he said, "You have my word, Ellenia. No trouble from us, and if any shows up, we'll handle it."

"Alrighty, I'll hold you to that," she said from over her shoulder, walking back down the hallway, waving for us to follow. "I only have one room open this late in the night. Will that be okay with you two?" Her eyes shift between us, an obvious question in her gaze.

My heart stumbled, but I ignored the implications that went with it and gave her a pleasant smile, nodding my head.

"That will be just fine, thank you." Kanan's face was blank, giving away nothing.

She led us down the hallway, where portraits, including one

of Ellenia, hung from the pale blue walls. She stopped at the first door on the left, opening it for us.

I stepped inside and the plush carpet sunk beneath my feet. The neutral walls held calm paintings of beautiful landscapes, the magic in the different places obvious through the colors. Relief hit me as I saw two full-sized beds were pushed up against the back wall, a night table inbetween them. A rug had been tossed at the foot of them.

A window on the far wall looked out towards the back, where a twisting tree grew right outside. A flicker of silver caught my eye, but it was only the moonlight cutting through the branches and into the room, throwing patterns all across the floor.

The beds weren't new, the wooden frames looking to be on their last leg, but pillows and dark green blankets covered any wear that might have been obvious. "The beds aren't the nicest we have, but they should be able to do the job." Elena's voice held a twinge of embarrassment. She probably hadn't been expecting the warlord of her people's army to stop by.

Not wanting the sweet woman to feel self-conscious, I turned and gave her my kindest smile—it was rusty, but it would have to do. "It's perfect. Thank you for housing us so late at night and on short notice. We really appreciate it."

She let out a little breath, happiness shining in her eyes. "Well, I'll leave you to it. I hope you have a good rest of your night here with us."

We said our goodnights before she left us alone, closing the door behind her. As soon as the door clicked shut, the tension that had mostly cooled in front of Ellenia came roaring back. It was so thick I could have cut it with my blades.

I did my best not to look at Kanan's broad shoulders, towering heads above me. I walked over to the closest bed and set my pack down, my entire body feeling beaten from the flight. I started digging through it for my canteen, trying my damndest not to listen to the near-silent footfalls of the man behind me.

The man I couldn't seem to keep out of my mind. He was so entrenched in my blood; I felt as if I would never rid myself of him. I must be completely insane to feel so much—understanding so little—for a man I had only known for a handful of weeks. Every second in his presence felt more right than the last.

Truly, it was the only thing in my world that felt completely right. There was confusion, sure, and I believed he did his best to drive me bat shit crazy with his secrets, but it only made me want to know more. He was the one unknown that I seemed to be okay with, which in and of itself drove me bonkers.

I had never gotten so wrapped up in boys—men—sticking to my quick liaisons that would never lead anywhere. I had always been content with that, scratching the raging itch and then moving on. I don't even truly remember having a crush—all the boys in the village were too much like their bigoted and abusive fathers for me to take interest.

I wonder if that's what this was, a crush. An infatuation was something I had simply never had. This was an overwhelming sense of drowning beneath feeling, every moment by his side like electricity beneath my skin.

Was I crazy to wish that he would reach over and touch me like he had in the piano room, hold me with those calloused hands, run those fingers across my skin as he had the keys? I thought so, and yet I couldn't help wishing it all the same.

A dull thud came from behind me, followed by the creek of bedsprings as he sat down. Seconds went by until he groaned, followed by a loud cracking, and then a boom.

Spinning around, I found Kanan stuck in the middle of the broken bed frame, the twin pieces sticking up into the air on either side of where he sat. The poor wooden legs that had probably seen better days, were unable to take the strain of his muscled frame.

I would never forget Kanan's look of astonished shock, frozen on the ground as if he couldn't believe what had just happened. Loud gasping laughs folded me in half, my stomach hurting from the force.

His peeved expression only set me off more as he pushed himself out of the wreckage. I tried to choke back my hysterics, only managing stifled giggles. Letting out a big sigh, which I couldn't help but notice was accompanied by smoke coming out of his mouth, he picked up his pack and a blanket, moving over to a clear spot on the floor.

"You can sleep with me." The words rushed out of my mouth before I could even think. His burning red stare met mine, not backing down, daring me to go through with it. Unable to back out now, I shrugged my shoulders. "It might be a tight fit, but it will be better than the floor."

I didn't think he even moved to breathe, going so deathly still it was almost unnerving. "Are you sure?" His dark voice was layered with an emotion I couldn't recognize.

Swallowing hard, I nodded. "Yeah, there's no reason for you to sleep on the floor when there is another perfectly good bed to share."

He gave me a teasing look from beneath his unfairly long lashes, raising an eyebrow. "What if I break that one, too?"

I looked back at the bed, not having actually considered that. My brow wrinkled, "Well, I guess then we'll both have to sleep on the floor, so do your best not to do that."

His shoulders shook with silent laughter as he moved over to the bed, sitting down with great care. He braced himself, ready to jump up at a moment's notice. I pressed my lips together, trying my hardest to not laugh again.

When the bed held beneath him, he relaxed, bending down to pull off his boots. Sitting down next to him, I did the same, untying the laces before placing them neatly under the bed frame next to his.

Pulling back the bedcover, I crawled under, facing away from him as he tossed his tunic to the foot of the mattress. I slid over to the wall as much as I could, and he fell in behind me after blowing out the candle. The dark of night surrounded us, and I could almost see the shadows undulating and writhing in Kanan's presence. I shook my head in amusement at their eagerness.

"Sorry, I can't always keep them back when I try to relax." His voice whispered into the darkness, brushing my ears like smoke from an ember.

"Don't, I like them," I chuckled softly. "And they seem to like me."

He let out an affirmative grunt that had me smiling a bit. Although it was invisible, I could almost feel him let his restraints go, finally relaxing fully into the mattress. The shadows crawled down the walls and across the floors, reaching out to touch the bed.

Some more adventurous tendrils tried to wrap around my ankles or play with my toes, which had me giggling, but he pulled them back. It was almost a reprimand, as if saying *no further than this, and don't mess with her.* It was kind of cute, in a *how is this my life* kind of way.

Closing my eyes, I tried to fall into the oblivion of sleep, but it refused to take me. My mind began to spin out of control with thoughts that only sought to torment me. Were my parents okay? Were they still alive, or had I acted too late to save them? Did Kanan's temperature just rise even more or was I just imagining things? Was the wraith infection going to become contagious? Would I need to prepare for an outbreak like Maris feared? Why was I different even among the Descendents?

I was spiraling before I could stop myself, shuffling around in the bed, trying my best not to bump into the living furnace next to me. I jumped as a large hand wrapped around my waist, settling under my tunic against my bare stomach. Pulling me back against his hard chest, pressing into my back, he tucked me in close.

His hot breath blew against my ear. "Sleep, or you'll be of no use to me tomorrow."

I wanted to say something snarky back, but my attention was fixated on his thumb rubbing back and forth against my skin. His heart beat loud enough for me to hear, the thumps slow and rhythmic, beating only every few seconds. His deep breaths were easy to match, slowing my own heart. I couldn't help but drift off into the dark emptiness.

CHAPTER TWENTY-NINE

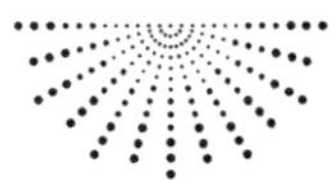

*S*obs *rocked my body, wails tore at my throat. I sat rocking in the corner, hidden behind the bed, not caring that the cold stone of the cell penetrated through the carpet and into my bones until my skin had turned to ice. I welcomed it, the cold, hoping it would numb me to the pain.*

Not the physical pain, the bites and wounds covering my too pale skin barely registered with the agony that encompassed my very being. I was screaming on the inside and yet no one could hear me, no one could hear my heart breaking with every breath I took.

Perhaps it would be a mercy to die, to forget what had been taken, but immortality would never allow such a thing. And yet I wished for it all the same; every move I made was too exhausting, too painful.

I hadn't broken until he left, but now I found I simply didn't care. Let them see. Let him see what he had done. But no one was around to witness, only the dark stone of my prison stood sentry to watch as I shattered.

There was only the four walls of my cage to echo the soul-deep agony that sprang forth from my mouth. The too-colorful carpet soaked up my tears as I rocked back and forth. Back and forth. I mumbled a quiet song, soft cracking sounds, in between the cries as I stared unseeing at the wall.

She was gone. Just gone.

"Atallia," a rough voice said, shaking me gently on the shoulder. "Atallia, love, wake up."

Startled, I jumped with a cry, looking around wildly. Kanan's hands kept me close, holding my shaking body to his own. Dread and sadness worked its way through me, the woman's agony becoming my own. I let out a few gentle sobs, the reason for them unknown, as a lullaby played through my head.

The walls of the inn surrounded me, shocking me back to reality. I looked down and realized I had been twisting and turning like a mad woman—no wonder Kanan had awoken—the sheets were a tangled mess around the both of us.

"Sorry, I was hoping I wouldn't have one of my nightmares," I said, embarrassed. I wasn't used to anyone but Maris and Geoff seeing me in such a way. At least I hadn't tried to sleepwalk.

His face was hidden in the shadows, the small window behind him still dark. We must have only been asleep for a few hours. Even through the darkness, I could see him narrow his eyes as he let out a quiet hum. "Do you always have these nightmares?"

Trying to shake off the lingering feeling of desolation, I rolled over onto my side to face him. "Most of the time, yeah." I shrugged my shoulders. "Sometimes they're not so bad, sometimes they're worse. It really depends on the day, I guess."

"You said you had seen things in them? Like the wraiths?" His voice was rough with sleep, but his gaze was clear, focused on me with an intensity that had my breath catching.

"Yes, but not—not like the ones that have been attacking us. The one in my dream a few weeks ago was still a person. I couldn't tell if it was an Aetherian or a Cynth, but it didn't function like these do. It wore armor and carried weapons like a guard, but it was basically a puppet on strings." I stared up at the ceiling, tracing the whorling pattern with my eyes and muttering to myself. "I don't think it could walk without being told to."

"And what was it guarding?"

"A cell of some sort." I looked at him. "A cell with me in it. Or someone in it. I don't really know; it has always been hard for me to pick out the details. Until recently, at least." I added, the sobs of a woman and a stone wall flashing through my mind.

He brought his hand up, running his fingers gently down my arm. "And it attacked you?"

"I think so." I squinted my eyes, trying to recall what had happened so long ago. "I'm really not sure."

I cleared my throat, trying my best not to shiver as he dragged his hand down to grip mine. His smoke and dark amber scent swirled around me, dragging me deep into his orbit.

He hummed again as he shifted his weight, causing the bed frame to creak threateningly. We both froze, looking at each other with wide eyes, waiting for the inevitable crack. A minute passed before we both breathed again.

"Maybe try not to move so much," I said teasingly.

He grunted, looking down at the foot of the bed. "Well, I'm already hanging off. I'm not sure what else I can do."

Sure enough, his legs stuck out of the blankets and were hanging off the end by about six inches. I buried my face into the pillow, shaking with laughter.

Brushing a strand of gold hair from my face, he lightly ran his thumb down my cheek. His brow wrinkled in a concern, a serious expression on his face.

"Are they all like that? Your nightmares?"

My breath came out shaky. I often tried to forget the small bits and pieces I remembered, the horrors they carried not something I wished to keep. "Not all of them," I whispered, picking at a loose thread on the blanket. "Sometimes they're … different, not so bad. Most of them though, like the one tonight, yeah. They're the stuff that keeps people up at night. Pain. Grief. War. Torture."

I couldn't help but think of Jasco, and the things that were done to him. Shadows rippled around his form, coming over the both of us, hiding us from the world.

"I'm sorry you had to see that." His eyes held mine, a question held in them, waiting for something.

"I'm not," I shook my head, hoping he didn't feel guilty for what he had to do. I only wish I'd been able to do it myself."

"Most would be surprised to find a healer so bloodthirsty," he said, sounding anything but.

"Most would be surprised to know that healers, although adept at putting people back together, are just as good at taking them apart." I knew without seeing that my eyes glowed with a viciousness that backed my words.

A ferocious smile that was more bared teeth than anything, brushed his lips. The dim light caught on his four canines, the daggers glinting. The smile of a dragon. Approval warmed his eyes as he spoke. "That they would. Still, I'm sorry if I added to your nightmares." His eyes grew dark, nearly black, lost in his own memories.

"Well, we all have our own nightmares," I said gently. "Don't we?"

His smile tightened in response. I reached out, brushing my hand down his side. The scars on his back just barely peeked out, the raised skin only a shade lighter than his own bronze tone.

"I saw them when you left the sparring ring," I prodded, my own curiosity getting in the way of politeness.

"Do you know how hard it is to scar Descendent skin?" he asked rhetorically, flipping onto his back staring out the window on the back wall. "It takes repetitive strikes of heartsglass or some sort of power—claws, elemental magic—you get the point. Even then, it still might heal and be nothing but a white line."

His entire back was a tapestry of white and pink lines, thick and thin. Some even puckered and raised as they criss-crossed his body like a quilted pattern of pain.

"But you see, before a Descendent Awakens, they're basically human. Stronger and healthier, but still nearly human." He rolled his head over and I could see it in his face how badly his walls wanted to come up. He was like me in almost every way. Better to lock the pain away than show it to anyone and let them think you're weak. That you needed pity.

"I was adopted too, except unlike your parents, my foster father hated me more than anything in the world. I think he saw what was inside me and feared me. But I also think it was sheer jealousy sometimes, like he knew I was going to have the one thing he couldn't."

"And what was that?" I boldly placed my hand over his chest, his strong, slow heart beating faster than I had ever felt it. It was stupid and reckless to get this close, but I couldn't get myself to pull away.

He looked down at my hand with an almost reverent gaze, playing with my fingers like he wasn't sure they were real. He stroked each one, tracing their shape, as if committing them to memory.

"Power. I would have a power that no matter what he did, he would never achieve. He was an average level Cynth who spent his entire life trying to make up for his lack of magic by becoming someone important. He ended up as the brigade leader of a smaller town not too far from here, and was working his way up to becoming a senior member of the leadership there."

I stayed quiet even though I was burning to know more. Despite being in Allasea for some time, I had yet to leave the borders of Eskira until now. I was dying to see more of the magical land, so different from the withered and mundane world beyond the Blackwood.

"When he was selected to be my guardian after I was found, he took it upon himself to train me in his image. By the time I was six I had seen a grown man skinned alive and had already been a part of a battle."

He stopped at my shocked and confused look. "We are isolated from the mortals, but there are other creatures and beings that walk these planes, and who only recognize the authority of The Divine. When they disappeared most stopped all contact with the Descendents. When my father came upon a group of Ratheons—big, intelligent creatures made of stone that crush you beneath their weight or impale you on their horns if they're provoked—and they refused to fall under his command, he had them killed. He justified it by saying they were actively threatening the lives and homes of Descendent civilians."

He spit the words out like a curse, his red eyes burning from within. "He was never a loving father, and as I got older, he began finding illogical reasons to punish me. I hadn't made my bed just so, I had sharpened his sword too sharp and the metal had become fragile. Anything to wield whatever power he had over me. And then one day he took me to our basement and put me in a cell that he had specially made for me."

The matter-of-fact way he said it nearly had me in tears, as if he had come to the conclusion that this was just something that had happened to him, and not a horrific crime to commit against a child.

"He locked me up in chains and muzzled me so I couldn't scream. He would only take them off to let me go to the bathroom and feed me the scraps from whatever of his meal he hadn't eaten that day. Whenever he was in a particularly bad mood, he would come down and whip me with steel-ended leather. I healed at an exceptionally fast rate even back then." He stared up at the ceiling, calm as could be as he told the story.

A small tear ran down my cheek. Anger filled my veins like lava, the boiling edge of rage curling in the corners of my mind.

"I think after a while I became more of an experiment to him than anything. He wanted to see what I could survive. I'm pretty sure he cut off my finger at some point," he said, holding up his right hand, showing the small white ring around the base of his second finger. "But I blacked out, so I'm not sure."

I was silenced by shock. The pain he had to endure at such a young age made my pitiful cynicism over my upbringing look like a paper cut. I wasn't one to compare, but I couldn't help but be humbled.

"I didn't have much to do in between the times when he visited, so I got good at listening through the floorboards. Learned to speak to the shadows and hear what they had to say." As if on cue, a tendril crawled up the bed, tangling around his fingers.

"They became my friends and my allies, bringing me information. I was silenced, but in that silence, I learned that being quiet meant you heard what wasn't always spoken aloud. That fading into the background was more beneficial sometimes than being in the spotlight."

"Is that why you're a man of few words, as you put it?" I asked quietly, almost too afraid to speak, as if speaking would bring about more torment than he had already faced.

He smiled softly, his chest lifting in a chuckle. "Yes, and no. I get more answers when I listen than when I speak. It aggravates me when people talk just to hear their own voice—it's a waste of time and energy. Not to mention, people typically start smelling of fear and piss the moment I open my mouth, so I prefer to let others, like Cashim, do all the talking. This also isn't my real voice, mine is much … louder, which seems to have an even worse effect, so I only use it when I need their attention."

Thinking back, I looked at him, surprised. "The echo. I thought it was just bouncing off the walls, but I heard it in the hall and at the funeral."

He nodded back. "And that's when I have it under control. When it first appeared I nearly made a town permanently deaf."

My eyebrows rose, and despite his warning, I kind of wanted to hear it. "So, what happened? How did you get away from him?"

He sighed heavily. "Well, he made the mistake of thinking no one would miss that I was gone. He told everyone he sent me to some training camp near the Northern Moors, but that only worked for a couple of years before a few of his commanders got suspicious. He wasn't very well liked to begin with, and they brought their concerns to Cashim, who happened to be stopping through."

"However, I got to him before they did," he said happily, his brutal side coming out to play in the darkness. "After a particularly bad beating, something in me just unlocked. I think it was a survival mechanism because sometimes I look back on it and I'm pretty sure he was going to kill me that night.

"Anyhow, he was laughing and laughing as I lay there a bleeding mess, and I just snapped. The shadows tore through my chains and held him to the ground. They squeezed so tight he started to turn blue all over, but even then, he was yelling at me, calling me ungrateful as if I had deserved all of it somehow. Next thing I knew, I was shifting, and I broke through the damn house. I burned it to the ground in front of Cashim and the commanders."

"And your foster father?" I asked, my hand still against his chest as I shifted closer, hoping my warmth, my touch, would give him something to hold on to while he dove through his own nightmares. More real than any of mine had been. "What happened to him?"

He looked me straight in the eyes. "I ate him."

I didn't think I could get more stunned, but I was proven wrong. He shook his head in annoyance, not the slightest bit concerned. "You wouldn't believe the indigestion he gave me afterward. The miserable bastard couldn't even die without one last punch to the gut."

A surprised laugh escaped me, not expecting that in the slightest. "What did everyone think when they saw you?"

Flipping onto his side, he chuckled in amusement. "They were surprised, to say the least. Some thought I was the child of The Divine, others a manifestation of the God's power. Cashim thought I was just an abused kid who had the unfortunate experience of Awakening at the ripe age of sixteen."

Thinking back to my own Awakening, I couldn't imagine what he had to have gone through. The pain he had to suffer after the abuse he had already experienced at the hands of his foster father.

I slid closer to him until our chests brushed. "I'm sorry you had to go through that. It took me a long time to figure out that the hate of others has little to do with the person it is directed at, and everything to do with the person it comes from. That the actions of those with hate in their hearts are not because of anything you have done or said, but simply because you exist and to them, that is enough. We're just the ones left to deal with the aftermath."

He looked at me in a way I'd come to realize was addictive. As if I were the only person in the world who had his attention. The full focus of a man like him was intoxicating in the worst way, making me desire to have it—to have him—all the time. I found myself lately fighting to get my next fix. He could enslave an entire people with that look, and something told me he knew exactly how it affected me.

Leaning in, his nose brushed mine, sprouting tingles from every soft touch as he spoke. "Yes, we are. It's just a shame that's how the world is. Leaving children so scarred that they become monsters like me, desperately wishing they weren't. Wishing that their hands weren't covered in blood, so that when they touched ivory skin such as yours," he whispered, dragging his knuckle down my arm, "they wouldn't leave a mark that stained something so beautiful."

"We're all scarred in some way or another, Kanan," I said, glancing down at his lips before whipping my eyes back up to his, both our gazes burning like stars. "Some of us just carry them on our hearts rather than our skin."

His hand grasped my waist, pulling me as close as possible, our skin only separated by our tunics. His breathing grew labored, his fingers clenching and releasing on my hip, as he fought himself.

I'm not sure who reached for who, but we came together in a clash, our lips joining us. He came over me, reaching up with a hand to grasp my cheek, tangling his fingers in my hair. Angling me, he dove deeper, nipping softly at my lips for permission. I granted it enthusiastically, and his tongue tangled with mine.

With gentle licks and strong strokes, he whipped me into a fury of desire. Moaning softly as he settled his weight in between my thighs, I wrapped a leg over his thigh. His large hand moved from my waist to grasp it, holding it tightly to him. His fingers dug in possessively, hard enough to leave marks tomorrow, but I couldn't find it in me to care all too much.

Groaning, he released my mouth, moving down my neck. I sighed with pleasure as he found that spot that dove me crazy, and couldn't help but roll my hips up, grinding against his hardening cock.

Gasping as he bit down in retaliation, I did it again just to torment him in return. For all the times I wished it was him as I touched myself in the darkest hours of night. For every touch he'd placed upon my skin. For the piano room.

Breathing wildly, he pulled down the v-shaped neckline of my tunic, palming one of my breasts through the bandeau wrapping, and I arched up into his grip with another moan of pleasure. As he played, he brought his mouth down to its forgotten twin, sucking on the hardened nipple. Crying out, my core clenched as each suck sent a bolt of need straight to my clit.

Bringing my hands up, I grasped onto his hair. I tugged on the strands as he tweaked one nipple while biting down on the other, whimpering as my body ignited under his touch. Each suck, lick, tug brought me closer to the edge, brought me closer to falling or flying.

Reaching up, he grasped my wrists, pinning them to the bed on either side of my head. Staring down at me, his eyes were wild with lust and desire. A desperate, wild look rose in his eyes as he leaned down, meeting me halfway. Lips connecting, we burned together, biting and teasing each other into oblivion.

I pulled against his grip just because I could, loving the feel of his strength holding me down. I knew if I said so, he would let me go immediately, but no part of me wished for that.

Chuckling against my mouth, I felt something cool slide around my wrists as he let go. Breaking apart, I looked up and saw that bands of shadows had pulled my hands above me, tying me to the bedposts.

Before I could even say anything, he grasped my jaw and forced my eyes back on him, kissing me with a bite of dominance to it. There was a lick of heat to every caress of his tongue against mine. The slight prick of claws dragged down my arm before reaching down to grasp my thighs, careful not to break my skin.

As he worked his way down, I couldn't help but writhe under his touch as he lifted the hem of my shirt, pressing a soft kiss below my navel. I watched in fascination as he grasped the laces of my trousers between his teeth, pulling them loose before slowly peeling the black leather off my legs. Lifting up onto his knees, he yanked them off the rest of the way, tossing them over his shoulder without looking.

There was nothing civilized or lordly in his gaze, as he smiled down at me wickedly. "Do you know how often I've thought about this? How many times I've dreamt of having you tied up and at my mercy? The things I've thought about doing to you"—he shook his head—"are depraved, but I don't care any longer. You have me so under your spell all I want is you. Your attention. Your touch. Your taste."

At that, he bent down, folding my legs over his shoulders, his hot breath against my core driving me wild. He looked up at me through those long, dark lashes, red eyes alight like stars, glowing so brightly his cheekbones also burned red; everything wicked and sinful, everything wild and feral in that one look. Even still, he waited. Waited for my permission.

He didn't have to wait long as I ground upwards, throwing my head back as I did my best not to scream my frustration. My breath came rushing out in gasps, my voice thick and heavy with emotions I couldn't untangle from the sensations wracking my body. I knew I must have been loud, some part of the little propriety I had shrieked in distress at waking someone up, but at this point I really didn't give a fuck as long as he touched me, licked me—did anything. I was burning alive, aching in a way that demanded to be sated or else it would take me with it. "Please, gods, just touch me. Please."

He smiled, a cat who got the cream, and with those simple, breathy words he was let off his leash. With a rip of his claws, he tore my underwear off like wet paper. Without a second's hesitation, he dove in, licking away at my core like a man possessed.

I cried out, electricity racing through my body as it tried and failed to process the sheer ecstasy it felt. Every lick sent me crashing underneath the waves, lost beneath his touch, sending me closer and closer to my end.

I yanked against my restraints, and they only pulled tighter.

Pulling me closer, he lifted me up, angling me better so he could feast upon me. He started sucking on my clit. At some point, I started moaning his name, which only seemed to drive him into a higher fever, as he buried his face between my thighs without a breath.

I pleaded and gasped, begging for him to stop, begging him for more. He was driving me to insanity, drinking me in the same way a man deprived of water would. I could do nothing, subjected to every long stroke, every breathtaking suck. It was too much, near blinding me with pleasure. I tried to pull away, just to release some of the pressure, but his grip only tightened, those claws digging in just enough that I felt the small drops of blood roll down my legs as he let out a hungry growl, angry that I would try to take away his meal. The bands of darkness around my hands pulled slightly, forcing me to arch further into his mouth, forcing me to take all the pleasure he was giving me.

I was teetering back and forth on the knife's edge that balanced between torture and rapture. "Please, Kanan. I need it." My voice was raw, my eyes rolling to the back of my head as I panted under his onslaught.

As if he heard the magic words, I felt pressure against my center as he thrust his finger in hard. Somehow, he found that small spot inside me immediately and rubbed. The air was taken right out of me as my whole body jerked at the touch, causing him to chuckle. He lifted his head up, lips glistening with my arousal as he dragged them along the inside of my thigh, a secret smile on his lips. "Right there?"

I moaned in reply, barely able to think, let alone speak as his thick finger stretched me, that torturous rubbing nearly sending me over the edge. Another dark shadow ran along my leg, darting down between my thighs until its cool touch started circling my clit. I gasped again, the strange feeling only sending me higher into the throes of passion.

Kanan bit the junction of my thigh as he pulled his finger

out, the sharp pain sending shockwaves through me even as I cried out at the loss; my attention shooting straight to him. "Answer me, love."

Climbing his way up my body, he hovered over my mouth as I breathed harshly, barely able to form words as his dark shadows released my wrists to run along my body, doing his bidding and ratcheting me higher and higher until I couldn't think, couldn't breathe. "Yes, yes, right there," I groaned out, the words barely making it past my lips.

He smiled again, his soft lips a sin of their own, as he mumbled against mine, "Good girl."

Capturing my lips with a groan, he plunged two fingers back in deeper. Harder. Every plunge, every stroke. I didn't care as long as he kept touching me. I could taste myself on him as I wrapped my hands deep into his thick hair and held him close. Those hard thrusts were my undoing. My release lit me on fire, shooting straight down my spine as I cried out. His lips covered mine, swallowing the sound, devouring it like it was his favorite thing in the world.

I shuddered around his fingers, my pussy clenching tight around them as he continued to thrust them in and out, drawing every gasp and shudder he could out of me until I was limp and shivering with aftershocks.

My breath came out in hard bursts as he sat up between my legs, pulling his fingers out. In the most debauched and sensual move I had ever seen, he stuck them between his lips, eyes locked on mine, as he licked them clean of every last drop of me.

As I caught my breath, I looked him up and down, not at all appreciating his state of dress. That being clothed and all. I reached down to the lacings of his pants, having every intention of fixing the problem and reciprocating, wanting to taste him just the same.

Grabbing my hand before it could touch him, he placed it on

the bed. "You have no idea how much I want you, but I have no intention of fucking you in a bed that is threatening to break down on us at any moment." He leaned down and kissed my lips, nipping at my bottom one.

My heart stumbled as he moved back behind me, pulling my still shivering body close and covering us with the blankets. "You need to sleep. We have a long day tomorrow."

How he thought I was going to be able to sleep after that, I had no idea. He was still hard as a rock behind me, his cock nestled into my ass, and yet his breathing slowed and his muscles relaxed. He started running his hands down my side, the gentle strokes lowering my heartbeat and forcing my muscles to relax.

Pressing a gentle kiss to my neck, he mumbled again, sleep already thick in his voice, "Sleep, love, or you'll be of no use to me."

Like my body was waiting for the command, my eyes closed. Pressed up against him like I was, his furnace-like heat drenched me, pulling me deep into the cozy warmth of his body. Sleep came for me, carrying me off gently in a way it never had before.

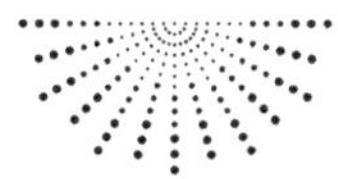

CHAPTER THIRTY

The village was even creepier in the daylight than it was at night, the silence that emanated from it more jarring. A village like this, no matter how small, should have people on their way to work, mothers hanging laundry on clotheslines, children playing ball in the clearing. There was none of that. There was just—

Nothing.

Entryways were not swept. The windows on all the buildings had a fine layer of dust on them, blocking our view of the insides, but I had no doubt they were just as desolate as the outsides. I would have thought it abandoned to time, the settlers having moved on to bigger and better things, yet it was as if they had simply stopped in the middle of their day.

Doors had been left ajar; the smell of ashes and smoke perfumed the air until I could taste it on my tongue. Several large areas of burnt ground must have been all that remained of the buildings that had been set ablaze, houses and businesses that had been left unattended with a fire still inside.

As we walked along the grass, I stopped to bend down, the sight of a small doll grabbing my attention. The burlap fabric, with its hand-stitched seams and button eyes, had seen better days, but it was the soft spots that had me grasping it to my chest. The places where a child would have repeatedly grabbed hold of it, held it to their cheek as they slept. The small rips and tears where they dragged it along the ground behind them as they chased the older kids, begging to play, too. This little doll had a person it belonged to, a young child that had a life, and now they were gone, having left the doll behind.

It was the doll that made me so sure that something bad had happened. Not the evil seeping into the very ground. Not the overwhelming silence that had my ears ringing to fill the gaps. No, it was the doll, soft from love that had been carelessly dropped along the ground.

Twisting my pack around, I undid the straps and stuffed the little doll inside, determination to find out what had happened to its owner flowing through my body like ice. The icy-cool fury burned like a blizzard would against skin; and for a split second, I felt that anger slip through the cracks in the barrier around my energy spark.

I felt it seep into the walls, freezing inside the shimmering power, before cracking it apart just slightly more. The trickle of aether that had sustained me grew into a stream, more powerful as the inside of my mind glowed with its power.

"Atallia?" The question came from beside me, breaking the eerie quiet like a glass shattering in an empty room.

Twisting around, I looked over at him, a flash of light catching my eye. Glancing down, I saw my hands cracking apart —breaking from within—golden light shooting out from beneath my skin. No blood or muscle or bone. Only the blazing, molten metal, and for a moment it burned so bright I saw an outline of a hand underneath. A hand made of gold energy, not corporeal or physical, but ethereal and hazy around the edge.

I blinked and it was gone, my hands back to normal as if nothing ever happened. I flipped them over, looking for the form I just saw, the magic that I hadn't seen since I had first Awakened.

"Atallia." Kanan's voice was firm, snapping me out of it. "Are you alright?"

I met his eyes, the red irises reminding me of the blood that had spilled along the grass the night I had been attacked. The night that changed everything for me. "Yeah, I'm fine, let's keep looking."

He stared at me for a second longer before looking away, a frown marring his savagely perfect face. Indicating with his chin, he started walking toward the far end of the clearing. "The meeting hall should be this way."

I followed behind, careful not to disturb anything lying on the ground, hoping one day that the people whose things they were would be back to pick them up. I was acutely aware of how unrealistic it was, but I couldn't stand one more fucking thing that made me sad, so I was going with optimism. My normal cynicism did not approve.

"What are we even looking for?" I asked as we picked our way along, the isolated village so far apart from the Eskira that there weren't even any proper roadways. The village people had plopped their houses in the clearing and called it that.

It reminded me of home in a way that made me sick for it. The peaceful view of the woods was so like the one outside my bedroom window, except these woods whispered horrid things; vile and rot slithering along my skin the longer we stayed.

"Anything that might lead us to whatever is causing these wraiths to be made. Or I guess I should say whoever is kidnapping Descendents and making them into these things." He snarled his frustration. Anger radiated from him at the situation, at himself for not being able to stop it from happening.

I nearly reached out for him, but thought better of it. Our interactions this morning had already thrown me for a loop. Both of us acting as if the night's activities hadn't happened, but also acknowledging that something had grown between us—a flower budding for the first time since its winter hibernation, the petals on the verge of opening yet waiting to see if a last frost would hit before it had its chance. Not a single word had been spoken as we left the inn, paying the blushing Ellenia for the night and for the broken bed, and I had no clue how to process everything.

We had been left on unsettled ground, unsure where we now stood, as too many things seemed to stand in our way. I had too many questions that I was sure he could answer but seemingly refused to. I was unsure of what to do next, so I defaulted to acting as if nothing was wrong.

Denial and I had become fast friends over the past few weeks, both of us working together to stop me from having to deal with all of my emotional damage. Wrynn thought I was deflecting my problems, and that it wasn't healthy. I thought it was great even though I knew that it would eventually come to bite me in the ass.

We made it to a long wooden building, spreading out before us in either direction. It was crafted in the same wood and thatch style as the rest of the village, but it was obvious as we stepped inside that it was a place of meeting for the people. Long tables lined with benches took up most of the space, facing a raised platform where the town elders and leaders would have most likely spoken.

Pushed into the corners were smaller tables made for the children, heavy with paints and brushes to keep them occupied during the long gatherings. Paintings had been hung up all around them, tacked to the wall with nails. Tiny, colored fingerprints marred the cream surfaces, streaks of color splashed wherever for the amusement of giggling kids.

My heart sat heavy in my chest, each slow thump more painful than the last. The village was empty, a remnant of what could have been. I think it was worse that it hadn't been destroyed. At the very least, then it wouldn't be a reminder of all that had been lost; instead, it stood like a stone over a grave.

It was a reminder to anyone who saw it that whatever you had that was good could be taken from you in a second, so quickly everything you loved could be wiped away and left like some dusty antique of the past.

"I should have been here," Kanan murmured quietly, pain clear and cutting in his words. "I should have been able to stop this, all of this, from happening."

"It's not your fault, Kanan, none of this is your fault."

He scoffed in disgust, fists clenched at his sides. "I'm good at this. I'm good at hunting down my prey and killing it. At serving justice, and fixing the problem; but I can't hunt ghosts. That's what we're going after, remnants of beings who once were. How do I find what cannot be found and still keep everyone safe? Families are gone without a trace, entire towns are going silent. How could I allow this all to happen?"

"You couldn't have known about any of this," I said, waving my hand around. "We don't even know what any of this is. How could you have known?"

His face grew dark as he shifted his eyes downward, running a hand over the back of his head. Looking back up at me, I saw it in his eyes, his posture. "Unless you do know what it is …" I tilted my head, outrage rising in my tone as I spoke. "Do you, Kanan?"

He kept his eyes locked on mine, something in his expression that I didn't like. "Kanan! Answer me!"

He opened his mouth—

A scream wrenched through the air. Whipping around, I faced the door, freezing in place. Quickly, another scream pierced through the silence that permeated the village clearing. Taking off at a run, Kanan not far behind, I dashed out into the sunlight, following the sound of crying and screeching into the woods.

I picked up my pace as another cry—female by the sound of it—shattered the air, thanking the Cosmos for the millionth time for the speed I was granted as I whipped past trees so fast their branches snapped at me. I blurred by so quickly I couldn't make out their shape, dodging them by mere inches.

I knew Kanan wasn't far behind me, snapping branches and an overwhelming sense of his location alerting me without having to look. We raced through the forest, the sounds of snapping branches and cracking bones getting closer and closer until we came upon it.

A young girl, not even twelve years of age, ran through the woods. Blood dripped down her skin from several cuts. Her red curls were a tangled mess around her heart-shaped face, blue eyes wide in fear. Without Awakening, she was as slow as a human, and the wraith chasing her was herding her through the woods, playing with its prey like a cat with a mouse.

The grotesque wolf carcass was nearly all bone, skin and muscle falling behind it even as it ran after her. Knowing now what I did—that it had once been a Descendent—made it all that much worse. Its broken-down body defied the laws of existence with the gaping holes in its side and its organs sloshing inside, black tar dripping to coat the ground.

"Get the girl back to the village," Kanan yelled at me, heading straight for the beast.

"Got it," I yelled back, trusting him to handle himself.

The girl saw us heading toward her and relief flashed over her face as she changed direction toward us. Holding out my arms, I waved her over to me, as Kanan took a running dive at the wraith, tackling it to the ground.

Grabbing hold of the girl, I picked her up and turned around without thought, heading back the way we came. "Are you okay?" I yelled at her, the snarls and roars behind me only forcing me forward faster.

"Thank you," she sobbed, tears running down her face. "Gods, thank you."

"It's okay now, I've got you." My breath rushed out of me in harsh gasps. "It's going to be okay, just hold on."

She did as she was told, tightening her arms around my neck and her legs around my waist; she buried her tear-stained face into my shoulder. I could see the village clearing in the distance, the sun starting to break through the canopy, and I ran as fast as possible towards it.

It was just within reach when a sudden force knocked me off my feet. The little girl was thrown from my arms as I crashed to the ground, my head smacking against something hard, disorienting me. My vision blurred as the air left my lungs in one big gasp.

Coughing, I blinked rapidly, trying to clear the stars from my eyes, my head pounding painfully as my chest felt like a thousand pound boulder had fallen on it. I shifted, trying to turn over and get up, but another blow knocked me flat on my stomach with a groan. It was followed quickly by a stabbing pain to my side that seared through me, causing me to cry out.

All my focus narrowed to that pain as my spark flickered weakly behind its barrier, the strength that made my bones steel strong turned to weakness. The fire that ignited my blood went dark, a smoldering ember at best.

Peering down through the haze, I saw a white heartsglass blade sticking out of my side, the hilt glowing fiercely as it drained my aether dry, chaining it down within me even worse than it already was. A bit of an overkill, I couldn't help but think, I barely had any access to my power as it was, and I got stabbed anyway. Motherfuckers.

Coughing again, I felt the blood speckle my lips as I tried to push up onto my knees. A foot kicked out, hitting me in the face, crushing my nose and causing blood to spurt out.

"That's enough, Hanson. The boss wants her presentable." The bored male voice sounded far off.

An annoyed grunt came from above, before a meaty hand grabbed my hair in a fist and yanked me up. I yelped in pain even though it was nothing compared to the soul-sucking feeling of the heartsglass blade in my side. Kicking out, I tried my best to fight the man's hard grip, but my strength was leaving me like a bucket with holes stabbed in it, the water leaking out faster than it could be filled. The sharp press of a blade to my throat had me frozen, a drop of blood sliding into the hollow of my throat. I didn't have to look down to know that the blade wasn't white this time. The other man, tall and blonde, came to crouch in front of me. I snarled in his face, bucking at the grip on my hair, scratching my nails against the man's—Hanson's—wrist at my throat.

His narrow face was full of sharp angles and shifting features, just like Jasco's. What I thought had been blonde hair was now black as night.

Blink. Brown.

Blink. Blue.

My vision was already having trouble keeping up, the man's face making me see double. Reaching out with his pale, tan, dark, hand, he gripped my chin tight, tilting it into the rays of light. Smiling cruelly, he looked up at Hanson, the big man yanking my hair tighter. "This is her, alright."

Smiling wickedly back at him, I spit my blood into his face. It struck him right on the cheek, and he turned to the side with a grimace as he wiped it off. Looking back at me, a sneer twisted his handsome, ugly, average face. I laughed weakly in his face, my own smile most likely painted with thick blood, the metallic taste heavy on my tongue.

Striking out fast, he backhanded me, whipping my head to the side and causing blood to drip down my chin. My shoulders shook with crazed laughter, giggles shaking raggedly out of my chest as I coughed, my ribs screaming in the process.

The man went to say something, but a yell—a war cry—that would have done any warrior proud interrupted him, and I saw over his shoulder the little girl careening toward him, a rock held high like some battle axe.

Her face held fear but also hardened anger, the kind of anger that brought people together in times of strife and war. The kind that made cowards into heroes. The kind that brought a child to the verge of murder, for the wrath of vengeance, the need for justice touched every soul no matter how young.

The strange man turned around swiftly, barely flinching at the ferocious sight of the brave child. Grabbing her wrist that held the rock high above, he swiftly pulled a steel dagger and shoved it underneath her jaw and straight through.

"NO!" I screamed, loud enough that the air wavered in front of me, as I watched her blood spill down his hand, her lips parted enough for me to see the blade breaking through her rosebud mouth. I gasped, tears running down my face as the light in her beautiful blue eyes went dark.

I stared open-mouthed in shock as he yanked the blade free, her small body falling backwards onto the dirty, leaf-strewn ground. The rock she wielded with such might fell uselessly beside her.

I didn't even know her name. This child that was willing to fight back to help me died trying to save me. Rain began to fall as surely as the tears fell down my face, the dark clouds covering all light from the sky. No colors would dance in this sky today.

The insidious feeling all around watched on in glee. Like a rising wave, it waited high above, ready to crash down upon the living, eating the magic—the sparks—of life. Another fallen warrior who shined so bright, so young, gone without a chance to begin.

Thunder boomed above as my anger tried to build, urging me to fight back, to not let her sacrifice be in vain, but I couldn't seem to move. The sight of the blade being shoved through her head played in my mind over and over again, like some sick game meant to torment me. I thought the heartsglass in my side was painful, but I was wrong.

I couldn't save her, I realized with a sob. I couldn't save her.

"We need to go now," the murderer said evenly, not at all affected by the choice he just made. "Our distraction will only last so long, and then we'll have to deal with him."

I could hear the words, knew they were talking about Kanan, but I couldn't bring myself to hear them, unable to take my eyes from the small, colorless body.

They started dragging me behind them, pulling me over behind a wide tree. There was a shimmer in the air. The space wavering, like a mirage on a hot day, showing a different view of dark sky and barren land before fluctuating back to the forest around us.

"Knock her out, Hanson," the featureless man said as he seemingly walked between two trees, wiping the blood off his hands with a white cloth, before disappearing into thin air.

I blinked rapidly, trying to clear my eyes, but just as the air shifted again, my hair was yanked, jerking my head back up to the sky just as a boulder-sized fist came down upon my face. I felt myself drop to the ground, my entire body throbbing in pain.

Blackness tinged the edge of my vision, and the last thing I saw before I fell unconscious was lifeless, blue eyes staring into mine.

CHAPTER THIRTY-ONE

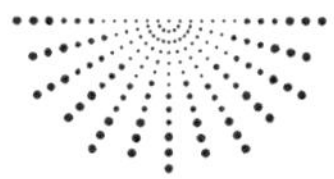

The rough rock beneath my cheek was cold enough to seep into my skin and send shivers through my bones as I woke from the foggy darkness of sleep.

Groaning softly, I closed my eyes as my head pounded incessantly, pain spearing through my skull right behind my eyes. I stretched out my sore legs, cramping from the weird position I must have been laid in, the harsh scrape of chain links forcing me to move.

Pushing up off the floor and stifling a yelp as my ribs gave an unnatural crunch, I peered down at my wrists. The glow from the white heartsglass shackles had me squinting, the light not helping the massive fucking headache that had shooting pains going down my spine.

The long chains that were attached to the manacles were hard iron tied into the ground by large stakes at four different points. Kneeling, I took a good look around, the nondescript chamber was filled to the brim with racks of weapons and implements. I didn't need to guess what their uses were, some still dipped in dried blood.

I swallowed the fear that tried to rise, not willing to give the bastards who had killed a little girl anything. My eyes closed at the reminder of the body in the woods, the empty eyes staring back at me, never to hold their spark again. Shaking my head, I forced myself to shove the image from my mind. Grief and sadness could come later when I wasn't being held captive chained to the floor of a torture chamber.

Taking the uninterrupted time free of any visitors, which I had a feeling wouldn't last long, I took stock of the room. Four plain walls, all stone, no windows and only one door. Escape wasn't looking good for me, at least not from this room.

The single exit at the far side of the room, directly in front of me, was wide, double wooden doors. The other side was without a doubt guarded, if the lengths that this person had gone to get me were any indication. Regardless, my first problem was the heartsglass manacles that were keeping not only me but whatever little power I had chained.

I was in no position to fight. The dagger had been removed from my side but if the bloodstain was any indication, my healing hadn't made a return yet, so I was a battered mess. My bare feet—where the hell were my shoes—were red and raw from the cold rock, and I could already see bruises forming from where the shackles had tightened.

I wasn't going anywhere. My only hope was that they would move me somewhere less protected and I could figure out a plan of escape then. Eventually the heartsglass would give out— at least that's what the woman in my dreams had said. Right? Or had it been something else? My memories of the dream were foggy at best. I couldn't rely on it though. Who knew if it was actually true?

My eyes caught the bloodstains that spotted the floor in puddles, too much of it for it to be fully cleaned out of the rough cracks. The stone was more red than gray, making me wonder how many times blood had to have been spilled to change the color of the rock. Would mine join the countless others'?

Pressing my lips together, shaking my head, I shoved the fearful thoughts away; instead, I did my best to steel myself for what was likely to come. I had no idea what they wanted from me, but I would be damned if I gave them anything that could be used to hurt the Descendents. To hurt the people who were quickly becoming just as much a part of my family as Maris and Geoff.

Cashim with his steadiness and wisdom.

Zanaya's wit and loyalty, always willing to lend a friendly hand.

Zander's infectious laughter and complete inability to allow anyone to be left out in the rain alone.

Nala with her crazy pyromania who didn't ask questions, but instead stood by you—sheltering and holding you up—until you were ready to face whatever it was that ate at you.

Saanvi, the quiet viper, who had seen too much, knew pain and understood loss; who never took credit for her kindness.

Orion, the silent sentry, waiting to be your rock in the storm, weathering any beating as long as it protected his family.

And Wrynn. Sweet Wrynn. With his hopeless inability to stay out of trouble, and the joy he brought in doing so.

The innkeeper, Ellenia, the children playing ball in Eskira's town square, the lovers dancing to the music in their souls. So many lives so full of life and wonder that could be hurt and damaged by the evil that was attempting to take their world from them.

And then there was Kanan. A man of few words, he said, but one of many actions. A man who saw behind the golden eyes that scared others—too many years in eyes so young—saw the scared, young girl who feared rejection over anything else. Feared the idea of being unloved even more than the power that slept inside of her. There was a bond between us, no doubt, of what I had no idea, but I wouldn't have the chance to explore it if this insidious evil was allowed to continue.

Clicking steps came from behind the door, shaking me free from my thoughts. My muscles tensed in preparation for what was to come. The wood groaned loudly as the doors pushed in, the sound echoing against the stone.

The clang of armor was next as several guards moved into the room, hands set on the hilts of their swords—black heartsglass, no doubt. Imposing silver helmets that covered everything except their eyes were an intimidating sight; every single one of them looked the exact same. It gave them a uniformity that spoke more of wiping away any self-expression or uniqueness than of unity between a people.

Their chest plates held an emblem that was even more bone-chilling. A dragon skeleton. The great beast's eye sockets were sunken in, its dagger-like fangs cracked and dull. Dead. The emblem was a twisted and demented twin to the Descendent Army emblem that waved high on every flag.

A man stepped into the room, followed by two more guards. His clipped steps were taken in shiny leather shoes. His lean, muscular frame was dressed in black trousers and a silver tunic decorated with golden thread.

The man's face was pretty, all sharp angles and chiseled features framed by straight, mahogany hair tucked just so behind his ears. His bird-like nose was slightly hooked at the end. His calm expression, soft lips curled in a pleasant smile, gave him an appearance that said he was on your side, ready to help; but it was the eyes that told a different story.

The pristine green was sharper than any blade, bright like summer grass. It was the toxic, infectious glow that reminded me of the disease that crawled beneath the skin of the sick, that had my hackles rising. My hair stood on end as I met his gaze, the insanity plain and clear, just as it had been in my dream.

The hazy memory came shooting to the front of my mind,

the once blurred image of the man in front of the heartsglass bars that held the woman sharpened, a pristine image of the man in my head. Her hate and disgust became my own as he walked closer.

A wave of rot followed on his heels, the smell so strong I nearly gagged. The overwhelming scent of infection and disease hit my nose stronger than even the wraith's odor had. At first, I thought it was the man himself, but as it spread around the large room, I realized it was the guards stationing themselves around the room.

The dream came to mind again, when the man had shown off his … creation. The chunks of skin that had fallen from the guard's face, the rotten muscle beneath. Looking around at the sentries, every inch of skin covered by armor, I wondered how decayed they were underneath all that metal.

It didn't get past me that as the man reached me he continued to stand, clearly placing himself above my kneeling form chained to the floor. His pleasant smile hadn't changed once, his expression frozen. It made me wonder if he had practiced it in a mirror. A false mask to hide where the true source of rot came from.

"Do you know who I am?" Smugness was clear in his voice, arrogance dripping from every word. He peered down at me with a superiority that made that of a king look childish. His pleasant façade couldn't hide the slight curl to his false smile.

The pieces had been coming together for weeks now. None of it made much sense to me, but then again, it was clear a lot had been forgotten. The dreams, the book that had been left for me, the gaps in history even Descendent children should know. I didn't know how it was possible, but it was the only conclusion that made sense.

"You're the God of Chaos. You began the War of Three."

His smile grew wide, a genuine one I think; truly a disturbing sight to behold. Approval shone in his pale eyes. "You can call me Kasis, though you should know that by now, Atallia."

I tried to stifle the chill that went down my spine as my name crossed his lips. Possession bordering on ownership twisted the words into stones that plummeted to the bottom of my stomach, the tone setting my nerves on edge. Disgust curdled in my stomach, my sheer repulsion towards him unlike anything I had ever experienced.

"What do you want from me?" I asked, masking my emotions with bluntness. "You've been kidnapping Descendents and turning them into your mindless monsters, for what? Power?"

Kasis laughed, big and loud, placing his hand on his chest. "My dear, I'm after the same thing I wanted two thousand years ago, the same thing I was after ten thousand years ago."

"And what's that?"

He smiled, and for a split second, his beautiful façade cracked, showing a sunken skull and rotted teeth. "Oh, this is just too good." He shook his head in disbelief. "I can't believe my luck." He looked at me, huffing out a chuckle. "I have no interest in spoiling all the fun just yet, but don't worry, love, it will be a fun surprise."

I narrowed my eyes at him, not at all liking the enjoyment he was having. A man like him was only happy when things were going his way, which didn't entail good things for my future. "And what does any of this have to do with me?"

He finally crouched down to my level, his hand reverently cupping my face, stroking my jawline. I couldn't stop the small flinch as his skin came in contact with mine; everything inside me tried to rear back as far as possible. My bones, my blood, my spark all shrieked as if in pain. Alarm bells went off in my head, my entire body going into a state of distress.

"This is all about you, don't you understand? It's always been about you, and what you carry inside." He smiled warmly, his face moving into all the right places to express normalcy, but it always went back to the eyes.

Their pristine green was more beautiful than any emerald or peridot, more vibrant than any forest or grassland. They could have been painted a thousand times over and not one of them would have truly captured all the hues, but it was what was underneath that had you pulling back in terror.

Dark, insidious madness lurked beneath the beautiful façade; just like everything else about him, it was a mask. A mask to hide the true nature of the man before me. It was an insanity that only came about from a fractured mind, shattered like glass into a million pieces and put back together, glued with corruption and rot.

The shards of that mind still stuck out though, still sharp and able to cut. Broken and fixed, but never the same. It made a person wonder what brought him to this point. Had he always been like this or was there something that pushed him off the edge, that broke him into those pieces and reshaped him into what he was now?

"You see, dearest," he continued uninterrupted, "Your mental barriers are naturally strong, even if you don't know how to use them to their full potential, and they're blocking me—and you—from accessing your power; so the only way to break them down is to, well … break you."

He actually sent me an apologetic smile, as if he had no control over this; as if this wasn't his decision. "I just want you to know that." He nodded encouragingly, trying to get me to understand. "So that you understand why I have to do this. I mean, surely you understand. You have to understand. She has to understand, she has to, that's what she said. She told me she would understand."

He trailed off, still mumbling the words to himself as he got up and walked away without looking back. With an offhanded wave that must be some kind of signal to the guards, he exited through the double doors, the suits full of rotten carcasses following close behind him.

A man I hadn't seen this entire time, so blended into the background he might as well have been invisible, stepped from the shadowy depths surrounding the edges of the room. He was covered head to toe in some sort of black suit, nothing visible but his red, scarred hands. He floated along the floor, moving like a ghost, his form flashing in and out of visibility as he crossed over to me, ripping the back of my tunic until my skin was exposed to the cool air. He made his way over to the racks of tools and instruments; all the sharp points now glinted even more menacingly in the torchlight.

I could do nothing but hold my trembling in, forcing a numbness to seep into my muscles, into my bones, my mind. Closing my eyes, I let my mind wander. Maybe if I could just go somewhere, somewhere far away where they could never find me, then I'd survive this. Maybe my soul would never be touched by this evil, my thoughts not edged with the screams this room would hold in a few short moments.

The clinking sound of a crystal-tipped whip hit the floor. No, it was the ringing of Maris's wind chimes coming in through the open window, the soft, cool breeze against my cheeks gently swaying the rods together to make beautiful music. I realized now that the sharp, metallic smell was actually the sweet, citrusy scent of the lemon balm and lavender that I was stringing together with a rough piece of twine.

Crack.

A scream off in the distance. No, a baby wailing in its mother's arms as they walk past our little cottage.

Crack. Crack.

It was raining, my back soaked in seconds as I leaned over the worktable, intent on my task. I looped the string around tighter, gritting my teeth as I did so.

Crack.

Another scream. Shifting, I elbowed a glass jar, knocking it to the ground where it shattered. A small shard jumped up and sliced me on the leg, a small cut, leaving little bubbles of blood behind. I wiped it away with a finger, closing the cut until the skin was smooth, the slight burn disappearing with it.

Crack.

A shriek of anguish. Maybe I should go check on the baby. They really shouldn't be out in the storm like this.

Crack. Crack.

The walls around me wavered as a storm raged above, water pouring down my back. The warm chestnut turned gray. I shook my head and smiled, the walls going back to normal.

Crack.

I cleared my throat, a sudden rawness to it. Setting the plant bundles down, I moved through the house. Wall shaking and rumbling. Gray, then brown. Gray. Brown.

Crack.

A whimper. When did we get a dog? I thought as I made my way up the stairs. I knew Geoff had always wanted one, but Maris always said no. I'm glad he got her to change her mind. I had always secretly wanted one as well.

Crack.

My bed. So warm and inviting, especially as the house was being weird. Maybe I would just sleep the storm away. It seemed like a better option than waiting for it to pass, I thought as my body started feeling very heavy.

Crack. Crack. Crack.

A nap sounded good, my eyes so tired as the walls around me wavered again. Even as I closed them, I could still hear the storm keeping me up, unable to sleep. I felt so heavy, like a rock instead of a feather dropping from a tremendous height. Free-falling instead of floating. I wonder what would happen when I hit the bottom. Would I stand strong or would I *crack* into a thousand pieces?

CHAPTER THIRTY-TWO

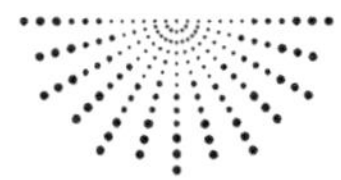

*P*ain. Such a simple, small word for something so all-encompassing. People put words to things in hopes of comprehending them, to help understand their place in our world. Pain was a short and sharp word, which always confused me. It came in too many different forms to be described in such a quick way—anguish, torment, agony—all of them provoking something different inside each person.

Pain was broad in a way that most things were not. Physical pain, mental pain, emotional pain, and it all could fall under that one small word; a word so easily said. I had faced it many times in my life before, and recently it had become something I knew all too well; but here, now, as I stared at this cell wall, unblinking because even that hurt, I realized I had never truly appreciated the word.

The word to describe the searing agony of having the flesh on my back flayed off. To describe the deep throbs where a mallet had been taken to my legs. The throbbing in my hand, bloody and raw and missing fingernails. The red and puffy slices decorating my stomach and chest from where the suited man had forced me on my back, ripped the rest of my tunic from my body and made me watch as he carved my skin to shreds.

The entire time my power had fought and battered the cage which held it, angrily beating and ramming into the wall—cracking that infuriating barrier further—and yet the incendiary, world-crushing power I had witnessed the night I had Awakened did not surface. I couldn't help but feel betrayed, my own power, which had started to feel less and less so, wouldn't even rise to protect me, to save me from the agony I had experienced in that blood-stained room.

I didn't remember how or when I had gotten into the small cell. Maybe it was sometime after the fourth time I had fallen unconscious only to be awoken by nearly drowning in a bucket of water. The bars were made of steel, one of the few like it, unlike the dozen others in the long hallway that made up the dungeon chamber. My guess as to why I had such nice accommodations was so that I would heal just enough to handle more of their ministrations.

I could already feel the skin on my chest closing up, knitting itself back together. I felt the slight prickling at my fingertips as nails regrew over exposed nerves. My back was being left alone, torn apart so badly that what little energy I did have was best used on fixing easier injuries. From what it felt like, it wouldn't matter if I had used all the energy I possessed, it wouldn't have made a dent in the burning wounds that had turned my back into a bloody pulp.

Which was why I was lying on my stomach, clad in only my bandeau and trousers which the torturer had left mostly alone. The icy stone actually felt good on my hot, inflamed skin, helping to cool down any fever that might arise from infection while my body did its best to heal.

I was left alone with my thoughts and the few sniffles and coughs that told me that, despite the relative quiet, there were others being kept down here. They had yet to say a single thing since I had come to, keeping quiet so as to not draw any unnecessary attention to themselves.

Which was why when I heard a small gasp, so close it might as well have been right next to me, that I assumed I was hearing things.

But no, it couldn't be fake unless my brain was making up the feeling of a little hand against my own, gently stroking it. A sniffle, a little sob. My eyebrows creased. *It couldn't be*, I thought, turning my head to look. With my luck it was a rat and my fucked up mind was trying to fool me into thinking otherwise.

But no, there he was, standing by my hand with tear-filled eyes as he gently rubbed the bloodied skin on my fingers. I had to blink a few times for my mind to finally catch up.

Wrynn.

Wrynn was here. I smiled as much as I could without grimacing.

It dropped quicker than it rose. Oh, my Divine. Wrynn was here.

"Wrynn?" I asked, suspicion thick in my voice, still not trusting my eyes to tell me the truth.

He jumped, gasping loudly as his white wings threw him up into the air like a glowing star. With wide eyes, hands pressed to his mouth, he flew straight at my face before kneeling on the cold floor, coming eye to eye with me.

"Atallia," he whisper-yelled. "Thank the Cosmos! I thought you were dead."

"I nearly am," I croaked back teasingly, which didn't go over well as his dark eyes—lit by the few torches outside the cells—overflowed with tears, dripping down his face like sad little rivers. "I'm still here, Wrynn, don't worry."

"How can I not worry?" he asked, looking down at my back. "This is bad. This is very, very bad. Your spark is very dull. I can barely see it."

"You can see my spark?" I said in confusion, before shaking my head and asking, "Wrynn, what are you doing here?"

He looked down at his hands, twisting them around and around. "Well, you see, uhm, I got concerned after you left, so I thought I would follow your trail. Just until you got to the town," he rushed out in explanation, waving his hands around wildly. "But then I was so tired after the flight. The warlord flies really fast, you know, and so I thought I would take a nap in the tree outside of your room at the inn. To listen for any trouble."

I narrowed my eyes. "Outside my room."

He swallowed, his cheeks going red. "Well, I heard some things, and I thought you were being attacked." He cleared his throat, his little pointed ears turning bright red in the firelight. "Then I realized you weren't and that maybe I shouldn't have been eavesdropping, but I really was trying to be on the lookout for bad guys."

I closed my eyes in mortification even as I tried my best not to laugh out loud, since Divine only knows how bad that would hurt. The thought of poor little Wrynn getting an eyeful of Kanan's and my nighttime activity was nearly too much for me to handle.

"And then by that point I didn't think it would hurt to make sure you were okay to get to the village in the morning, and then I thought it wouldn't hurt to just keep watch from a distance, and then I got curious and started looking in the houses, it was so sad," he mumbled off-handedly before continuing on. "And then you ran into the woods and I nearly lost you, but then I caught up to you when those men attacked," he finished, gasping for air by the end.

"So let me get this straight," I said, shifting, groaning as my ribs, my back, my everything protested the movement. "You decided that after everything I told you, how dangerous it was and that I needed you to stay behind so that you wouldn't get hurt or captured"—I stared at him hard—"you would do the exact opposite."

His mouth opened and closed like a fish before he crossed his arms over his chest, a look of indignation on his face. "Well, didn't Lord Kanan and Lord Cashim say the exact same thing to you? And I don't want to rub it in, but isn't this the exact situation they wanted you to avoid?"

I pursed my lips, frustration bubbling up inside me at the hard look in the mirror Wrynn was forcing on me. It's not like I knew they would use a little girl as a trap. I closed my eyes. "You're not wrong," I admitted. I wasn't that much of a bitch to deny it, but it didn't mean I had to like it. "But you still shouldn't be here. I don't want you to get hurt, Wrynn," I said, even as I lay there confused. "How did you get here, anyway? I know you said you followed us, but what happened afterward? Did you see Kanan?"

Concern flashed through me as I realized I hadn't even considered what might have happened to him. The man who had powers like Jasco had mentioned a distraction, which could only mean that they had been lying in wait for us, ready to take Kanan out of the equation so that they could snatch me.

But I couldn't for the life of me figure out why. If anything, they should want him. With his dragon form and immense power and importance, he was worth so much more than I was. My broken power and complete inexperience wouldn't be worth much to anyone.

Except maybe if Kasis was correct in his theory that he could break my spark out of its cage by literally beating it out of me. If my Awakening was indicative of what my spark's true breadth was, then at full power and under Kasis's control, he could use me as a weapon of mass destruction, and then rebuild the world as he liked.

I couldn't help the shiver of dread that worked its way through me. Wrynn moved closer, his glow nearly blinding, he was so close to me. "I only saw them take you through the weird shimmery air. That thing had a strange feeling to it, by the way. I'm not sure what happened to the lord while you were attacked —I only saw the aftermath."

"Then how did you find me?" I asked, moving myself gently onto my side, wincing as I hit one of the cuts.

"Well, that's the thing, those bad men, the big dumb one and the other one with the shifty face," he said, describing Hanson and the illusionist with amusing detail. "They had another friend, who I guess had been waiting for Kanan before releasing a pack of wraiths; I saw the bodies." He shook his head, eyes wide and serious. "It did not end well for them. Anyway, the lord was able to catch the guy and knock him out before trying to reach you. We heard you scream for that little girl."

His eyes filled with sympathy, reaching down to pat my undamaged cheek; my face was the only part that hadn't been touched other than by Hanson who had used it as a punching bag. Another set of eyes flashed in my mind, blue and dull and filled with fear and bravery alike. Gods, I wished I had been able to save her.

"Lord Kanan tortured information out of the bad guy. I listened and heard that they were keeping you in the Gravelands. I didn't wait around to hear the rest of it before flying out this way. It took me a day and a half, but I did it." I couldn't help the smile that cracked my dry lips at the proud set of his shoulders.

My brain snagged on what he said, though. "The Gravelands? I read about it in a book. Isn't it the barren area where the war was fought against Chaos?"

He nodded his head violently, big eyes going wide. "Yes, we're inside the mountain range here. I saw a lot of it when I was looking for you. It reminds me of Eskira."

"Wrynn, that was reckless, you could have been caught. I don't know what I would do with myself if you had been hurt because of me." I reached out with my hand, my arm shaking with exhaustion, grabbing onto his with two of my fingers. I gave it a squeeze, which he returned before my arm stopped working.

He gave me an uncharacteristically serious smile, no teasing remarks or actions waves of the hand in sight. "Friends don't leave friends, My Lady."

"Oh, are we being formal now, Lord Wrynn?" I retorted back sarcastically, another smile curling the edges of my mouth.

He only smiled, a mix of emotions behind his eyes before he moved on. "Well, regardless, you should feel lucky that I'm here. Now I can help you escape."

I looked around the cell as best as I could, unable to pick my head up from where it rested on my outstretched arm. No windows, a single straw mattress in the corner which I hadn't had the energy to crawl to after being thrown in here, and a pot in the corner.

The steel bars were as thick, if not thicker, than my forearms and did not have a door, which made me think you needed magic to open it. Looking back at Wrynn, I raised an eyebrow. "And how do you plan to do that, because unless you have a card you can pull out of your ass, I think we're stuck here."

He grinned like a fiend, flying straight up and through the bars at the front, slipping between the two like it was nothing. Flying back, he landed in front of me and sat cross-legged. "It's a good thing that they didn't put you in one of those cells," he said, nodding to the ones across from me that glowed with white heartsglass.

I cracked a real smile for the first time since I had been thrown in here. If anyone could find us a way out, it would be Wrynn. "Everyone always underestimates sprites," I said with conviction.

He laughed. "Yes they do, My Lady."

A loud cough, sharp and guttural, broke the deafening

silence from the front of the chamber. It was followed by the sounds of a dozen feet shifting in their cells. The mood in the room shifted, going from a tense exhaustion that could be felt in waves to a cautious waiting that had the hair on my bruised arms prickling.

"Wrynn, hide. Now," I whispered quickly as I kept an eye on the hallway in front of me. I was grateful that for once he did as I said, shooting up to the ceiling before disappearing into a small crevice I could barely see in the dreary light. I don't know what he did, but his ever-present glow went nearly nonexistent, the barest hint of silver peeking out, and even then I struggled to find it.

Satisfied that he was hidden away from whatever danger had the room on high alert, I forced my screaming body to move forward ever so slightly, getting a view of the front where the only doors were. Falling flat, ignoring my protesting back, I did my best to pretend I was still uncon-scious, closing my eyes as much as I could while still watching the doors.

I waited with bated breath, just like the rest of the room, it seemed. It wasn't long before the short, clipped steps, along with the clang of armor, announced the presence of guards. The doors were flung open with a bang as two silver armored guards stepped through, dragging a large body between them.

I had to give the man some credit—he was still struggling, yanking every few seconds at the guards' grip even as his feet dragged behind him, fatigue weighing him down. His head was hanging low and his long brown hair was greasy and tangled, concealing his face as they stopped at the cell diagonal from mine.

The guard waved something I couldn't see and the hearts-glass bars shot up into the ceiling, allowing them to barely toss the man in before closing the bars back down.

"Fuck," the male spat out as he landed hard in his cell, venom and fury twin flames in his tone as he spat curses at the rotting creatures that would have made a sailor proud.

A shock of electricity raced through me, more surprising than even Wrynn showing up. I nearly moved, but I stopped myself at the last minute. I held my breath, anxiety and hope warring inside me, causing my heart to race inside my chest.

The guards moved out with an eerie precision, taking the same clipped steps. Ten seconds had never felt so long, as the thick doors slammed closed behind them. The room held its breath for five more seconds before the sounds of shuffling started as people moved to the front of their cells.

"Are you alright there, Commander?" a male voice asked in concern from my left.

There was more shuffling as the big male that had just been tossed moved to the front as well, and peered between the bars. The torch above his cell gave off enough light to see his features. The familiar blue eyes sparkled with the same roguishness as they had every time we sparred as the voice that used to sing me lullabies as he rocked me to sleep spoke up. "I'm just fine there, Anderson. A little beating can't break me."

I gasped loudly, the entire room going silent as I pulled myself up, ignoring the fire racing down my back as I used the bars as a rest. My eyes met his, going wide with I didn't know what. Shock. Relief. I nearly choked on the word as tears started filling up my eyes. "Geoff."

CHAPTER THIRTY-THREE

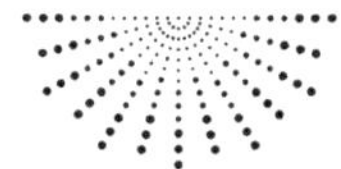

"Cub?" he asked, mouth open in shock, grasping onto the white bars even though it must have felt like a thousand needles stabbing into his hands, slowly leeching him of his spark.

"Geoff, get away from the bars," I yelled at a whisper, whipping my eyes to the door, waiting for the guards to burst back in.

He thankfully listened, releasing the bars and pulling himself back just barely. He stared at me in disbelief, shaking his head back and forth. "No, no, no, no, no! You shouldn't be here." He ran his hands through his limp hair. "How are you here, cub? Didn't the Council send someone to find you after we were taken?"

"Oh, they found me alright," I said accusingly, narrowing my eyes at him. "Only after I had been torn apart by wraiths and destroyed several miles of the Blackwood during my Awakening." I couldn't help the small amount of satisfaction I got seeing him avert his eyes from mine, shame crossing his face. "Funny how you both never mentioned that family secret."

The others in the chamber fell silent, moving back to their places in the corners of their cells, letting us have our conversation in as much privacy as we could.

I couldn't find it in me to feel sympathy for him, even all bloodied and beaten—his face and arms a myriad of bruises and cuts—the anger and indignation that had been building for weeks finally rose to the forefront.

He went to speak, but I beat him to it. "This is not the time nor the place for this conversation. We're too deep in shit to be having this talk, but let me make one thing very clear." I don't know what he saw on my face, but it had him swallowing hard, guilt riding hard on his shoulders. "The minute we are out of this hellhole, we're going to be having a family meeting. The first topic of discussion will be what the definition of family means to you two, because I'm afraid we have drastically different opinions on that matter."

He closed his eyes, facing pinching in pain. "Cub, there's just so much you don't understand."

I scoffed in frustration. "Yeah, so everyone keeps telling me, and yet no one seems to be willing to fill me in on it."

He locked eyes with me before looking away after a few seconds. "There's so much you don't know, so much that I can't explain to you, not if you haven't figured it out yet," he whispered quietly over to me, his voice pleading with me to understand. "You just have to trust me."

I shook my head sadly, my heart hurting with a pain that couldn't be seen as I quietly replied back, "I don't know if I can anymore."

His face fell, and a wetness shined in his eyes. I looked away, never having seen him cry before. My adoptive father had always been my rock, so strong and unbreakable that knowing I was the one to finally break him down nearly did the same to me.

"Where's Maris?" I asked, the words catching in my throat as I tried to change the subject so that the tears that threatened to spill over wouldn't fall.

I saw him look over to his left, towards the back of the cell. "She's in here with me, but they've been feeding her to the wraiths, siphoning her energy almost every day for the past couple weeks." Angry tremors shook in his voice as he spoke, as obvious as the heartbreak he must feel looking at his wife—drained and exhausted—and not being able to stop the torture. "That or they have her healing other Descendents so that they can be tortured again or worse. She hasn't woken up in days."

"Why is she helping them?" There had to be a good reason for Maris to use her power to help Kasis. I may not know her like I thought I did, but I knew that she was tougher than anyone would have guessed. She would have laughed in anyone's face if they tried forcing her to do something.

I could practically hear Geoff's teeth grinding together as he spit out, "They have children. Young ones from some of the outer villages. They keep them separated from us and only bring them out to threaten us to comply with their orders."

I could hear stifled sobs coming from some of the neighboring cells and knew that some of those children's parents were sitting right next to me, unable to help their babies. My heart broke all over again, the image of the little redheaded girl flashing in my mind. Were her parents here? Did they know their daughter was dead?

I nearly doubled over, gasping as the opalescent barrier around my spark shook with the force of my power hammering away from the inside. I could hardly feel my screaming back, all my attention focused on the cracking in the wall as it splintered and groaned.

For a split second everything went still inside me before the gold mass of energy, so large and encompassing I couldn't see its blurred edges, smashed up against it, sending a jagged line through the shimmering obstacle that stood in its way to revenge. Then everything went quiet again.

Gasping for breath, I looked down at my hands, expecting half grown nails and scraped skin, not the perfectly smooth ivory with pink nails perfectly cut and shaped. My ribs throbbed and I could almost feel the bone knitting itself together faster and faster. Turning my hands over, I caught the quickest glimpse of gold beneath my skin before it disappeared.

The extra strength, however, stayed, filling my fatigued and beaten body. Closing my eyes, I leaned back against the bars, breathing in my first unhindered breath, sighing in relief as the pain in my side started to fade.

"Cub, you alright over there?" Geoff asked, concern heavy on his words.

I cleared my throat, leaning heavier on the bars. "Oh yeah, you know how it goes; get the shit beat out of you and then have your magical powers fix it all up lickety split." I shrugged my shoulders, looking at him with a deadpan look. "Normal day of the week."

He cracked a small smile, looking down at his hands as he twisted his wedding band around and around his fourth finger. "It's not all bad, you know. I mean, you have to admit the super strength is kind of fun, and I guess the magic is kind of cool," he said, wrinkling his nose and rolling his eyes.

I chuckled, not at all surprised to find it didn't hurt. "Let me guess," I said wryly, shooting him a glance. "You're a Cynth."

He laughed, more of a croak than anything. "What gave it away?"

I let myself smile, enjoying the moment even if it was inside a dungeon of horror. I hadn't let myself dwell on it, but I had missed this. Missed these easy conversations that I had always been able to have with him, but it was hard to mistake the underlying tension in our words. Like two people in a new relationship that didn't know what the rules were. It made me unbearably sad.

My smile dropped. When he saw my face, his followed. A palpable silence filled the space. Not like it had before, when everyone was just trying to survive. This was a silence that said more than words, said that there was something broken and I didn't know if it would ever go back to the way it was.

Some part of me I guess had hoped that when I found them that all of this would be explained away, and we would be able to go back to our old life. Even as hellish as the village had made it, those moments when it was just me and my small little family, life was perfect. Our cozy cottage, the peaceful forest, the quiet nights I would wake up in a pool of my own sweat after a nightmare and just listen to the crickets and the owls going on with their night.

But it was all tainted now. I had been through too much, seen horrors that would haunt me forever. I wasn't the woman I used to be. That woman had been content to live her life as an outcast so long as she was left alone, but now I had sipped on the addictive taste of friendship, of a bond beyond a quick dalliance in the woods.

I didn't think I could go back to that empty life. I had been loved by Maris and Geoff and nothing I could say or do could ever repay them for their kindness, for taking in a little girl with golden, fearsome eyes and raising her like their own. For showing her what affection was. But for the first time in my life, I think I wanted more for myself.

That I deserved more than that.

"Do we like him?" a small voice asked from right next to my ear.

Jumping, I nearly let out a scream, Wrynn's body jolting up in the air from his seat on my shoulder. "Cosmos, Wrynn, warn a girl, would you?"

He blushed, glowing wings fluttering behind him in embarrassment as he squeaked, "Sorry."

"This is my foster dad, Wrynn, and we usually like him," I said, answering his question and shooting a glance over at Geoff before whispering quietly, "But right now I'm not so sure."

Even with his handsome features, mouth pursed in understanding, he couldn't look anything but adorable. Lifting his hand up to block his face from Geoff's view, he leaned in conspiratorially, but forgot to lower his voice. "Got it, so do we want to help him escape as well or no, because we can just you know"—he mimed us walking out with two fingers—"and never have to see him again if you want."

Geoff's head whipped around, hearing Wrynn's loud plan. I closed my eyes, shoulders shaking with barely contained amusement. I found it impossible to be mad at him. His innocence was one of the only bright spots in my life at the moment.

"Everyone can hear you, Wrynn, you kind of need to whisper our secret plans," I said, tilting my head at him in faux exasperation. Even in the dim light, his silver-white glow bounced off his hair and let me see his dark skin deepen in blush. "But yes, we're going to help him and everyone else escape if we can."

He nodded his head, seriously looking around the room, holding up two thumbs before leaning in once again—as if to prove he could—quietly saying, "Got it."

"Cub, who's in there with you?" Geoff asked, trying to peer through the bars of his cell and into mine.

I gestured behind me with my thumb. "This is my friend, Wrynn. He's going to help get us out of here."

Said friend hung out from between the bars with a huge smile on his face, waving his hand wildly. "Hi, nice to meet you. So sorry about the whole leaving you behind thing, but you see, Tali is kind of my best friend and you hurt her feelings very badly, so I have to be on her side. You understand right?"

he said, nodding earnestly. "Good news is, we've had a little chat, and she says we're going to try to get all of you out of here."

"Is that a sprite?" someone asked from the cell next to Geoff's.

"Yes, I am! Thank you for noticing." Wrynn's wings flapped happily, his silver glow getting just the tiniest bit brighter. "You know, not everyone gets it right away. I'm not as colorful as some of my brethren."

"It won't work," a male said from the farthest cell to my right, hidden deep in the shadows. His accent was unlike anything I had ever heard. It was gritty and full, an underlying musical tone to it that I couldn't place. It sounded like the burning sun on hot sand, an empty desert turning into an oasis before your eyes. His voice was like a mirage, and it was one of the most beautiful things I had ever heard.

"And why is that?" I asked, curious to see what he had to say, this newcomer with a strange accent. I hadn't been to many places across the content, which was wide and vast in its diversity, so it wouldn't surprise me if he hailed from one of the southern borders; but there was just something about him, something different that I couldn't figure out. I pushed it aside for now. Bigger and more important questions needed answering.

He chuckled darkly. "You really think that you'll be able to do anything that hasn't been tried a dozen times before?"

"I think you're underestimating him and his skillset," I retorted, only receiving a snort before his cell went silent again.

I didn't have time to say anything else before another warning cough came from the front, sending anyone not at the back of their cell scurrying into the shadows. Wrynn, without being told, shot back up into his crevice.

I stayed where I was, leaning as far as I could to see who was coming down the aisle. I heard his shoes first, then smelled the rotten stench, Geoff's face twisting in rage and disgust, and then finally I saw him.

His slicked-back hair, bright smile, and clear, green eyes. Handsome and perfectly put together in an almost unnerving way, not a strand or thread out of place. I looked like a fucking mess in comparison: dried blood covering every inch of my body, my golden hair coated in dried blood and grime, curly strands shooting out in every direction, but considering he had put me in this position, I honestly couldn't give a shit if I looked presentable.

His smile didn't drop one an inch as he looked down at me like I was the rarest prize in the world that he had just won. "How are you doing, dearest? My apologies about the dreadful accommodations. I told them to put you in one of our better rooms, but it is so hard to make good help these days."

He whipped around to the two guards who had followed him, striking out lightning fast and punching his hand through the armored chest plate of the one on the left and yanking out his still beating heart, blood spurting out from the arteries. He dropped it unceremoniously to the ground as the guard—who hadn't made a sound the entire time—stood completely still and unmoving.

"I told you not to put her in here," Kasis screamed in its face, before turning back to me, a bright smile firmly back in place as he took a white kerchief out of his pocket and slowly wiped the blood from his hand.

"I see you got to catch up with your"—he curled his lip at Geoff—"rearer. Has he filled you in on everything or has he continued to keep secrets, just like everyone else in your life, I've been told?"

I stayed quiet and ignored him, turning to look at the wall in front of me. Engaging with him would only feed into his psychopathy, and I also wanted to see what he would do; and like I expected, he didn't take it very well.

He scrunched his face, an expression of rage appearing and disappearing underneath his placid one as he struggled to keep his facade up. "Has he not told you the big secret?" he yelled loudly, anger thrumming through his voice. "Has he told you what happened twenty-one years ago, what about twenty-six years ago, or how about two thousand years ago? Did he mention any of that?"

He spread his arms out, green eyes wide, sparking with madness. The creeping insanity that he kept under wraps started to peek through, vibrant green turning to a noxious, putrid color. Tapping at his chest wildly, he continued. "I'm trying to help you here, show you what you could have always been, what you can be now. Don't you see?" he implored, bending down to nearly touch the floor, reaching for me through the bars. "I've only ever wanted to help you, to show you what we could be together. She said you would understand, she said you would understand!" he shouted, beating his hands against his head.

I turned, unflinching, in his direction, holding his gaze in mine and freezing him with a look. Then I said the only words that came to mind, my mouth curving into a wicked smile. "Careful, your crazy is showing."

His mask cracked like glass, falling around him like shards of rain, the tears in his mind filling with a madness that couldn't be hidden any longer. I thought I knew rage, knew evil, but nothing had ever compared to the twisted look on his face. His handsome face faded into a malicious depiction of horror.

His eye sockets caved in, leaving behind only an infectious, green glow. His skin had veins of black running all across it, the pallor underneath sickly compared to the youthful paleness of before. He snarled, and I could almost feel the black, rotting spittle hit my face; but between one blink and the next, his face was back to normal save for a slight twitch.

Standing to his full height, he straightened the bottom of his dress coat, carefully brushing invisible lint from his arm. "You will understand one day, be able to see that I did all of this for you, for us; but until then, I see we still have a lot of work to do."

He turned and walked down the hall, hands casually shoved in his pockets. "Take her to the room," he said without a backward glance, waving at the two guards.

They moved as one, automatons without any real thought, even the one with a hole in its chest still missing its heart, which lay cold on the stone floor in a small puddle of blood. One of them pulled something from its pocket, a green crystal, and waved it over the bars. The steel bars shot into the ceiling with a clang.

I was already fighting as they stepped in, even as my exhausted muscles begged for me to stop, because I knew where I was going. The thought of being put back in that place without a fight was too depressing of a thought.

Unfortunately, even with my body healing, the barrier around my spark grew weaker every second; I had been using all my energy to heal and now I had none left. They easily subdued me, stronger than any rotting corpse had a right to be.

I could hear Geoff shouting expletives as they put the heartsglass shackles back on my wrists, seemingly unaffected by the crystal's power through their thick armor. The second they touched my skin, I cried out in pain. The soul-sucking feeling came back with a force, feeding off the extra power that now circulated in my blood.

They dragged me out by the chains, my knees scraping against the floor as I stumbled. I jerked against their hold on me, gritting my teeth as I fought to break free, but nothing worked and slowly I was pulled closer and closer to the double doors.

Dread filled my stomach like a lead weight, dragging me down into that dark abyss, that fevered dream I went to, to survive. The place where my mind kept my soul from breaking, from being touched by such a penetrating horror that it could leave a scar that would never fade. I didn't know if I would make it through untouched this time. As I got closer, I let the numbness set in.

The last thing I heard as I was pulled out was the sound of Geoff. "Please, no," he begged, praying. "Take me, please. Cosmos, please."

CHAPTER THIRTY-FOUR

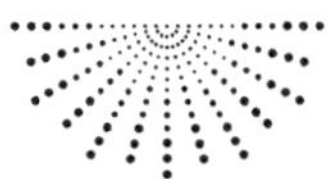

I was staring up at the barrier, waves of color undulating through the opalescent wall. I felt small in comparison; it went so high up it disappeared into a foggy abyss. Small specks of gold dust spattered the great structure like paint on a canvas.

It was beautiful in a way that not many things were. A testament of strength and undeniable power that made the large splintering cracks that marred its surface all the more terrifying. I approached it and the shine from the different colors and energy that it was made of danced across my body, turning my skin into a myriad of peaceful light; it felt like being underwater and looking up to see the sun shattering into beams of light that broke through the water.

Through the opaque barrier I saw my spark, so different from what I had seen before, only making the slightest movements. I felt its watchful presence as if it was waiting, observing me and my choices. The gold power was unlike anything I had ever seen. Its unending vastness was almost terrifying to witness; so much power in one little space.

A part of me wondered if it was better to keep it locked up, but the other part knew better. Knew that power like that couldn't be contained forever. It felt strange looking at it like this, with a curious, awe-filled detachment, like I knew it wasn't yet mine. Maybe that was why it hadn't hit me, that this much power lived in me, in my body, simmering and waiting for the right moment to come forth. The only problem was I didn't know what that moment was, or how I could fully comprehend what this power could do, what it could mean.

The golden fog, full of light and life and color, separated, allowing a form to step through the amassed power. It was the body of a woman, and she was made of our energy. Every curve was gilded power, pure aether given form. Her features were suggested outlines, but nothing more. Her steps were soft, light, as she made her way toward me. Waist-length hair flowed around her on the breeze.

Her form was faded around the edges, a fuzzy glow surrounding her like she wasn't truly a part of this realm, a piece of her still somewhere else. Small glowing specks lifted from her nebulous body and danced in the air like tiny embers.

She reached the wall, stopping the same distance from it as me. Even without definitive eyes, I could feel her watching me, her gaze brushing over my skin as we took one another in. My heart pounded in my chest, an overwhelming sense of knowing filling me.

I lifted my hand up, placing my palm lightly on the barrier between us. A pulse went through it, slight and barely noticeable, but I watched as the colors twitched and felt it tremble beneath my touch. On the other side, she lifted her palm up, placing it directly over mine. A boom sounded, the wall undulating between us as the crack above fractured the wall into millions of tiny pieces until it was only held together by the barest fragment of power.

I looked back at the woman in front of me. Her visage broken into a million pieces, splitting and refracting her image. She stared back at me, unmoving in the face of the breaking but not broken barrier.

"You must see." Her voice reverberated through the cavernous space, galaxies and planets and stars held in her words. The echo in her voice made it sound as if two people were speaking. "You must hear. You must listen. It is time, you must remember," she said, removing her hand from the wall.

As she did, I was pulled back, a tether in my chest yanking away from the wall and into the real world.

My eyes flickered open slowly, blinking away the haze as the torturer's room came into view. My cheek was once again pressed to the cold, stone floor. The fire from the torches placed around the room sent a fiery orange tone across the floor, complementing the blood-stained stone.

He must have not bothered to bring me back to the cell, probably assuming he would be back for another session soon. As if the last one hadn't been enough. He had reopened all the old wounds before adding more, and the last thing I remembered before I passed out was him rubbing salt into them; the burning was so intense that I lay motionless in order to not break out into tears of agony.

Laying in a pool of your own blood had to change a person, there was no way it couldn't. It was like watching yourself die, feeling the lifeblood that you so desperately needed to live, only for it to go cold mere inches from your face. Watching as it crawled away from you only to stain the floor that so many others had died on.

It was a torture all on its own to be left like this, with only your thoughts and the screams of other victims that echoed in the very stone your ear was pressed to. I could hear their wails and cries of pain, begging The Divine, the Cosmos, anyone to make it stop. My heart hurt for them. It ached knowing that their voices, their souls, were trapped here in this place of evil and pain.

If I got out, I would find a way to release them, to set them free so that they could maybe find some slice of peace after being stuck in a hell for who knows how long. I whispered it over and over, letting them know they weren't alone anymore, until finally, one by one, they believed me and the screams stopped.

Then I was left with the silence, wondering if I had just

made it all up in my head, but regardless, this place needed to be purged like the rotting infection it was. I would treat it just like I would any disease, by cutting it out and making sure it could never grow again. Nothing this insidious deserved to be in this world, feeding off of its people, its magic.

I didn't know how long I lay there, falling in and out of consciousness too many times to count, but a resounding thunder had me jolting from the hazy limbo. The following vibrations in the stone had me looking around as much as I could, searching for the source of the commotion and finding nothing.

I heard the stomping boots of corrupted soldiers running past the doorway. It went on for several minutes, the grumbles and yowling of animals mixed in with the uniform steps, orders being shouted by those with their minds still intact.

It went on and on until it finally fell silent once more, the stray vibration rocking the mountain fortress. Flecks of dust and rock fell from the ceiling. The door to the torture room opened, my head whipping up to see who it was.

Nothing came through the small crack, the empty hallway just behind it, until finally the distinct silver glow of sprite wings flew through, slamming the door shut behind him.

I let out an exhausted chuckle, relief racing through me knowing Wrynn hadn't been found. He came down to his knees, seemingly unbothered by the blood soaking into his tiny trousers. He grasped my splayed arm, the bruises and slashes much more pronounced than before, and his big, brown eyes watered at the sight of me.

I cracked a smile as big as I could, hoping he couldn't see the pain and fatigue in my eyes. "Hey, you," I croaked, my voice cracking as I swallowed hard, trying to relieve the parched dryness in my mouth.

"I'm sorry," he whispered. "I'm so sorry. They told me we had to let you figure it out, but I can't do it anymore. I can't watch them do this to you, and we don't have any more time to wait."

My brow creased in confusion. "Wrynn, what is it?" I asked, but he kept rambling on, his anxiety palpable.

"I was able to get one of those crystal thingies from the guards and unlocked everyone's cell"—a boom in the distance—"but you were gone and I was the only one fast enough to find you." He started breathing heavily. "I tried everything, I really did, and the warlord led the army here, but there's too many of them and we've run out of time. I did what they said, tried steering you in the right direction, but there's no more time and now they're overrun." His eyes were wide, staring straight through me, fear running wild in his gaze. "I've never seen so many. The Lord, he doesn't know, doesn't know how many. There's about to be a massacre and he doesn't know it." He was gasping, tugging at his white hair until it stood straight up. "This wasn't the plan; this wasn't the plan."

He was talking so fast I could hardly keep up, but the bits and pieces I caught are enough to have me reach out and grasp him. "Wrynn," I shouted, shocking him out of his panicked state, "What is going on? You said the army is here?"

He nodded his head and another wave of relief rolled through me, but then I put the rest of what he said together. "Wrynn." I stared at him hard, suspicion clear in my voice. "What plan?"

He pressed his lips together, looking down at the floor, guilt pinching at his face. "Wrynn," I said louder, making him jump a little in my hand. I felt bad being so forceful with him, but at the same time, I needed to know what the hell was going on.

"I gave you the book," he squeaked out.

I stared at him in confusion, mouth gaping. "What."

"I gave you our history. The account of events that happened at the beginning of our history and then subsequently the war two thousand years ago." He searched my face, a seriousness on his own I had never seen. "It was written by the sprites because no one else remembers."

"Why?" I asked, feeling as though I was on the cusp of so many answers I had long desired. "Why the secrecy? Why not give me the book yourself, instead of leaving it at my door? Why does no one remember, Wrynn?"

So many whys, so many questions that had been bouncing around in my head for weeks just waiting for their answers to step into the light.

He swallowed, his throat bobbing in nervousness. Straightening his shoulders, he looked me dead in the eye. "Because after the war ended, and the Goddess of Beginnings left this realm, Death erased parts of history before building the barrier and isolating the Descendents in Allasea."

I gaped at him, shock coursed through me like electricity. I opened and closed my mouth several times, words failing me. Nowhere in the book—that Wrynn had left me, apparently— had that been written down. For weeks, I had been wondering why no one seemed to talk about the war in great detail, even though it wasn't that long ago for the Descendants. I mean, surely there had to be people still alive from when the war had been fought. There was no way it would have been forgotten by them.

And then I remembered, there was at least one person I knew of who had been there. Cashim had been just a boy, barely Awakened, when the war was being fought, but I can't imagine it was ever something you forgot about.

So why? Why did no one seem to remember anything specific from back then? How come there weren't more stories being shared or written down as legends for children to read about? How was it that there was story after story of The Divine's descent to this world, and yet not a single person had ever mentioned what they looked like despite the fact that they were known for being involved with their people? How come no one knew their names?

Because Death himself willed it to be so.

"But … But what reason did he have to do that? They were beloved! They would have been remembered as the great rulers of our planet, not just some lore that has all but become fiction in barely two thousand years. Why would he want them to be forgotten, for them to disappear from history?"

He shifted in my grip, and I opened my hand, letting him into the air. Coming down to the ground, his white-silver glow threw him into a hazy view standing so close. He reached down to pat my cheek in sympathy, pressing his lips together. "To protect them"—his gaze bounced around the room, looking anywhere but at me as he whispered quietly—"To protect them for when … for when they were born again."

He could have told me anything but that, and I would have been in less disbelief. I had heard the theories the people had, that The Divine had returned to the original state—pure energy that represented two fundamental pillars of the universe—others thought they had chosen to sleep as the Cosmos had, and many more assumed they had passed their power on to someone new; to imbue their energies in order to keep the peace.

The idea of their rebirth was only spoken on the tongues of the hopeful, the traditionalists who prayed for the day their true rulers would return. That looked back on the olden days where peace, prosperity, and equality were the cornerstones of society, not this bleak facade of one that was moving more and more towards a society ruled by the elite. Where power was the only real currency, and only those that had it would amount to anything in this new world.

Now, according to Wrynn, those that looked for the return of Life and Death were correct. That they had indeed returned, or would.

"Why would you tell me this? Why give me the book if they need to stay a secret?"

He looked at me, tilting his head sadly as he searched my face, looking for something. Looking me directly in the eye, his dark, doe eyes were serious and compassionate. "You know why."

I froze, my body going still, as if not moving would make it all go away. He pressed his lips together. "You've always known why, you just refuse to accept it. You think if you don't dwell on it that it won't be real, and then you can continue trying to force yourself to be normal." I flinched at his harsh words, and how close to home they really hit. "But you have known what you are since the moment you were old enough to understand. Deep down inside of you, you knew. Well, it's time now. You need to remember who you are."

He breathed out heavily, as if a large weight had just been taken from his shoulders. "I wanted to tell you for so long, but I wasn't allowed to. The other sprites said it was best if you found out yourself, put the pieces together, you know, but we don't have any more time for you to do that."

"How do you know about this?" I gasped out, my mind shooting from one thought to the next, trying to connect the dots. "How do the other sprites know about this? I thought Death erased history." So many things were no longer what they seemed, and now I was left questioning everything once again.

He smiled sadly, a tiny curl to his mouth that was nothing compared to his normal jovial expression. And to the distinct sounds of shattershells exploding somewhere far off, he whispered, "A sprite never forgets, My Lady." And with that, he folded his small body over into a bow, tilting his head to the floor in respect.

Rolling onto my back, ignoring the pain and the bite of my chains digging into the wounds, I closed my eyes. Maybe that would shut everything off, stop the world from closing in around me. Maybe if I couldn't see it, then maybe it wasn't there. What if all of this was just some weird dream that I was waiting to wake up from? What if all my suspicions weren't coming true and the universe itself wasn't crumbling around me?

But no, it was all real. All of it. Everything that I had hidden deep inside me, every thought that crossed my mind that I had thrown away under the pretense of insanity, came rushing to the forefront, eager to connect everything together. To show me all the signs I had missed, and all the ones I hadn't wanted to confront, that I refused to acknowledge.

The dreams that didn't feel like dreams, all the secrecy—from my family, from everyone around me—Kasis and his crazy plan he still wanted to enact two thousand years later. Everything. Everything I thought I had known was a lie.

Why I thought I could have a normal life—why I even wanted one in the first place—was beyond me. I had shoved everything down, denied it to my last breath, refusing to confront what I knew to be true head on. I could feel the tears falling down my face, feel Wrynn's silent presence next to me, as the life I had created in my head crumbled to pieces in my hand. None of it mattered as I was sucked in, a tether tugging deep in my very being, refusing to let me ignore the obvious any longer.

And there she was. The woman in gold behind the broken wall. Appearing from the golden mist on the other side, an embodiment of power and strength. The cracked barrier fractured her, like pieces of a shattered mirror seconds away from crashing down all around me. And that is when it hit me.

It was a mirror.

The whole thing was one big mirror. Reflecting everything I was, everything I had been and would be; making me confront all that made me who I was. All the things that I had never wanted to be in fear of rejection. I had locked it all inside, never letting it rise to the surface, terrified that I would be hated even more.

Because deep down, I was scared and lonely, missing a part of myself so integral that I felt its absence even without knowing what it was. Scared of myself, of what I was and refused to accept who I could become; all of it. I was just so scared.

No more.

I had spent my entire life worried about who I truly was, but no more. I was the waves that rocked the ocean, the wind that carried the storm, the hot burn of a wildfire, and the everlasting rock that kept our world spinning in a vast space. The light of the universe could not compare to me, for I was the light. Life, the very essence of all that we were, flowed through my veins. I was the Aether, and it was time I stopped hiding from that fact.

The gilded woman stepped up to the crumbling barrier, pieces falling down around us. Placing her hand on the wall, she asked, "Who are we?" Her voice, that once held the echo of two people, melded into one and echoed all around the cavern of my soul.

It was my voice, I realized, my voice that echoed from the golden form. It had always been me on the other side of that wall, waiting and waiting for me to finally understand; and now I did. Straightening my spine, head held high as the last pieces of the wall came crashing around me, my mind disappearing under the swell of gold.

I opened my eyes and spoke the words out loud.

"Atallia. Goddess of Beginnings."

CHAPTER THIRTY-FIVE

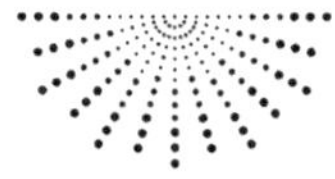

*P*ower crackled under my skin, filling every nook and cranny until it finally burst free. It exploded from my chest with more strength than anything I had ever felt before. It twisted through the dark room, lighting it up with golden fire.

The reds and blues, greens and purples that played within its gilded depths were like a painter's brush strokes, chaotic and without care and so consumingly beautiful. I could see trees and forests, rivers, lakes, and the creatures that lived within them. The magic, the aether, the power transforming into anything and everything. It twisted and twirled above me like a storm of creation as more and more poured out of my veins, my skin.

It was everything and nothing. The Beginning of something that had no start, that never stopped, even at its Ending. The universe, expansive and uncontrollable, appeared in my mind as I watched, more and more power leaving my body. Great galaxies of light and life, planets and moons and stars. Everything that began with me, whose energy flowed through my very being and into existence.

I was the Goddess of Beginnings. Lady Life. The hearts of

planets beat because of me. From the smallest leaf to the largest oak, the tiniest insect to the largest mammal, they had all passed through my gate; every being connected to me intrinsically.

I had been the Beginning for thousands of years, and it was time I became it once more.

Reaching my hand into the air, I tugged on an invisible thin string, the last bit of power connecting me to the pillar of energy that the very Cosmos had ripped from their being. I yanked hard on that string, and with a final swoop, the gold entity rushed straight into me.

The second it touched my fingers, the heartsglass shackles not only went dim, they shattered, spraying me with gray crystal shards. My cells glowed gold, my eyes, my hair, my form blurred around the edges, just like I had seen behind the barrier.

Underneath the aura, I saw my skin cracking apart, the glowing core beneath trying to slip out between the cracks, and I felt as if at any moment I could leave this body behind and become what I had been before.

A pure energy that moved through space as easily as the sun.

Standing, I tilted my head back, closing my eyes as I absorbed every last drop. My back knit back together in seconds; every wound, every ache and pain disappeared as if it were never there. My trousers and bandeau crumbled, turning to ash and floating to the ground. Flakes of dried blood burned away from my skin as the cracks traveled all across my naked body.

I stood bare, power surging off me in waves, my vision golden-tinted as my aura grew stronger. My hair drifted on an invisible breeze, the glowing, golden strands like individual beams of light.

I looked down, eyes burning like the sun, and saw Wrynn having fallen to his knees, head bowed. I recognized him as my friend, but I felt nothing but pure power, so much that had been shoved down for so long. The pressure was unbearable, the need to let it all go nearly too much to handle so soon after absorbing it all.

"Show me the way, Wrynn," my voice boomed, backed by power that shook mountains.

"Yes, My Lady," he replied quickly, flying straight for the wooden door. I followed behind, my feet barely touching the ground.

I rested my hand on the door, about to exit, but I turned around, peering at the blood-stained room that echoed back so much pain. I tapped my foot slightly on the stone floor.

The rock shook and grumbled before a large resounding crack filled the space as the floor broke in half and the ceiling started to crumble. Rock after rock, the room collapsed in on itself and I could almost feel the relief of the lost souls—stuck in this place of hell—as they were finally set free. Their prison, this place of torture, destroyed and never to be used again.

It wasn't until it went quiet again, nothing but boulders and dust left, that I turned and followed Wrynn out.

I always kept my vows, and those lives would never again be stuck screaming for eternity.

Following the silver glow of Wrynn's wings, we took several turns, passing down many stone hallways. I caught my reflection in a puddle of water. I was all-consuming strength, power personified. My ivory skin was barely visible beneath my aura of gold, throwing light in every direction. Aether poured out of my eyes like smoke, my irises bare outlines, the whites completely gone, having been consumed by the power that had replaced my blood.

I couldn't find it within me to care that I didn't have a speck of clothing on me, my magic so pent up from being locked away for so long it seemingly refused to go back inside my mortal form. I had more important things to worry about than finding clothes.

Like the explosions that had yet to cease, the warlord and his army somewhere battling outside, having no idea they were about to be swarmed.

I could tell Wyrnn was taking us away from the direction of the dungeons. The torture room had been close enough that it had only taken a few short turns to get from the cells to it. The halls were getting considerably less musty. The damp walls and moldy smell had slowly turned into something resembling more of what I expected from Kasis and his obsessiveness.

The fortress was made of warm-toned walls and floors of deep chestnut wood. While each hall looked nearly identical, each was pristinely decorated with lush carpets and colorful tapestries. It reminded me of Eskira, but the beauty and uniqueness of each room and hall of the Allasean capital were incomparable. Certainly not by this poor mimicry of it, the rot soaked so deep into its bones that no mask could cover the stains it left behind.

A scream had me moving quickly down the hall, Wrynn's wings helping him keep pace. Several more shrieks of alarm, high pitched and fearful, had me running, the sounds reminding me of the little girl in the woods.

Turning the corner, I saw wraiths, both animal and guard, cornering a group of Descendents in the dead-ended corridor. Children, some younger, some older, were being shielded behind the adults, tears streaming down their faces as they wailed in fear. The youngest looked barely old enough to walk and was having to be held by his mother.

Their shackles hadn't been removed, the heartsglass still draining them, making them powerless to protect themselves. Several were holding wooden chair legs and metal rods up like bludgeons, but those would do nothing but serve to piss the starving wraiths off.

The inhuman creatures turned, having felt my presence. I slowed to a stop at the start of the hall, and the Descendents' looked stunned by my appearance, my golden form reflecting in their eyes. The wraiths snarled in rage and hunger, their never-ending desire and need for energy flaring up into a wild storm, my boundless energy ready for them to consume.

Like they had at one point, I thought, remembering the dream I had at the start of all this. My energy spark turned them full fleshed creatures, no rotting muscle or black tar in sight. I couldn't allow that to happen again. Their strength would be too great, and those children wouldn't stand a chance against them even with their parents. My heart clenched in pain at that thought.

I narrowed my eyes at the wraiths. Their corpses no longer held the people they once were; I was doing them a mercy by ending their existence. I had no doubt in my mind as they charged towards me that the people they once had been would be horrified by what had been done to them and what they had become.

And so, I let out a breath for those that had been forced to become mindless monsters, for those that had become everything they stood against, and for those that had lost someone to this pitiful existence. I let out a breath, and the beasts turned to cinders, from the touch of an energy that helped craft the universe..

Leftover skin and fur, mottled and patchy and covered in tar and blood, dissipated into nothing. Eyes burned red before melting into a river of goo, turning black and floating away. Within seconds, all that was left was a slight smoky smell and a few ashes drifting along before falling onto the black rug uselessly.

As I stared at the small flecks, I felt hope for the lives once contained in those bodies. That they would find the peace they deserved, and I hoped they knew they would never again be used in such a horrific way.

I walked over to the small group, ignoring their awe-filled

faces—tinged with the slightest bit of fear—as I stepped up to them. "Where are Geoff and Maris?"

One of the males stepped forward, and it didn't escape my notice that he stepped in front of a smaller female, his wife judging by the ring on her hand. "When the sprite let us out we had all nearly made it out of the cells when Kasis found us. Maris was so weak, he grabbed her." The man rambles on under the weight of my gaze. He swallowed hard, taking a deep breath as he continued, "Geoff told us to find the kids, and that's where we last saw them."

"Get them out of here," I told Wrynn as I took off back in the direction of the dungeon.

"What about you?" he asked, silver wings flapping anxiously.

I gave him a smile, letting my power flare as I turned the corner. "I'll be just fine."

I raced through the halls, faster than we had coming out now that I didn't have to worry about Wrynn keeping up. Turn after turn, it all blurred together until the walls once again turned dark and damp.

A rumble stopped me in my tracks, the sound low and agonizing. Turning to look, I saw a hallway leading into nothing, the darkness so overwhelming it appeared to be a void in the world, so empty it shouldn't have existed. Even my golden aura seemed to be snuffed out by its sheer nothingness. Chills raced down my spine as a feeling of anxiety settled over me. The emptiness…not even near-death had felt like this.

The muffled sounds of an argument drew me away, and I turned to run. I couldn't help the last look I threw over my shoulder, the hallway slowly disappearing from view, but the feeling of terror stayed. Shaking it off, I followed the sounds as the light dimmed, and the rotten smell became nearly overwhelming.

The source of it was pouring out of the doorway to the dungeon cells. All the cells had been opened and emptied, but standing at the back of the room was Kasis with Maris held against his chest. A black dagger, glinting menacingly, was pressed precariously to her throat. Geoff stood opposite them, hands outstretched in a surrendering gesture. Desperation seeped from his pores.

They all startled at my entry. Kasis stood up straighter, puffing his chest out, which caused the blade to dig into Maris's neck, a single drop of blood dripping down into the hollow of her throat, pooling there like some blood-ruby necklace.

Maris's eyes flashed wide in disbelief, tears welling as she took me in. Blinking rapidly, she released a shallow breath, a beautiful smile stretching the corners of her eyes as happiness shined brightly.

Geoff spun around, a range of emotions flashing quickly across his face one after the other. Relief followed by unadulterated shock, which was then replaced quickly with understanding and awe. He knew this was coming and had expected this outcome. Maybe not the setting, but it was the absolute proof I needed to know that they both had known who I was well before I had.

"Well, well, well," Kasis crooned creepily. "Looks like someone finally remembered who they were. I must say, my plan worked excellently. I had expected this to take much longer."

He rambled on as I stepped further into the cramped space, stepping in front of Geoff, blocking Kasis's view of him slightly. There was no way to cover the giant, but at the very least, I could intercept any blow thrown at him.

"Do you understand now? I explained it all that first night—do you remember what I told you?" Kasis asked, eyes wild as snakes of poison slithered under his skin.

"I think you've misled yourself," I said carefully, fully aware of the risk at stake, glancing down at Maris. "I broke through the barrier around my spark, and I know that I was reincarnated, but my memories from before did not carry over. This is my new life. It's supposed to be a fresh start, so whatever hope you had that I would remember you was incorrect."

And yet memories from my past had come back to haunt me, became my nightly horrors and dreams. Now here stood the man who had started them all two thousand years ago, having nearly the same conversations over and over again. History seemed inclined to repeat itself, which didn't bode well for my future.

I, however, had no intention of losing my second chance at life to some fucking creep with an obsession, regardless of if the creep was the God of Chaos.

He started shaking his head immediately, his mouth agape in disbelief. "No, no, that's not right. You were supposed to remember, you were supposed to understand," he screamed, running a hand harshly through his perfectly positioned hair and making it stick up in all directions before hitting his forehead over and over again.

"We were supposed to be a pair, not you and him," he spit out the word, making no mistake as to who he was referring to. "We were supposed to bond, to be together, and rule this world. Now it's all wrong," he mumbled, looking off into the distance.

"I was never yours, Kasis, you know this; and you know it's over, you don't have to do this. Aren't you tired of war?" An explosion rocked the mountainside in response, shaking the ground and nearly sending me over.

Using the distraction, Maris reached up with one hand to sweep the blade away from her throat while simultaneously knocking her elbow back into his stomach. Doubling over, coughing from her surprisingly strong blow, he whipped his hand out, grasping her tunic.

Rushing forward. I went to grab her, but he pulled her close again, a wickedly evil smile spreading across his face. "It's too late. They'll all be dead in minutes." And with that, he stabbed straight up into her side with the dagger. I gasped in shock, feeling her life force start to slowly drain away. She had mere minutes, if that, already weakened by her time spent in this place.

"NO!" Geoff screamed, catching her falling body as Kasis pushed her away. Kneeling next to her, Geoff pulled her limp body into his lap, yanking the dagger out of her side and putting pressure on the wound. Normally it would have been better to leave the blade in, but with it eating away at her spark, I would take blood loss over it any day.

Anger charged through me, my aura flaring up, lighting up the entire room with its power. I moved towards Kasis, but Geoff grabbed my legs, ignoring the burning he must feel from being so close to my unrestrained aether. I looked down at him, his pleading eyes, and then back at Kasis. Frustration raged within me, but I had already made my choice. And Kasis knew that.

I slowly backed up, noticing the air was shimmering like it had in the forest. I thought it was just the haze over my eyes then, but the view changed from the rough stone of the prison walls to an ocean, water so teal and clear it was unlike any ocean I had ever seen, and then it changed again to another forest. This one I knew, the trunks made of black bark, their roots jutting up into the air like arms and legs. The Blackwood.

He gave me one last smile, a promise held in his gaze as he said, "And no, I'm not tired of it at all. In fact, I'm just getting started." And with that he disappeared through the rift, the quivering air going still behind him, the gray stone of the cell walls reappearing.

I gave a snarl of frustration, hating that he got away, but moved next to Maris. Her face was pale and sunken in, the weeks spent in this dark hellhole being fed upon by corrupted creatures had done a number on her. Her green eyes still held their usual fiery spark, though, which gave me hope.

Moving Geoff's, I placed my hand over her gaping wound, blood pouring out into a large pool around us. I shot her a hard look. "You just had to go and get stabbed, huh?"

Her chuckle was weak, blood tinging her pale lips. "I knew you could fix me." She smiled softly. "You could always fix everything, even when I first met you so very long ago." She coughed, more blood spurting out to fleck her chin.

"Yeah, well, you don't get to die on me. We still need to have a talk about keeping secrets." I looked at her pointedly before turning my attention back to the task at hand.

Closing my eyes, my lids translucent through the gold shimmer, I focused on her spark. Innately I knew what to do, following my instincts as I felt out the dark, draining force the black glass had on my people. Guiding her weakened aether to the wound, I strengthened it with my own, pushing out the looming shade of death. It was not *his* time to have her; she still belonged to me, her spark unwilling to release from her body despite the wound.

With precision, I knit the gaping hole together, like a needle and thread through cloth, pulling the individual strands of muscle together and binding the spot they were cut. When her own magic faltered, I picked up the slack, and within seconds the once deadly injury closed. A pink scar marred her previously unblemished skin, a reminder that Death had come calling for her once, and he might not be so willing to let her slip by again. I'd have to talk to him about that, but first I had to get to him. To tell him who he was.

With a weeping gasp, Geoff pulled her up, digging his face into her neck, and even as she winced in pain, she folded her arms over his back, pulling him into her. I could see it now, their bond. A wave of relief rushed through me, knowing I had just saved them both. No matter how mad I might be at them right now, neither of them deserved to lose the other, not when they were each a piece of the other's soul.

Standing, I moved over the back wall, inspecting it. No sign of the rip in space that had just been there, no sign of Kasis or where he had gone, nothing. A growl ripped through my chest, irritation bubbling to the forefront.

All was silent, Geoff and Maris still engrossed in each other, but then I heard it. The snarls and growls, shattershells exploding, and the roar of a dragon. The battle was still raging on, and Kasis's warning came rushing to my mind. They would all be dead in minutes.

Placing my hand on the wall, the rough stone biting into my hand, I sent a pulse through the mountain. Searching, searching, and then I felt it. The cool breeze, the smell of iron and blood, the ground vibrating with the pounding steps of battle.

My friends were out there, fighting for their lives. The people who had welcomed me as one of them, who tried to stand by me as my entire life was turned upside down. The Descendents, my people, were out there. They were possibly dying right this second, lying motionless on some barren field, alone. They were on the other side of this mountain, facing an insurmountable challenge. These warriors who would lay their lives down for Allasea and their loved ones.

They were all mine, and I had to protect them.

"Atallia?" I heard Geoff cautiously ask. I knew the golden aether swarming me must have frightened them, but I didn't care. I had to protect my people; it was an instinct inside me that couldn't be stopped.

Peeking over my shoulder, the rage bubbling inside me nearly ready to burst, I nodded down at Maris, who would still be weak from everything. "Pick her up and get ready to move."

Something in my face must have told him to listen, because he lifted her into his arms with ease despite his own injuries and moved back a few feet.

Facing the wall, I pooled energy into my hand, all of it coalescing into a single point. I molded it smaller and smaller until it was the size of a pinprick, and then, with a narrowed glance at the wall, I shoved it through my hand and straight into the wall.

I pushed the power through the rock, waves and pulses of magic shaking the foundations of this millennia old mountain, as the entire cliffside blew outward in a cacophonous, booming rumble. The rocks slid down fast, barreling to the ground, thundering as they bounced and cracked and broke. Thousand-pound boulders smashed to dust beneath the weight of my blow.

The entire side of the mountain was cut away in one single blast, the ground disappeared beneath my feet so quickly it was nearly unnerving. Unnerving that something that had stood since the beginning of this planet had just been irrevocably changed by a single thought from me; but I couldn't find it in me to dwell on it.

The battlefield had grown silent, not a single glance of a sword or claw to be heard. Every entity on the barren wasteland turned in my direction. I felt my body lift up, floating above the rocky ledge. Unflinching, I stepped out into open air, nothing but silence and the gray, cloudy sky above to greet me.

The beasts of Chaos would bow to my burning rage today, and nothing would stop me from unleashing it.

CHAPTER THIRTY-SIX

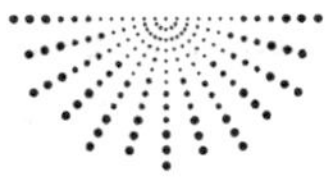

The Gravelands was an apt name for the barren waste that lay before me. My entire view was made up of various shades of gray: the ground, the mountain range that spread behind me like the maw of some giant that shot up sharply into the colorless sky. Thin, sickly trees stuck up through the ash-covered earth in sparse patches, several crackled and snapped from the fire eating away at their spindle-like branches.

It went on for miles in every direction, a scar on the world. It appeared to be wasting away, broken down to the bedrock underneath, ash and rubble covering most of what I could see. But it was what lay underneath the soot and cracked, jagged pieces of mountain that made me understand why it was called as such.

Blood, rusted and dark from time, smeared the dark terrain. Bones were scattered amongst the debris, and that's when it hit me. The gray layer that covered everything in a fine dust and floated through the air wasn't embers or soot from the small fires, it was the ground dust of thousands of bones.

And now thousands more stood to have their bones added to

the mass grave beneath their feet. When Wrynn said Kanan had brought the army, he hadn't been exaggerating. Thousands of troops in black armor were congested together in a group. Red flags, the dragon emblem waving in the air proudly, were being used as javelins, a sharp wall for the amassing horde of wraiths to impale themselves on.

The wraiths … gods, I had never seen so many. Rotting corpses of Aetherians and Cynths alike surrounded and dwarfed the Descendent Army. I had no idea how Kasis had been able to gather such a group under the Descendents' noses?

In the middle of the clustered army, I saw Kanan pushing to get to the outside, but his soldiers refused, shoving him further into the middle. If he shifted now, he would crush hundreds beneath his weight. If only he knew who he truly was, he could have destroyed them all in seconds.

Too little, too late. It was my turn to shake the world.

I sent a beam of energy straight into the planet, entering with a boom, the ground around cracking under the force.

In mere seconds, I felt it. A thump, a pulse, beating wildly as it felt my tether, the very core of the planet responding to its queen. I didn't need my memories to know that I had a connection to the celestial rock that kept us all afloat in the drifts of space. Since the first moment I had stepped on its grass, had felt its cool springs, and colorful skies, I had loved it; and it had loved me in return.

And as such, when I called, it answered.

Spreading my arms wide, I unleashed everything. I let go and felt the freedom of opening the hatch on the forbidden well of power. Anger. Pain. Grief. Guilt. Relief. Happiness. Love. All of it rushed out of me in a scream that echoed across the world. Across the galaxies.

Golden power, mixed with every other color imaginable, exploded out of me in all directions, filling the sky until I overcame the gray, nothing else existing but me and magic.

I was infinite.

It erupted and spread, slashing down from high above, barreling through the lines of rotting corpses, waves of power tearing through them in seconds.

Shards of rock broke through the crust, impaling dozens upon the sharp peaks. Cracks appeared randomly across the dead land, hundreds falling within the gaping chasms before the ground swallowed them whole, closing behind like they were never there, before reopening on the opposite side.

Vines studded with wickedly sharp thorns, the only specks of green on the whole of the field, reached up through the garden of bones. They wrapped around limbs and muzzles, crawling up bodies and dragged them to the ground. They tightened like curling snakes and cut through skin without resistance. Heads were decapitated from shoulders, hindquarters with tails hanging limp lay still, feet away from their other half. Thicker and thicker they grew, feeding off the blood of their victims.

I kept pushing, every bad emotion or thought I ever had, every time I felt rejected or hated. It poured out of me, ripping through the corrupted husks that locked the lives of who they once were inside. I threw it out, unable to hold anything back.

Everything left me in a rush, all in protection of the people I had come to love for the second time. They deserved my everything. These people and this place that had become my home again.

It was over within minutes. The dead now at rest, free of their prison. True ash rained down around us, the breeze making light work of the dusty battlefield.

I watched as my power slowly filled back into the cracks breaking my skin. The rocks disappeared back under the ground, the vines laying still as small, blue flowers bloomed along their green stems as they held on to their skeletal meals.

And in the middle of the destruction was my army,

unharmed and staring up at me with shock and awe on their faces. Blood-spattered and sweaty, blades hung limp from their hands. Floating to the ground, I landed gently on my feet in front of them, the sharp edges of bone and rock dug into my skin, but I hardly felt it.

I walked towards them, some falling to their knees weeping. Compassion filled my veins, my heart aching for each and every one of them. They had fought for so long the first time, and now I was here, about to ask them to do so once again. Their queen, their Goddess, who had failed in her duties to them; who was I to ask this of them?

But I had something more pressing to handle at the moment.

So as the crowd parted, most dropping to one knee, bowing their heads as I passed, I stared straight ahead. And then I saw him. Standing like a beacon of strength amongst his warriors. Black armor glistened with the dark blood, his shadows curling around him, whipping out in agitation. His face was blank, and I saw it in his eyes when his gaze locked with mine, red meeting the impenetrable gold wall that I had become. I saw it, and a new rage filled me.

The wind brushed my skin, blowing my hair across my still naked body—I should really do something about that—and yet I was locked in. Everything blurred away until it was only he and I and nothing else. The only two beings in the world, the universe. The one person I thought I could learn to trust.

His onyx claws were clenched into fists, blood leaking to the ground. His perfect face was almost annoying as I came upon him, stopping a foot away. Chiseled cheekbones, sharp jawline, soft lips so frustratingly out of character for such a rugged man. His red eyes flashed wildly, and I knew it was taking everything in him to not reach out and take me.

The tether in my chest, which I now realized was connected to him on so many other levels than just that of a simple relationship, thumped and pulsed and beat like a living, breathing

thing in my chest. I ignored it all, staring straight-faced. Unflinching under his watch, something I should have recognized sooner, I simply stood. Unable to grasp the reality of what he had done.

More and more, the soldiers around us fell to their knees, most too young to have ever met me in my previous life and yet still recognizing who I was to them. The only people left on their feet were the ones I wanted to see the most, for many different reasons.

All of them stood with the same expression, but it was the slight shift in some of their eyes, the press of their lips that told me which ones had known. Guilt and shame emanated from those most responsible.

The slightest flare of anger burned in the pit of my stomach, so apparent was the emotion that it even fought through the utter emotional exhaustion I faced.

Kanan opened his mouth to speak, but I cut him off. For too long had I let others decide when it was my time to know things. No more.

"You know what I find interesting?" I posed, looking around at the kneeling soldiers, their faces upturned to face me. "You all know who I am, but for the past two thousand years, not a single one of you could have told me my name. Told me the name of my pair." I spoke, staring straight into Kanan's eyes. I saw it. The guilt that spread across his face before I could even say the words, my voice underlined with heady power. My skin crackling across my face, my gilded eyes blurring with energy.

"Tell me, Warlord," I played the title over my tongue. "What is the name of the God of Death?

CHAPTER THIRTY-SEVEN

KANAN

he knew.

ACKNOWLEDGMENTS

Here I am writing this and it is beyond surreal. Firstly I want to say how immensely grateful I am to everyone who showed support to me on this wild journey.

Thank you to my mom who encouraged me every step of the way, for cheering me on even when I thought every word I wrote was garbage. Thank you for supporting me five years ago when I first had this idea, and for supporting me when five years later I finally decided to finish it. This book wouldn't have become a reality without your love and belief that I could do anything I set my mind to.

Thank you to my dad who taught me that what you wish for yourself, and what you set as your goals, are what become your reality. That every step you take is just one step closer to reaching what you made for yourself, and that setbacks are just stepping stones on your path there.

Thank you to my grandparents who found a way to support anything and everything I ever tried or accomplished. My grandma who shares my love of different worlds and magic, and who was one of the first people to read my book; and my grandfather who has told me from day one that I would write a book.

Thank you to my friends who listened to me carry on about things that probably made no sense, and still smiling about it anyway. There are only so many times you can hear about the astronomy of a fictional world without going crazy, or on this plothole or that, but they somehow did it. Putting up with me, especially crazy book me, is no easy feat.

Thank you to all the wonderful people on Bookstagram who have probably seen this journey up close and personal. A little over a year ago I couldn't have imagined where my little page would take me. I originally started as a way to stay connected to my passion for books and reading while I traversed my first year of college, but through it all I have found true friends and an entire community who have supported and advised me this entire time.

Thank you to my editors Taylor Robinson(@tayloretext) and Ciara Lewis(@clewis.edits), and to my cover artist Rebecca Frank (@BewitchingBookCovers) for assisting me in bringing my book and all the wonderful things I see in my head come to life.

Lastly, thank you to anyone who gives Atallia's story a chance, whether that be reading a single word or patiently waiting for book 2. Without you, none of this would be possible. I will never be able to express how truly grateful for each and every one of you.

BOOKS BY ASHLYN B. RUDD

Beginnings and Endings

Of Secrets and Beginnings

Of Memories and Endings

Book 3 Coming Soon

ABOUT THE AUTHOR

Ashlyn B. Rudd is the American author of the captivating and enthralling romantic fantasy, Of Secrets and Beginnings.

She lives in the States and is currently working on her degree in nursing. She spends her days in scrubs going through classes, and at night, in between bouts of studying, she lives in the fictional worlds in her head, kicking ass with a sword and casting magic.

When she's not with her friends and family she enjoys stormy days with her animals, a good book, a cozy blanket, and a fireplace. Outside of books, her interests lie in a whole host of things including: gardening, horseback riding, cooking, and binging a good show.

If she could she'd live on a farm in the middle of nowhere, so when she finally takes the dive deep into the woods, don't be surprised if she only comes out for trips to the bookstore and to stock up on snacks.

www.ingramcontent.com/pod-product-compliance
Lightning Source LLC
Chambersburg PA
CBHW060607300726
48975CB00005B/1480